The Sinner's Mark

Also by S. W. Perry

The Sinner's Mark

S. W. PERRY

CORVUS

First published in hardback in Great Britain in 2023 by Corvus,
an imprint of Atlantic Books Ltd

This paperback edition published in 2024 by Corvus

10 9 8 7 6 5 4 3 2 1

A CIP catalogue record for this book is available from the British Library.

Paperback ISBN: 978 1 83895 403 1
E-book ISBN: 978 1 83895 402 4

Printed by CPI Group (UK) Ltd, Croydon CR0 4YY

Corvus
An imprint of Atlantic Books Ltd
Ormond House
26–27 Boswell Street
London
WC1N 3JZ

www.atlantic-books.co.uk

For Jane, as always.

... And some that smile have in their hearts, I fear,
Millions of mischiefs.

OCTAVIUS IN WILLIAM SHAKESPEARE'S
THE TRAGEDY OF JULIUS CAESAR

PART 1

✠

Old Friends

1

London, Summer 1600

His plan is to slip into the city unobserved and unremarked. He has chosen the place carefully. The gatehouse guarding the road from the east is bound to be busy at this time of day, a chokepoint for Londoners hurrying home for the shelter of the hencoop before the light fades and the foxes begin to prowl.

A group of gentlemen on horseback, returning from a day's hawking in the fields beyond St Botolph's, provides the perfect cover. He falls in between them and a gaggle of servant women bringing in bundles of washing that has dried on the hedgerows in the uncertain June sunshine. A procession of the damned, he thinks, looking up at the raised portcullis hanging above his head like a row of teeth in a dragon's jaw.

In appearance he is forgettable. The only flesh he carries is in his face, as though God hadn't allowed enough clay from which to make the rest of him. What remains of his hair is as sparse and wiry as dune grass after a North Sea gale. It is as white as a cold Waddenzee mist. All he possesses are the clothes on his back, the boots that trouble his raw feet, a set of keys, and the ghosts he carries in his pack.

Only in name is he rich.

Petrus Eusebius Schenk.

Petrus after St Peter, long dead. Eusebius in honour of the great Christian theologian from Caesarea, also dead.

And Schenk?

What is there to say about the Schenks? Little enough, other than that they are an honest if unremarkable family from Sulzbach, a one-spire little place astride a crossroads of no note, barely two leagues to the west of Frankfurt.

But this is not Frankfurt. This is London. Aldgate, to be precise, one of the four original towered gatehouses in the ancient wall that the exiled Trojan, Brutus, raised when he founded the city a thousand years ago. A city he named New Troy. Or so it goes.

After all, what are we if not the sum of the myths we tell ourselves?

The short tunnel stinks of horse-dung. From the narrow ledge where the walls reach the domed ceiling an accretion of pigeon-shit hangs like clusters of pale grapes. Slipping out of the crowd as easily as he entered, Schenk drops to his haunches, wincing. It has taken him five days to walk from the place he came ashore – Woodbridge in the county of Suffolk. As he wiggles his feet to ease the cramp in his calves, the sole of his right boot flaps like a wagging tongue. A rivulet of grit trickles down under the instep, adding to the torment. He sits down on the trampled earth and unlaces the boot to inspect the damage. The glue holding the sole in place has split and a few nails have worked loose. It's nothing a cobbler couldn't put right in a moment, although Schenk's coin is all but spent. He won't receive more until he finds the man he has come to see. Turning side-on to the wall, he hammers the boot against the indifferent stone, silently chanting words from a verse in the Old Testament with each strike: *Enticers... to... idolatry... must... be... slain...*

Biting against the pain of his blisters, Schenk squeezes his foot back inside the leather and reties the laces. A temporary fix, but it should last until he reaches the Steelyard.

In Schenk's mind it is always the *Stalhof*, from the archaic German. His English friends have told him that 'Steelyard' is a corruption of an old term for a measuring balance, or a distortion of the name of the ancient fellow who once owned that stretch of land on the north bank of the Thames close to where the Walbrook empties into the river. One thing alone is indisputable: no steel is sold there now, not since the queen's Privy Council expelled the Hansa merchants from Lübeck, Stade and Cologne.

Schenk knows the story well. For more than three centuries – since the time of England's third Henry – generations of Hansa merchants have made the little self-contained enclave beside the Thames their home. They have built their houses and their businesses, paid their taxes and worshipped God in their own churches. But they are not wanted in England now. The English can make their own trade in pitch, sailcloth, rope and tar. England has no need of the Hansa merchants any more.

It might be empty, its houses boarded up, but the Steelyard offers Petrus Eusebius Schenk something he craves: undisturbed shelter. Now almost deserted, the warren of warehouses, storage sheds and private homes is the perfect place for a man to hide.

But the echoes of his boot striking the wall have attracted one of the gate-guards, set there to raise and lower the portcullis and to watch for vagrants, papists and other undesirables attempting to enter the city. He walks over. Schenk watches him approach, alarm spiking in his veins.

'God give you a good evening, friend,' the man says, smiling without merriment. 'Do we have a name, perchance?'

A name? Why yes, we have a name fit for a Bohemian prince, thinks Petrus Eusebius Schenk. But these days we must be careful about proclaiming it, in case we linger in the memory of a man such as this. Schenk's English is good enough to pass muster, though a little too guttural for general taste. As he answers, he prays his accent won't prick the guard's suspicion.

'Shelby,' he says. 'My name is Nicholas Shelby, of Bankside.'

✠

William Baronsdale, the queen's senior physician, breaks his stride halfway down the long, panelled gallery. His gown – a sinister corvine black – flaps around a frame as angular as a sculptor's armature. The sudden halt releases a faint scent of rosewater from the rushes underfoot, anointed by the grooms to keep the coarser smells from the royal nostrils. In his long professional life, Baronsdale has held every major office the College of Physicians has in its gift to bestow: censor, treasurer, consiliarius, even president. Clad in his formal robe and in the grip of a fearsome indignation, he reminds Nicholas Shelby of nothing so much as a man caught by the sudden urge to burst the swelling head of a particularly uncomfortable boil. Baronsdale's usually placid Gloucestershire tones tighten in concert with his features.

'I can remain silent no longer, sirrah. She will die one day. And when she is with God in His Heaven, enjoying the holy balm of His reward, who will abide your heresies then?'

There was a time – and not so long ago, Nicholas recalls – when to give voice to the very thought of Elizabeth's demise was treason. In the taverns, the dice-dens, the playhouses and the bear-gardens, suggesting that the queen might be anything other than immortal would draw the unwelcome attention of the secret listeners placed there by the Privy Council. But today we need stay silent no longer. Now even the unspeakable may be imagined, made corporeal. Faced. Accepted. Not even those anointed by

God can live for ever. At least, not on this earth. Mercy, thinks Nicholas, how times have changed.

Through the open windows the spring sunshine dances an energetic volta on the brown face of the Thames, racing the breeze upriver towards Windsor. The priceless Flemish hangings fidget gently against the wainscoting, caught by the waft from the open windows. And at the end of the corridor: two yeomen ushers in full harness, barring the way. Nicholas can make out the Tudor rose woven in red and white thread into the breasts of each tunic, and in the polished blades of their axes the reflections of himself and Baronsdale, two tiny curvaceous gargoyles with enormous heads. He waits for Baronsdale to resume his march. But Baronsdale seems reluctant to move, glancing at the yeoman ushers to gauge how long he can delay. I understand, thinks Nicholas – there is still a little pus left to squeeze from the boil.

'I confess it willingly, before my maker,' Baronsdale announces as if it were a last testament. 'I have *never* liked you, Mister Shelby. *Never*. Your arrogant rejection of the discipline you took an oath to uphold... your contempt for tradition, precedence and custom... Who are *you*, sirrah, to scoff at the writings of the learned ancients?'

The thin lips fold in on themselves as though sucking water through a reed. The jowls wobble. They have grown pendulous over the years, the only weight Baronsdale carries. They're where he keeps his store of vitriol, Nicholas decides.

If Baronsdale is expecting an answer, Nicholas is not of a mind to provide one.

'To my mind, sirrah, you are no better than a mountebank,' the senior physician continues petulantly. 'If men of your ilk represent the future of medicine, I see little hope for the continuing survival of Adam's progeny. I prophesy that within a generation it will be an easier thing in England to find the fabled basilisk than an honest doctor. You could at least have worn your physician's gown. You look like a... like a...'

Baronsdale has a lexicon that would stretch around Richmond Palace twice over, most of it medical, much of it Latin. But he seems at a loss to find the right words for the hardy-framed man of middling height with the wiry black hair who stands beside him, a look of weary sufferance on his face.

'An actor from the playhouse?' Nicholas suggests. 'A cashiered pistoleer?'

'Are you mocking me, Shelby?'

'Not at all. I'm merely repeating what Her Majesty has said to me on more than one occasion. Anyway, I wouldn't worry. She's in rude health. She hunts, she dances—'

Yes, and she also ages, Nicholas tells himself. In a few months she'll be sixty-seven. It could happen at any time. But he's damned if he's going to give Baronsdale the slightest satisfaction.

'If she tires of me, I'll live with it.'

Baronsdale wags an accusing finger at him. 'You revel in this, don't you? Despising your betters, laughing at us, as though you have some superior right to question all we hold to be the truth – a truth revealed to us by the Almighty.'

Nicholas responds with a casual shrug. He's growing tired of the lecture. 'I hear you prescribed a freshly killed pigeon to be lain across the ankles of the Countess of Warwick last week, to relieve the swelling,' he says.

'Meat that is still warm draws to it the heat of inflammation,' Baronsdale says defensively. 'I would have thought you'd have learned that at... Where was it you studied medicine: the butcher's shambles on Bankside?'

'Cambridge. And Padua. But the best of it I learned in the Low Countries, on the field of battle. Couldn't get a pigeon for love nor money: the Spanish had eaten them all.'

Nicholas sets off again towards the yeomen ushers guarding the privy chamber. He wishes to God he hadn't bumped into Baronsdale in his hurry to answer the summons. He has no stomach for this fight. His wife Bianca, being half Italian, would blaze with anger, were she here. But Nicholas is made of calmer clay. Acting the firebrand will only confirm Baronsdale in his prejudice. And besides, there's bound to be a prohibition against brawling within the royal verge.

But Baronsdale is right about the queen's favour. The mercurial nature of her interest in young men with good calves and passable looks is legendary. Soldiers, poets, physicians... if you last long enough to receive a nickname, you're doing well. As far as Nicholas is aware, he has not yet been honoured with one. He knows that the time will come when her interest in him wanes. The calls to discuss advances in physic and the natural philosophies will become more infrequent. Then they will cease altogether, and Baronsdale – along with all the other elderly worthies of the College of Physicians – will be ready for his revenge. Their spite will be as sharp as any scalpel. They'll probably drag him before the Censors and have him struck off on some trumped-up accusation that he's practised witchcraft.

'I cannot keep Her Majesty waiting,' he says, laying just enough emphasis on the I to remind Baronsdale that he is not invited. 'Is there anything you wish me to ask her – while we're speaking?'

✠

Safely past the first obstacle, Petrus Eusebius Schenk hoists his heavy pack over his shoulder and sets off towards the Aldgate pump. Looking back, he sees the guard trying to settle an altercation between two waggoners over who has right of way through the arch. A cold trickle of sweat makes its way down his spine as he considers how close he had come to disaster.

'And where are you bound, Master Shelby?' the guard had asked.

'The Dutch church at Austin Friars, to give thanks to God for seeing me safely home.'

'And why would an Englishman named Shelby pray in a church for aliens? Besides, you don't sound English.'

'Because I was Dutch before I was English,' Schenk had explained, struggling to keep his nerve and trusting the man couldn't tell the difference between a Dutch accent and a Hessian one. 'I became an Englishman by letters patent from the Privy Council. Cost me more money than I shall likely see again this side of heaven. And I have friends amongst the Calvinist refugee families who live in the Broad Street Ward. It's good to catch up with old friends after a sermon.'

'Where have you been, then, to get so dusty and travel-worn?' the guard had asked, still not entirely convinced.

'Does it matter?'

'It might. We've been told to keep an eye open for fellows carrying pamphlets.'

'Pamphlets? What manner of pamphlets?'

The guard had lowered his voice, leaning towards Schenk as though to impart a great secret. 'Seditious tracts. Puritan tracts. Tracts that denounce the queen's bishops as corrupters of God's word.'

'Mercy,' Schenk had replied, fearing the guard was about to demand that he open his pack to see if he was carrying such incendiary items. 'Things *have* taken a turn for the worse while I've been gone.'

And then God had sent a brace of angels to save him – in the shape of two particularly stubborn waggoners, whose irate voices are even now echoing around the interior of the Aldgate arch, to the annoyance of the gate-guard.

Schenk's thirst is raging now. Once, he would have stopped at the sign of the King's Head on Fenchurch Street for ale and a bed, but no longer. Too many questioning eyes. Besides, ale is a sinful intoxicant that allows the Devil a way into your soul. Schenk will take honest, God-given water at the Aldgate pump. Then he will walk south along Gracechurch Street towards the river, cut west into Candlewick Street before making his way through the narrow lanes of Dowgate Ward to the Steelyard. How far must he walk before he spots another of his secret companions?

They are always with him. He has seen two on the road from Woodbridge, where he came ashore. The first was a pretty fair-haired youth, the second a woman of around fifty who carried a goose in a wooden cage. He hadn't spoken to either. He knows it is improper to speak to the dead unless they invite you. Schenk is nothing if not polite, an English habit he is proud to have adopted.

After quenching his thirst at the pump, he encounters the next one between the church of St Gabriel and the junction with Lime Street. She cannot be more than seven years old. She walks with a swaying, merry gait. Her arm is raised so that she may hold the hand of the woman beside her. The child's dark hair is tucked up in a French coif, a miniature version of the one favoured by the adult – her mother, Schenk assumes.

There was a time when he would have slowed his pace, held back, perhaps even dived down a lane if there was one to hand – anything but face what he knew was about to happen. But no longer. Now he has learned to embrace the inevitable. It is his way of testing himself against the punishment he knows will one day come.

As the woman senses his presence behind her, she turns. Not caring much for what she sees, her grasp on the child's hand tightens. She steps out across Fenchurch Street, the child stumbling along after her, confused by the sudden change in direction. Just before the woman steers her charge around two apprentice tanners bent under a canopy of hides, the child glances back at him.

Her eyes are exactly what he was expecting: blank, filled with dirt, a worm twining its way out of the corner of one bleached socket. The child smiles up at him, her gums studded not with teeth but with gravel. The tongue lolls – a devil's tongue, the maggots writhing upwards towards the dark safety of the throat. The dead, Petrus Eusebius Schenk knows, enjoy nothing better than to play their little games with the living.

That was probably me, he thinks.

I did that.

⊁

In size, the room Nicholas Shelby is standing in is modest. Barely fifteen paces square, he reckons, with painted panelling and a row of windows looking out over an orchard. Save for a pair of heavy, overly carved sideboards, it is furnished with satin and damask in the style of the Turk, fashionable amongst the quality these days, now that there are exciting new markets in Barbary and the Orient to explore, and an alliance against Spain with the King of Morocco. Instead of chairs or benches to sit upon, a profusion of cushions covers the floor. Nesting amongst them, propped languorously on one elbow, is the majesty of England personified, a potentate in flowing cloth-of-gold, pearls gleaming like the dew on a spider's web. Her white face tilts thoughtfully towards her breast as one of the ladies grouped around her reads in a soft voice from a leather-bound book.

After what seems like half an hour, but is probably only a minute or two, she looks up.

'Marry,' she says, observing the waiting Nicholas and waving away her coterie with the merest spreading of the fingers of her right hand, 'I see my Heretic has arrived.'

She saw me enter, Nicholas thinks, but I did not exist until she had need of me. In this chamber, time itself is at Elizabeth's command. She beckons to him to join her. He kneels beside her, a pose he will have to maintain for as long as it pleases her, regardless of the limitations of his commoner's knees.

'God give you good morrow, Dr Shelby.'

Nicholas bows his head. 'Majesty, I came the moment I was summoned. I feared perhaps you might—'

'Have no concern, sirrah, England is well.'

By 'England', she means, of course, herself. And indeed, she looks well enough. But then she always does. The Venetian ceruse is laid on like mortar, the hair as authentic as the mock-Turkish cushions she reclines upon.

'Then how may I serve, Majesty?'

'Lady Sarah was reading to me from a new translation of *De Rerum Natura*. Did you study Lucretius, when you were in... where was it now?'

'Padua, Majesty.'

'Yes, Padua. Do you know his work?'

'I do, Majesty.'

'And do you believe his claim?'

'Which claim in particular?'

'That everything in the world – rocks, trees, animals,' she gives a regal frown of distaste, '*ourselves* – is in truth made from tiny particles so small that our eyes cannot see them.'

'I am familiar with the opinion, Your Majesty,' Nicholas says. 'Master Shakespeare, in his work *The Tragedy of Romeo and Juliet*, has one of his players speak of tiny *atomi*, creatures so small that they can draw Queen Mab's fairy chariot up men's noses and into their brains whilst they sleep, to make them dream.'

'And Master Shakespeare is naught but a saucy rogue,' the queen tells him firmly. 'It is a blasphemous suggestion. We are made in God's image, not Queen Mab's. Besides, if it were true that we are no more than piles of dust, we would each blow away at the first breeze.'

'Only a week ago I heard the Bishop of London giving a sermon, Majesty,' Nicholas says, without adding that he had been forced to attend because the service had been to inaugurate a new president of the College of Physicians. 'He quoted from Genesis, about us being from dust, and to dust returning.'

'That's not the point, Dr Shelby. While I concede Bishop Bancroft may at times be a little dry, I refuse to believe he is made of soil. More to the point, God is most certainly not made of dust and *therefore*' – a pause to makes sure there can be no debate – 'neither is His anointed, the Queen of England.'

'I'm sure you are right, Majesty,' Nicholas says. He is accustomed now to the inevitable consequence of these conversations: there is only ever one opinion that prevails.

'I recall you did us some small service with the Moors a while back,' Elizabeth says, changing the subject now that victory is hers.

'That was some seven or so years ago, Majesty – Morocco.'

'Sir Robert Cecil told me you made a goodly impression on our behalf, with the sultan and his vizier, Master Anoun.'

'Abd el-Ouahed ben Massaoud ben Muhammed Anoun,' Nicholas says, giving the man he remembers the courtesy of his full appellation. 'I believe it is also acceptable to call him by the shorter style: Muhammed al-Annuri.'

Given the Moorish nature of the furnishings, this chamber would well suit al-Annuri well, Nicholas thinks. He can picture the tall, imposing figure lying back on the cushions, his stern features relieved only by the merest twinkle in the hawkish eyes, like the sultan waiting for Scheherazade to tell him another story.

'You are familiar with Master Anoun?' the queen asks, as if renaming him by royal decree.

'I have met him, Your Grace.'

'You are friends?'

'I wouldn't say that. We did each other some useful service.'

At once Nicholas is back standing in the shade of the red walls of Marrakech, parched and dusty after the camel journey from Safi. The sharif's most trusted minister, he is being told in a reverent tone, as he watches the stately man in the simple white *djellaba* stalk away. Not that al-Annuri had needed identifying. Nicholas would have known him at once, from the warning he'd received before he'd even set foot on the Barbary shore: *Cold bugger... Eyes like a peregrine's... Not the sort of Moor you'd care to cross...* It had never occurred to him at that moment that in a matter of days he would owe al-Annuri his life.

'Sir Robert told me you wouldn't be here now, were it not for Master Anoun,' the queen says, breaking into his thoughts.

'That is so, Majesty. But nor might he be living in peace and comfort in Marrakech.'

'So, you understand each other?'

'Not in our native tongues, Majesty. But we both speak Italian to some degree, though not with the competency I understand Your Majesty possesses. He also has some Spanish.'

Elizabeth eases her position on the cushions. Nicholas thinks he detects the slightest wince of discomfort. He would ask if she was well, but that is not the kind of question a man asks his queen, even if he is one of her physicians. If she is ailing, he will have to wait for her to tell him so.

He remembers the day last year when he caught his one and only sight of the truth behind the royal mask. He had been just behind Robert Devereux, the Earl of Essex, when Devereux had committed the unpardonable insult of throwing open the doors to the queen's privy chamber at Nonsuch Palace and bursting in upon her. Before the ladies-in-waiting had slammed those doors shut again, Nicholas had caught a glimpse of an elderly woman with taut, pockmarked skin and thinning hair, as unroyal as the humblest Bankside washerwoman. Fortunate, he thinks, that the queen hadn't caught sight of him, or else he'd probably be under house-arrest like the unhappy earl.

'Master Anoun is to be received at our court, as the Moroccan king's ambassador. I want you, Dr Shelby, to be my ears and my eyes in his entourage.'

'Me, Majesty?'

'Is there a problem?'

'No, of course not. When does he arrive?'

'Not for a while. I am told he is yet to leave the Barbary shore. With fair winds and God's grace, sometime in August, I would hazard.'

Nicholas mumbles something about how honoured he is to be entrusted with Her Majesty's commission. In his heart, it is not a task he relishes. Until he had met Muhammed al-Annuri, he had never fully appreciated how much menace one man can exude from beneath an otherwise humble white robe.

'It will require a display of humility on your part, I think.'

Nicholas eases himself on his haunches. How can Elizabeth be so perceptive when his last encounter with the Moor took place seven years past and more than four hundred leagues away? Then he realizes she is not speaking of al-Annuri at all. She fixes him with a cold gaze.

'If you are to please us in this matter,' the queen says, staring at him with a look that is even more unnerving for the false whiteness of her complexion, 'you must lay aside this petty quarrel you appear to have with Sir Robert Cecil.'

✠

It is raining when Schenk reaches the Steelyard, a sudden hard summer shower. Overhead the clouds are as black as coal, a halo of dying sunlight edging the rooftops and the spires and the darkness of the river where it turns at Westminster. The cobbles shine like polished tin. Now it's not rainwater but grit that torments Schenk's right foot; he is walking as though lame.

To his relief, he finds the Lord Mayor's men failed to put a lock on the Steelyard gate when they expelled the foreign merchants the year before last. The omission saves him having to scale the outer wall that was once the frontier between English London and the mysteries of the foreign Hansa. Pushing through, Schenk heads directly towards his destination. The way is familiar to him. Some of the storehouses and dwellings he passes show signs of recent occupancy. He spots an overturned stool-pot outside one door, a broom propped beside another. One or two have doors forced open, where some of the city's vagrants have sought shelter, regardless of who once lived here. But most of the properties are just as he expects: dark, empty and abandoned, their occupants banished for ever by royal decree.

On the wharf, wheeling gulls shriek at him, though whether in welcome or in warning he cannot be certain. A skeletal wooden crane still stands forlornly on the quayside, waiting to unload cargoes from the Baltic that will never arrive.

Schenk stops before a modest but neatly timbered house that looks out over the empty wharf and across the water to Bankside. The shadows are lengthening towards night. To his left, stretching across the river like a barrier planted to prevent tomorrow's dawn from coming too soon, he can make out the mass of buildings on London Bridge and the massive stone piers they stand upon. He has arrived in the nick of time. Any later and there would be no light to see what he was doing.

Dropping his pack, he takes the heavy key from his purse. In the gloom, with the rain now streaming down his face, it takes a while to find the keyhole in the square iron lock-plate. But when he does, the key turns with ease. Count on old Aksel Leezen to oil the lock regularly. Who did he think was likely to come here again when he'd gone? Certainly not the fellow presently standing at his door, one foot tilted to let the rainwater drain out of his boot.

Schenk tugs at the door. But it does not open.

He tries again. The solid Baltic birch planks remain firmly in the frame.

He tries the key again. Once more it turns without resistance. But still the door does not open.

Then Schenk notices a second lock-plate, set a foot or so below the first. He had missed it in the shadows. Someone – either Aksel Leezen himself, or a locksmith sent by the Lord Mayor's men – has installed another lock. A lock for which he has no key.

Schenk looks up. The little window in the overhanging upper floor is latched shut. Through glass that hasn't been cleaned in some while, he can make out the interior shutters. He remembers the solid wooden beam that bars them from within – Leezen trusted his fellow merchants even less than he trusted his English customers. It would require a battering ram to break through.

The light is fading fast. Soaked by the shower, Schenk begins to shiver. He fortifies himself by recalling that he has known worse discomforts in his time than a summer shower. Abandoning the house, he searches for an alternative place to hide.

It doesn't take him long to find one: an empty storehouse near that part of the Steelyard wall that borders All Hallows Lane to the east. Inside, the air is stagnant, oily with the smell of pitch. The barrels themselves have gone, either sold before the enclave closed or stolen afterwards. The place has no windows, but that suits him. If he keeps the door shut, he will be invisible, and invisibility is what Schenk needs as much as he needs food and rest.

He retrieves a tinderbox from his pack and a stub of tallow candle. Its meagre flame shows him a glimpse of brickwork with mould sprouting from the mortar. He makes a slow progress around his new realm, holding the candle before him like a priest's censer, oblivious to the stink of burning animal fat that make a rancid incense of the smoke. He finds nothing of use; the storehouse has been stripped bare. He will have to look elsewhere, when the rain stops.

The only other illumination is a grey splash of light on the earthen floor. It leads his eyes upwards to a small hole in the roof where a tile or two has blown away. He considers searching some of the other buildings to find enough dry detritus to get a fire going; the hole will make a vent to stop him choking in the smoke. He could do with the warmth, and he doesn't care to sleep in the dark. That is when his secret companions are more likely to visit him. There are nights when they cluster around him like desperate beggars.

But there are dangers to consider. The Steelyard is not entirely abandoned. Smoke rising from the roof might attract unwelcome attention. When the sun rises, the vagrants sheltering here might come calling. He has nothing of value for them to steal, and though he might once have looked like a diffident chorister, now his plump cheeks have hollowed somewhat, giving him a harder, tougher look. If they are merely curious, he'll tell them he's a masterless labourer thrown off the fields for lack of work. Should they come with evil intent, he knows how to use the knife he carries.

Schenk sits down for a while to rest his feet and wait for the rain to ease. He pulls his pack towards him, folding it to his exhausted body as a miser might hug his hoard of gold. From a pouch on the side, he retrieves the remains of the hunk of bread he stole from an unguarded saddle-pack outside an inn at Chelmsford. The bread is coarse-grained and hard, but it goes a little way towards easing his hunger. He begins to plan.

Tomorrow he will go to see the banker. He won't ask for much. If he has coin, he will be tempted to spend it. Profligacy will only get him noticed. He can wait for his reward. It will be enough just to be dry, less hungry and a few more steps closer to forgiveness.

Returning the last of the bread to the pouch, he starts to unlace the pack's leather flap. His fingers work cautiously, like those of a man about to open the door upon a scene he dreads but knows he cannot escape witnessing. When the flap is at last free, Petrus Eusebius Schenk draws it back and waits for his secret companions – the little girl with the earthen eyes and the maggots in her mouth... the old woman with the goose in a cage... and all the others – to come crawling out to keep him company.

2

The morning after his audience with the queen, Nicholas makes his way towards the Richmond Palace water-gate, praying with almost every step that he doesn't bump into William Baronsdale again. His thoughts are anywhere other than on the wherry waiting to return him to Bankside. Thus it is only when he gets close to the jetty that the casual way the oarsmen watch him approach causes a flicker of concern in his mind. Something is not quite right. Nicholas is used to raised eyebrows and doubting looks from the royal servants. Judged against the satins and velvets preferred by other visitors to the queen's palaces, he knows his plumage is decidedly dowdy – a simple olive-green doublet laced with scarlet points and black Venetian hose, his knee-high boots no better polished than those of the stable-lad at the Tabard inn on Long Southwark. He prefers to leave the collar of his shirt loose, finding a ruff an irritation against his close-cut beard. It's not that he's making a point about his humble origins, he doesn't have the money to dress more fashionably. If he wanted, he could remedy that lack in an instant. His occasional audiences with the queen have enticed a regular stream of courtiers out of the woodwork, most of them presenting with imagined ailments just so that they can dig for titbits of information or use him to curry favour. He refuses to indulge them. Let them whine, he thinks; it's ordinary Banksiders who have real need of his physic.

But while he might dress like a stable groom, the bargemen at Richmond, Whitehall and Greenwich know him well enough by now. They should be preparing to cast off from the jetty the moment he settles into the cushions, treating him with the urgency their richer passengers expect. Yet they show no signs of alacrity. They sit on their benches as if enjoying a pleasant day out on the river.

Is he to share the ride with someone more important, someone who has yet to arrive? He looks back over his shoulder. Beyond the orchard wall the many towers of Richmond Palace soar into the misty air, each one capped with a burnished dome like an onion stuck atop a painted pole. The multitude of windows gleam like pearls against the red brickwork. It looks to Nicholas as bejewelled as its owner. But the path behind him is empty. He is alone.

'Are we waiting for someone?' he asks when he reaches the wherry.

'Aye, sir. You.'

The lead oarsman doffs his cap.

Nicholas waits for something to happen. But the oarsman does not reach out for the bag that contains his overnight things.

'I'm ready, if you are,' he says, beginning to feel a little foolish.

'A message from Sir Robert, Dr Shelby,' the oarsman says. 'We are not to take you to Bankside until you have seen him.'

How petty, thinks Nicholas, to let me find out just as I was about to climb aboard. Could Mr Secretary not have sent word directly to my chamber? Does my refusal to be his intelligencer still rankle?

It will take him a good four hours to walk back to Bankside. He considers going to the stables and asking for a horse. But he suspects Cecil will have sent the groom there, too, with the same message he gave to the wherryman. The only other option is to wait for a public wherry to put in at the Richmond water-stairs.

But that might mean a long wait, and the sooner he is back on Bankside with Bianca and little Bruno, the better he will feel.

But the truth is – and Nicholas knows it only too well – to walk, sail or ride is a freedom he does not enjoy. No one in his right mind would so contemptuously disobey a command from the queen's principal Secretary of State.

Letting out a weary sigh, he turns back towards the palace.

✠

Robert Cecil is standing over a trestle-table in a plain chamber in the Middle Court, the view from the window half-obscured by the pyramid roof of the great kitchen. A chest full of papers lies open beside the table, a small part of the travelling fair of state business that must catch up with Mr Secretary Cecil wherever he happens to be. Watching him from the open doorway, Nicholas imagines he's looking at a five-foot-tall raven with a pale face and an injured wing, a pint-sized Mephistopheles in a black velvet half-cape tailored to minimise his ill-formed shoulders. He is the bane of Nicholas's life.

As Nicholas enters, Cecil looks up.

'What was it this time?' he asks pleasantly. 'Lucretius and his nonsense?'

'She did mention Lucretius, yes.'

Cecil is Nicholas's age, but he carries himself as if all the wisdom of the ages is contained within his little, damaged frame. It is an intensity that Nicholas always finds unsettling.

'I haven't seen you for a while,' Cecil says.

And that's the way I like it, thinks Nicholas. He still can't quite believe that Sir Robert has truly released him from his role as intelligencer. The Crab's claw is not known for its willingness to let go of anything he might find useful, even if it is in exchange for having Nicholas remain as his family physician. 'Then let us give thanks that you and young Master William are in good health, Sir Robert. You've had no need of me.'

'I saw Baronsdale a short while ago, though.'

'I'm sure he sang my praises.'

'To be honest, he had the look of a whoremaster whose vixens had all decided to run away. Have you upset him?'

'No more than usual, Sir Robert.'

'And what of me? How have I offended?'

The question comes as a surprise to Nicholas. Given Cecil's lofty position, why would he care? It can't be down to a generosity of spirit; Cecil isn't that sort of man.

'I have always been grateful for the favour you have shown me, Sir Robert,' Nicholas says cautiously. 'I am happy to tend your boy, should the need arise. Let us both pray that will be seldom, if ever.'

But in the meantime I'd rather you found some other sap to risk his life, and those of his wife and son, in the service of your darker self.

'Still aggrieved about Ireland?' Cecil asks smoothly, as though he can read Nicholas's thoughts.

'If I'd known you were sending me there merely in order to weaken the Earl of Essex in the eyes of Her Majesty while bolstering your own position, I would have thought twice about going.'

Cecil gives him a cold smile. 'Still the same plain-speaking yeoman's son, I see.'

'I believe it right to be honest in all things, Sir Robert.'

'Very laudable, if somewhat priggish,' Cecil observes. 'Advancement of position without the attendant advancement of manners – that way lies catastrophe, Nicholas. Essex was – still is – a danger to this realm. His ambition will end badly for him.'

'Robert Devereux's ambitions were no concern of mine, Sir Robert.'

'But they are the realm's concern, Nicholas. That's why I sent you to Ireland. In these times it is not for a man to decide which duty he will, or will not, honour. When called, he must rise to the moment.'

'I was called to be a physician, Sir Robert, not an agent of intrigue, politics or deceit.'

'A physician who cannot afford a new doublet.'

'I'm a yeoman farmer's son; we tend to make do with only what we need.'

Nicholas is aware it sounds pompous, but he's damned if he's going to let Cecil know that he sends what money he can spare to his father at Barnthorpe. It was only by mortgaging his land that Yeoman Shelby had been able to send Nicholas to study medicine at Cambridge in the first place. With a row of bad harvests giving his parents sleepless nights, a plain doublet is no price to pay at all.

'If you're hoping the queen will shower you with riches,' Cecil says with a wry smile, 'I can tell you you'll end up paying far more for the privilege of her occasional interest than you will ever earn from it. My father, Lord Burghley, knew all about that.'

Nicholas considers pointing out that Burghley House and all the other properties the Cecils own didn't build themselves. But he keeps his peace.

'I think you should see this,' Cecil says, taking a sheet of paper from the desk and handing it to Nicholas. 'It's an appeal to the queen.'

Nicholas takes the document. The writing is that of someone of modest but thorough education, neat but not flamboyant:

Whereas the Queen's majesty, tendering the good and welfare of her own natural subjects, greatly distressed in these hard times of dearth, is highly discontented to understand the great number of

Negroes and Blackamoors which, as she is informed,
are carried into this realm since the troubles between
Her Highness and the King of Spain...

Nicholas lets his eyes run on over the list of grievances.

... to the great annoyance of her own liege people
that covet the relief which these people consume...
most of them are infidels, having no understanding
of Christ or His Gospel... the said kind of people
shall be with all speed avoided and discharged out
of this, Her Majesty's realm...

'Unusually for one of these diatribes, this one is actually signed,' Cecil points out. 'One Casper van Senden, a merchant, apparently. On the surface, it's an attack against foreigners, which I consider somewhat rich, given that he's originally from Lübeck.'

'And below the surface?'

'Little more than an attempt to get Her Majesty's permission to take up those same Blackamoors and transport them out of the realm, for his own profit. The point is, "highly discontented" is a fair assessment of many of those same "natural subjects" he seeks to champion; at least those natural subjects who happen to be members of the city's worshipful companies.'

'The guilds?'

'It was their anger that persuaded the Privy Council and the Lord Mayor to eject the Hansa merchants from the Steelyard.'

'On what grounds?'

'They objected to what they believed to be underhand and deceitful foreign practices, undermining the toil of honest Englishmen.'

Cecil tugs at one sleeve of his black velvet gown. Nicholas has seen him do it often, a surreptitious habit to make his crooked shoulders look like those of a better-made man.

'There is a cold current running beneath the surface of this realm, Nicholas,' Cecil continues, 'a current I don't much care for. People have come to the realization that the queen cannot live for ever. They can smell change coming. And change can be fertile ground for trouble. There are some in this realm looking for an opportunity to make mischief – dangerous mischief. It won't take much to turn the merely discontented into the violent mob.'

Nicholas recalls what Baronsdale had said to him in the corridor before his audience with the queen: *And when she is with God in His Heaven, enjoying the holy balm of His reward, who will abide your heresies then?* Perhaps Cecil is conscious that when the queen is no longer alive, he too will have to ride out the rough waters of change, unprotected.

'This is all very interesting, Sir Robert. But why call for me? I'm no longer your intelligencer. If you want to sniff out mischief, I suggest you buy yourself another scent-hound.'

Cecil seems amused by Nicholas's show of defiance. He feigns hurt. 'Mercy, how ungenerous. I summoned you because I thought I could do you a favour, Nicholas.'

'A favour?'

'I still hold you in high regard, even if you are somewhat fiery and stubborn. I suppose we must put that down to the influence of your wife's Italian blood.'

Here it comes, thinks Nicholas: the poisoned chalice. 'And does that favour require me to travel to, say, Marrakech? Or back to the Irish forests? Will I come away from it thankful to still have my life – *if* I'm lucky enough to come away from it?'

Cecil smiles. 'Come now, this is hyperbole. Last time I heard, Suffolk was at peace.'

'Suffolk?' Nicholas echoes.

'Yes, Barnthorpe. That is where Yeoman Shelby farms?'

'You know it is.'

Cecil gives a little shrug. 'If you'd prefer not to bother, then so be it. 'Tis no concern of mine.' He rummages through the papers on the table. Nicholas watches him with mounting unease. Finding what he's looking for, Cecil lifts another document, this time a small sheet of cheap paper with neatly printed lines of text on it. He waves it leisurely in Nicholas's direction. 'I thought you'd be more grateful for the effort I put in,' he says, in mock disappointment.

'Effort? Into what?'

'Why, stopping the magistrates lopping off your father's right hand for spreading sedition like this, of course.'

3

Even as Nicholas reaches out to take the little sheet of paper, he imagines the axe blade smashing not into his father's wrist but his own. The physician in him sees in stark but prosaic detail the flesh parting, the tendons severing, the bones splitting. Forcing a professional detachment upon himself, he studies the document.

The first thing that strikes him is the quality of the print. While the paper might be coarse and cheap, the lines of type would pass scrutiny by the Stationers' Company, whose printers go about their business in the precincts of St Paul's. The lines are square on the page, regular and clear. But what makes Nicholas's mouth sag in disbelief are the words themselves. They begin with a rousing call to arms:

A cry to all God-fearing Englishmen...

From there on, the message is uncompromising, chilling in its implacability. It is nothing less than a call to overthrow the very foundations of the queen's realm:

Away with the vile servile dunghill of those ministers of damnation, the queen's bishops! Destroy that viperous generation, those scorpions, those puppets of the Antichrist, the murderers of the soul. Let God's hand strike those who worship false gods, even as they weep pious tears of lying falsity. All will be damned, save those whom God has already chosen. Prayer is not enough; only a pure and sinless heart will speed your reward in heaven. Be our masters ever so mighty, their pride and their vanity will destroy them. Cast them down into the fires of hell where they belong. Let Hooper, the glorious Martyr, be thy touchstone and thy comfort, even when the task seems beyond the strength of thine arm. Deut. XIII.

Be the first to raise thy hand.

'I presume you studied John Foxe at school in Barnthorpe, if they have such things as schools there?' Cecil says, reaching out to retrieve the pamphlet. '*Actes and Monuments?*'

Nicholas nods. Being forced to read Foxe's account of the burning of Protestant martyrs on Queen Mary's Catholic pyres had kept him awake at night, especially the case of John Hooper. It had taken the pious Hooper almost an hour to die, calling all the while for God to receive his soul, until his jaw burned away. Even then he fought against the torment, flailing his hands against his breast in supplication, until one arm burned clean through at the elbow joint and fell off into the flames.

'What has this paper got to do with my father?' Nicholas asks, handing back the tract to Cecil.

'An identical one was found in his possession.'

'Found? Where? By whom?'

'I am not aware of the precise details. All I know is that the magistrates at Ipswich are ready to cut off his hand for disseminating such monstrous sentiments. One is even calling for his execution. Fortunately, when Yeoman Shelby mentioned your name in his defence, they thought it best to consult me first.'

Nicholas stares at Cecil, confused and afraid.

'Then the magistrates have made a mistake. My father would never be party to something like this. Who arrested him?'

'Sir Thomas Wragby of Framlingham, Her Majesty's local justice of the peace.'

'I know that name,' Nicholas says, searching his memory. 'He was a magistrate when I was a boy, then went off to fight with the army of the House of Orange. When I was in Holland, they called him Wrath-of-God Wragby.'

'You've met him then?'

'No, Sir Robert. By '87 he was safely tucked away in Delft, on the staff of the late Earl of Leicester.'

'Well, he returned to England last year, while you were in Ireland.' Cecil jabs at the document on his desk as if to run it through. 'And Wragby's piety seems to have thrived in the damp Dutch soil, because he wasn't much impressed when your father was brought before him in possession of material like that.'

'My father isn't a seditionist, Sir Robert,' Nicholas insists. 'He's a loyal subject of the queen.'

'Has he never expressed such sentiments to you before?'

'Of course not! He has enough on his mind trying to make a living from the land he holds. Puppets of the Antichrist? Murderers of the soul? If a bishop dropped by to help my father with the ploughing, he'd be as civil to him as the next man.'

'This isn't trivial, Nicholas,' Cecil cautions. 'This is extreme Puritanism. You can forget all about observing the Sabbath more properly or eschewing the playhouse and the tavern. You can ignore refusing to wear the white surplice in the pulpit. *This*' – another thrust at the tract – 'this is what the zealots of Puritanism would have come to pass, if they could: the overthrow of bishops and princes. They would have the common people believe that they should have no leader other than God Himself, and that they are the ones who should determine His will on earth. And to promote such nonsense is punishable by death.'

Nicholas tries to imagine his father as a Puritan rebel. He fails utterly. True, he has occasionally heard his father grumble at his lot, but is there a farmer's son anywhere in England who hasn't? Besides, Yeoman Shelby has witnessed the realm's religion change, sometimes violently, from Protestant to Catholic and back again, yet never once has Nicholas heard him criticize the eternal order imposed upon him by God and his sovereign.

'Did you notice the reference at the end: *Deut.* followed by the Roman numerals for thirteen?' Cecil asks, breaking into his thoughts.

'I assume it refers to the thirteenth chapter in the Book of Deuteronomy.'

'Correct. And do you happen to know what we would find in Deuteronomy thirteen, were we to look?'

'I cannot say that I do, Sir Robert. I tended to fall asleep during old Parson Olicott's sermons.'

Cecil takes a small volume bound in expensive black leather from the desk and hands it to Nicholas. 'I had to send to Her Majesty's chaplain for this,' he says. 'Finding a copy of the Old Testament, it appears, is like trying to find a physician who gives you a straight answer.'

Nicholas opens the book at the place indicated by a gilded ribbon. Letting his eyes move quickly over the dense print, he soon reads enough to understand why Cecil is worried:

*The enticers to idolatry must be slain, seem they never so holy...
If thy brother, the son of thy mother, or thine own son, or thy
daughter, or the wife, that lieth in thy bosom... entice thee
secretly, saying, Let us go and serve other gods... thine hand shall
be first upon him to put him to death...*

'Papist credo – that I can deal with,' Cecil says when Nicholas
looks up. 'But this is something else, something perhaps even
more troubling. This is the queen's own religion distorted into
something dark and very dangerous.'

Nicholas points to the single sheet of printed text, the document that could mean his father's mutilation, or worse. 'That
thing, is it the actual one found in my father's possession?'

'Yes. But what troubles me most is that it's not the only one.'

'You mean there are others?'

'We've had a few turn up here in the city, in churches mostly.
Fortunately they were swiftly handed in. But it's only a matter
of time before news of this... this...' – Cecil struggles for a word
bearing the necessary heft – 'this plot begins to spread.'

'I presume you're searching for the culprit.'

'Oh, indeed we are. But that's not as easy as you might think.
We've been to every printer licensed by the Stationers' Company,
with no luck. Now we must look further afield, for a secret, unlicensed press. There are more than two hundred thousand people
in this city. What are the chances of catching the perpetrator
with the ink still wet on his fingers?'

Nicholas shakes his head. 'I don't understand, Sir Robert. My
father would never subscribe to such notions. I cannot believe
he would embrace this nonsense, let alone proclaim it in public.'

'Your father is a lucky man. If the Ipswich magistrates had
ignored him when he claimed his son was physician to Her
Majesty – something we both know is not strictly true – then

Yeoman Shelby could already be missing a hand, at the very least. Earning a living from the soil is hard enough at the best of times, but a missing right hand could be enough to bring the spectre of penury and starvation into view.'

'Where is he being held?'

'Framlingham Castle.'

'If I went there, do you think I could effect his release?'

A rare smile plays at the corner of Robert Cecil's mouth. 'Are you asking for my help, Nicholas? I thought you had dispensed with me.'

He's going to make me beg, Nicholas thinks. He's going to punish me for daring to break free of him. 'Only in the matter of acting as one of your intelligencers, Sir Robert. You know of the regard I hold for you in all other matters.'

'Prettily said. I have already written a letter instructing Yeoman Shelby to be released on your recognizance, pending further investigation. You can carry it to Wragby yourself – take a horse from the stables, if you want; tell the grooms you are about my business. When you get to Framlingham, I recommend you take your father home and talk some sense into him.'

Fumbling his words in reply, Nicholas manages, 'That's... that's... very generous of you, Sir Robert.'

'I am not one to forget past services, Nicholas. In this uncertain world, you may at least rely on that.'

Perhaps Mr Secretary Cecil's appetite for duplicity is waning with the passing years, Nicholas thinks. Or is there something else behind this sudden generosity?

'I'm certain I can resolve this, Sir Robert,' he says. 'I know my father had nothing to do with whoever is printing these pamphlets.'

'I believe you, Nicholas. Caution your father to take more care. And perhaps tell him to avoid the local ale. If, as you say, his behaviour is out of character, they must be brewing some very fiery stuff in Barnthorpe.'

'He no longer drinks strong ale,' Nicholas says.

Cecil rolls his eyes. 'Christ's wounds! That won't count in his favour, not if you're trying to convince Wrath-of-God Wragby that he's no Puritan. When you see him, I suggest you advise your father to indulge in as many earthly vices as a man of his age may enjoy without injury to his body or his soul.'

Nicholas finds himself replying with an unexpected laugh.

'If it does not offend, I may disregard that advice, Sir Robert. I think my mother will have had enough shocks already.'

✠

Bianca Merton's apothecary shop on Dice Lane, between St Saviour's church and the bear-garden, is doing brisk business. Despite the good weather, Bankside is experiencing one of its frequent outbreaks of troublesome coughs on the lungs. The patent electuary she offers is a mixture of anise, celery seeds and pepper. It is bound in honey, taken from the hives she and her Carib assistant, Cachorra, have recently set up in Bianca's hidden physic garden down by the river on Black Bull Alley. And Bianca has almost sold out of it. When the door opens for the twentieth time this afternoon, she looks up from her mixing table, prepared to disappoint.

The young fellow making his way towards her seems to be in better health than many in Southwark, and certainly more prosperous. The velveteen shine of his black lawyer's gown is matched only by the gleam on his plump cheeks and the wide barren stripe that runs between the two halves of his spiky brown hair, like a firebreak between two clumps of gorse. Ducking around the clusters of dried herbs and plants that hang from the ceiling beams and make a heavily scented arbour of the little shop, he stops before her and makes a passable bend of the knee.

'Mistress Merton?' he enquires, his eyes uncertain whether to settle on Bianca or Cachorra.

'This is Mistress Merton,' Cachorra says, her English tinged with a strong Spanish accent.

The stranger seems almost relieved. But Cachorra is used to that. In her short time on Bankside, she has learned that many Englishmen are a little discomforted when encountering a striking, strongly built Carib woman a good head higher than they are.

'Good morrow, sir. How may I be of service?' Bianca says, starting to run her fingers through the thick dark waves of her hair, a habit she has had since childhood. She stops herself. Last week when she did the same thing, she found a grey hair entwined around her fingers. She is almost thirty-eight, but she cannot imagine wearing a wig like the queen is said to do, because her hair is too thick and untamed to abide it. She might consider dye, but that would be an expensive luxury if she didn't want to smell of charcoal and pig fat. 'Are you ill?' she enquires. 'You don't look ill.'

'Perhaps a privy word might be in order,' the fellow says, casting a sideways glance at Cachorra. 'A person might wish to keep certain things from a Blackamoor.'

'I'm not a *Blackamoor*,' Cachorra says, seeming to gain an inch or two as she rouses herself. 'I'm from Hispaniola – via the household of the late illustrious gentleman Don Rodriquez Calva de Sagrada.'

'Cachorra is my friend and my apprentice,' Bianca explains in a tight voice, suddenly very close to losing her temper. She can already feel the Italian phrases forming in her mind, ready to receive the burning match. 'Anything you have to say to me, sir, you may say in Cachorra's presence also.'

'It's a legal matter, to your direct benefit. I'm simply trying to be discreet, lest any seek to take advantage.'

Bianca puts her hands on her hips. 'The last person who tried to take advantage of *me*, sirrah, was the Earl of Tyrone – and *he's* a wanted fugitive with a bounty on his head. Now, out with it.'

Wisely accepting defeat, the visitor announces himself to be Master Nathaniel Woolrich, clerk to Their Honours at the Consistory Court.

'And what does that have to do with me, pray?' Bianca asks.

'Were you ever acquainted with a man named Aksel Leezen?'

Bianca remembers the white-bearded old Hansa merchant who – before his death last year – had imported many of the more exotic ingredients for her distillations, infusions and medicaments. 'Dearest Aksel, yes, of course. What of him?'

'I am pleased to be able to inform you that although it has taken a while for Their Honours to come to an agreement, they have managed it at last.'

'Agreement? Managed what?'

Woolrich opens his hands as if to say, *Where to begin?*

'Firstly, the Consistory Court deemed that Leezen wasn't a proper person to make the bequest, given that he was a foreigner. But then we discovered that two days before his demise he was made one of Her Majesty's subjects by Patent of Denization—'

Bianca resists the urge to lift Master Woolrich of the Consistory Court by his collar and shake him like one of her jars of medicinal decoction. 'I'm expecting more customers soon,' she says evenly. 'If you could just get to the point...'

'Yes, of course,' Woolrich says. 'Aksel Leezen has left you something in his Will.'

Bianca puts her hands together in surprised appreciation. 'How thoughtful of him. Aksel was such a kind, generous man, and he had little enough to give away. I don't know what to say. Have you brought it with you?'

'I should be a veritable Hercules if I had,' Woolrich says with a condescending smile. 'He's left you his house.'

✠

Leaving Cachorra in charge of the shop, Bianca takes a detour on her way to the Jackdaw, the tavern she purchased near the Mutton Lane shambles when she first arrived in London some twelve years ago. She stops off at her secluded physic garden to do some tidying, before prising her son Bruno away from the attentions of Ned and Rose Monkton, who now manage the Jackdaw for her.

Cutting a sprig of eglantine (which she intends to mix with ashes and honey to halt the hair loss so afflicting Mary Spindle, the churchwarden's wife), she ponders upon her contumacious husband. She can understand his discomfort at accepting financial help from a woman – even if that woman is his wife – but the tavern is turning a good profit these days. More than once Bianca has offered to send money to his father in Barnthorpe, but Nicholas has always refused, preferring instead to dip into the modest returns he makes as a physician.

A lesser man would be rich by now, pandering to the over-indulged, selling doubtful cures to those attracted by his association with Sir Robert Cecil and his not infrequent summonses to Whitehall, Greenwich, Hampton Court or Richmond. His rejection of so much of the physic he had been taught – labelling it misguided or just plain wrong – hasn't helped. It has made him enemies amongst many of the elder fellows of the College of Physicians. Save for a few trusted patients, his only income is the stipend he gets for attending Robert Cecil and his young son, and the sixpence a session Nicholas makes from St Thomas's Hospital for the poor, which pays him a pittance once a week to provide medical care to the destitute of Southwark.

As for the rest of Bankside, most of them can only pay him in vegetables, a chicken or two, eels, or a side of mutton when things are looking up. *We should have stayed in Padua,* she has thought more than once, though she's never dared suggest it to him. *You might have made lecturer at the university.*

She knows for a fact that the great Fabricius, professor of anatomy at the Palazzo Bo, certainly thought highly of her husband. He still does, it seems. Every few months Nicholas receives a letter from the old gentleman, his face lighting up as he reads of some new advance or discovery. But the joy is fleeting. She knows he wants to discuss these matters with his colleagues, but the likes of old Baronsdale have so tarnished his standing within the College that no one wants to be seen discussing their profession with a heretic. Now when the letters arrive, Nicholas will invariably withdraw to Nonsuch Palace for a day or two, where he can be sure of the sympathetic – and knowledgeable – ear of Lord Lumley, the two friends strolling through Lumley's immense library together, discussing the contents of the letters in detail, which is often frankly beyond her.

As if her thoughts of Nicholas have magically conjured him up, she hears his voice: 'I thought I'd find you here, sweet.'

Looking up, she sees him stepping through the doorway in the ancient and sagging brick wall that separates the physic garden from Black Bull Alley. Laying down her trimming knife, she stands up and greets him, reaching out to throw her arms around him. She checks herself at the last moment, preventing her muddy hands from clasping his shoulders. Instead she holds them palms together, as though in prayer.

'So the queen has tired of her plaything, my husband,' she says, a mischievous glint in her eyes as she leans forward to kiss him.

'As is her royal prerogative.'

'And what was it this time? Master Copernicus and his model of the cosmos, or Dr Dee and his necromancy?'

'We spoke at length of *atomi*.'

'*Atomi*? And who might he be, pray?'

'Not a "he" – tiny particles, small beyond the eye's ability to see, but which are deep in all things in nature. They dance about, their motion giving rise to all natural disturbances.'

Noticing the troubled look in his eyes, Bianca says, 'You mean like Robert Cecil?'

'Indeed,' Nicholas says, laughing.

'I have some goodly news, Husband.'

'I'm mighty glad to hear it.'

'Do you recall old Aksel Leezen?'

'I cannot say I do. But I, myself, have something to—'

In her eagerness, she cuts him off.

'I used to buy Muscovy rowanberry from him, for quickening the digestion; birch sap for kidney stones; aralia for those afflicted by a slowing of the thoughts – lots of ingredients. Never once cheated me with crushed bark or coloured water. He died last year, while we were away in Ireland.'

'Now you mention it, I do vaguely remember him,' Nicholas says, accepting defeat and nodding as the image of an unremarkable fellow in a coat of plain Flemish frieze, a mournful face rimmed with a white beard, comes to his mind.

'A lawyer came to see me on Dice Lane today. Aksel has remembered me in his Will. Apparently it's all been somewhat complicated. You see, Aksel was born in Saxony—'

'Is that so?' Nicholas interjects. He knows, from experience, that when Bianca Merton is in flood, there's no dam yet built that can halt her. But he tries. 'I really must tell you—'

'Anyway, because he was a foreigner, the Consistory Court deemed that he didn't actually own his property. But then they got confirmation from the Privy Council that Aksel had become an Englishman by Patent of Denization. So the archbishop finally gets round to deciding that dear Aksel was neither a usurer nor a convicted heretic, that he's not a child, a woman or a felon and that, as he wasn't an apostate, a sodomite or raving drunk, he was entitled under English law to make a Will—'

In desperation, Nicholas takes her by the shoulders. 'Bianca, I must go to Barnthorpe. It's my father—'

This, at last, brings her to a halt. She sees the anxiety in her husband's eyes.

'Oh, Nicholas – I'm sorry. Is everything alright? He hasn't—?'

'No, sweet. He hasn't died.'

'Oh, thank Jesu for that.'

'But he's imprisoned in Framlingham Castle. He's in grave danger of losing his right hand for having possession of a seditious pamphlet.'

Bianca listens, appalled, while Nicholas tells her of the tract his father is supposed to have had about him when he was arrested.

'Did Sir Robert say where these tracts were coming from?' she asks.

Nicholas raises his eyes to heaven and spreads his hands, as if to tell her that the answer is unknowable this side of the Resurrection. 'A secret, unlicensed press *somewhere* in the city,' he says ponderously, imitating Robert Cecil at his most formal.

'There's a printer on Gravel Lane,' Bianca says. 'I remember someone saying he'd brought his press across from the north bank two winters back. Keeps himself very much to himself, from what I understand. He wouldn't be on Bankside if he was authorized by the Stationers' Company. Do you think it might be him?'

Nicholas laughs. 'This is Bankside. He's probably here because he's printing questionable Italian tales of love – with accompanying illustrations.'

'But he might be able to help you, Nicholas. He might have heard something. Rumours, perhaps. Anything that could help you prove your father isn't the source would make it easier to get him out of prison.'

Nicholas's instinct is to ride for Suffolk immediately, but on reflection he thinks her suggestion sound. 'Robert Cecil has already written a letter ordering my father's release. But I still need to prove his innocence. Those tracts didn't just flutter down from the sky like falling leaves. At least this printer fellow might be able to tell me where to start looking for their source.'

Bianca frowns as a thought occurs to her. 'This isn't one of the Crab's ploys to drag you back into his service, is it? That's how you were lured into his web in the first place – when he threatened to hang me for a papist if you didn't spy on Lord Lumley at Nonsuch Palace for him.'

Nicholas gives her an appeasing smile. 'It's nothing like that. I think his offer to help was genuine. He hasn't asked for a single thing in return.'

'Not yet. Wait till you get back. I don't trust that little anatomy—'

'Atomi.'

'I still don't trust him.' Bianca takes him by the sleeve of his doublet, getting dirt on the cuff. She brushes it off with the back of her hand. 'I'll help you pack. There's some mutton and bread at the Paris Garden lodgings. You can take that with you. Hire a horse from the stables at the Tabard. Tell them to send the account to the Jackdaw.'

'I've already got a horse,' he says with a knowing smile.

'What do you mean you've *got a horse*? You've got two doublets – one of them as patched as Bruno's toy deer – two sets of Venetian hose and a physician's chest that I dare not look in. You don't even have your physician's gown. You threw it away in disgust, remember? If there's one possession I know you to be lacking, it's a horse.'

'Cecil offered me one from the stables at Richmond.'

Bianca gives him a look of deep suspicion. 'Are you *sure* this isn't some deceit he's playing on you, for his own ends?'

'You might be right. But for the present I must get my father out of danger. He and my brother Jack have enough to worry about at Barnthorpe, as it is. A yeoman farmer with one hand is about as useful as a physician who thinks you can cure a sprained ankle with a still-warm dead pigeon.'

Bianca gives him a quizzical look.

'Baronsdale,' Nicholas explains with a roll of his eyes.

'Oh. You've had *another* argument with the former president of the College of Physicians?'

'He made it clear that if it weren't for the queen's interest in me, he'd be relishing the Censors stripping me from the College roll.'

'Well then, you'd best keep yourself in Her Majesty's affections, hadn't you?' Bianca tells him with a grin. She gives the broadcloth sleeve of his doublet a disapproving tug. 'Adopt the style of a court gallant.'

'Utterly beyond me, I fear.'

'Oh, I don't know. I'm sure there's a courtier hiding somewhere under that bluff yeoman's exterior.'

Nicholas laughs. 'Do you really think so? I don't recall that it was my ability to dance a pavane or read verse that made you fall in love with me.'

'Must have been *something*,' Bianca says teasingly as she makes a point of studying the way his thighs fill the woollen Venetians he's wearing.

As she locks the door to the physic garden behind her and they step out into Black Bull Alley, Nicholas says, 'You haven't told me what old Aksel Leezen left you in his Will. A nice little memento, I hope.'

'Oh, it was much more than a memento, Husband. He left me his house.'

Nicholas stops in his tracks. 'His *house*?'

'Worth fifty pounds, according to the lawyer who brought me the news.'

Nicholas whistles. 'That is some bequest.'

'Aksel had no family in England,' Bianca explains. 'His wife and daughter died in '93, when the plague came. You were in Morocco at the time, cavorting with those alluring Moor sirens.' She makes a play of coquettishly drawing a veil across her face, remembering the Eastern women she had seen in Venice.

'I'm from Suffolk,' Nicholas says. 'Morocco was too hot for cavorting. Will you rent it out or sell it?'

'I haven't decided yet.'

'Somewhere pleasant, I hope. It would be good for you to have a property away from London, should the plague ever return. Essex is too flat. Suffolk's too marshy. Kent's too quarrelsome. Surrey would be nice. We could visit John Lumley more often.'

Bianca lets out a peal of laughter.

'Nowhere so tranquil,' she says. 'It's here in the city, across the river. It's in the Steelyard.'

4

P etrus Eusebius Schenk stands in the neat porch while a servant's eyes range contemptuously over him in the fading light. The property is a smart, timbered town house on Milk Lane, just off Cheapside, not far from Goldsmiths' Row where the seriously wealthy financiers live. The owner has made a careful choice. The Royal Exchange is barely five minutes' walk away, but the house is secluded enough not to attract an angry mob whenever the price of grain rises too steeply.

'We give no relief to vagabonds here,' the man says, preparing to slam the door in Schenk's face. 'Be gone.'

Schenk returns the stare with interest. He notes the fancy tunic and the Florentine-style boots. *Bankers*, he thinks; even their servants consider themselves mighty.

'I'm here on business,' he says.

'I doubt it,' the servant sneers. 'The only business a fellow like you will be about round here is house-diving. Away with you, or I'll fetch the constable to give you an ear-trimming.'

Schenk bites his tongue. 'Tell Silvan Gaspari that someone from Zurich is here to see him. Tell him I'm a friend – of the brothers.'

'Master Gaspari doesn't have a brother,' the servant says, his eyebrows almost meeting as he frowns.

'He's a banker – he probably doesn't have any friends, either. But he'll see me. He'll understand.'

A deep voice, syrupy with affluence, calls from inside the house. 'Who is it, Jonas?'

'A man who says he's from Zurich. He says he's a friend of the brothers.'

'Not here,' growls the voice. 'Tell him to wait by the garden door at the end of the lane.'

The servant repeats the instructions, then closes the door in Schenk's face, though not with the slam he was expecting. Schenk hears an ostentatious rattle of the lock, as if the servant still isn't wholly convinced the visitor isn't here to steal the plate and jewellery.

A few moments later the man who opens the garden door to Schenk is a very different order of creature altogether: a large, glossy monument to hard business and easy living. His coat of Bruges taffeta sparkles in the light. On his head he wears a black velvet cap with a broad fringe of white goose feathers along one side. Luxurious silver locks tumble around his shoulders. The sheen on his plump features comes not from the exertion of hurrying to this pleasant corner of his garden, but from the regular application of expensive balms and ointments.

Although they have never met, Schenk knows at once that this is Silvan Gaspari, one of a numerous tribe scattered across the principalities of Europe. The Gaspari – Swiss bankers to a man – may not be as rich as the Fuggers, but they can claim to be longer-lasting than the Medici or the Bardi, having been sensible enough never to have loaned money to England's Edward III, who at a stroke ruined most of the Italian banking families by refusing to pay back the half-million crowns he'd borrowed. While the Hansa merchants may no longer be welcome in London, foreign crowns, florins and écus – in vast amounts – will always find a welcoming hearth.

'Don't tell me your name. I don't want to know who you are,' Gaspari says in a low voice, seizing Schenk by the sleeve and almost pulling him into the orchard garden. 'I am not supposed to meet any of you. It was agreed.' He shuts the door, carefully sliding home a long iron bolt. He looks around at the apple trees as though expecting them to turn their backs on him and allow him a little privacy.

'You have a nice place here, Master Gaspari,' Schenk says as he admires the orchard. Through an open window in the back of the house, he can hear someone practising on a viol. A piercing cry of complaint whenever a bad note is struck tells him it's a girl, presumably a Gaspari daughter acquiring the social accomplishments of a banker's daughter. 'I need coin, or else I'll starve before I can fulfil what has been entrusted to me,' he says.

'Did they not provide for you, when you left Zurich? It was all included in the agreement.'

'I was robbed, at Rotterdam. I had to sell most of what was left for the passage.'

'How much do you need?'

'Just enough to keep my belly from complaining for a month or so. Oh, and some new boots.'

'I don't want you coming back for more.'

'Don't fret, I'll have the rest of my reward in heaven.'

'Good, because you can't stay here,' Gaspari says, catching Schenk looking admiringly at the neatly kept garden and the trim red brickwork of the house, its timber frame freshly painted. 'It is a condition of my loan to the Brotherhood that I am kept utterly apart from all this. There can be no connection made. That fool of a printer is already drawing unwelcome attention.'

'Don't worry, he'll be taken care of. Besides, I've found somewhere,' Schenk assures him, 'though it's not quite where I planned. The Lord Mayor's people changed the locks while I was away.'

Gaspari raises one manicured hand. 'Don't tell me where; I don't want to know. How much do you need?'

'Six will be enough,' Schenk says.

'Six pounds? Gaspari protests. 'Do you plan to sleep on goose-down pillows?'

'Shillings! Six shillings. That will keep me for a month or two. My needs are simple.'

'You people make such a virtue of austerity,' Gaspari says contemptuously. 'You'll all be different when it's over. You'll be wanting your palaces, just like all the other princes. And you'll need people like me to help you pay for them.'

'You wouldn't miss six pounds if it fell out of your purse,' Schenk says icily. 'One day you will be held to account, Master Gaspari. Covetousness is a sin. And each man's sins will be laid before him at the final reckoning. You're a banker – I trust you can count quickly. God does not like to be kept waiting.'

The stare that his visitor gives him starts a cold knot of fear unravelling in Silvan Gaspari's stomach. 'I am a good man,' he protests. 'I go to church. I pray. I give to the poor. I have as much expectation of entering heaven as you or the Brotherhood.'

The whisper that issues from Schenk's mouth strikes Gaspari's flesh like a cold wind on a dark night: *'God spared not the Angels that had sinned, but cast them down into hell, and delivered them into chains of darkness, to be kept unto damnation…'*

It's you, Gaspari tells himself, his mouth suddenly dry, the comfort of his rich clothes and his fine house suddenly somehow far less protective than it was before the knock on his door. You're the first. It's begun.

'Wait here,' he says, all his previous assuredness gone. 'I'll fetch what you've come for.'

✠

48

'The last building on Gravel Lane. You can't miss it,' Nicholas had been told when he'd asked for directions from the staff at the bear-garden kennels. 'If you can see the sign of the swan, you'll almost be in the river.'

Now, looking down the side of the wall facing the sloping riverbank, he can see the still-discernible image of a giant, long-necked bird, painted in fading whitewash. Even though the image is flaking, it's probably still visible from the far bank, and most certainly to anyone in a boat on the river. It tells him that the building had once been a bawdy-house, the bird a nod to the myth of Leda, seduced by Zeus in the guise of a swan.

The street door is grey and weathered, reinforced with iron bands. Nicholas's rapping against the timber is met by no response other than the murmur of the river twenty paces away to his right. He knocks twice more. Still no answer.

He is about to give up when he hears the slide of a bolt. The door swings open and he finds himself looking at a man in his late fifties with a high, balding crown smudged with ink. He wears an apron similarly befouled. His eyes scan the lane, as though he suspects his visitor has not come alone. Perhaps I was right, Nicholas thinks: this is a purveyor of questionable Italian verse with illustrations, the sort to be found in the libraries of gentlemen with prurient tastes, or in the salons of London's more expensive bawdy-houses. The sort of thing a member of the Stationers' Company wouldn't touch, at least not in public – material that would have the Bishop of London in a lather.

'Good morrow, friend,' Nicholas says. 'May I speak with you on a matter of commerce? I might have need of your services.'

'That depends,' the man says, using the hem of his apron to wipe a black smudge off the edge of one hand. 'Who are you?'

'I'm not a churchwarden or an officer of the parish, if that's what you're concerned about,' Nicholas says, smiling to show he has the same regard for the Lord Mayor's dominion as any other true Banksider. 'May I come in?'

The printer shrugs and turns back inside. Nicholas follows.

The room is sparse: flagstones and plain plaster walls. It would be an unremarkable space – just one of thousands across the city – were it not for the machine that dominates it. Nicholas has never seen a printing press before. He had imagined something much smaller.

In the centre of the floor is an H-frame of solid oak, almost as tall as its owner. The frame has a wooden screw the thickness of a man's arm running vertically through the crossbeam. A pole – Nicholas assumes it to be the operating handle – sticks out from the screw like an oar frozen in mid-sweep. The H-frame straddles a low, horizontal carriage. Nicholas can see rows of metal type, glistening with ink, laid out in what he assumes is a sliding frame. At one end of the carriage, like an open window laid on its side, is a device for holding a sheet of paper. The design is clear to a practically minded yeoman's son: the paper is lowered onto the lines of inked characters and slid directly under the crossbar of the frame. The handle is turned... the screw revolves... and drives a block down to press the paper firmly onto the faces of the type. He can't help thinking that the whole contraption looks like an engine of torture.

Robert Cecil's voice barges its way into his thoughts: *We must look further afield, for a secret, unlicensed press... What are the chances of catching the perpetrator with the ink still wet on his fingers?*

Nicholas glances at the small brick furnace in the corner. The coals glow brightly, sending out waves of heat that make the chamber unbearably stuffy. *What were you doing while I waited outside? Stuffing sedition into the flames to destroy the evidence?*

Almost as if he can read Nicholas's thoughts, the printer says, 'I apologize for it being so hot in here; I was casting some new type. You need a fierce heat to meld lead and antimony together.'

Nicholas turns his attention from the furnace back to the printer. He is an insignificant man. He doesn't for a moment look like a zealot.

'What are you printing?'

'Oh, just passages from the Holy Book. I sell them at markets, in the playhouses, the bear-garden and the taverns.'

'A hard trade on Bankside, I imagine.'

The printer lets out a snort of cold laughter. 'You're a perceptive man, Master—'

'Shelby. Nicholas Shelby. I'm a physician.'

A flicker of understanding crosses the printer's face. 'Ah, you're the fellow whose wife is mistress at the sign of the Jackdaw.'

Nicholas smiles as he nods. 'There are few on Bankside who don't know Bianca.'

'What is it you want, Dr Shelby? I don't have need of a physician. I'm not sick.'

Nicholas falls back on the prepared story he's constructed for this very question.

'You might not need a physician, but I have need of a printer. I'm considering writing a medical book. Something along the lines of *The Method of Physic* by Master Barrough – a compendium of treatments, for the apothecaries to use as a guide.'

The printer looks unconvinced. 'So why come to me? There are plenty of printers in the city, around St Paul's. Besides, it would have to be approved by the Stationers' Company. And I am not.'

'I'd prefer the profit to go to a Banksider,' Nicholas says. Then he grabs the chance to steer the conversation towards the real reason he's come to Gravel Lane. 'But while we're speaking of printing without approval, have you heard about the tracts they're finding in churches in the city?'

'I don't attend sermons across the river. Why would I pray in another parish? I don't know what tracts you're talking about.'

The denial is so abrupt that Nicholas wonders if there is more behind it than a mere protestation of ignorance.

'Seditious ones, calling on the people to rise up and do away with those set over them. Some fire-and-brimstone nonsense from the Old Testament. You haven't heard any rumours about where they're being printed?'

The printer's demeanour hardens. 'Is that why you've come here? As a provocateur? I'll tell you again, I know nothing about any seditious tracts.'

'No, of course not,' Nicholas protests, wishing he had learned to be a better liar.

'You'll find nothing here that isn't in the Book of Common Prayer,' the printer says. 'Look around, if you must.'

Nicholas colours. 'I wasn't implying—'

The printer picks up a pair of ink-blackened gloves lying on the carriage of the press. He slides them on, to signify he has work to attend to. 'We're not all rogues and criminals on Bankside,' he says. 'Some of us are decent, God-fearing fellows. I don't suppose you encounter many of those in your wife's tavern.'

As a dismissal, it is both comprehensive and effective.

'It's true, I've been less than honest with you,' Nicholas admits. 'The truth is, my father has been arrested for being in possession of one such paper. I'm trying to discover where it came from.'

'I'm sorry, Dr Shelby, but you've had a wasted journey. I cannot help you. I prefer that you leave me to my work.'

Walking back up Gravel Lane, Nicholas considers the likely consequences of mentioning the printer to Robert Cecil. Bianca was right when she'd said that locating a press on Bankside was suspicious. But he has no proof that the man is responsible for the tracts that have got Yeoman Shelby into such trouble. And if he were to denounce him, Cecil would certainly have the printer arrested and most likely put to hard questioning. Even if he were innocent, he might confess in order to stop the pain. The penalty would be a severed hand if he was lucky, execution if he wasn't. And that is not something Nicholas wants on his conscience.

With the cold river wind fretting at his back, he hurries towards the Paris Garden and the house he shares with Bianca and little Bruno. She should be back from her shop on Dice Lane by now, having planned to give herself a night off from helping Rose Monkton at the Jackdaw. The thought of having a few free hours with his wife and son lifts Nicholas's spirits.

But even that joy cannot entirely banish the knowledge that he also has a journey for which he must prepare, and the nagging worry about what he will find at the end of it.

5

There is no proper road to Barnthorpe. To reach it, Nicholas must take the ancient, rutted way from Aldgate in the London Wall to Colchester, then north-east to Ipswich, striking across the flat, marshy farmland to Woodbridge. In the late afternoon of the first day, barely twenty miles from the city, he reaches the little town of Brentwood. The way is still busy with market-day traffic. Nicholas dismounts and leads his horse to the public trough to quench its thirst. As he waits, he hears a familiar voice hailing him.

'Jesu! The Devil's own luck! Who'd have believed it?'

Looking up, he sees his older brother, riding wearily towards him astride a mud-spattered horse, the reins loose in his hands.

'Jack! What are you doing here?'

Jack Shelby swings out of the saddle and drops stiffly to the ground. Guiding his horse to join Nicholas's mount at the trough, he flexes his legs to ease the ache of hard riding. The two brothers embrace, each oblivious to the sweaty stink of man and beast.

Drawing back, Jack wipes the dirt from his face with a brush of his sleeve. 'Do I take it by your presence here that you've heard the news, little brother?'

He has lost weight, Nicholas notices – hard work on the farm and worry, he suspects.

'The news about Father? Yes, I have. Have you seen him?'

'Aye. We brought him food and some fresh straw to sleep on.

Knowing the jailers, they've probably already stolen it to sell to some other poor bugger.'

'But is he well, Jack?'

A sliver of dried mud flakes off Jack's cheek as he pulls a sour face. 'As well as any man constrained like the most dangerous felon in the world. He has no company but the rats. How did you hear he was taken up? I was on my way to tell you. I thought it quicker than sending a letter.'

'I heard it from Sir Robert Cecil.'

'That's bad, if the Privy Council is involved,' Jack says, frowning.

'What in Christ's wounds has he been up to?'

With a doleful shake of his head, Jack says, 'It all started with us getting a new parson at Barnthorpe, now that old Olicott's up there boring the cassock off St Peter. This new fellow – Parson Asher Montague – he's young, one of those hot prophesiers who refuses to wear a surplice. He delivers his sermons all in plain black.'

'A Puritan?' Nicholas asks as his horse lifts its head from the trough, sending a cascade of water over the right shin of his breeches.

'Too much of the fire and brimstone for me and my Faith, to be honest. Mother thinks he's in need of a strong wife to take his mind off sin and damnation.'

'How is Faith?' Nicholas asks, knowing his sister-in-law is pregnant again.

'Bonny as ever. But I don't like her hearing all this end-of-days, repent-thy-sins stuff. It's not good for her humours. A woman with child doesn't go to sermon to be assailed with tales of graves gaping open and sinners being cast into hell; she wants to hear about the lamb of God.'

'And Mother?'

'Worried sick.'

'I should think so. None of this sounds much like Father's meat,' Nicholas says doubtfully.

Jack shakes his head. 'You know what it's like, Nick. These past few harvests, the bad winters, the loans – they wear a man down. Father has long struggled to ensure the farm feeds us all. And now here's Parson Montague telling him that it's not God's will that life has been hard, it's the fault of those who've put themselves between a man and his maker: the rich merchants in Ipswich, the foreigners in London, the Privy Council... It's hardly surprising if he now starts looking for someone to blame.'

'How did Father come to be arrested?' Nicholas says.

'He finds this tract in the church, hands it to Asher Montague and the next thing we know, he's being taken up for sedition.'

'I'm not surprised, if it was the same tract as the ones that have been turning up in London. It's strong stuff – about as incendiary as throwing black powder on burning coals. Did you read it?'

'No,' says Jack. 'Parson Montague took it straightway to Sir Thomas Wragby, the magistrate.'

'What else do we know about Parson Montague, Jack? You said he arrived from the Low Countries.'

'He's been learning from the Calvinists in Frankfurt, Zurich and Basle, or so he tells us. He's very knowledgeable about the great martyrs.'

'Like John Hooper,' Nicholas suggests, remembering the tract's call to let the faithful take Hooper and his torment in the flames as their guide.

'Aye. He's very keen on Hooper. Scared the women and the little ones to death with that stuff about his arm burning through and dropping off. You know how that church echoes – I'd warrant God Himself could hear the screams.'

'If Montague's such a firebrand, maybe he's responsible for

these tracts that are appearing. Perhaps he's trying to deflect attention.'

Jack thinks for a moment, then says, 'Too canny, I reckon. He'd just have burned it.'

'But instead he hands it to the justice of the peace. I understand Wragby's another one returned from across the Narrow Sea.'

Jack nods. 'Old Wrath-of-God Wragby. Thought we'd seen the last of him, years ago, when he went off to fight the Dons in Holland. You were probably too young to remember much about him.'

'I have a vague memory of seeing him around Hasketon Manor,' Nicholas recalls. 'We had to pass it on the way to petty school. But when I was serving as surgeon to Sir Joshua Wylde's company in the Low Countries I never got to meet him.'

'Well, he's back at Hasketon now – arrived last winter.'

'The English captains in Holland always said he was a Puritan, very pious.'

'You wouldn't think it to look at him,' Jack says. 'And folks say he's fair enough – no tormentor of the ordinary man. We haven't had any hangings for stealing bread. Seems Wragby draws the line at seditionists, though. Well, he would, wouldn't he?'

'Things aren't quite as bad as they might appear, Jack,' Nicholas says, patting the leather of his saddle-pack. 'In here I have a letter to Sir Thomas, signed by Mr Secretary Cecil. It releases Father into my custody, pending further investigation. Let's get the ankle-irons taken off and have a good talk to him – find out what's going on.'

✛

Nicholas rides out of the courtyard at the Bell tavern in Ingatestone before dawn next morning, leaving Jack sound asleep in the communal lodging bed. He makes the remainder of the journey in two days. Yeoman Shelby might be hardy from working the land, but he's also nearing seventy years of age. Even a few days longer in harsh confinement could prove fatal. The ride gives Nicholas time to dwell on how to tackle Sir Thomas Wragby. Should he bluster? Should he wave Cecil's letter in the magistrate's face and demand instant obedience? Suffolk is far from London, and even Mr Secretary's writ can be weakened by distance. Besides, Nicholas has no authority there other than whatever his occasional audiences with the queen might fool Wragby into giving him.

Sir Thomas receives him in the main hall of a sagging-roofed, plaster-fronted manor house just outside Woodbridge. A sword in a practical leather military scabbard hangs from a peg by the door. Below it, a pair of battered cavalryman's riding boots stand sentry.

Nicholas remembers Hasketon Manor from his childhood, when he passed it daily on his way to school. It had seemed to him, then, an outer gatehouse of a prison of the spirit. He still knows exactly how many paces he would have to make from there before reaching the school. The house had been a signpost, pointing to what lay ahead: long hours of sitting on hard benches while the masters and the ushers droned through their lessons on Latin grammar, Hebrew and Greek. He had not been a natural student. At times he had wanted to smash his hornbook on the floor and burst free of the place to go hawking with Jack and his father in the fields around Barnthorpe. But his father had been wise enough to see something in his younger son that Nicholas himself could not yet see: a bright mind only temporarily dulled by rote and repetition. When Nicholas had at last begun to excel, no one was surprised but him. Five years later Yeoman Shelby had mortgaged his farm to send his sixteen-year-old son to study medicine at Cambridge, and the old manor house had soon slipped from Nicholas's consciousness.

And now he is back, shaking his head in amused disbelief at where the years have gone, wondering how such an ordinary place as this had loomed so large in his childhood imagination.

Wragby is a fizzing fuse of a man in his early fifties, wiry, hot in movement and temperament, but civil with it. He seems almost glad that Nicholas has come. He reads Robert Cecil's letter as if he were a captain digesting an order from his general.

'It seemed clear-cut to me: possession of seditious material – fellow deserved to have his right arm trimmed a little,' Wragby says. 'Still, if Mr Secretary Cecil commands him released, then released he must be.'

Nicholas struggles not to wince as he imagines the pain of the axe smashing through flesh and bone, wielded by someone no better practised in amputations than the local blacksmith.

'I'm sure you were only doing what you thought was your duty, Sir Thomas.'

Wragby calls a servant to bring two glasses of sack. 'When the magistrates at Ipswich assizes told me the accused was claiming his son was the queen's physician, I wasn't inclined to believe him at first. Some rogues will swear they're Her Majesty's long-lost brother to avoid the sting of the blade.'

'I'm sure they will,' Nicholas says, as though all that stands between order and criminality are the two men drinking expensive imported Spanish wine in a Suffolk manor house.

'But I had my lads ask around,' Wragby continues. 'Seems everyone in the parish is mightily proud of Yeoman Shelby's son.' He gives Nicholas – doublet and breeches stained by hard riding; wiry black hair dishevelled – a faintly disbelieving look. 'That is you, is it? Only I'd expected someone older, more bookish.'

'I *am* a physician, Sir Thomas. And yes, I have the honour to be called to Her Majesty's side on occasions.'

'And a friend of Mr Secretary Cecil to boot,' Wragby observes, waving the letter as if it were an ensign, and ahead of him was a well-defended bastion that needed charging.

'He engages me to attend to his son. Infrequently, I'm pleased to say. The lad is robust.'

'Pleased to hear it,' Wragby says. 'Odd little fellow, Sir Robert, or so I hear. And ill made, too, they say.'

'But he is Her Majesty's principal Secretary of State,' Nicholas says, to remove any remaining resistance Wragby might have about letting Yeoman Shelby go.

'The fact remains that your father was found with vile, seditious material in his possession.'

'That, Sir Thomas, is disputed. I understand from my brother that the offending tract was found, but not actually possessed. It sounds to me as if conclusions have been reached somewhat prematurely.'

'I can't simply drop the charges; it would set a poor example. Your father will still have to appear before the Ipswich assizes.'

'I'm confident I can show that this was all a mistake,' Nicholas says. And then, to capitalize on the hand he's playing, 'And of course I'll ensure my father gets good legal representation.'

A flicker of doubt – the first sign of weakness in Wragby's armour. 'I suppose you'll have the Attorney General take the suit. That's what you do, you fellows at court: stick together.'

Nicholas tries not to grin. Sir Edward Coke thinks not much better of him than William Baronsdale. And as for the notion of Nicholas's influence at court, Wragby couldn't be further from the truth if he walked all the way to Muscovy.

'I shall certainly consult him,' he says, trying to sound suitably ominous.

'Fellows in silk and ribbons spending their days listening to poetry. Look at the way they've abandoned the Earl of Essex. Only proper soldier amongst the lot of them. I'd like to see Coke stand against those rebels in Ireland.'

Nicholas seizes the opportunity Wragby had just given him.

'I was physician to the army of His Grace, the Earl of Essex – during last year's campaign in Ireland.'

Wragby stares at him. 'Christ's nails, is that so?'

'When I left Cambridge, I spent a season as surgeon with Sir Joshua Wylde's company in the Low Countries.'

Wragby rubs his beard so vigorously that Nicholas fears it will begin to smoulder. He almost throws aside his glass of sack, seizes Nicholas's hand and begins to pump it vigorously. 'When I was at Delft in '87, I remember hearing about a clever young surgeon Wylde had in his company. Was that you?'

'It was, Sir Thomas.'

'God's bollocks!' Wragby cries. 'We must away to Framlingham at once. I can smell injustice in the air.'

✠

Finding the time to visit the house Aksel bequeathed her has not been easy for Bianca. Little Bruno, five years old and possessed of even more energy and inquisitiveness than Buffle, the Jackdaw's dog, can steal away her hours without her even noticing. Then there's the constant demand for her skills as an apothecary. Business on Dice Lane is brisk, and Cachorra is still learning the ropes. Thus it is three days after Nicholas left for Suffolk before she and Ned Monkton finally walk across London Bridge, up past the fishmongers' stalls to Gracechurch Street and on to the Dutch church in Austin Friars. Here, to the south of All Hallows in the Wall, where the city spills out into Moor Fields, Bianca presents the document with the Archbishop of Canterbury's Court of Prerogative wax seal attached, which proves her entitlement to the bequest. She receives the keys from a young priest with a boxy face and moist blue eyes, whose name, she discovers, is Father Auguste Beauchêne, a refugee Huguenot from the borderland between Brabant and France.

'I hadn't expected so many keys,' she tells him. 'It's not a very large house.'

'There are two spare sets,' Beauchêne explains. 'The Consistory Court demanded one, and the Lord Mayor's people another. It wouldn't surprise me if they both wanted access, just in case Aksel had anything left that they might appropriate. They should have remembered him more honourably.'

'Dear, kind Aksel,' Bianca agrees. 'Always full of hope for a better life, even as he suffered great loss. At least he has gone now to a better reward.'

Beauchêne identifies the two largest of the keys hanging from the ring he has given her.

'This is for the original lock. Its companion is for the one installed by the Lord Mayor's people. They didn't want anyone getting in until they'd confirmed Aksel had settled any outstanding debts.' He sighs. 'Some people won't trust a foreigner, even in death.'

As Bianca leaves the church, a thought comes into her mind: she could lease the house to the local parish for a nominal rent – say, a shilling per year – on the condition that they turn it into an almshouse for the poor of Dowgate Ward. After all, she has enough income from the shop and the Jackdaw to live a comfortable, if modest life.

It takes almost twenty minutes to walk from Austin Friars south along Walbrook and so to the river and the Steelyard. The roads are busy with people and waggons. Where Dowgate Street opens out as it meets the Thames, Bianca sees that the tide is almost in flood. A drayman and his apprentice are watering their horses in the shallows. Cutting east past a house built on wooden piles festooned with seaweed, she and Ned emerge onto the wharf. Soon Bianca is standing outside a familiar door at the end of a row of four connected properties.

'So this is it?' rumbles Ned appreciatively as he stands four-square on the cobbles, looking at the house. Ned, whose father spent much of what little he earned on charlatans' cures for Ned's sickly younger brother, finds the notion that someone could gift an entire house to another almost incomprehensible.

'Yes, this is it,' Bianca agrees.

The building has a lower storey of brick – the warehouse part – with an overhanging upper floor fronted with plaster. In the months since Aksel's death and the expulsion of the Hansa merchants, it has weathered somewhat. But Aksel's pride in it is still evident; it is one of the better-kept properties in the Steelyard. Turning the keys in the locks, Bianca is about to open the door when Ned bars the way, one arm out like the bough of a sturdy tree.

'This requires a ceremony,' he says, grinning. He makes a gallant bend of the knee, sweeping his extended arms back to invite her to enter. 'Your new palace 'waits you, my lady,' he says, feigning the manners of a duke. In return Bianca favours him with a suitably austere look of condescension, hoists the hem of her gown and strides imperiously across the threshold in her best impression of the queen.

✠

It is dark in the storeroom. Ned leaves the door open so they can see where they're treading.

'I can 'ear the river,' he says. 'I can smell it, too.'

'There's a hatch by the far wall, leading down to a culvert,' Bianca explains. 'It runs to the edge of the wharf, about fifty feet away. It's for bringing in light cargo. Don't think of going down – the tide's almost in.'

'I weren't plannin' on it,' Ned says with a grim laugh.

Bianca replies with an embarrassed smile. After his years working in the mortuary crypt at St Thomas's, Ned has an aversion to dank, underground spaces. She looks around the long storeroom. The place has been stripped bare, the contents sold off – she assumes – by a man who knew his time on earth was fast coming to an end: a closing of the ledger, a settling of accounts. She had been told by Master Woolrich, the lawyer from the Consistory Court, that Aksel had left all his coin and his scant possessions to the parish for poor relief. Then – without fuss or complaint – he had retired to his bed to await the end, mostly alone except for visits from Father Beauchêne.

Climbing the stairs to the upper chambers, Bianca half-expects to hear the creaking of floorboards in the living area and Aksel calling out a greeting in his Saxon-accented English. It may be her house now, but she can't help feeling as if she's trespassing.

The main chamber is also in semi-darkness, the single window shuttered. Ned goes ahead of her to remove the bar and let in some light. As he moves, the sagging floor objects to his tread with a series of despondent creaks.

'It's got a lock on the shutter bar,' Ned calls out. 'Cautious bugger, your friend, weren't 'e?'

'He'd been robbed before,' Bianca says, handing him the keys. It takes Ned a while to identify the right one, but eventually the latch on the shutter bar is unlocked and light spills into the chamber.

Looking around, Bianca sees that this room too is almost empty. On one wall hangs a plain wooden cross, reminding her that Aksel was a pious Calvinist. In front of the window – which now gives a narrow view over the wharf – stands a plain rosewood chest, its lid closed. The repository for Aksel's meagre collection of clothes, she assumes. Moving into the next room, she discovers that the only remaining trace of the former occupant is a double bed, its planks sitting in the frame like the bare ribs of a shipwreck. She stands beside it for a while in silence while she gives up a prayer for Aksel Leezen's soul. She knows that praying for dead souls is a Catholic abomination, to the queen's religion. But Ned isn't going to object. He waits in silence one step behind her.

When Bianca comes to the second bedroom, she finds the door locked. Taking back the keys from Ned, she tries several before the mechanism at last makes a disturbed metallic groan, like a wild animal waking after a long hibernation.

The room she enters has a cold, sepulchral smell about it. It's as though it hasn't been aired in years or – and here Bianca chides herself for letting her imagination run away with itself – as if it were the first of a body's limbs to feel the chill of encroaching death. When she opens the shutters, the light seems strangely disinclined to spill in.

Like the first sleeping chamber, this one too has a bed. But this bed is partly made up. Draped over the end of an old straw mattress, whose innards hang out in places like the toy soldiers she makes out of discarded rushes and sackcloth for Bruno, is a threadbare woollen blanket. As her eyes track up the length of the bed towards the bolster she freezes, letting out an involuntary 'Oh!'

An improbably small child is staring directly at her, leaning back against the wall, two tiny feet protruding from the hem of its gown. It is a girl child in a blue dress. A child with half its face missing.

The child stares back at her out of its half of a face. Unmoving. Silent. Dead.

And then Bianca lets out a bark of relieved, nervous laughter. The thing is nothing more sinister than a painted cutout, an effigy, barely eighteen inches tall, the face only half-complete, one side of it merely an outline drawn over whitewash.

She moves to the head of the bed to get a better look. Now she can see it is made from cheap timber, barely thicker than veneer. The half-painted face wears a look of immeasurable sadness. Even in her relief, Bianca cannot stop an awful image forcing its way into her mind: the chubby face of Bruno, her five-year-old son, the form and colour of him leaching away to nothingness as he dissolves before her mind's eye. She is suddenly overwhelmed by a sense of inevitable and agonizing loss, like watching someone die in your arms.

'What in the name of Lucifer be *that*?' she hears Ned Monkton ask. He too has been transfixed by the image.

'I'm not sure,' Bianca answers.

Despite her imagination returning to a semblance of calm, she cannot drag her eyes away from the thing on the bed. Should she revise her opinion of her old friend, the Hansa merchant?

She remembers when she had first come here. She had learned of Aksel Leezen from a Venetian spice merchant living on Petty Wales. She'd been seeking out importers of the more exotic ingredients that she required for the illicit physic she practised in the cellar of the Jackdaw. That must be a good ten years ago, she thinks – before Nicholas had come into her life; before Lord Lumley had used his influence to get the Grocers' Guild to license her as an apothecary. She recalls how she had found Aksel in a jubilant mood. He was getting married to the daughter of a fellow merchant, a woman much younger than himself whose first husband had drowned falling off the wharf after an overindulgence in Rhenish wine. The result of the union had been a bright, joyful little girl named Vreni. But this half-painted face cannot be Vreni's. Not unless the artist had never met her.

'That's witchcraft, that is,' Ned growls. 'We should 'ave none of it. Burn it, that's what I'd do – throw it on a fire.'

'Aksel lost his wife and daughter to the pestilence,' Bianca explains, trying to be rational. 'Perhaps it's a shrine.'

But then where is the effigy of the mother, Goodwife Leezen? And what manner of grieving father commissions an effigy of his dead daughter and has the artist paint an entirely different child's face?

Sensing Ned turning to leave, Bianca is only too happy to follow him out of the chamber. She emerges into the living space with the relief of someone hauled out of a freshly dug grave.

It was nothing but a harmless piece of painted boxwood, she tells herself, making a show of searching the space again to prove to Ned that she's mistress of her emotions. Striding as boldly as she can manage, she goes to the rosewood chest standing in front of the single window.

To her surprise, the chest is unlocked. Lifting the lid, she peers inside with a breezy, 'Let's see if Aksel has left anything behind.'

And it appears that Aksel has – although not the spare clothes or pewter Bianca was expecting. Instead the chest contains only a bundle wrapped in the same coarse cloth as the blanket in the chamber she has just fled. Lifting it out, Bianca pulls back the wrapping.

For one awful moment, disgust – and yes, fear – freezes her limbs, so that the contents of the parcel seem bonded to her hands. As if she herself had wielded the blade that severed the disjointed human limb she is holding. A forearm, complete from fingertips to the elbow joint. Complete, save for the skin – stripped away along one side to reveal the bones, muscle and tendons beneath.

For an instant it lies in her open palms, cold and hard. Then she screams.

Repelled by the thing's icy hardness, by the faded red of the inner flesh, the yellow of the fat, and the cream of the bones visible where the muscle has been cut away, her hands reject the hideous object with an explosive jerk. It cartwheels through the air, striking the wall with a solid thump, like the discarded remnants of a carcass carelessly tossed aside by a slaughterman in the Mutton Lane shambles. The hand and arm separate at the wrist. The two pieces tumble to the floor, where – to Bianca's horror and astonishment – they shatter into fragments, leaving a ghostly cloud of plaster dust drifting on the cold air.

6

Framlingham is a dour, flinty fortress some three leagues north of Woodbridge. Once the place where Mary Tudor gathered support before marching on London, today it is a prison for felons, recusants and Catholics. As Nicholas rides beneath the down-at-heel gatehouse, he pulls the sheet of paper with Robert Cecil's seal on it from his doublet. Will it be enough to bring his father out of the castle's stinking cellars?

In the event, the warden takes one look at it, declares himself Mr Secretary's obedient servant and sends for the keys.

When Yeoman Shelby is brought out into the light, Nicholas stifles a gasp. His father is as pale as a ghost, hollow-cheeked and smeared with God-knows-what filth. His ankles are raw from the shackles that have only recently been removed. Stumbling into Nicholas's outstretched arms, he looks as though he's been incarcerated for years instead of days. There are tears in his frightened, red-rimmed eyes. 'I knew you'd come, boy. I knew you'd come,' he says in a pained whisper.

Nicholas, too, is moved to tears. He holds his father close, oblivious to the stink of him. Despite his position as head of the family and his reputation as a practical, unimaginative man, Yeoman Shelby has always been a loving, tactile father. The reversal of roles is not lost on his son.

After days languishing in a dark dungeon, Yeoman Shelby must get used to the sunlight. His eyes soothed by cool water from the deep Framlingham well, he can soon take in his surroundings without discomfort. Then he stretches his limbs to ease the pains of lying on a hard, damp stone floor. Soon Nicholas is escorting him around the inner walls of Framlingham as he regains the use of his legs, letting him find his own pace, but always ready to lend support.

'I'm sure this confusion can easily be resolved,' says Sir Thomas Wragby, as they pass him sitting astride his horse just inside the gatehouse. He seems in a hurry to be gone. 'I'm sorry Yeoman Shelby was handled roughly; the jailers here are rogues. I'll have a word or two to say to the steward about that. Give my regards to Sir Joshua Wylde, should you encounter him. You can't be one of those medical charlatans if Sir Joshua had you for a surgeon.'

Then Wragby tips his cap, turns his horse in a passable pirouette and spurs away through the gatehouse with a theatrical clatter, as though he has better things to do.

Nicholas bites his tongue as he helps his father into the saddle of the mount that Robert Cecil has loaned him. On foot, he leads Yeoman Shelby through the gatehouse, away from the flinty walls of his captivity. Soon they are on the track towards Barnthorpe, passing lush meadows where labourers wield their scythes, cutting down the tall summer grass for hay. Perhaps this harvest will at last be a good one, Nicholas thinks. If it is, it will be deserved.

As he walks, he looks at the men working in the fields. They don't look like seditionists. They look exactly what he knows them to be, what their predecessors have been for centuries, what those who come after them will be for centuries more: humble men trying to eke out a living from the uncaring land. Then he hears Robert Cecil's voice scratching at the inside of his skull: *It won't take much to turn the merely discontented into the violent mob.*

With the horse walking obediently beside him on a loose rein, Nicholas glances up at his father in the saddle, whose face is turned to the sun, revelling in his freedom. How can it be that words printed on paper can have such cruel consequences? How can a man face incarceration, mutilation or even death simply for reading them? How can the man who printed them deserve to die for turning the handle on a press? Nicholas is sure now that he did the right thing when he chose not to denounce the printer on Gravel Lane.

But then a cloud covers the sun. In the sudden shadow cast by horse and rider, Nicholas senses a chill that is more than simply external. It is the chill of doubt.

What if Robert Cecil has good cause to be afraid? What if each turn of that handle not only presses the paper to the ink, but also crushes one of those little *atomi* of order and stability on which the realm is built? What if there comes a day when so many have been destroyed that – as Elizabeth herself told him at Richmond – *we would each blow away at the first breeze?*

✠

Two hands, a second forearm, a lower leg, complete with foot, and a jawbone – all with the muscles and tendons attached. And all so lifelike that Bianca cannot stop her stomach giving a little lurch as she pulls back the cloth covering.

Now that the Jackdaw tavern has closed for the night, she has decided it's safe to show Rose Monkton the haul of plaster body parts that she and Ned recovered from Aksel's house in the Steelyard. Rose pushes aside her dark ringlets to get a closer look. She is a buxom, mischievous soul with an inexhaustible well of good humour. She is also in possession of a lurid imagination.

'They look like the leftovers of a quarterin' at the scaffold on Tower Hill.'

Buffle, the Jackdaw's dog – half spaniel, half lord-only-knows-what – wanders over, on the chance that the bones might be real. She tilts her head, wondering why she can't smell meat.

'I still thinks it's witchcraft,' Ned says.

Rose, who believes herself as educated as any on Bankside, if not beyond – an opinion she has held ever since Bianca taught her to read and write – says, "Ush, Ned Monkton, you thinks a door 'inge is witchcraft. Us what comprehends the new sciences, like Master Nicholas an' me, *we* use our reason.' She scratches her cheek and looks to Bianca for help. 'But at present I can't see the reason in any of *these*.'

'I think they might be anatomical,' Bianca says, recalling a book of medical drawings Nicholas had shown her in Padua. 'For the instruction of anatomists.'

'Then what was they doin' in the home of a merchant what dealt in tar and furs?' Ned enquires.

'That's not all that Aksel imported, by any measure, or else I'd likely never have met him,' Bianca says. 'He had a good reputation for the trading of spices, plants, oils – all manner of things useful to medicine. Everything from whale tusks to foreign books on physic.' Re-covering the objects with the cloth, she feels a sense of relief when they disappear from view, much as she does when waking from a disturbing dream. 'Master Nicholas will be back from Suffolk soon enough. I'm sure he'll be able to tell us what they are.'

And so he might, she thinks again when she settles herself to sleep a while later. But even if the plaster limbs are what she thinks they are, that doesn't explain the unfinished effigy of the little girl. And until she can come up with an explanation, she's of a mind not to return to the gloomy house in the Steelyard. Come to think of it, she'd feel a lot happier staying at the Jackdaw with Ned and Rose until Nicholas returns. Being alone with only

Bruno for company in their lodgings in the Paris Garden is one thing. Sharing the place with a dismembered corpse is quite another – even if it is only a plaster one.

✠

Yeoman Shelby has been magically returned almost to his former imperturbable self. Like a prize bull about to go to market, he has been washed, brushed, fed and generally pampered. Goodwife Shelby has now passed from tearful joy at her husband's return to quiet displeasure at how he could have got himself into such a predicament in the first place.

Alerted by Jack to her husband's imminent release, she has prepared a hearty pottage. Rejecting his favourite ingredient – silvery eels caught that morning from the brook below the tithe barn, still hanging in the buttery like slippery ribbons – she fills the cooking pot with blood-thickening mutton. Now that the bowls are put away and the malmsey poured in celebration, the men of the household sit around the fire in the main hall and do what men everywhere are inclined to do after a good meal – mull over the current state of things and how to put them right.

'Tell us again, Father, is there anything more you can tell me about how you came by this pamphlet?' Nicholas says. 'When precisely did you find it?'

'At Sunday sermon, three weeks ago. It was lying right where our family pew is, just behind where the squire and his family have their seats.'

'Did you read it before you handed it to Parson Montague?'

'Course I read it, boy. "Away with the vile servile dunghill of those ministers of damnation." Words like that tend to catch a fellow's eye.'

'And you didn't think of tearing it up or burning it?'

'Why should I, when there's sentiments there I agree with?'

'Which ones in particular, Father?'

Yeoman Shelby's face takes on a fervour that makes Nicholas uncomfortable. '"Be our masters ever so mighty, their pride and their vanity will destroy them. Cast them down into the fires of hell where they belong,"' his father quotes.

'I suppose that's slightly more reassuring to hear. It might have been the part about the bishops being puppets of the Antichrist and murderers of the soul.'

'Can't say that I disagree with that, either,' Yeoman Shelby says reasonably.

'Why in the name of Jesu's wounds did you show it to other people? It wasn't only Parson Montague, was it? Jack tells me you showed it to several people in the congregation.'

'People need to hear the truth, boy. And I'd trouble you not to blaspheme in my house.'

'It's the truth according to one man, Father,' Nicholas says. Until now, he has never heard his father object to cursing.

'There is only one truth, lad. And that's God's.'

'What happened when you handed the tract to Parson Montague?'

'Nothing – at first. He asked if I would like to read scripture with him.'

'Which you did?'

'It's good to hear a fellow who believes in what he's saying. Can't say that about most of those set over us: the earls and the dukes, the justices and the magistrates. They put themselves up as demigods, eat venison off silver plate, parade their false piety in silk and fur, while all the time the truly godly – the common folk – must beg for alms or starve. But God *sees* them, Nick. God will punish them for their pride and vanity. He will not abide the worship of false gods or graven images. There's a reckoning coming, boy, and soon. Prayer won't save the sinners; the damned have already been marked for hell.'

From the corner of the room, Goodwife Shelby lays down a smock she is repairing. 'Hush now, Father. Enough of this foolishness. If you don't lower your voice, they'll hear you in Ipswich. Then not even Nicholas will be able to save your sorry skull. Don't you think I have enough work to do around here as it is, without you getting yourself carted away and leaving me a man down?'

His wife's admonition has more effect on Yeoman Shelby than a magistrate could ever bring to bear. Grumbling, he ladles himself more pottage.

But Nicholas is speechless. Never has he heard his father express such seditious thoughts. In his long life, Yeoman Shelby has witnessed the forcible change of his religion from Protestant to Catholic and back to Protestant. He has seen the whitewash stripped from the walls of Barnthorpe's little church to reveal the painted images of the saints beneath, and then seen them painted over again. He has borne this with quiet obedience, content to believe that his monarch and her ministers know what is best for his soul. Now he's talking as though he can barely wait for the rebellion to start.

'When did they come for you, Father?' he asks, reluctant to defy his mother, but needing to hear the story to its end.

'A few days after I handed Parson Montague the paper. Two of Sir Thomas Wragby's fellows took me to Framlingham. Then Wragby came and told me I was to be committed to the Ipswich assizes. When I heard what they had in store for me, I used your name. It was a weakness. I should have faced them with the courage of John Hooper – told them to do their worst.'

From her mending, Goodwife Shelby pipes up, 'John Hooper was a brave martyr for the one true faith – not some addle-pated old fool who can't see when he's being used.'

A stony silence falls, until Nicholas says, 'This Montague, how can you be sure it wasn't him who denounced you to Wragby?'

'Why would he do that?' his father asks, through a mouthful of pottage.

'To divert attention from his own hot preaching?'

Yeoman Shelby shakes his head. 'Montague is a true man of God. It has to be someone else – someone I showed the paper to. There's more than a few around here with an eye on this farm; even in these hard times, we do better than most.'

Jack's wife Faith, dandling their latest infant on her lap, says softly, 'I think I might have been inclined to leave the vile thing where I found it. Can we talk about something else? The midsummer fair, perhaps. Anything that isn't likely to get us hanged would be nice.'

But Nicholas hasn't finished. 'Has Parson Montague ever preached from the Book of Deuteronomy in his sermons?'

His father's runnelled face creases into a frown. 'Why do you want to know that?'

'There's a verse in it, one saying that if your brother or your wife entices you to worship false gods, your own hand should be the first raised to put them to death. Has Montague ever preached that from the pulpit?'

Goodwife Shelby almost throws her mending work to the floor. She stands up, her face flushed with anger.

'That's enough from all of you. Father, finish your pottage and go to bed. As for you, Nicholas, any more talk like that and it will be *me* raising a hand to put a blush on your backside – even if you *are* the queen's physician!'

✠

'Apart from what you told me at Brentwood, what else do we know of this new parson, other than his propensity for inflammatory sermons?' Nicholas asks his brother a while later in the cool seclusion of the buttery. 'I'm surprised he hasn't been arrested, too.'

'For a start, Montague's a wise one for such a young fellow. Walks a very clever line,' Jack tells him, taking some cheese from the shelf, breaking it in two and handing half to Nicholas. He chews as he speaks. 'After old Olicott died, we had no one to give us sermon. Then the churchwarden told us someone was coming to keep the pulpit warm until the bishop could find a replacement – someone properly ordained. Next thing we know, there's Asher Montague doling out the fire and brimstone.'

'And Father bought what he was selling.'

'Not only Father. After old Olicott, it was a shock for everyone. I'd never seen so many people awake in a church before. From only attending Sunday sermon, Father was soon listening to Montague whenever he could find the time: morning prayer, evensong... And when he wasn't either with the parson or with me and the boys in the fields, he'd have his nose in the scriptures. Faith made the mistake of telling Father he was becoming a preachy Moses. We thought he was going to chase her clean out of Suffolk. Took all Mother's honeying to calm him down.'

'You told me Montague was preaching in Europe before he came here.'

'Aye. I reckon the Barnthorpe congregation now knows more about the teachings of the great Protestant preachers of Zurich, Basle, Geneva and Frankfurt than any bishop in this realm. He's very big on martyrs, young Montague. It's almost as if he's been trained to it, like the papists train their priests at Douai and Rome.'

'And like those papist priests,' Nicholas muses, 'Montague chooses to come back into England somewhere he might expect to avoid the eyes of the watch or Privy Council searchers—'

Jack smacks his lips as he finishes the cheese. 'I take your point, Brother. Somewhere like Woodbridge, rather than Harwich or Ipswich.'

'It's just a thought,' says Nicholas. He is remembering what Robert Cecil had told him at Richmond: *There are some in this realm looking for an opportunity to make mischief – dangerous mischief. It won't take much to turn the merely discontented into the violent mob...*

Tired from the long walk back from Framlingham, he feels his eyelids growing heavier than lead. He lays aside the cheese Jack handed him, uneaten. 'I think I ought to pay Asher Montague a visit later,' he says, yawning. He pats his brother on the shoulder. 'If only to suggest he stops filling the good hearts of venerable yeomen with sentiments that are guaranteed to get them into trouble.'

7

Nicholas bides his time. A discreet conversation with Asher Montague after sermon is better than outright confrontation, and Sunday is only three days away. Besides, it is good to be back with his family. News of his arrival and of the freeing of Yeoman Shelby has spread across the pastures and marshes around Barnthorpe in that mysteriously efficient way common to the wilder parts of England, as though carried on the breeze, in the ebb and flow of the water in the creeks and estuaries, and on the wings of the wildfowl that skim low over the flat landscape. Nicholas is in demand. In this part of the realm, a lad and his love out walking are more likely to encounter the fearsome Black Shuck than a qualified physician. Even if they were to come across one, the chances of being able to pay for his services are remote. But Nicholas is a son of Barnthorpe and well known for his charity. By sunrise next morning a quiet, orderly queue of men, women and children has assembled in the yard of the Shelby farmhouse. Having stocked his doctor's travelling chest in anticipation, he is well provisioned to accept them. What he cannot provide, he will prescribe. In every hamlet, village and town in the county there will be a wise-woman or a caster of spells, a diviner or a herbalist to mix, boil, distil and dispense according to his instructions. After watching Bianca at work, he trusts them more than most fellows of the College of Physicians.

He treats a ploughman's daughter suffering from a suppurating pustule on the right elbow, lancing the crown, evacuating the interior, washing the cavity and applying the yolk of an egg sprinkled with crystals of sugar alum. To the badly burnt arm of the son of the Barnthorpe blacksmith, Nicholas applies a balm of egg-white, turpentine and rosewater. For the mother of an infant with an infestation of pinworm, he advises milk diluted with the juice of wormwood. The treatments that he finds most satisfying are the practical ones usually entrusted to a barber-surgeon: the splinting, the reduction of a dislocation, the removal of foreign objects from inappropriate places, the stitching and the setting. In these procedures he is particularly adept, having learned his skills on the battlefields of the Low Countries. They are the ones that no amount of dubious philosophy in Latin or Greek can influence for the better.

In the evenings, he plays with Jack and Faith's children, who seem to have no need of his physic, but an inexhaustible need of his attention. Though he is suspicious of the efficacy of studying urine, he is persuaded to check his sister-in-law's. 'If it makes you happy,' he tells her as he sends her to the jakes. When she returns with the bowl, he applies the measure he learned not at Cambridge, but in Morocco, preferring to rely on the great Ibn Sina's judgement. 'There's a nice hint of blue in there, which I'd expect in the early stages of a healthy pregnancy,' he observes. 'And overall, there is a good blush to it. I'm looking for the colour of water that's had a pig's trotter boiled in it. I see that. And it's clear. That's good.'

'Test mine, too,' says Jack.

'Just pour a glass of knock-down,' Nicholas replies, landing a friendly punch on his brother's arm. 'I'll learn as much by looking at that.'

At mealtimes, no one is permitted to discuss Asher Montague or his religious convictions. Goodwife Shelby has spoken, and she is one authority that not even her husband is prepared to challenge.

✠

Sunday arrives with a pall of low grey cloud, trapping the smell of the river and the marshes between the land and the sky, a pungent scent left by the ancient cycle of decay and regrowth. Nicholas follows his brother, his parents and the rest of the family to join Barnthorpe's inhabitants at the little church by the estuary. If Yeoman Shelby has reservations about meeting again the man who was at least partly responsible for his incarceration, he does not show it. Several men among the congregation press in upon him to offer their sympathy, expressing loud outrage at his recent ordeal. If he suspects any of them to be the cause of it, again he gives no sign.

Without the sun to light its narrow interior, the church has a cold, dank feel to it, as though only recently reclaimed from the flood. The ancient beams that arch overhead are as dark as the petrified tree stumps that sometime emerge from the mudflats when the tide is unusually low. The only brightness in the place beams from Parson Montague's eager young eyes. He has the smooth, rapturous face of a poet. If he's older than twenty-three, thinks Nicholas, then prayer is as good for the complexion as it is for the soul. He wears a plain black gown – not the white surplice of the queen's official religion – and the joyous expression of a child who has just dug a purse full of shiny golden half-angels from the mud and, in his innocence, wants to share his good fortune with everyone he meets.

The congregation takes its place as required by proper social order: the minor gentry at the front, Yeoman Shelby and his family one row back, the farm labourers and village artisans next, and the lean, hollow-eyed folk who make their precarious living cutting reeds and catching eels in the marshes last. The size of the congregation tells Nicholas nothing about Asher Montague's appeal as a preacher: attendance is compulsory, on pain of a fine that few gathered here could afford.

At last Montague enters the pulpit. His eyes begin to range over the congregation, taking note of each expectant face, smiling as though they are dearest friends restored to him after a long absence. Then heads begin to drop. Surprised, Nicholas remembers what Jack had said to him: *I'd never seen so many people awake in a church before.* Then he realizes that this is not the result of boredom, or weariness from a week of labour in the fields; it is something closer to subservience. He notices that only Jack, his mother and a few others still possess the animation with which they entered the church.

When Parson Montague's beneficent smile has subdued the congregation to his satisfaction, he says softly but clearly – for, in the silence, you could hear a mouse scurrying under the pews even if it went on tiptoe – 'Behold, I was born in iniquity, and in sin hath my mother conceived me.'

Psalm something-or-other, Nicholas recalls as he hears a muttered chorus of 'Amen', each sounding in his ears like an admission of unpardonable guilt.

From this soft but uncompromising beginning, Parson Montague begins to climb. His voice has a chorister's sweetness, clear and sharp. Yet it has a strength that belies its youthfulness. From the slight accent, Nicholas puts its genesis somewhere in the wilds of the West Country.

The higher Montague goes, the more breathless he becomes. Soon he is fighting his way through black clouds of sin, parting them with the lightning of his oratory. He flails his audience mercilessly, and by extension all those whose sinfulness blinds them to the true glory of God. They are seduced, he tells them, by lavish display and luxury, though Nicholas wonders where in hard-pressed Suffolk all this lavish display and luxury are to be found. Then he realizes that what Montague really means are the fine copes of the bishops and the rich trappings of the nobility. Clever, he thinks. Accused of incitement, Montague can protest that he was only speaking of his congregation's own vanities.

Looking around, Nicholas sees that by now some amongst the congregation have taken on the manner of those condemned to imminent execution. But Asher Montague has a sliver of hope to offer. Nothing but perfect obedience to a humble and austere love for their creator will save them from the unimaginable horrors that await them in hell. The path to salvation, Montague tells them, is as narrow and treacherous as a high mountain track. Look down, and you might stumble and plunge into the abyss. Look up, and the summit seems too far away ever to reach. It is a picture Nicholas suspects many of the parishioners in flat Suffolk might find hard to imagine, but he senses that more than a few of them are up there on the precipice with their parson.

If anyone is expecting the path to be easy, Asher Montague warns, they should think again. There are dangers waiting to sweep them over the edge. Dangers such as music: music is the Devil singing to you. And dancing: dancing is an abhorrent, pagan frenzy.

Montague turns his glare on the fathers amongst the congregation. Their daughters' hair must be always covered, he thunders. Display is nothing more than vanity. That too offends the Almighty. If anyone should be in any doubt about the authority behind his instruction, he cites Proverbs, Chapter 31, as proof. 'Beauty is vanity,' he tells them, his voice close to breaking with pity for those who might still hanker after a few lace trimmings. 'But a woman that feareth the Lord, she shall be praised!'

From the Book of Corinthians, Montague picks a passage to remind the women in the congregation of their place. 'For the man was not created for the woman's sake, but the woman for the man's sake,' he proclaims, pointing at random – but accusingly – at some of the female members of the congregation. Nicholas is relieved to see his mother has her head up and a dangerous determination in the set of her jaw. He's thankful Bianca is not here beside him, though he does wonder how Montague would respond to a fiery stream of Paduan street-Italian hurled in his direction.

Thinking of Bianca, he recalls the story she told him of the firebrand priest Savonarola, whose preaching turned the people of Florence against their duke, turned servants against their masters, children against their parents. Savonarola too had railed against vanities and luxury. Cecil's words at Richmond spring into Nicholas's mind: *the queen cannot live for ever... Change can be fertile ground for trouble...*

When Asher Montague has finished, his congregation seems wrung out, exhausted, as though every one of them has been battling sin alongside their preacher. It takes some time for people to find the use of their tongues, their limbs, their independent will. Only a few – his mother and Jack amongst them – appear unmoved. Nicholas dares to glance at his father. His jaw has a resolved set to it, his eyes still fixed approvingly on Asher Montague.

The service over, Nicholas tells his family he will join them presently. He waits awhile by the porch while the congregation disperses. Out on the estuary the dunlins and the oystercatchers wander, pricking the mud banks for prey. A cold wind rustles the leaves of the crack-willows in the graveyard. When he is alone, Nicholas opens the door and steps back inside the little church.

✠

'May I be of service, Brother?' Asher Montague asks, looking up from the heavy Bible spread open on the lectern. His voice echoes down the empty nave. 'Have you perhaps left something behind?'

Nicholas walks towards the priest, his boot heels clacking on the stone floor. 'I'm Nicholas Shelby, Yeoman Shelby's son.'

Montague slowly closes the Bible. His smile is that of the artless innocent, yet Nicholas thinks he detects a flicker of alarm in the soft brown eyes.

'Ah, yes, the royal physician. I was pleased to see Yeoman Shelby free and in the congregation. It was all very unfortunate.'

He extends his hand, his grasp soft but purposeful.

'He told me he found the seditious paper here, in this church,' Nicholas says, coming straight to the point. 'How could that be?'

'I fear I have no idea, Doctor.'

'Nevertheless, you decided to pass it to Sir Thomas Wragby – without enquiring further.'

Nicholas might have invited him on a tour of the Bankside stews and dice-dens, given the appalled look on Montague's face. 'I had no option,' he protests. 'It was seditious.'

'Yes, but it wasn't my father's. He didn't print or distribute it.'

'I did make that point to Sir Thomas. But sedition is sedition.'

'And you, I think, are quite the expert on the subject. Or should I say, "expert at staying the right side of it"?'

'There is no right side to God's word, Dr Shelby. His word is law. And laws are there to be obeyed. The alternative is simple: the Devil reigns.'

'You're a Puritan, I take it.'

Montague almost smiles, though there's none of the innocent warmth in his face that was evident before the service. 'I am pure in my heart, if that's what you mean. Can *you* say the same thing?'

Nicholas clears his throat. He hopes he can get through what he has to say without error.

'"Prayer is not enough; only a pure and sinless heart will speed your reward in heaven. Be our masters ever so mighty, their pride and their vanity will destroy them. Cast them down into the fires of hell where they belong." Do those words sound familiar to you, Parson Montague?'

The jawline of this lamb of God suddenly takes on the hardness of a wolf's. He gives Nicholas a direct stare. 'As soon as I read that blasphemous screed, I took it straight to Sir Thomas. But I'll take your recital as accurate; I did not commit it to memory.'

'You weren't afraid, by any chance, that the discovery of such a tract in your church might throw suspicion on *you* – as the real author? Listening to your sermon today, I could describe it as somewhat inflammatory.'

Montague's youthful cheeks colour. 'I have told my parishioners nothing that is not written in the Holy Book. And I did not write the sacrilege on that paper your father gave me.'

Nicholas has the uncomfortable feeling that he's being out-manoeuvred by this deceptively callow-looking young man. Asher Montague is tougher than he'd expected. 'The bishops and the Privy Council get very nervous when the very reason behind their existence is questioned, particularly when the Bible is used as evidence,' he says, acutely aware he's beginning to sound like Robert Cecil. 'It won't be just you who pays the price, it will be the ordinary folk who get fired up by your preaching.'

Asher Montague seems unmoved. 'Martyrdom is a glorious reward, Dr Shelby. If we are called to it, we should embrace it.'

'Like John Hooper did?'

Nicholas watches Montague's face to see if his question strikes a chord. But Montague's stare is uncompromising. The certainty in one so young troubles him.

'My father was a follower of John Hooper, Dr Shelby,' the priest tells him proudly. 'When Hooper burned, he fled across the Narrow Sea – first to the Low Countries, then to Frankfurt. I watched the hope fade in his eyes as a Catholic Queen of England tried to burn the one true faith out of these isles. I know well enough the terrible price God sometimes asks us to pay for entry into His glory. I can assure you I am not at all afraid to pay it. Now, if I can be of no further service to you, Dr Shelby, I have the scriptures to read and my next sermon to prepare.'

✠

Nicholas finds his father in the barn, tending to the apple press that sits in one corner. As he turns the quernstone to check it is rotating freely, the tart scent of crushed fruit rises on the warm air. If he is aware of Nicholas's presence, he does not look up.

Nicholas cannot enter this place without remembering the rainy day – almost a decade ago now – when he clung to his father like an infant, weeping out the pain of losing Eleanor, his first wife, and the child she was carrying. Until that moment he had never imagined that this stoic man, who had always seemed to him like a gnarled bough that no tempest could ever break, had such an understanding heart. It pains him now to see it falling before such a loud but essentially transient breeze as Asher Montague.

'A word if I may, Father,' he says.

Yeoman Shelby turns, wipes a hand across his forehead and sits down on the quernstone.

'Has my son the courtier come to tell me the queen's ministers wish me to bend a more reverent knee and have better regard to my place?'

'They do it to me, Father, whenever I arrive for an audience without a physician's gown.'

'I suppose you're here to give me your learned opinion on the sermon.'

'If you want me to. I had intended to let you know I'm return-ing to London tomorrow.'

Yeoman Shelby toys with the rusted bolt he's removed from the press. 'I don't know how long God intends me to dwell upon this earth, Nick – none of us do. But it would be good to see a better world for the likes of folk around here before I leave it.'

'That's not what Asher Montague is offering, Father; nor the author of the tract that got you into so much peril.'

His father lays the bolt aside and looks Nicholas in the eye. 'What's wrong with making us face our sins?'

'Bianca told me of a priest in Florence named Savonarola. He was a pious force, too. He convinced the young to turn against their parents, brother against brother, wife against husband. And all in the name of confronting sin.'

'What happened to him?'

'In the end, they burned him. All he really wanted was power over his followers.'

'And you think that's Asher Montague?'

'When my first wife died, I would have taken a sword to the queen herself if a Montague or a Savonarola had told me it would bring Eleanor back. Men like that are always on the watch for such a fracture in a person's soul. They use it as tinder to start a torch burning. The next thing you know, they're telling you to burn down your neighbour's house because they've convinced you he's somehow responsible for your hurt.'

Yeoman Shelby rises from the press and takes his son by the arm. 'There's no cause for you to worry, Nick. Parson Montague will be gone soon.'

'That's a blessed relief. Where's he going – back to the Low Countries?'

His father's reply is not what Nicholas is expecting.

'Our parson is going down to London, to preach at the foreigners' church. I didn't know they had such a thing there.'

'Yes, it's part of Austin Friars, up by Bishopsgate,' says Nicholas, his brow creasing with surprise.

'So you don't have to worry, boy. I'm sure whoever comes to replace him will be as unoffending as old Olicott.'

'Promise me one thing, Father...'

'If it's within my power.'

'Forget any notion of championing Montague's sermonizing. Your liberty is conditional, and I'm responsible for your parole.'

Yeoman Shelby's acquiescence is signalled by no more than a deep-throated grunt and an almost imperceptible nod of his head.

'There's still the Ipswich assizes to consider,' Nicholas explains. 'Sir Robert Cecil may have got you released, but he can't simply make the charges vanish. I'll need to tell him what I've learned, so that he can speak to Attorney General Coke.'

'Very well, boy. I promise I'll keep my peace and pretend that all in the queen's realm is justice and tranquillity.'

Ignoring the sarcasm in his father's voice, Nicholas says, 'Have you thought of the ill effect all this is having on Mother? Or on Jack and Faith?'

'Your mother is a strong woman, Nick. She's buried two other sons and a daughter.'

'I know. Perhaps, now, she deserves a little peace.'

Yeoman Shelby draws his son into an embrace. 'It's them I want this better England for, Nick. And for you and Bianca, and young Bruno.'

'I know,' Nicholas says, surprised to find his throat tightening. 'But I always thought it was the young who wanted to change the world.'

✣

From the pressing barn, Nicholas goes in search of his brother. He finds Jack mending the sluice at Barnthorpe mere.

I'd almost forgotten how the work never stops, he thinks. The mown grass will need drying, then collecting for storage; the sheep will require shearing; before you know it, harvest time will arrive. 'You should have asked me. I could have helped,' he calls out. 'I think I've made progress with Father. If we can just keep him out of trouble—'

Jack does not reply. He lays down his iron crowbar and lifts out the length of rotten wood he has come to replace. Water spills through the gap in a muddy torrent. Jack slips the replacement into place between the iron stems and slams it home. The torrent reduces to a trickle.

'Did you hear me?' Nicholas says.

Jack looks up, drying his hands on his jerkin. 'Aye, I heard you. What do you want me to do – lock him in the stocks?'

'Just do the best you can. I'm returning to Bankside tomorrow. If it doesn't rain, the prospects for the ride back to London look good.'

'Back to your fancy life at court.'

Nicholas rolls his eyes. 'I don't *have* a fancy life at court, Jack.'

'Will you be back for the assizes?'

'I'm hoping Father won't have to appear. We should be able to get the charges dropped.'

'How?'

'I'm counting on Sir Robert Cecil to speak to the Attorney General. After all, there's no real evidence of sedition. All that Father could be accused of is having a loose tongue, repeating something he'd read on an anonymous sheet of paper.'

'He's old and tired, Nick,' Jack says. 'And he worries about keeping the farm. It hasn't been easy, these last few harvests. Without the coin you send, I'm not sure we could have fed every-one this winter past.'

'I'll send more. I don't want Father's reward in life to be the gallows, for spreading sedition.'

'I think he's looking for his reward elsewhere.'

'So are a lot of people, Jack. And fellows like Asher Montague are taking advantage of them,' Nicholas says. 'But make no mistake, the Privy Council is on the watch for any sign that the people might not be as biddable as it would wish.'

'Her Majesty told you that, did she?' Jack asks with a laugh.

'Close enough. It was Robert Cecil.'

'And has Mr Secretary Cecil told you who will reign when the queen dies? I could make some money wagering on that at Woodbridge market.'

Nicholas reaches down to help his brother up out of the stream. 'Not in so many words. Cecil and most of the Privy Council seem to favour James of Scotland.'

'A king would be proper,' Jack says, nodding. 'Being ruled by a queen gives my Faith a certain sense of liberty that I sometimes think she could do well without.'

Nicholas grins. 'Know your place, Jack. It's the way things are.'

'So we'll be governed by the wild Scots then?'

'Not necessarily. There are others being spoken of, discreetly. The Lady Arbella Stuart... Edward Seymour... Anne Stanley – her father was grandson to Mary Tudor, the sister of the queen's late father. Some among the peace faction at court are even suggesting Isabella, the Spanish *infanta*.'

Jack stares at him in astonishment. 'The queen tells you all this, does she, while you're studying a flask of the royal piss – *my* little brother?'

Nicholas laughs roundly. 'She doesn't tell me anything of the sort. But you'd be surprised what the servants say when they think you can't hear. The point is, such uncertainty can lead some into rashness. Firebrands like Asher Montague don't help. The very last thing we need in these troubled days is the slightest incitement to insurrection. The result could be a bloodbath – civil war.'

Arm-in-arm, they walk back to the farmhouse. The old uneven walls of whitewashed plaster, the thatch and the beams of weathered oak are as familiar to Nicholas as his own skin. But suddenly the place no longer seems to promise the same safety and shelter it had when he was a boy. Is that because he's no longer a child? Or has the world changed while he was looking in the other direction?

8

Nicholas has ridden the horse he borrowed from the Richmond Palace stables as hard as he dares. He had feared at the outset that a mount from the royal stables would prove to be all coat and no lungs, showy but unsound. In fact the bay mare has done him proud. Reaching Southwark, he stables her at the Tabard. Tomorrow he will have to return her to Richmond before taking a wherry back, all at his own expense. He knows he could probably get away with charging everything to Cecil's account, but although he's lived amongst Banksiders for a decade, he draws the line at venality. He gives the ostler threepence for the livery and the best feed he can provide and then, weary and sore from the journey, he goes directly to Bianca's shop on Dice Lane.

'She is at the Jackdaw, Master Nicholas,' Cachorra tells him, breaking off from mixing ingredients for one of Bianca's medicinal pastes. 'Is all well with your father? He is safe, yes?'

'Safe enough at present, thank you,' Nicholas says. He watches as she continues her work, grinding the pestle in the mortar, the sinews in her arms tautening. 'But it might help if you could mix a good specific for stubbornness.'

'Stubbornness is illness, yes?' Cachorra asks, giving him a doubting glance. After only a few months in England, she is still making sense of the subtleties of the language.

'In my father's case, apparently incurable.'

At the Jackdaw, he finds Bianca sitting at one of the tables with Rose, going through the previous day's reckoning. Ned, not having a faculty with words or numbers, is scrubbing the pewter jugs and tankards until they shine.

'I wasn't expecting you so soon,' Bianca says, jumping up to embrace him. 'Do I take your presence here to imply good news, Husband?'

'Good enough.'

'Your father is free?'

'And, in my opinion, entirely innocent of anything other than suddenly becoming easily led, which is most unlike him.'

'I never doubted it,' Bianca says. 'Now that you're here, I want to show you something.'

'A surprise? Has Rose managed to stop Buffle stealing scraps? Or has the queen sent word to tell me I'm not required any more? Either would be welcome.'

'Things, actually,' she tells him. 'Things that Ned and I found while you were away. I don't want them up here in the taproom, lest anyone comes in and catches a glimpse of them. I don't want to be accused of witchery – again.'

'That sounds ominous. I thought the Turk's Head was the place for passing off stolen property.'

'Come with me, Husband.'

Lighting a tallow candle, Bianca leads Nicholas to the stone steps that disappear into the cellar, calling on Ned to follow. They descend into the dark, low-ceilinged chamber where she used to mix her medicines before the move to Dice Lane. At the foot of the steps, she says, 'Will you fetch them for me, please, Ned? I really don't like touching them. Put them on the top of that cask over there.'

When he has unwrapped the cloth and laid out the contents, Bianca says to Nicholas, 'We found them in a locked room at

Aksel Leezen's house in the Steelyard. At first I thought they were real. But I dropped one in fright. It shattered all over the floor.'

Nicholas picks up each item in turn, a look of appreciation spreading across his face.

'Écorché pieces,' he says at length.

'They're *what*?'

'Écorché models – for teaching anatomy.'

'I thought they might be something of that nature. Ned here thinks they're for the practise of devilry.'

Glancing at Ned, Nicholas replies, 'Nothing so curious, Ned – just plaster, artfully crafted and painted.'

'Well, I'm on Ned's side,' Bianca says. 'I think they're unnatural, too. I'd rather have left them in Aksel's house, but I thought I'd best show them to you. I thought you might know what to do with them.'

Nicholas doesn't answer her directly. He holds one of the pieces – a hand – up to the candlelight again. The tendons and the flayed flesh gleam as though the blood is still flowing through vein and artery. He can't help but think of how close his father had come to having his own hand detached. 'They're not English,' he says. 'We don't make anything as accurate as this. From the duchy of Hesse, I would imagine.'

Bianca looks impressed. 'Are you a divinator now? Have you developed the second sight on the road to Barnthorpe?'

He shows her the plaster palm, pointing to the plump section below the thumb where the artist – for in Nicholas's mind, this is a fine piece of statuary – has left a portion of flesh on the otherwise flayed hand. 'Look,' he says, 'here's an L. Then another letter I can't read. Then: FR.FUR.TENS.'

Bianca studies the tiny letters etched into the plaster, brushing away a heavy lock of dark hair that insists on swinging down over one eye. 'What does it mean?' she asks.

'The L and whatever comes next – I can't quite make it out – could be initials. Then there's the FR.FUR.TENS. Either the owner or the maker could be L-somebody, of Francofurtensis: Frankfurt.'

Bianca claps her hands in pleasure. 'My clever husband!' she teases.

'You say you found these in Aksel Leezen's house?'

'Yes. I thought I'd stumbled into a butcher's shambles. I got the fright of my life.'

'To the right person, they're valuable. If Leezen was importing them, I'd have thought he would have sold them on quickly.'

'Perhaps he died before the customer could collect them.'

'Leezen isn't a name familiar to me as an importer of materials of physic,' Nicholas says, turning the flayed hand over in the candlelight and inspecting it with more admiration than Bianca feels is called for, given the macabre nature of the thing. 'But I could ask John Lumley at Nonsuch. He's still the patron of the chair of anatomy at the College. The question is: what are you going to do with them?'

'Me? I hadn't thought – other than to get rid of them.'

'Aksel left you the house. Presumably he also wanted you to have what was in it.'

'I don't want them,' Bianca says, horrified. 'They're grotesque.'

Nicholas lays the hand back amongst the other parts. Out of the candlelight, they look like the sad debris of a pillaged grave. 'When I return Cecil's horse to Richmond, I'll go by way of Nonsuch. I'll speak to Lumley.'

'You can give them to him, if you want; he can add them to the collection of strange marvels he keeps in his library. As long as they're not with us at the Paris Garden. I don't want Bruno seeing or touching them.' She gives Ned Monkton a hard stare. 'And while they remain here, make sure Rose doesn't get one of her daft fancies – such as sneaking up behind the customers while they're playing *primero* and sticking that horrible arm out, with a King card wedged between the fingers. You know what she's like.'

'I'll put 'em in the brew-'ouse, Mistress,' Ned promises, wisely suppressing a grin. 'They'll teach the rats a lesson if they try to take a bite.'

'There was something else we found at the Steelyard,' she tells Nicholas when Ned has scooped up the parcel and climbed the steps out of the cellar. 'Something equally odd. There was a painted image of a little girl propped up on the bed. I thought at first it might be a shrine to the daughter Aksel lost to the pestilence, little Vreni. Now I'm not so sure. It was all rather sinister, to tell the truth.'

'I take it Aksel Leezen's bequest is not quite the gift you thought it to be,' Nicholas says.

Bianca nods. The house in the Steelyard has been much in her thoughts of late. It has been hard for her to have to reconsider her opinion of the old Hansa merchant. But then, she supposes, we can never truly know the shadows that haunt someone else's mind. Could it be that losing his wife and daughter had taken Aksel down a darker path than his outwardly gentle persona might have suggested? That, she can understand. Nicholas himself only came into her life because he had once tried to drown his own grief in the cold waters of the Thames. Nevertheless, she is forced to admit there was something about that room in the little house that discomforted her. Why was it the only interior chamber with a locked door? And what was Aksel's motive for placing the effigy of the child where he did, a blank-eyed, unfinished sentinel?

As she follows Nicholas back up the steps towards the daylight and the comforting normality of the Jackdaw's taproom, Bianca shivers. The cellar had been cold, as cold as that room in the Steelyard when she had first entered it. But whether it's the chill of the cellar or her memory of walking into that room that makes her flesh pucker, at this precise moment she finds it impossible to say.

✠

The Jackdaw is busy tonight, the taproom full of drinkers, dice-rollers and card-players. The hard work allows Bianca a temporary reprieve from her uncomfortable thoughts. Soon she has put Aksel Leezen and the bundle that is now lying in the brewhouse out of her mind completely.

When Constable Osborne, leader of the Southwark nightwatch, enters accompanied by two of his men, she is helping Rose clear away a table recently vacated by a group of apprentice butcher boys who'd come across the river from the scalding houses on Eastcheap for a night of youthful riot on Bankside. In truth, they hadn't been much trouble. The tricksters, whores and sleight-of-hand merchants had left them with precious little coin on which to get rowdy drunk.

'God give you a good evening, Mistress Merton,' Osborne says, making a polite little bow that sets his leather jerkin squeaking over his broad back. He is a well-set fellow, tall, with a calmness that not even the most truculent apprentices up for a fight can disquiet.

'A cup of warm hippocras for you and your bold fellows, Constable?' Bianca suggests, giving him a broad smile.

'Marry, no, not tonight, thank you all the same,' he says, declining the offer.

'Then what can I do for you?' Bianca asks, noting the look of disappointment on the faces of the two watchmen.

'Do you know Jed Trindle's lad, Gideon?'

Bianca searches her memory. 'Jed Trindle... the broiderer on Kent Street?'

'Aye, him. We was wondering if Gideon might have been in here recently.'

'Gideon? On his own?'

'Or perhaps in the company of someone other than his father.'

'Gideon can't be more than twelve,' Bianca says disapprovingly. 'You know me better than that, Constable Osborne. This might be Bankside, but the Jackdaw draws the line at allowing twelve-year-olds to sup. We're not the Chapel Royal, you know.'

'I ask, Mistress Merton, because he's been missing for a couple of days.'

'Missing? Has he run away? Jed Trindle isn't a rough fellow, is he?'

'Mercy, no. Dotes on his boy. Jed sent him across the river to buy some ribbons from the haberdashers up by Cripplegate. Gideon hasn't returned.'

'Well, he's certainly not been here. Rose or I would have seen him.'

Constable Osborne sighs dispiritedly. 'I reckoned on you telling me as much. Maybe you could ask around – talk to your customers... keep an eye out.'

'Of course. Have you spoken to the landlords of the Turk's Head and the Good Husband?'

'Not yet, but we are resolved to do so before the night is out.'

'I'm sure young Gideon will turn up before long,' Bianca says.

She watches the three men push their way through the taproom throng towards the door. She knows that what has passed between her and Constable Osborne is notable only for what each has left unsaid. There are reasons enough in London why young boys go missing. Some do so voluntarily, signing up on one of the ships moored in the river in the expectation of profit and adventure. Others take to the road to join the roving gangs of tinkers and vagrants. But then there are the lads sold into false apprenticeships, whose only schooling turns out to be in debauchery, or who end up in private houses playing Ganymede for wealthy gentlemen who like their actors smooth and their masques performed behind locked doors. Then there are the most pitiful of all: the ones who end up giving themselves in dark alleys for little more than the cost of the wherry that brought their customer across the river, and who will never in their short lives earn enough to buy themselves a comb to scrape the lice out of their hair.

Bianca gives up a silent prayer that Gideon Trindle does not fall amongst them; that he is soon reunited with his father. Then she goes back to work. She has long since learned that if she allowed herself to dwell on the fate of every unfortunate who fell into the darker shadows of Bankside, she would never sleep at all.

✠

On the shelves and in the newfangled display cases built after the Italian style, Lord Lumley has assembled a collection of learning that is the equal of any library in Europe. From the Book of Genesis in Hebrew, through Latin translations of Plato and Hippocrates, to the latest works of natural philosophy, Lumley likes to claim – as modestly as he can, for he is by nature a modest man – that the whole span of human learning is contained within it. Amongst the collection, Nicholas knows, are several books depicting the workings of the human body stripped of its veil of skin, écorché drawings by the great masters of the art, Leonardo, Alberti and Vesalius.

The owner of this fabulous collection is a lean, dour Northumbrian with a spade-cut beard, whose perpetual look of disappointment hides a gentle nature and an inquisitive mind. Nicholas has known John Lumley for a decade. They share the bond forged between survivors – Cecil intrigue has touched them both.

'Your assumption that these pieces are not English is correct,' Lumley says after studying the objects Nicholas has brought him. 'And I agree with your hypothesis that they have a connection with Frankfurt. But they may not have been made there. Follow me.'

Lumley leads Nicholas to the collection of volumes on medicine.

'Let us see what we can find,' he says, beginning to pull heavy leather-bound tomes from the shelves. He hands them to Nicholas, who carries them to an oak table by the window. Through the glass, he catches glimpses of animated servants hurrying to and fro against the beautiful white stucco walls. Lumley has learned that the official talks between ambassador al-Annuri and the Privy Council are to take place at Nonsuch. It will not be the first time a major treaty has been signed here, and Lumley likes to have the preparations for the festivities well in hand.

When a small pile of books has been assembled, Lumley picks one and begins to thumb through the thick sheets of parchment. As the pages turn, Nicholas is presented with a procession of extraordinary figures. Some are marching, some sitting, some prone, one frozen in the act of throwing a discus, another sitting on a plinth, deep in contemplation. The only difference between these figures and the ones hurrying about outside is that the écorché figures show their inner selves. Peeled of their protective skin, the bones, muscles, tendons and sinews are all perfectly described by an artist's hand – a procession of cadavers, dead and yet vibrantly alive.

'Here,' says Lumley triumphantly. 'These might be what we're after.'

The images Nicholas is looking at now are not whole bodies, but rather their constituent parts: a knee joint with a section of femur, tibia and fibula attached; a shoulder with the deltoid muscle portrayed; a foot flayed of skin to reveal every bone, down to the distal phalanx of the little toe.

'Could this be your artist?' Lumley asks.

Nicholas takes his time studying the images. 'I suppose he might,' he says at length. 'There can't be many exponents of such fine work.'

He turns back to the title page. The illustration is a woodcut, showing an imagined lecture by a physician of ancient Greece. The great man stands on a platform between two Doric columns while his students look up admiringly. The text is in Latin, a eulogy to the skill of the artist whose work is contained within.

'Johann van Calcar,' Lumley announces. 'A pupil of Titian, said by some to be the illustrator for the great Vesalius,' he adds, tapping a copy of *De Humani Corporis Fabrica* that he had previously rejected.

'From the Low Countries?'

'German – from the duchy of Cleves.' Lumley points to the small lines of type set into the plinth on which the physician stands. 'The book itself is printed by Johannes Oporinus in Basle, Switzerland, in the year of our Lord 1545. Oporinus printed the *Fabrica*, so it's hardly surprising he also printed Calcar's work.'

'But these écorchés are statuary, not drawings. Someone else might have made them from Calcar's illustrations.'

'That's possible.' Lumley gives Nicholas a look of regret. 'But a sculptor is not mentioned here. If it was not Calcar himself who crafted these items, then I fear we have reached a dead end. Is it important?'

'Bianca finds these somewhat distressing. Ned Monkton and Rose think they're witchcraft. I thought the more I knew about the provenance of these items, the easier it will be to reassure them.'

Lumley's melancholy face breaks into a rare smile. 'And how are Ned and Rose? The household at Nonsuch is sadly the quieter for their absence.'

'They're in good health, thank you. No children of their own yet, but they still hope.'

'I could use them here, during the revels planned for the Moor ambassador. Master Ned is one of the few souls I've met not intimidated by royal servants. Extra hands would be invaluable.'

'I'll ask them,' Nicholas says. 'I'm sure they'd be honoured.'

'I cannot believe it is very nearly seven years since they came here for refuge during the pestilence, while you were away in Barbary. How fast the years speed by. And Bianca – she is well?'

'Very well indeed, my lord. She teases me endlessly about my conversations with the queen.'

'That is a good thing, Nicholas. Closeness to Her Majesty does sometimes tend to encourage overweening pride in a man. Such vanity needs regular pricking. Fortunately, God has given womankind a mysterious skill with the needle.'

Nicholas goes to the cabinet on which the écorché figures are laid out, taking the book of Calcar's drawings with him.

'They're certainly in Calcar's style,' he says, after a careful comparison. 'I wonder who they were intended for – on the assumption, that is, that Aksel Leezen was indeed the importer.'

'Why not ask your fellows at the College?'

Nicholas gives Lumley a rueful smile. 'I'm about as popular there as an outbreak of the French gout at Lambeth Palace.'

'Still upsetting them with your heresies?'

'I had an argument with Baronsdale not so long ago, when I told him about an English student at Padua named Harvey. Professor Fabricius is generous enough to write to me occasionally; Harvey is studying under him. He has a conviction that the heart is central to the circulation of the blood around the body.'

'And Baronsdale told you that was nonsense?'

'Baronsdale is a liver man. He believes that's where the blood is controlled from. I, on the other hand, favour Harvey.'

'Well, we've had that conversation before, Nicholas. And I still refuse to believe that the seat of courage and love is nothing more than a pump.' He gives the younger man a clap on the shoulder by way of encouragement. 'Still, Baronsdale won't be around for ever.'

'The point is, neither will the queen. And when she goes, so does my protection from the august fellows of the College of Physicians. Sometimes I'm certain I can hear them sharpening their knives already.'

'Then I shall do the asking for you, Nicholas,' Lumley says, 'when I'm next in London.'

Nicholas makes to wrap the écorché figures, but Lumley raises a hand to stop him.

'If you wish, you may leave them here. If we cannot find out for whom they were intended, then I would like to purchase them for my collection of curiosities. Will that satisfy Mistress Bianca?'

'That's kind of you, my lord,' Nicholas says. 'It will.'

'Will you dine before you leave? I can ask Farzad Gul to prepare something for you.'

Nicholas smiles as he recalls the young Persian lad who had washed up on Bankside after an English ship had rescued him from Moorish pirates – again a memory from years that have passed too swiftly. 'It would be an honour,' he says. 'And how does Farzad these days?'

'I've made him my head cook,' Lumley tells him. 'When Her Majesty comes, she insists on at least one of his exotic dishes with her meal. He's to be married to Abigail Small, one of my wife's maids. I'm sure he'll tell you himself when he sees you. He wants you and Mistress Bianca to attend.'

'We would be honoured,' Nicholas says, remembering the smell of warm beeswax on the wainscoting of the private Nonsuch chapel where their own wedding took place.

'He's a good lad,' says Lumley, 'though I must confess that I still wince when I hear him cursing the Pope as he joints a carcass of venison.'

Nicholas smiles. Lumley is a recusant, a Catholic who must practise his faith discreetly. 'It was how Farzad learned his first English phrases – from the Protestant sailors who saved him from Moorish slavers.'

'I can forgive him,' Lumley says. 'Besides, with Farzad's cooking to sustain her whenever she comes here, the queen is bound to live to be one hundred. Baronsdale will be long gone by then. You won't have to worry.'

Nicholas hands him the book he's holding. As Lumley's long fingers close around the leather spine, he says, 'Wait a moment, Nicholas. I've just thought of something.' He reopens the book at the illustrated frontispiece. 'It must be the advancing years – I failed to register it at first.' He holds the page up for Nicholas to see.

'What am I supposed to be looking at?'

'There – the printed lines set into the plinth on which the Greek physician stands. The dedication.' Lumley turns the book and proceeds to translate from the Latin. '"In honour of our most illustrious benefactor of learning and physic, he who caused this folio to prosper by his gracious favour: Aurelio Nicolò Gaspari."'

'I see it,' says Nicholas. 'But I don't understand how it helps?'

'We established that the fellow who printed this book was Johannes Oporinus—'

'You established it, my lord.'

'Well, Oporinus was Swiss. And it would make sense that the Gaspari would patronize a Swiss printer,' Lumley says, the merest hint of triumphalism breaking through his dour carapace. 'The Gaspari is a prominent banking family, also from Switzerland. They have agents in almost every major city in Europe. There's even one here in London: Silvan Gaspari. There's a good chance *he* might know who your écorché figures belong to.'

✠

The printer is a man of habit. He likes to be abed before sunset. This evening, as on every evening, when he has finished the work to hand he will prepare himself for sleep by ensuring that he has not inadvertently left anything lying about that might incriminate him. He has good cause to be careful. If they are going to come for him, they will strike in the hour before dawn. There will be no sound in the lane to give him warning. They will tie cloths around their boots and stuff rags into their scabbards to prevent the clash of steel blade against buckle. Mindful of this, he has long found it impossible to rise late. The moment he opens his eyes he becomes attuned to every little groan and sigh emitted by the narrow, three-storey tenement on Gravel Lane that he has leased since he made the move to Southwark from St Paul's, where most of London's respectable printers reside.

He had first learned the dangers of his trade in the closing years of Queen Mary's reign, a period he considers the tangible manifestation of the Devil's rule on earth. He had been a young apprentice then, helping to produce Protestant counter-attacks against the spread of papist idolatry, a loathsome superstition spread by Mary herself and those demons with human faces in the Catholic Church who enabled her.

When Elizabeth had come to the throne, the printer had thought the task God had given him was over. But then came Archbishop Whitgift and the crackdown on the truly pure of thought. Now, while the Church does little but wring its hands in the face of spreading sin, bawdiness and licentiousness are everywhere. Even the bishops souse themselves in luxury and display. And Whitgift and the Privy Council – even the queen – do nothing but persecute Puritans, when they should be driving the people to penance and a proper obedience to holy law.

The printer has long known the penalty for being caught. He has witnessed more than one of his number lose a hand to the axe, or even – during Mary's reign – go to the flames. For his own protection he moved to Southwark, where the Lord Mayor's writ runs tenuously and the officers of the Stationers' Company seldom go – unless to attend the playhouse, the stew or the bear-baiting. True, the rewards for his skill and labour here on Bankside are minimal, and he must daily endure the depravity and blasphemy of the ungodly. But he considers these trials simply the Almighty's way of testing his soul. All he really needs is food to feed his hunger, and water to quench his thirst – and paper and ink with which to ensure, when the time comes, his admittance into heaven.

He is running a little late this evening. He has been pressing extracts from the Old Testament, which he plans to offer in the markets of Southwark and the surrounding Surrey countryside for a farthing a sheet, or a ha'penny if he's lucky. Nothing provocative. Nothing they won't hear at Sunday sermon.

Again, by habit, he remains vigilant. The street door is bolted, to give him time. If he was in the process of printing his forbidden work and the Privy Council searchers were to break their usual custom and come for him at this moment, he knows he can have the galleys of composed type jumbled into a meaningless heap of individual letters within a score of heartbeats. In less than two minutes he could have the completed pages safely hidden under a flagstone beneath the privy pot in his sleeping chamber. He is always ready. It is the only way to stay alive.

Picking up two inking pads – leather balls stuffed with horse-hair – he grips their long wooden handles tightly. Rolling them in the viscous ink he has spread over the inking table, he ensures each ball has a consistent black coat – no gaps, no blots. Then he crosses to the frames of metal type lying in the cradle of the press. He begins to bat the inkballs down firmly, like a washer-woman striking wet laundry against a stone. They make a sticky, kissing noise as they meet the typeface.

As he works, he recalls the recent visit from Mistress Merton's husband – the physician. Like most people on Bankside, he has heard the rumours that Dr Shelby is sometimes called upon to visit the queen, and that he has more to do with Cecil House than merely prescribing physic for Mr Secretary Cecil's son. As a result, he hadn't believed for a moment that nonsense about Shelby requiring a printer for a proposed book of cures. The moment the physician had left, the printer had burned in the furnace every remaining copy of his declaration – just in case.

Yet the expected subsequent raid hasn't materialised. Either Dr Shelby isn't a very competent intelligencer or the rumours are merely the usual Bankside miasma of speculation and downright fiction. He feels safe enough now to reassemble the galleys and print another run – when he's finished the job in hand.

Once he has the type inked to his satisfaction, the printer returns the inkballs to the inking table. He is about to swing the frame containing the paper down onto the type, prior to running it under the heavy wooden platen and turning the screw to impress the first copy, when he hears a soft knocking at the door. Making his habitually careful check of the chamber, the printer walks over and slides the bolt.

The man standing in the alley is of middling height, well framed and wearing a plain broadcloth jerkin. The light is fading and it is not easy for the printer to judge what trade or station he occupies. Nor is he able to distinguish much of a face. The fellow wears a simple buckram cap with sides that hang down around his cheeks, and a cloth tippet around the lower part of his face, protection – the printer assumes – from the dust of the road and the stink of Bankside's open drains. Only his eyes are truly visible, pale and careworn. Looking directly into them is like peering over the edge of a very deep well.

'You are the printer, Symcot, yes?' the man asks.

Because of the tippet across his mouth, and because the printer is untravelled, he finds the accent hard to place.

'Aye. Josiah Symcot. Do I know you?'

'I bring you a message, from the Brotherhood,' the man says through the cloth. '"Whatever you shall ask in prayer, if you believe, you shall receive it."'

For a moment the printer does not answer. It is enough for him just to let the joy surge in his heart. He has always known this day would come, that the Brotherhood would not forget him; that one day they would reward his devotion by calling him to his duty. To enlist him as one of God's warriors, though he has never wielded more than a table knife and abhors violence. This is it, he thinks: the call to arms. The beacon that flares on the distant hill, telling you that you've been following the right road, even though in recent days you might have begun to doubt it. Taking a breath to steady himself, the printer gives the reply he knows the stranger is expecting to hear: 'I ask for nothing but for the glory of God to reign on earth. I am of the Brotherhood of the First Hand. And I am ready.'

9

Today, beneath a coverlet of cloud, the Thames is a sullen grey-brown. The tide is ebbing, the gulls wheeling and screeching over the spreading ribbons of ooze along either bank. Standing on the empty Steelyard wharf, Nicholas looks across to Southwark. The tenements around the Clink and Winchester House stand like tombstones seen from a distance in a misty churchyard. He can just make out the thatched roofs of the Rose and the Globe playhouses rising above the riverfront.

Bianca has brought him here to make a further inspection of Aksel's gift. Being a practical and educated man and therefore less susceptible to credulity, he is less likely to feed her sense of disquiet than Ned Monkton.

'It might not be Nonsuch Palace,' he says as he turns his back on the river to approach the house, 'but fifty pounds is fifty pounds.' Almost two years' yield at Barnthorpe, he thinks – but only with good harvests.

'Watch out for rats,' Bianca warns him as she steps across the threshold and into the cold semi-darkness of the storeroom. She hurries to the stairs and begins to climb, only partially comforted by the accompanying creaks of Nicholas's footsteps behind her. Wrinkling her nose again at the dank, melancholy smell of a place that has stood empty too long, she says without turning her head, 'I was fine until we found that effigy and those horrible plaster things. Now I don't know what to think about Aksel.'

'I've told you, they're nothing to be troubled by,' Nicholas says, trying again to reassure her. 'If John Lumley can find out who they were procured for, then you'll have helped Aksel complete one of his last commissions.'

'I hadn't thought of it that way.'

Reaching the upper floor, Bianca crosses to the window and opens the shutters. On the floor beside one wall lies the debris from the plaster limb she propelled across the chamber in disgust. She points to the chest beneath the window. 'That's where we found the other écorché figures.'

'Was there nothing else inside? Nothing to indicate where they might have come from or who they were meant for?'

'To be truthful, as soon as Ned had taken them out, I closed the lid. But I don't think so.'

Nicholas opens the chest. Stuck to the felt lining are remnants of what he takes to be straw packing. Otherwise, the chest is as empty as Bianca had said. He follows her to the second bedchamber.

'Did you ask your friend Lord Lumley what he would make of *that*?' she says, throwing open the door.

On the bed, the painted effigy of the little girl leans against the wall where Bianca left it.

For a moment Nicholas says nothing. Then: 'No. No, I didn't ask him. I didn't think to. It doesn't appear to have any connection to the écorché figures.'

'Well, I still don't like it, Nicholas. It troubles me,' Bianca says. 'She's like a fragment of memory that never changes, never moves, no matter how often or for how long you dwell upon it.'

'Perhaps you're right. Perhaps Aksel had it made so that he could remember his daughter,' Nicholas says, trying to sound the practical man. In truth, he too finds the effigy unsettling.

'Then why wasn't it finished? Why make a shrine out of a half-finished image?'

He has no answer. 'It's of no value. Burn it, if it displeases you so.'

Bianca moves closer to the bed. She stops short, unwilling – for a reason she cannot explain – to touch the painted image. She has the unfathomable sense that were she to do so, the little girl would suddenly come to life, drawing her animation from Bianca's own body. And in exchange, like a turning tide, a terrible sadness would flow in the opposite direction.

From what she considers to be a safe distance – two paces – Bianca takes in the pale-blue dress with its ruffed collar, the little pink hands poking out of sleeves that are too wide to keep out a breeze, the plain blank face staring out on a view she does not seem to recognize. 'There's another reason it concerns me,' she says. 'Look at the side of her head, the finished side.'

Nicholas moves nearer.

'The hair,' Bianca says. 'It's dark.'

'Yes, I can see that.'

'It should be fair. Whoever this is, it isn't Vreni Leezen.'

Returning to the ground floor, Nicholas suggests opening the double doors to let in the light. He makes a careful inspection of the storeroom, finding nothing but a few rusted iron hoops and rotten wooden staves left over from old barrels, and the desiccated corpse of a rat. As he reaches the wall facing the wharf, the floor changes from flagstones to planks. 'There's a trapdoor here,' he calls.

'I know. There's a place under the wharf where a little skiff can bring in smaller cargo, right up to the house.'

'Did you look in there?'

'The tide was in when Ned and I were here,' Bianca tells him. 'There's a ladder, but there was water at the bottom, so we didn't climb down.'

'Does it have a lock?'

'Yes.'

She identifies the key on her chatelaine's ring and holds it out towards Nicholas. He takes it from her and kneels to get a better look at the mechanism. The bolt holding the trapdoor shut is old but clean. He inserts the key vertically into the plate. Pulling at the bolt, he finds it slides open easily. Lifting the hatch releases a gust of damp air that stinks of river mud. Looking into the space, Nicholas sees nothing but darkness. As his eyes adjust, detail begins to emerge, as if the tide was still ebbing.

Just as Bianca had told him, a wooden ladder descends to a stone base slippery with waterweed. He is looking down into a culvert perhaps six feet wide and ten feet deep. If the tide was in, he reckons the water in the culvert would be just deep enough to bring a small boat in and still leave sufficient headroom for a couple of men to hoist the cargo up through the trapdoor. Putting his back to the void, he seizes the cold, slick sides of the ladder, eases himself into the space and begins to descend.

'Nicholas, you'll get filthy,' Bianca protests. 'You'll hurt yourself. Come out. Please!'

But her words are muffled the moment his head drops below the beams of the storeroom floor.

When he reaches the base of the ladder, he turns to face in the direction of the river. Now he can see a square opening where he judges the edge of the wharf to be. Even with the river to reflect it, the light barely penetrates to where he stands on the slimy, dank floor of the culvert. But he can make out enough to see that the channel is empty.

Grey-brown kelp hangs in festoons from the walls on either side of him. Set into the brickwork to his right is a rusty iron hoop, the first of a line that runs towards the river – handholds for drawing in a boat when the water is high. He positions himself beneath the nearest, reaching up to see if it's within his grasp, intending to use them as handholds, because about fifteen paces ahead he has spotted a dark bundle lashed to one of the heavy crossbeams that supports the roof.

The ring is just beyond his grasp. He will have to reach the bundle unaided. He starts to make his way cautiously towards the package. The sludge beneath his feet is treacherous, a black liquid-glass floor that gives off the stink of the river with each footstep. This is not, he thinks, the place in which to fall flat on your face.

Reaching the bundle, he looks up. It appears to be wrapped in dirty canvas. It looks as though it has hung here for years, slightly above the band of green slime in the brickwork that marks high water. Again it is beyond his immediate reach.

Bending his knees to provide extra impetus, Nicholas jumps up and grasps the edge of the bundle. But the fabric is as slippery as the muck that he has walked through to get here. His fingers slide off the cold, hard folds. As he lands he struggles to keep his balance.

'What are you doing?' Bianca calls from the hatch.

'I might have found another package of écorché figures.'

'Leave it be. I don't want any more of the horrible things.'

But Nicholas is determined to make one last attempt. Bending again, he launches himself upwards. His fingers close on the dank canvas. As the bundle comes away and he falls back onto his feet, a human hand – partly skeletal, partly covered with a grey flesh – slides out of the wrapping as if to take him by the shoulder. And Nicholas has just enough time to make the oddly professional observation that real bone feels absolutely nothing like the plaster imitation.

10

It takes almost an hour to find the Dowgate Ward parish constable, and another for him to summon the coroner. In the meantime, Nicholas – with the assistance of three men from the local watch – removes the body from its resting place in the culvert. They lay it out on the flagstones of Aksel's storehouse. The watch has access to a lantern, and by its meagre illumination Nicholas is able to arrive at a preliminary judgement, at least enough to present to the coroner when he arrives.

The first is that the body is that of a young male, evidenced by its size and its ruined tunic. The second is that it has been in the culvert for some time. This Nicholas can easily determine by the advanced state of decay. The corpse has been reduced almost to a skeleton. This brings Bianca a modicum of relief. The remains cannot be those of Gideon Trindle, the lad who set off across the river in search of ribbons and hasn't yet returned.

The coroner is a harried-looking man in his sixties with a lazy eye and the habit of holding his arms tightly against his sides, as though he's only just been released from his infant swaddling bands.

'Dankyn – Thomas Dankyn,' he says to Nicholas. 'Are you the owner of the property?'

'I am,' Bianca says, stepping forward. 'I'm Bianca Merton.'

Dankyn looks at her askance. 'Merton? That's an English name. This was a foreign enclave, before the Lord Mayor closed it down. Are you foreign?'

'I sometimes think so,' Bianca replies wearily, not caring much for Coroner Dankyn's abrupt tone.

'How does an Englishwoman come to own a house in the Steelyard?'

'It's a long story. It used to be owned by a Master Leezen, a merchant—'

'Is this Leezen to hand?' the coroner asks, clearly preferring to speak to a man.

'Not in any practical sense,' Bianca says. 'He's buried in the churchyard at Austin Friars. He left the property to me in his Will.'

'Did you know the body was here?'

'Yes. I always insist upon a corpse with every house I inherit.'

Dankyn looks at her as though he half-suspects she's being serious.

'I found the corpse,' Nicholas says hurriedly. He points to the trapdoor. 'It had snagged on a beam in the roof of the culvert that runs from there to the edge of the wharf. It had been wrapped in the canvas sheet it's lying on now. The sheet was secured with a chain that had caught around an iron hook set into a ceiling beam. It was sort of suspended.'

'I would like to inspect the rest of the premises,' Dankyn announces.

'Why?' asks Bianca. 'Aksel hasn't left me any more bodies upstairs, if that's what you're concerned about.'

'It is my duty to make a thorough inspection,' Dankyn says sternly. 'You'd be surprised what some people fail to mention.'

As the coroner climbs the stairs to the upper floor, Bianca seizes Nicholas by the arm. 'Oh, Jesu's holy wounds, he's going to notice the effigy. How do I explain that?'

Nicholas winces. 'I fear there's nothing much we can do about it.' He returns to the body, intent on making another examination, just to be sure he hasn't missed anything. Overhead he can hear a meandering creaking as Dankyn goes about his inspection. He has little confidence the official will draw anything concrete either from his search or from the body itself, for that matter. He's been on enough coroners' juries to know that unless the killer is caught in the act, denounced soon afterwards or easily identifiable through motive, the crime will remain a mystery. In London there are too many quarrels and too few coroners for it to be any other way. Which is why Nicholas has sometimes taken matters into his own hands – as he has now.

Dankyn returns a few moments later. 'You claimed this was your property, Mistress?' he says, fixing Bianca with what she assumes is his official look.

'It is. I told you, it was left to me in the owner's will.'

'The foreign owner—'

'Yes. But I don't live here. I've never lived here.'

'So that... that *thing* in the chamber upstairs...'

Bianca has rehearsed her explanation. 'It's a memento mori, of Aksel's daughter. She and her mother died in the pestilence of '93.'

Apparently satisfied with her explanation, Dankyn says, 'Then I think all is done. I see no point in setting up a jury to debate the matter. I'll have the watch carry the remains to All Hallows for interment.'

'You're not interested in how he died?' Nicholas asks, confirmed now in his suspicions.

'Why should I be? The body has clearly been here a long while. The former owner of the property is dead, and any witnesses to the crime – if it *is* a crime – have been expelled from the realm.

What possible benefit could come from wasting the time of decent folk on a coroner's jury?'

'Don't you want to know how he died, for your report?'

Dankyn shrugs. 'Drowned, I suppose. You're a physician, I understand?'

'Yes, I am.'

'Then while I instruct the watchmen what to do with' – a glance at the body lying on the flagstones – 'with that, perhaps you'd be good enough to confirm my conclusion. For the record, you understand. Nothing complicated. A simple examination will do.' He pauses while he gives Nicholas an imperious stare. 'Followed by an opinion that won't waste my clerk's time.'

✠

'Are you going to tell me what you found?' Bianca says as they walk along Thames Street towards London Bridge. 'I know you've found something. I can tell when you're keeping secrets.'

Nicholas can sense the rage in her. Since leaving the Steelyard, she has brought down more bloodcurdling retribution on Coroner Dankyn than any sinner in Purgatory could reasonably expect, mostly in muttered street-Italian. He suggests they stop at the sign of the Boar's Head on the corner of Thames Street and New Fish Hill. Ordering two glasses of hippocras from the public counter, he takes a wrapped kerchief from his belt pouch. Carefully unwrapping it, he shows Bianca a length of discoloured steel about five inches long. Even in its poor state, she can tell it's the blade of a knife, complete with tang, but missing the wooden handle. The tip of the blade is missing, too.

'It fell out while the watchmen were removing the body from the culvert. They were too busy to notice. But I did.'

'Why didn't you tell Dankyn?'

'I've met his type before. You heard what he said: "An opinion that won't waste my clerk's time." Remember how little interest the queen's coroner showed when Ralph Cullen's body was found? I refuse to go through that again.'

Bianca nods, remembering the events that had brought her and Nicholas together, ten years ago. Without Nicholas's stubborn determination, the killer of little Ralph – and only God knows how many others – would still be at large. No one in authority then had been even remotely interested in the unidentified child whose body had been taken from the river.

'I think he was killed with his own knife,' Nicholas says, interrupting her thoughts. 'There was a leather belt keeping his tunic in place. It had an empty sheath attached.'

'Couldn't this have just fallen out of it?' Bianca asks, looking at the muddy blade but unwilling to touch it.

'I found the point embedded in his spine, just below the seventh rib, when I carried out my *simple* examination. If the thrust didn't kill him outright, then he either drowned or his skull was fractured – there's evidence of that amongst the tufts of hair still on what remains of the scalp.' Nicholas pauses, marshalling his thoughts. He can see the events unfolding in his mind's eye. 'I think he was stabbed by someone he knew, probably during what he thought was a friendly embrace. The killer slid the knife out of the sheath and thrust it up into his back. Then he wrapped him in a sheet of canvas, secured it with a length of chain and dropped him into the culvert.'

'But how did the poor boy end up suspended from a ceiling beam?'

'It took me a while to piece that together,' Nicholas says. 'When the killer put the body in the culvert, he probably expected it to wash out into the river with the first tide. But you and I both know the river can be fickle. Sometimes a body can carry away on the current and end up at Tilbury or Gravesend – perhaps even further. But it can also stay close to where it went into the water. My guess is that this one went in around the time of an exceptionally high tide. A surge lifted it up, close enough to the ceiling to—'

'Catch on that hook,' Bianca says, shuddering as she completes the imagined picture.

'That's probably what caused the fracture to the skull.'

'And it's just hung there ever since?'

'A year or two would be my best judgement. Lower tides wouldn't have disturbed it. The water wouldn't have reached high enough to carry it off.'

'You're saying it could have been there when I visited Aksel?' Bianca says, horrified.

'Did you ever smell anything odd?'

She lets out a harsh laugh, leaving a sheen of wine on her lips. 'Civet oil... tar... pitch... animal pelts from Muscovy... the spices I bought from him – there was always a stink in Aksel's house. Most of what he imported had a reek to it. It drove his wife to distraction.' She raises her eyes to his. 'We must go back and demand Dankyn convenes a coroner's jury.'

'I have no such authority. I'm a physician, he's a lawyer.'

'He's a cold-hearted, dissembling rogue; that's what he is.'

'As I say, he's a lawyer.'

Bianca glances at the ring of keys attached to Nicholas's belt. She had pressed them upon him when she'd locked up the house in the Steelyard. They no longer hold the promise they once had. She has half a mind to hand them back to Beauchêne, make an apology so that she doesn't sound ungrateful and have nothing more to do with Aksel Leezen's bequest. It's a sad end to his generosity, but there it is. She drains her glass. 'How old do you think the lad was?'

'Twelve to fifteen, I reckon.'

'When you called out that you'd found a body, I had the terrible feeling it was going to be Gideon Trindle's.'

'Well, you can put your mind at rest on that score,' Nicholas says, laying a hand on her wrist.

Bianca looks at him. She seems almost close to tears. 'Aksel wasn't a murderer,' she says in a small voice. 'I *know* he wasn't.'

'I'm not saying he was. And I could be wrong. The body could have gone into the river somewhere else entirely. The tide might have carried it into that culvert. Either way, I'm sorry it's rather spoiled your inheritance.'

'Why did you take the knife? Why not leave it there?'

Nicholas has asked himself the same question more than once since leaving the Steelyard. The question has brought back uncomfortable memories of the Cullen murder. He has not forgotten how his obsession with the case had taken him to places darker than he could ever have imagined.

'I don't know. It probably won't be of any use. Perhaps I just don't want the victim to be forgotten so easily. Call it an antidote to Dankyn's indifference.'

'*Basta!*' Bianca says, raising a hand. 'If you don't mind, I'd like to stop talking about death. I've had enough melancholy for one day. To be honest, I think I'd rather sell Aksel Leezen's house to whoever will take it from me. He was a good man, but I'm starting to wish he'd left it to someone else.'

✠

That evening Constable Osborne stops at the Jackdaw to fortify himself for the rigours of the night-watch with a glass of hot hippocras.

'Is there news of Jed Trindle's boy?' Bianca asks. 'Have they found him yet?'

'Not yet, Mistress.'

'There's still hope, though.'

'Aye, with God's mercy there's always hope,' Osborne says with a smack of his lips as he empties the glass.

Neither chooses to pursue the conversation. The longer Gideon Trindle is missing, the less chance there is of a safe return. Better to avoid the subject than to tempt the Devil. Nor does Bianca share with him news of the macabre discovery she and Nicholas made at the Steelyard earlier in the day, because Osborne's authority does not extend beyond Bankside and there is nothing he can do. The tale will already be common gossip around Dowgate Ward. She can see no benefit in having it spread around Southwark, too – not when there's a Bankside lad missing in the city across the river.

Settling Bruno down for the night, she tells him a tale of a brave knight sent on a quest to battle a dragon that has no manners and is unpardonably rude to the peasantry. Instead of drawing the moral from the story, Bruno insists on being the dragon. He turns Buffle into cinders by breathing imaginary fire over the poor dog, even though he loves her to distraction.

'What are you going to do now, sweet? You can't sleep beside a pile of ashes.'

'Cast a spell, Mama,' Bruno insists, on the verge of tears as he realizes the implications of what he's done. 'Make her better. Please.'

When he falls asleep, Bianca helps tidy the taproom before she and Nicholas retire to their chamber.

'Why don't you give me that blade,' she says as he closes the curtain of the tester bed. 'I'll take it to Dice Lane tomorrow and put it in some *aqua fortis.*'

'Why?'

'In Padua the boys always had their nicknames or some personal device etched into their blades.'

'And what if we find something? What do we do then? Aksel is dead, the Hansa merchants dispersed. I hate to admit it, but Dankyn was right.'

When Bianca falls asleep, she dreams. She is in Aksel's house, sitting by his bed and holding his hand as he dies – while below her she can sense the painted figures of children, flat wooden puppets, marching to and fro and hanging skeletons from hooks, as if they were the sprigs and sprays that hang from the rafters in her apothecary shop on Dice Lane.

✠

Schenk wakes to the smell of burning thatch. Blazing fragments of straw drift on the wind. Against a sky of smoke, he can just make out the shape of a barn. Yet even as his throat tightens against the acrid taste, he knows he is still asleep and dreaming the old dream.

I did that.

He steps cautiously over the bodies lying around the barn's entrance: a greybeard and a greybeard's plump wife. He looks down at his crimson sword blade.

I did that, too.

Pay them no mind, his sleeping self tells him. They are heretics. Lucifer will look after them. More important to search out the youngsters. They're the dangerous ones. Let them live, let them breed, and their heretic blood will one day poison the whole world.

The entrance to the barn is a blazing wall of fire, impenetrable. By the smoking timbers to its left, a young lad – as young as I was when I first came here to the Spanish Netherlands, thinks Petrus – had managed to claw a space under the barn wall, freeing his upper torso before a rafter fell in and trapped him. His dead face is half-turned to the sky, the frozen mouth gasping for air that his lungs can no longer use. Petrus stands as close as he can to the burning barn and studies the boy with casual interest, as if he were no more than a curiosity at a fair.

I herded you in there. I called you a heretic dog before I set the torch to the thatch.

And then, to his horror, the head turns towards him. The torso begins to move. The open mouth sucks in life. The eyes bulge with determination and the fingers, their nails thick with earth and desperation, give the body purchase. It hauls the rest of its blackened body out from the scrape it has made, in its desperate bid for life. It rises up, takes Petrus Eusebius Schenk by the throat and, howling against the noise of the fire, demands to know: *Why did you do this to us?*

As Petrus wakes – into the dawn gloom of his Steelyard hiding place – he realizes the scream is coming out of his own mouth. He looks around, wild-eyed. For a moment he fears the ghost has followed him out of his dream, because hunched in the corner of the storehouse, arms hugging his own body, is a terrified young boy who appears to be cowering from the imminent assault of a madman.

'Master... Master... forgive me,' whimpers the lad. 'I meant you no harm, I swear it on my life.'

As his senses settle, Schenk recognizes the messenger from Silvan Gaspari. He curses himself. In the grip of exhaustion, he had forgotten to slide the stout length of timber into the iron hoops that secure the door from the inside. What if Gaspari had betrayed him and, instead of sending his messenger, had despatched a band of Privy Council searchers?

I will not make that mistake again, he tells himself.

The lad holds out a leather pouch, like a peace offering. Schenk takes it, unlaces the cord and pulls out a sealed letter and a box of writing implements. Breaking the wax seal, he unfolds the parchment. In the semi-darkness it is hard to make out what the dozen or so lines of German script say, but that does not concern him at this moment. What they say is not what they mean. The bland statements of everyday commerce will have a hidden meaning known only to himself and the writer. He will scrutinize them later, when the lad has gone. For now, it is enough to know that the contact has been made.

'Did you hear, they found a body down at the Steelyard yesterday?' the lad asks nervously, to mollify. 'It was at the house of the merchant, Leezen.'

'Is that so?'

'They do say the Hansa practised witchcraft to discomfort our English commerce. Perhaps they made a sacrifice.'

'Perhaps. A sacrifice of the over-inquisitive,' Schenk says coldly.

Deciding it might be unwise to linger, the boy says, 'Is there anything I should convey to my master in return?'

'Give him this,' Schenk says, handing over the brief note he committed to paper late the previous night, using paper, ink and pen purchased with the money Gaspari gave him. The sheet is sealed with wax, but for Schenk the words are as visible as if they were encased in glass: *Our friend is no longer in business. Physic is working well. Anticipate full recovery.* 'Tell Master Gaspari to send it to the brothers in Zurich by his fastest courier,' he adds.

The lad gets to his feet and heads for the open door. He has taken barely two paces before he stops, his attention caught by a series of darker shadows in the corner of the storeroom. He stares at them, then back at Schenk.

'*Holy Jesu,*' he whispers.

'Don't worry,' Schenk says, almost laughing. 'They're only ghosts.'

The lad turns again towards the door, his desire to be away from this tattered apparition and his strange companions evidenced by the hurried jerkiness of his body.

'Tarry a moment,' Schenk calls after him. 'There is something you can tell Master Gaspari.'

The boy looks back at him, his eyes wide with unease.

'Tell him this, from the Book of Matthew,' Schenk calls out from his mattress. 'A man cannot serve both God *and* riches.'

11

I t has taken Nicholas some time to find the house on Milk
Lane. In this part of the city strangers are almost as unwelcome as vagrants and are likely to be reported to the watch.
After several rebuffs, he'd done what the Banksider in him was
telling him he should have done at the start: try a tavern.

The liveried servant wears a smart jerkin of cream buff cloth.
On his left breast, an elaborately woven G trails curlicues and
coils of red thread. He shows Nicholas to a smart panelled
chamber with views over a well-tended orchard garden, saying
nothing and maintaining an aloofness that would put the staff
at Richmond or Greenwich to shame. *Bankers*, thinks Nicholas,
the new royalty.

A young girl of about twelve is seated in the corner practising
intently on a viol. Nicholas makes a gallant knee, but she takes
no notice of him. He waits for about ten minutes, according
to the hour hand on the expensive imported German clock on
the window ledge, before a balding man in a plain dark gown
appears in the doorway.

'That will do, Marie,' the man says, addressing the player of the
viol. 'You may continue your practice upstairs before Monsieur
Aubert arrives to determine if the cost of your tuition is a wise
investment for your father, or money sunk in a hopeless folly.'

Not Silvan Gaspari then, thinks Nicholas with disappointment. Presumably I'm not deemed worthy of meeting the great

banker face-to-face. He remembers what his father had told him, when Yeoman Shelby had finally admitted he'd mortgaged Barnthorpe to send Nicholas to Cambridge University: *Bankers! They'll sell you a cow with plump pink udders – but when you get to pull on the teat, all she'll give you is piss.*

The child takes her viol by the neck and, without a word, removes herself from the chamber.

'I am Signor Gaspari's secretary,' the man says without disclosing his name. 'I understand you are a physician.'

'Yes, Dr Nicholas Shelby.'

Again, the usual disbelieving scrutiny of the eyes.

'Signor Gaspari has no requirement for a doctor. He is in the best of health. Were he not, he would summon William Baronsdale, the queen's physician. Do you know Master Baronsdale?'

The question is framed as though to catch Nicholas out.

'Yes, I know of William Baronsdale. Indeed I expect to be seeing him shortly. But I haven't come here seeking tenure. I wish to speak to Master Gaspari on a private matter.'

'That will not be possible,' the secretary says.

'Does he not deign to speak to mortals?' Nicholas asks, angry with himself for rising to the bait.

'He's at the Royal Exchange.'

'When will he return?'

'When he wishes.'

Nicholas is about to invoke John Lumley's name, but the secretary's hauteur has rankled so much that he's having difficulty keeping his temper in check. Thankful that the écorché figures aren't the only cause of his journey across the river, he declines to leave a message and leaves with as much stoic dignity as he can manage.

In Milk Lane he almost collides with a beady-eyed fellow about half his height. He hopes it might be Silvan Gaspari. But upon enquiring, he learns it's only Monsieur Aubert, hurrying to assess the Gaspari daughter on the merits – or otherwise – of her viol-playing.

From Cheapside, Nicholas makes his way to the guildhall of the College of Physicians on Knightrider Street. Baronsdale is delivering a lecture to the Fellows on advances being made in the Italian states on surgery to correct facial disfigurement suffered in a quarrel or in battle. Even though Nicholas knows of the procedures from his time in Padua, he feels he must attend. His absence would be noted – snubbing the former president of the College just another black mark to be added to the extensive list already set against his reputation.

Baronsdale has received a woodcut illustration of the procedure for replacing entire noses lost to blade or shot. It shows the patient sitting upright in bed. But he is far from comfortable. One arm is bent, elbow straight ahead, with the hand fixed over the top of the scalp, as if the patient was slapping himself on the head. The position is maintained by a harness around arm, head and chest. A thin, rectangular flap of skin from around the bicep has been cut away on three sides and attached to the area around the missing nose, the source end of it still firmly part of the arm.

'Over a period of some forty days and nights,' Baronsdale announces, as though he's performed the operation a thousand times, 'the flap may be moulded into the form of a new nose, until the base can be sliced free of the arm.'

The Fellows pore eagerly over the illustration, like players at the Globe handed a new script by Will Shakespeare.

'Forty days, you say,' calls one. 'How is the pain mitigated?'

Nicholas considers telling the audience, 'It isn't mitigated, it's borne. Even with a strong sedative, the experience is a drawn-out torture.' But he keeps quiet. They all know he's a contrarian.

'Can the new nose perform its previous function?' Censor Braithwaite asks.

Not a chance, thinks Nicholas. The stink of the London streets will never trouble you again, but you'll never be able to smell the scent of rosewater in your lover's hair, and your new nose will flap like a turkey's wattle.

In the end, the discussion takes the course Nicholas always knew it would. The procedure requires surgery, and surgery is not what physicians – schooled in the medicine of the ancients – sully themselves with. Surgery is meat-work, not diagnosis, best left to butchers, or to the tradesmen of the Worshipful Company of Barber-Surgeons – and to misfits like Nicholas Shelby, who have learned their skills on the battlefield.

When the lecture is over, he approaches anyone prepared to talk to the one person in the chamber not wearing a physician's black gown, enquiring if they know anyone who has ordered a collection of écorché figures. The result is exactly what Nicholas expects:

'Are you still on Bankside, with all those cut-purses, whores and actors?'

'Still tupping that tavern wench, Shelby?'

'Can you get me an audience with Robert Cecil?'

During the after-lecture supper, a senior Fellow whose name he cannot remember leans across and says, 'Sirrah, do you think yourself so superior to these gentlemen that wearing the gown that signifies your doctorate is somehow beneath you?'

'No,' Nicholas answers. 'I threw it away ten years ago. I don't want my patients to think I'm a lawyer come to charge them ten shillings for bad advice.'

Leaving the guildhall on Knightrider Street, Nicholas considers returning to Milk Lane. Perhaps Silvan Gaspari has returned from the Royal Exchange. But after his experience there, he doesn't think he can bear the condescension. He'd rather be back on Bankside. Besides, the écorché figures are little more than a distraction to him. He couldn't afford them even if he wanted them, and Bianca loathes the sight of them. They're best left with John Lumley, he decides. Setting his feet in the direction of Bread Street Hill and Queenhythe, he heads for the river, hoping the wherrymen aren't too busy at this hour.

✠

Bianca has spent the day with Cachorra at the shop in Dice Lane. One of her first tasks is to place the blade Nicholas found at the Steelyard into a jar of diluted *aqua fortis*. She watches the slow release of bubbles for a minute or so – to ensure the solution is not too fierce – then walks away, leaving the metal to clean. She doesn't expect to find anything significant when the process is complete, and certainly nothing that might easily identify the corpse now already interred at the All Hallows churchyard in Dowgate Ward.

Trade is brisk, and it is several hours before she returns to the blade. Taking it from the acid with a set of tongs, Bianca looks at the broken length of steel, now shining almost like new. If Nicholas is hoping to find a name etched into the metal, he will be disappointed. The only mark on the blade, other than a few pitted indentations and scratches, is what looks to her like the curling stem of a leaf, meandering from the fractured end down about an inch towards the tip, which is itself broken away and presumably still embedded in the victim's ribs. Satisfied she has done all she can, she goes back to her work.

As evening approaches, Bianca closes the shop. With herself on one side, Bruno in the middle and Cachorra on the other, they walk hand-in-hand towards the Jackdaw. On the riverbank, Bruno pulls free and points across the water at almost every other place, calling out loudly, 'Look, my Sir Papa!' – a form of address he has invented for himself, by combining Ned Monkton's injunction that he should call Nicholas 'sir' – as befits the son of a gentleman – and Bianca's Italian habit of referring to Nicholas in his presence as 'Papa'. It takes Bianca five minutes to realize that Bruno is pointing at every wherry and tilt-boat he sees, regardless of who is in it.

At the Jackdaw she spends a while helping Bruno copy the letters in his absey-book. He chalks A... B... C... on his slate with pleasing accuracy. He is growing into a bright, receptive boy with all the charm of her dear dead cousin for whom he is named, but with none of his improvidence. When he has eaten a bowl of Rose's pottage and settled down with Buffle to sleep, she goes downstairs to help Rose, Ned and Timothy, the taproom steward, and the trencher-lads, potboys and serving maids, with the delivery of ale, food, comfort, a compassionate ear and blunt advice to the Jackdaw's customers. She fends off a brace of drunken student lawyers from the Inns of Court, who've come across the river in search of excitement a little more fulfilling than studying tort, amercement, pannage or trespass; and advises John Cottrell the wherryman on how he might repair his recently fractured romance with Abigail Truxton, daughter of the churchwarden at St Olave's.

'There's someone askin' for Master Nicholas,' Rose tells her, after Bianca has spent more time than she can truly afford with one arm around old Tim Gilpern, consoling him for the loss of Margaret, his wife of forty years. 'What shall I tell 'im?'

'Tell him he can wait, if he wants. Nicholas shouldn't be much longer.'

And, indeed, as the St Saviour's bell chimes nine, Nicholas returns from his ordeal on Knightrider Street. Bianca is too busy to do more than welcome him with a chaste kiss. He is about to climb the stairs to kiss the sleeping Bruno goodnight when she remembers the visitor Rose told her about.

'Someone came in a while ago, asking for you,' she says. 'Rose doesn't think he's a patient, and I certainly haven't seen him before.' She nods in the direction of a booth beside the chimney. 'He's over there, by the hearth. He's had two bowls of Rose's pottage already. You'd think he hasn't eaten in a month.'

In the far corner of the taproom Nicholas can just make out a man sitting guard over a clay pot, cloaked, solitary and – in the shadows cast by the booth – almost formless. The only distinguishing features Nicholas can make out are the high brow and the pale tufts of hair lit by the firelight spilling over the shoulder-high partition. Yet there is something about him that is familiar.

Nicholas walks over. The closer he gets, the more certain he is that he knows this man. If he's right, he hasn't seen him in more than a decade, and certainly not in London – least of all on Bankside. This memory, if it is true, belongs to his time on campaign in the Low Countries.

At Nicholas's approach, the man puts down his spoon and turns his pale, bloodless face in his direction. 'Good morrow, Nicholas, old friend,' he says. 'Took me a while to find you. But here I am.'

For a moment Nicholas just stares in disbelief. When he speaks it is with great care, as though he feels the need to give the name enough weight to stop its owner evaporating before his eyes.

'Petrus Eusebius Schenk! What in the name of all that's holy are you doing on Bankside?'

PART 2

�֍

Reunion

12

Where have the years gone? And how is it that a man can age a lifetime in the passing of only thirteen of them? Nicholas remembers something his grandfather told him when the great confusion descended upon the old man: that for him, Henry Shelby, time no longer trod its reliable familiar path, and faces too often fell out of the memory.

Nicholas tries to match the face before him with his recollection of the smiling man-child whose eyes once looked out on the world with the innocence of a cherub. The passing years have not been kind to Petrus Eusebius Schenk. The halo of fair hair that had once framed the head is now tufted and sparse. The plump cheeks have hollowed, the smooth flesh runnelled like badly tilled soil. The eyes still gleam, though, Nicholas notices. But a cold weariness has replaced the innocent, insatiable curiosity he remembers.

'Why so surprised, Nicholas?' Schenk says, pushing aside his bowl and rising to his feet. 'You look as though you've seen a ghost.'

'I can't believe... I didn't expect...'

And then the two men are embracing like brothers. Bianca watches from a few paces away, smiling, glad to see the pleasure in Nicholas's every word and gesture, but wondering in the depths of her mind why he has never once mentioned to her – even in passing – a friend with such an unforgettable name.

✠

The trio are sitting together in the alcove beside the hearth: Nicholas, Bianca and Petrus Eusebius Schenk. On the table lies a plate of hot coney pasties fetched from the kitchen. Schenk's hunger seems insatiable. But he has refused the offer of ale, even though it's on the house. Nicholas is so surprised and delighted at seeing Petrus again that this minor abjuration barely registers.

'Here's the story,' he begins. 'We met in the Low Countries, back in '87—'

'Nick was a physician straight out of swaddling,' Schenk interrupts helpfully. 'And I, well, I was what you see now – a poor fellow of no account.'

'So humble, in fact, that he was on the staff of the emissary of the House of Orange to the Earl of Leicester,' Nicholas says, clapping his old friend on the shoulders.

'In a very minor capacity, Mistress Bianca,' Schenk protests, lowering his eyes and shaking his head in a gesture of humility. 'My role was essentially to ask the English not to steal all the oatmeal. That, and showing them the way when they got lost.'

Nicholas gives Schenk a disapproving look. 'Which required him to risk his life keeping up with the army and evading Spanish patrols.'

'Well, I'm pleased to see that in the end you came safe home, like my husband,' Bianca says. 'Is this your first time on Bankside?'

'In all London, Mistress. Indeed, in all England.'

'How did you find us?'

'Simple – I asked Nicholas's father,' Schenk says.

Nicholas stares at him blankly. 'My father? You've been to Barnthorpe?'

'You always spoke of Barnthorpe with fondness. I remembered the name of the village. The vessel I took from Rotterdam docked at Woodbridge, which I also recall you speaking of. So I searched him out. Imagine my surprise – and indeed my pleasure – when I learn that young Nicholas is now physician to the English queen.'

'I'm not really. Not officially,' Nicholas protests.

Bianca gives him a kiss on the cheek. She smiles at Schenk. 'If you'll forgive me, Master Petrus, I should be helping Rose and Ned. I'll leave you two lads to catch up with the years and fight over which of you is the more modest. Please, you must lodge here tonight as our guest; we have a chamber free.'

When Bianca is out of hearing, Schenk leans across the table. 'A Bianca, not an Eleanor?'

'You remember?' says Nicholas, surprised.

'You never stopped talking about your Eleanor – Eleanor this... Eleanor that... We used to tease you for it.'

'I recall.'

'Well?'

'She died, a couple of years after I returned.'

'I'm so sorry to hear that,' says Schenk. 'But you were able still to find great love – I can tell. You have children, yes?'

'A boy. Bruno. He's five.'

'A strange name for an English son.'

'Named after Bianca's Italian cousin.'

'Ah, I thought I heard an accent.'

'My father didn't mention her, when you spoke to him?'

'No, we met only briefly.'

'Before or after he was arrested?'

Schenk's arched eyebrows make two pale half-hoops in the firelight. 'Arrested? I didn't know. For what?'

'Oh, it's a long tale. I'll save it for another time. What have you been doing all this while? You're not still fighting the Spanish, are you?'

'No, not now. But after you returned to England, I stayed on with the army of Prince Maurice. I had decided to stop being a child and take the defence of our faith seriously. I grew up.'

'I think we all did, that summer,' Nicholas says ruefully.

'It got worse.'

'I hear that.'

'Much worse,' Schenk says darkly. 'The Devil has had great sport in Holland. You were wise to leave.'

'Were you at Breda?'

'Aye, and Deventer and Oldenzaal, and a dozen other places where Lucifer and Beelzebub stirred the pot, so that their master could gorge himself on the lumps of meat that rose to the surface.'

'But you're out of it now, and safe, thank God. What brings you to England?'

'Well, in the end I went back home to Sulzbach and sought to find my fortune—'

'And have you?'

Schenk gives a sour laugh. 'What do you think? Look at me. Still, you know me – ever the optimist, the fellow with a plan.'

'You were, indeed. I remember it well.'

'So now I have come into England to see what luck, or Fate, might have in store for me.'

'Have you come alone or do you have a family?'

Schenk's smile cannot hide the solitude in his eyes. 'No family, Nick. Never had the time.'

'But you do have a plan?'

Schenk looks thoughtful. 'I heard how England had decided to shut down the Steelyard,' he says, 'so I came to see if I could perhaps establish myself as a factor, selling English wares to the Hansa – instead of the other way round. There are few enough English merchants who speak German or Dutch, so I think perhaps I may have a usefulness in this grand new world of ours – now that I've played my part in putting a stop to Hapsburg ambitions.'

'Here's to it,' Nicholas says, raising his tankard in a toast and nodding his approval, though he fears Petrus will find success elusive – the city's guilds and companies are notoriously protective. 'It may take a while to feel your way around,' he adds, trying not to sound discouraging. 'How well do you know the city?'

Schenk laughs. 'By reputation alone! I heard tell the streets were paved with gold, but all I find are open sewers.'

'But I trust your lodgings are comfortable? You could always stay awhile at ours, at the Paris Garden. It's been thirteen years; it's going to take some while to recount our tales in full to each other. And perhaps I'll be able to find you someone to speak to at the Muscovy Company, or the Eastland, or the Dansk. I'm sure we can find you a merchant venturer who could offer employment for a fellow of your skills.' He grins. 'Remind me again, what were they: drinking ale and chasing Dutch maids?'

A swirl of movement around the street door draws Nicholas's attention across the taproom. For a moment he thinks a quarrel might be about to erupt. Quarrels can swiftly lead to drawn steel. He looks for Ned Monkton – Ned can stop a fight merely by taking one of those slow, deep breaths that makes his great chest expand like a wind-filled sail. Nicholas spots him at the taproom counter, calmly filling jugs of stitch-back from the cask. Not a fight then. Ned would have caught the ripples of dispute even before Bianca did.

And then he hears the cry go up.

'Dr Shelby! Dr Shelby, you're called away. There's murder! Murder on Gravel Lane!'

13

The wind rips sparks from the burning torch Nicholas carries, sending them into the night to vanish like lost spirits dropped into Purgatory. At the end of Gravel Lane, where it spills out onto the riverbank, a small crowd has gathered around the door to the printer's house. Constable Osborne blocks the doorway.

'Thank you for coming so promptly, Dr Shelby,' he says, before a look of fatherly concern clouds his usually imperturbable face. 'But I can't let you in, Mistress Bianca. It's not a sight for gentle eyes.'

'I wasn't brought up in a *monastero*,' Bianca tells him firmly. 'I'm not a nun. I don't spend my time sewing and reading psalms from a psalter. My stomach is as strong as a Thames oystercatcher's.'

Constable Osborne looks to Nicholas for help. 'I think you should instruct your wife to return to the Jackdaw, Dr Shelby. Do you truly wish her to see this?'

'Of course I don't wish her to see it,' Nicholas says. 'But you've more chance of running across the river to the Vintry without getting your feet wet than you have of stopping her. Besides, if there's poison involved, Bianca's skill as an apothecary might well prove useful. She's very good at spotting the signs. The women of her family in Padua all have a long association with the poisoner's art.'

Osborne looks at Nicholas as though he can't quite be sure whether he's joking. 'If you insist, Dr Shelby,' he says wearily. 'But

I'm confident poison wasn't the cause of this fellow's demise. Follow me.'

The chamber is lit only by a watchman's lantern. Nicholas's torch doubles the illumination at a stroke. The shifting pools of yellow light cause the printing press to loom out of the darkness like the altar of some pagan temple.

The printer's body is spreadeagled on the carriage of his press, belly up, the wrists and ankles secured to the frame by strips torn from the ink-stained apron. His hands are balled into tight fists – evidence that his final moments on earth were filled with agony. But it is the victim's head that shows the true brutality of this killing, wedged beneath the thick wooden platen used to press the paper down upon the type. The heavy block hides the damage done to the front of the skull, but the cause of death is clear from the distorted shape of what remains visible at the sides of the platen – and from the black, frozen rivulets running down over the bottom legs of the H-frame.

Nicholas's stomach churns as he imagines those last terrible moments: the killer hauling on the handle protruding from the vertical wooden screw, driving the platen relentlessly downwards, crushing first the nose, next the chin, then the brow...

He hears Bianca's gasp at his shoulder.

'*Santa madre di Dio!*'

Constable Osborne gives a discreet cough, looking away so that he doesn't have to see Bianca make the Catholic sign of the cross. He confines himself to a sotto voce, 'I did suggest your presence was not a wise idea, Mistress.'

How long did the killer make it last? A minute? An hour? A lifetime? The pain must have been unendurable, Nicholas thinks. 'Did no one hear the screams?'

'The river is on one side and an empty house on the other,' Osborne says. 'If you look closely – which I wouldn't recommend

– you'll see a scrap of cloth between the jaw and the block. I think his mouth was probably stuffed.'

Nicholas gives voice to the question that has nagged him since leaving the Jackdaw. 'Why did you call me? It's not as if I could have prescribed a cure.'

Even in the dancing torchlight the conspiratorial look on the constable's face is clear.

'I thought you might want to see the body before the parish authorities or the Surrey coroner were called – seeing as how you have the ear of a certain Principal Secretary.'

Nicholas waits a moment before answering.

'Is that what you've heard?' he says with a wry smile.

'A very *short* Principal Secretary, with a crooked back.'

'I cannot imagine what you mean, Constable Osborne. I'm his son's physician; nothing more.'

'If you say so, Dr Shelby.'

It occurs to Nicholas that perhaps the quality of Bankside constables is improving. Osborne seems a deal sharper than his predecessor.

'In the entirely hypothetical case that I did, perhaps, have contact with Mr Secretary Cecil – in a capacity other than as physician to his son – why do you think this man's murder might interest him?'

'A printer who chooses to ply his trade on Bankside rather than around St Paul's... seditious tracts that we've been told to be on the lookout for...' Osborne gives Nicholas a conspiratorial smile. 'I've asked around, Dr Shelby. This fellow had no known quarrels, and he certainly wasn't killed for his riches. He had something someone wanted badly enough to attempt to squeeze it out of him – literally.'

'Who found him?'

'The landlord's boy. He'd been sent to tell the fellow his rent was going up,' says Osborne. 'I've spoken to him. He's innocent – or as innocent as any Bankside boy of that age can be.'

'Well, I'd best have a look around,' Nicholas says, 'to see if there were signs of a struggle elsewhere – for the inquest, of course.'

'Of course,' echoes Constable Osborne archly.

'I think I'll wait outside – for the air,' Bianca says. 'I've seen enough.'

'It might be wise not to speak to the crowd of what you've seen,' Nicholas suggests.

'It might have been wiser if I'd listened to Constable Osborne,' Bianca says with a grim smile as she turns to leave. The sight of the printer's head partly crushed beneath the platen has made her realize that a woman can sometimes overestimate her own fortitude.

When Bianca has gone, Constable Osborne says to Nicholas, 'She's a brave one, I'll give her that. I've had stout watchmen faint like maids at far less than this.' He frowns. 'But her family in Padua – they weren't really all poisoners, were they?'

'It's just a family tale.'

'I'm relieved to hear it,' Osborne says. He glances at the elderly watchman holding the lantern. 'In future, I'll have young Master Chincroft over there be the first to taste the Jackdaw's pottage next time we stop by for a bite.'

Nicholas makes a swift examination of the body. Other than the bloody mess around the platen, he can see no obvious wounds, no sign that the victim put up a fight. He reckons the man has been dead for about two days. The smell of decay is already beginning to leach out, the skin yellowing. He knows he will have to report what he has witnessed here to Robert Cecil, in case this press is indeed the source of the seditious tracts.

Next, Nicholas explores the rest of the tenement. He discovers nothing to contradict Osborne's suggestion that the printer was not murdered for his possessions. The man had few enough of them, and none worth killing for. He sees no evidence of family life, or even a nod to comfort; if the two upper floors had once been occupied, nothing remains to suggest it. Nicholas forms the impression of a man living alone in almost monk-like simplicity.

He is about to leave the sleeping chamber next to the room with the printing press in it when he hears voices and sees moving shadows cast by watchman Chincroft's lantern. The authority of the parish has arrived, in the form of a churchwarden and two aldermen. At least there's no chance of another Dankyn turning up; it is the Surrey coroner who has jurisdiction in Southwark, and he lives in distant Guilford.

With his eyes no longer focused on where he's treading, something makes Nicholas stumble. He almost drops his torch. Looking down, he sees that he has stepped into the depression left by a missing flagstone.

Even in the unreliable light, Nicholas can see the row of gouges in the dirt where the slab once lay. He steps back, then kneels for a better look. He knows at once what he's seeing: finger marks made by the repeated lifting and replacing of the flagstone.

And – just at the edge of the pool of light cast by the torch – a deeper recess scraped out of the earth. A convenient hiding place, about the size of a printed folio. And deep enough to take a stack of them.

✠

Leaving Gravel Lane behind, Nicholas and Bianca walk back towards the Jackdaw. The night is moonless and the lanes dark, but they have the torch, they know the way and the presence of the watch will have scared away any cut-purses.

'Two bodies in almost as many days,' Nicholas muses.

'Let's hope they will be the last. By the way, I forgot to tell you: there was nothing of interest on the blade of that knife, other than a short curlicue – a leaf or something.'

'I wasn't holding much hope.'

'But at least you can tell the Crab you've found his seditious printer, can't you?' Bianca says, her voice echoing quietly in the closeness of the narrow street.

'It would appear so. If the printer was going to be found at all, it was always likely to be in one of the wards beyond the authority of the Lord Mayor.'

'But you didn't find anything you could call real proof?'

'If you mean a pile of those seditious tracts, no. But I found where they might have been hidden.'

'Why would the killer take them?' Bianca asks. 'If he found them objectionable enough to kill their creator, why not just burn them in that furnace?'

'I don't know,' Nicholas says with a shrug. 'Nor do I really care. The most important thing for me is that it goes a long way towards proving my father had nothing whatsoever to do with them.'

'Well, whatever the truth, we know what Bankside will be thinking by sunrise. It will be a Catholic assassin sent to stop the printing of Protestant Bibles... or the French... or the Pope himself. A cache of gold will have gone missing... a jealous lover will have taken revenge – you know what Southwark is like.'

Nicholas laughs. He knows she's right. The house on Gravel Lane will turn from one man's cold, lonely compass to the centre of a wide-ranging web of intrigue. Tomorrow, in the taproom, someone is almost guaranteed to claim they saw Lucifer himself being rowed across the river, his sulphurous eyes fixed on that flaking image of the swan.

The candles are still burning at the Jackdaw when they return, though Rose has closed the tavern for the night. She lets them in and finds enough hot hippocras left in the jug to fill two glasses. 'You look as though you might welcome these,' she says. 'Was it bad?'

'Bad enough,' Bianca says, trying to block out the image of the printer's skull pinned beneath the platen of the bloodstained printing press.

'Where's Petrus?' Nicholas enquires.

'I've made 'im comfortable in the empty lodgin' room. I've never seen anyone eat two bowls of pottage *and* a coney pie afore. You'd think 'e'd come close to starving. By the way, 'ave you 'eard the news?'

Thinking Rose means the murder on Gravel Lane, Bianca gives her a look of bewilderment. 'Where do you think we've been this last hour or more, Mistress Moonbeam?'

'No, not the murder, silly,' Rose says with a toss of her black curls. 'The missin' lad.'

Bianca's hands fly to her cold cheeks. 'They've found Gideon Trindle! Is he safe?'

'No, Mistress, not Jed's boy – the other one.'

'Other one? What other one?' Bianca asks, her brow tightening into a frown of confusion.

'The carpenter's apprentice, Hugh Mould. While you was away, 'is master was in 'ere wantin' to know if anyone's 'ad sight of him. 'E was sent across the river to Leadenhall on an errand. That was last Monday. 'E hasn't been seen since.'

14

The Thames gleams like polished steel as the sun rises over the Essex marshes. Throughout the dark hours the men whom Londoners call night-scavengers and gong-farmers have been at work, carrying the city's emanations to the cesspits in the surrounding countryside. For a short interlude just after sunrise the air is almost sweet, cleansed by their labours, the rising tide and a gentle breeze. On Bankside the new day pokes about in the crevices of the crowded half-timbered tenements with thin, bright fingers. Soon it is warm enough to unlace the doublet and the jerkin, loosen the collar and the ruff, ease the points of the bodice and dispense with the cloak. Gaudy blossoms of colour sprout from drab broadcloth, frieze and russet. The rich, whose display needs no season, are as brilliantly in bloom as ever.

'It's a fine place indeed,' observes Petrus as he and Nicholas emerge from the north end of London Bridge into the city proper. 'Finer even than Frankfurt, though the sewer ditches would benefit from dredging, I think.'

At the corner of Old Swan Lane and Thames Street, by a stall selling salted stockfish, Nicholas says, 'The offer is still there, Petrus – lodge with us. You'd be welcome.'

Petrus gives him a sad look. 'It's generous of you and your lady, Nick, but I won't impose.'

'It's no imposition; it truly isn't.'

Petrus breaks his stride, as if he needs to unburden himself of a secret. 'It's not that I'm ungrateful, I assure you. But to tell you the truth, I have become somewhat uncompanionable over the years. I think I might have forgotten how to enjoy company.'

'You were on fine form last night,' Nicholas points out. 'Until the... upset. I'm sorry your visit was soured.'

'It wasn't soured, Nick.'

'A murder? You don't call that souring?'

Petrus gives a dismissive shrug. 'The bigger the city, the more opportunities for quarrels. I don't mean to insult, but I'm sure it's not the first on Bankside.'

'I would have preferred we had had more time to talk. Why not stay?'

Petrus lays one hand on Nicholas's shoulder. 'Mistress Bianca would soon tire of me. Sometimes I get unreasonably angry. I make some noise. I am not a fellow who sleeps well.'

Nicholas rubs away a trickle of sweat from his neck. 'You've brought the Low Countries back with you, in your head. Haven't you? You're not the first.'

Petrus shrugs. 'Whatever we say in the company of others, it was not good when you and I were there together. It got worse after you left.'

'Yes, you said.'

'I meant it.'

Nicholas remembers another man troubled by what he had seen of war – Porter Bell. Bell had almost destroyed himself through ale and anger. But now he's restored and making a decent living as a boatman at Gravesend. 'If it's melancholy that troubles you,' Nicholas says, 'then friendship might prove a helpful curative. Tell me where you are living; I could visit you. We could talk.'

Playing with the sleeve of his jerkin, Petrus says, 'I lodge with an intemperate old rogue who shouts at visitors. You wouldn't like it.'

Nicholas suspects he's stepping on ground that his friend would rather he kept clear of. He doesn't press further.

'Well, you know where to find us. If not at the Jackdaw, then our lodgings at the Paris Garden, not far from the Falcon stairs. Ask for us – everyone knows the house.'

'The house of the famous physician to the queen, eh?' says Petrus with a shy smile.

'I keep telling you, she simply asks for my opinion.'

'Is that where you're going now? At breakfast you said only that you had to go across the river.'

'If it was to the queen, I'd be walking faster,' Nicholas says with a grin. 'I'm on my way to the Strand.'

Petrus taps a finger against the side of his nose conspiratorially. 'Ah, Mr Secretary Cecil calls. Mercy, in what high circles my old friend moves.'

'I didn't say it was Robert Cecil, did I?'

'You didn't have to.'

'Then how do you know if I'm on my way to Cecil House?'

Teasingly Schenk gives him a look of feigned hurt. 'Oh, don't be so reticent. I heard the stories about you and Cecil when I was seeking you out on Bankside.'

'I'm just his son's physician. That's all.'

'That's not what I heard.'

This is getting a little too close to the truth for comfort, Nicholas thinks. He looks towards St Martin in the Vintry, as though gauging the battle that he will face with the morning traffic. The street ahead is a melee of people, carts, horses, geese, sheep and waggons, all seemingly heading in conflicting directions. 'If you believed only one-tenth of what you hear on Bankside, Petrus, you'd believe the Thames is full of mermaids and the Pope has cloven feet. Don't listen to gossip.'

'I shall take your advice,' Petrus says, laughing.

'The truth is, I do have some business with Mr Secretary Cecil. I am to play a very minor part in the arrival of the Moroccan ambassador to Her Majesty's court.'

Petrus makes a show of being impressed. 'I knew you'd make something of yourself, Nick. But this—'

Nicholas blushes. 'I didn't mean to boast. It will be mostly listening to tedious discussions on trade, I imagine.' He is about to bid farewell to his friend when a thought strikes him. 'I'm surprised my father didn't mention you asking after me.'

'I'm a forgettable sort of fellow,' Schenk tells him with a self-deprecating smile.

'I suppose he had other things on his mind, like keeping his right hand attached to his wrist.'

Petrus frowns. 'That sounds ominous to me, Nick. What has he done to risk such a punishment?'

'Nothing, that's the point. He was falsely accused of spreading sedition,' Nicholas says. 'It's a long story. But he's free now.'

'I'm glad to hear it. He seemed a goodly man.'

Nicholas grips his friend's hand. 'Anyway, I must be on my way. Remember, there will always be a hearth, a bed, a meal and good ale for you, either at the Jackdaw or the Paris Garden. And a friendly ear, if you feel inclined to talk.'

Petrus smiles. A trace of the young innocent Nicholas remembers finds its way through the carapace. 'Don't fret. I'll come to the Jackdaw when I'm feeling in the mood for reminiscence.' Then he gives Nicholas's hand a brief pump and bustles away with a satisfied, rolling gait in the direction of All Hallows Lane.

And in the moment before his friend disappears around the corner, Nicholas observes a fleeting, almost imperceptible phenomenon that will lodge in the back of his mind until Bianca causes him to bring it out into the light. Coming in the opposite direction is a young lad, around twelve or thirteen. The boy carries a basket of medlars at his hip, one hand on the wicker rim to steady it, the other cupping the strap that crosses his chest. The lad does not look at Schenk, not even for an instant. But Petrus falters. His body gives a sudden, involuntary jolt – as though he has taken a shot to the chest.

Or seen a ghost in broad daylight.

✠

The gatekeepers at Mr Secretary's grand redbrick mansion to the south of Covent Garden know Nicholas well. He is through the first line of defence in less time than it takes to reassure them that he hasn't come because Robert Cecil's son is ill. But where Cecil servants are concerned, a broad courtyard can be as wide as a county. They cannot confirm Sir Robert himself is in residence.

Passing through an archway flanked by towers pierced with tiers of latticed windows, Nicholas reaches the second line: the grooms of the hall. Here he learns that he is in luck. Mr Secretary returned from Richmond last night. But he is presently engaged in a meeting with representatives of the Lieutenant General of the Ordnance, who have come over from Ireland to discuss the present ongoing rebellion there.

'I really do think he'll want to see me,' Nicholas tells a minor secretary, summoned when Nicholas stands his ground. 'Tell him it's about the illegal press.'

He is ordered to wait on the terrace behind the house. Beyond the neatly boxed shrubs and the border of trees, he can hear faintly the sound of women singing as they weed the crops in Covent Garden and Long Acre. He sits down on a low wall and enjoys the soft, companionable sound. After what he judges to be about half an hour, a door opens and six gentlemen spill out onto the terrace – military men, judging by their plain fustian doublets and the unadorned guards of the swords they wear at their belts. Nicholas recognizes some of them from his time in Ireland the year before, supporters of the fallen Earl of Essex. Then, they'd considered Nicholas a traitor. Today they acknowledge him civilly enough, before disappearing in a huddle around the side of the house. When it comes to pleasing Mr Secretary Cecil, thinks Nicholas, loyalty can be as malleable as wet clay.

A black-gowned secretary pokes his head through the door and summons Nicholas inside.

'My apologies,' says Cecil from behind his desk. 'I didn't know it was possible to spend an entire hour discussing the merits of differing irons in forging cannon shot. I can spare you only a moment. Her Majesty is returning to Whitehall, and I must be there to greet her.'

'I think I've located the source of the seditious tracts, Sir Robert,' Nicholas says, coming straight to the point. He recounts the events on Gravel Lane, omitting none of the gory detail.

When Cecil has heard all Nicholas has to say, he spends a few moments deep in thought before he speaks. 'But you found no actual *proof*? No copies of that blasphemous tract that I could show to the Privy Council and say, "There you are, we caught the rogue in the act"?'

'No, Sir Robert. Sadly not. But the pieces fit neatly. The illegal press was always likely to be hidden somewhere like Southwark... Finsbury Fields... Moorgate. It would be a brave fellow who worked his press directly under the Lord Mayor's illustrious nose.'

'Have you given thought as to why the killer acted with such malevolence?' enquires Cecil, leaning forward across his desk like a raven scenting carrion. 'Perhaps he was trying to make a point: that extreme sedition deserves extreme punishment.'

'An eye for an eye?'

'That tract was an outrage to all decent Christian men. Had we taken him, your printer would have faced no lesser punishment on Tower Hill.'

'No, Sir Robert, I don't think that was the killer's motive,' Nicholas says. 'I think he wanted information. But what manner of information, or whether the printer surrendered it before he died, I cannot say.'

Cecil claps his little hands impatiently. 'Well, we shall soon see if the killer got the right man. If the tracts stop turning up, we may assume your printer was indeed the culprit.'

Taking the audience to be at an end, Nicholas makes a formal bow and starts for the door.

'Just a moment, Nicholas,' Cecil calls after him.

'Mr Secretary?'

'That preacher fellow, the one who helped get your father into trouble—'

'Montague, Sir Robert. Parson Asher Montague. At least I've proved him wrong – my father clearly had nothing to do with those tracts.'

Cecil rises from his desk, lacing his gown below the ruff in preparation for his own departure to Whitehall. 'I'm sure it won't surprise you to learn that we keep an ear out for new voices in the city's pulpits. Mostly it's to catch Jesuits; they can be adept at sounding like true Christians at first, before they start their proselytizing in secret. But there are Protestant troublemakers, too: Anabaptists... Puritans... I've received word that this Montague is preaching at the foreigners' church in Austin Friars. What do you know of him?'

'I knew he was coming. My father told me.'

'Should I be concerned?'

'He's a firebrand, I'll admit. And he plays on people's fears. He's provocative but clever. He knows how to stay just on the right side of lawful.'

'Well, as long as he keeps his sermons scrubbed clean of papistry and doesn't call for the Privy Council's collective heads to be arrayed on spikes on Tower Hill, then the content of his preaching is a matter between himself, the Bishop of London and the Almighty,' Cecil says as he steps past Nicholas and out into the gallery where a clutch of secretaries await him. He looks back over his shoulder. 'Don't fret, we'll soon hear if this Montague fellow is overstepping the mark.'

✠

'Do you care to disrobe, Husband,' Bianca says with a raised eyebrow when Nicholas returns from Cecil House that afternoon.

Surprised by her sudden forwardness, he almost blushes. 'I fear it must be later, sweet. I saw Ben Sumner on Long Southwark just now. His little daughter has a sore ear. He's convinced it's due to a phlegmatic humour of the blood. If you ask me, her brother's been sticking things in her ear again. But I said I'd attend.'

With a knowing smile playing at the corners of her mouth, Bianca says, 'You mistake me, Husband. I thought I might look for bruises.'

'Bruises?'

'In case Mr Secretary Crab has sunk his sharp claws into you again.'

Nicholas laughs. 'Surprisingly, I am unmarked. But he did tell me that fellow Montague – the one who got my father into so much trouble – is to preach at the foreigners' church at Austin Friars.'

'Better here than at Barnthorpe,' Bianca says. 'Wouldn't you agree?'

'Indeed. If he oversteps the approved ministry, Cecil's people will soon clip his wings.'

'Is your friend Petrus safely lodged?'

'I don't know. I don't think he's telling me the whole story.'

'You mean he's lying to you?'

'I mean he's ashamed.'

'He can stay at the Jackdaw, if he wants.'

Smiling at her kindness, Nicholas says, 'I did tell him so, but at the moment I think he'd rather be left alone to lick his wounds.'

'I admit I sensed he was troubled,' Bianca says.

Nicholas takes his physician's chest, places it on the table and begins to check the contents: lancet... thread for tying off blood vessels... a small length of iron with a handle at one end, flattened to a pad at the other, for cauterizing wounds...

'I'm surprised my father didn't mention Petrus when I was in Suffolk, though. And Petrus must have done some asking, because he knew all about my audiences with the queen – and that if I was on my way to the Strand, then I was probably going to visit Robert Cecil.' He closes the lid of the small chest and pulls the strap over his head and across his shoulders. 'Still, I suppose he must have learned that here on Bankside, while he was trying to find the Jackdaw.'

A sudden wail of misery from the chamber above announces that Bruno has managed to inflict some minor catastrophe on himself.

'Hurry back,' Bianca says, quickly kissing Nicholas on the cheek and heading for the stairs. 'I shall still need to inspect you for bruises.'

'I shall look forward to it,' he replies with a grin as he opens the street door. 'I'm sure I can feel some aches springing up somewhere.'

But by then Bianca is halfway up the stairs and calling out soothing reassurances to her son. And so it is only later that she has the opportunity to recall the exchange in much detail – and to reflect that despite Nicholas's association with Cecil being well known on Bankside, its denizens are seldom in the habit of making so free with their knowledge to total strangers.

✠

The evening shadows are lengthening across the Paris Garden. Bianca leaves the house by the Falcon stairs and heads to the public cistern to fetch water before Nicholas returns. A laden ewer and a five-year-old with the mischievous proclivities of little Bruno require more hands than God has seen fit to bestow upon her, so she takes Cachorra, who lodges with her and Nicholas, for support. Bianca leaves later than usual – deliberately – because the path to the cistern passes the bear-garden, and today there has been a baiting.

The first time she had taken Bruno with her on such a day, they had encountered the parade: one shackled bear with mournful eyes and nostrils scenting for a hint of forest in barren Bankside; one bearward with just three teeth in his gums at the other end of the chain; a musician to snatch a catchy tune from his hurdy-gurdy; five wild-eyed and frothing mastiffs dragging the kennel-lads for a walk; the manager with his cap held out for the wagers; and a crowd of Londoners from across the river up for a wild time and a bit of blood. Bruno had shrieked with a mixture of fear and delighted curiosity. But then he had demanded to know where the beasts were going and what was going to happen to them when they got there. Now, rather than invent some sugared lie, as she had on that occasion, Bianca prefers to wait until the crowd has dispersed and the beasts are out of sight, licking their bloody wounds in the misery of their captivity.

'I have the feeling that Master Nicholas's friend is a very troubled man,' she says as Cachorra begins to fill the ewer from the spring water at the cistern. 'It is my guess he's suffering from bad memories, acquired during his time in the Low Countries.'

'My dear friend, Don Rodriquez, knew a fellow much like that,' Cachorra says. 'This man, when he was young, had sailed to Nueva España with Cortés. His sleep was forever thereafter troubled by what he had seen done there.'

Bianca splashes some of the water on her face to soothe her smarting eyes. She wonders if it's the summer dust thrown up by the people around the spring or too long spent peering into a mixing bowl on Dice Lane. 'At breakfast, I thought I might offer to make Master Petrus a decoction of French wheat, madder and thistle for the melancholy. But you know what men are like. It would be, "There's naught wrong with me that a full jug of mad-dog can't cure" or "I'm not a babe that needs swaddling." Nicholas is just the same.'

Leaving the cistern, Bianca carries the heavy ewer while Cachorra leads Bruno by the hand. At the corner of Mouse Alley their way is blocked by two men, both around her own age, one with a ruddy complexion and a broad, country chin, the other with a high forehead and a perceptive gaze that sparkles mischievously as he gives Bianca a direct smile.

'Good morrow, Mistress Kate, the prettiest Kate in Christendom... Kate of my consolation,' the latter says.

Shifting the ewer so that she can get a clear view of the speaker, Bianca returns his greeting as if it were a fast serve in a tennis match. 'Good morrow, one half-lunatic.'

He bows, making an exaggerated knee to her.

'Why does Master Shakespeare always call you Kate?' Cachorra asks.

Bianca's response is delivered in a stage whisper behind a raised hand. 'Because he wrote a very poor play about the taming of a shrewish woman. The shrew was supposed to be me. But he hadn't the courage to give her my name, so he called her Kate instead. He named the sister Bianca – lest I should fail to spot the amusement. And now that he's found a little fame, he's suddenly come over all courageous.' She drops the hand and gives the fellow a direct look. 'Isn't that so, Master William?'

'You were a gift I could not pass, Mistress. 'Tis my regret I never did unwrap you.'

In reply, Bianca gives him a bright laugh. 'Mercy, but you're a saucy rogue, Will Shakespeare. And by next Michaelmas, London will have forgotten about you entirely.'

'"Her name is Katherina... renowned in Padua for her scolding tongue,"' Shakespeare says with a grin.

Bianca tilts her head in Cachorra's direction, her voice cutting. 'I was born in Padua, you see. I find I often must explain Master Shakespeare's lines – most frequently to the people who go to see his entertainments.'

The older man has watched the exchange with amusement. 'God give you good morrow, Mistress Merton,' he says, tipping his cap.

'And to you, John Heminges,' Bianca says with studied courtesy.

Bruno pulls away from Cachorra and almost throws himself upon Will Shakespeare, who bends down and lifts the boy to his chest. 'Swordfight! Swordfight!' Bruno cries happily.

'Master William has no strength left for swordplay, Bruno,' Bianca says. 'I think he is already comprehensively defeated.'

Shakespeare bows his head in surrender.

'But I want to be Henry Frith!' shrieks Bruno.

'It's Henry the Fifth, sweet. Not Henry Frith,' Bianca explains to her son in a laboured tone. 'And Master William doesn't have the time, I'm sure.'

'I always have time to indulge the son of Mistress Bianca and Dr Nicholas,' Shakespeare says fondly.

'And how goes the new play?' she asks, lowering the ewer to the ground.

'The Stationers' Company will receive it in the summer, if all goes well.'

'Well, good luck if you want it printed around here.'

'I heard. To have one's pate crushed beneath a platen – a most terrible murder, terrible indeed.'

'I'm sure you can make use of it. Perhaps in one of your comedies.'

Shakespeare gives Heminges a weary look. 'Pity we don't have saints in England any more, John. If anyone deserves beatification, it's Dr Nicholas.'

'May I carry your load for you, Mistress Bianca?' Heminges asks. 'We're going to the Falcon, so we can pass your lodgings without going out of our way.'

'That's kind of you, John Heminges.'

'And I shall carry young Hal, here,' says Shakespeare, hoisting Bruno onto his shoulders to an accompanying peal of delight.

As they set off, Bianca says, 'I hope our happy exchanges haven't driven you to sup at the Falcon rather than the Jackdaw, Master William. I'd hate to think you took them to heart.'

Shakespeare laughs. 'Mercy, no, Mistress. John and I are off to drag young Oliver Sly out of the Falcon's taproom. We sent him there with five shillings to pay Mistress Cox for two yards of Bruges satin, for costumes. We must presume sly little Sly has spent our coin not on satin but stitch-back. We're off to haul him away by his ears.'

With a sinking feeling in her heart, Bianca asks, 'How long has he been gone, Master Will?'

'A good four hours,' Shakespeare tells her. 'He's probably cup-shot, fast asleep under a table. He's an actor. It won't be the first time.'

✠

'Gideon Trindle a few days ago; the carpenter's lad, Hugh Mould, yesterday; and today it's Oliver Sly. Three lads missing in quick succession,' Nicholas says later that evening at the Paris Garden lodgings when Bianca tells him of her conversation with Will Shakespeare and John Heminges. Bruno has been put to bed, having proudly and repeatedly informed his father that Master Shakespeare thinks him a far greater monarch than Henry Frith ever was. 'I suppose we should take comfort from the fact no bodies have been discovered – apart from the one we found at the Steelyard. Which could have everything to do with the rest or nothing at all.'

'That reminds me,' Bianca says, clearing away the plates. 'I haven't shown you the broken blade I took out of the *aqua fortis*.' She goes to the box where she keeps her perfumes and unguents. 'Look, do you see? Nothing to identify the owner,' she says, holding out the small length of cleaned steel for Nicholas to take. 'Be careful, it's still sharp.'

He turns it over in his hand. 'There's a design on it, or part of a design,' he observes.

'I know. It's a curling leaf stem or a monkey's tail,' Bianca says.

'Pity there's not a name.'

'What do we do with it?'

'I'll keep it,' he says. 'You never know.'

'I'm more concerned for Gideon, Hugh and Oliver than for a lad whose name we'll most likely never learn.'

'I suppose we could go across the river and ask to search the Bills of Mortality. Of course we'd have to inspect the records for every parish in all twenty-six wards. Twenty-five, discounting Southwark.'

'Why can we discount Southwark?'

'Because Gideon Trindle went across the river on an errand to Cripplegate, and Hugh Mould was sent to Leadenhall. Only

162

Oliver Sly disappeared here on Bankside, and if there is a common thread, he's probably been taken over to the north bank, too.'

Bianca remembers Hugh Mould's master. She's had him ejected from the Jackdaw more than once. 'I suppose Hugh could simply have run away. Carpenter Bowright is a known bully and a drunkard. If I were his apprentice, I believe I'd run away.'

'And Oliver Sly is a boy-player. The playhouse doesn't exactly attract fellows known for their unadventurous dependability,' Nicholas points out. 'They could return at any time. There's certainly no proof they're dead.'

'I suppose you're right,' Bianca says. 'At least I hope you are.'

But in her heart, she is not persuaded. Old memories – dark memories – have resurfaced. Memories a decade old. Memories of a killer who stalked Bankside in the very year that she and Nicholas met.

15

The church at Austin Friars lies in Broad Street Ward, in the north of the city close to Bishopsgate. Forty years ago, during the reign of the sixth Edward, it was gifted as a place of prayer to the Dutch, though given Londoners' imprecise grasp of geography, that could mean worshippers from as far afield as Krakow. The one thing the congregation – and those buried in the churchyard – have in common is that they are all firmly Calvinist.

Bianca finds Father Beauchêne in the churchyard, trimming the holly around the lychgate, set there to keep the witches out.

'Mistress Merton, what a happy surprise! I had not expected to encounter you again,' he says, putting aside his knife and wiping the back of one hand across his solid, open face. 'Have you brought a touch of homeliness to Master Leezen's old house? A place of sadness can so often bloom into one of happiness and tranquillity, with a woman's touch.'

Before she speaks, Bianca draws a calming breath. She knows that what she intends to say next might well change Father Beauchêne's opinion of a former member of his flock.

'We found a body there,' she says brutally. 'In the culvert that runs to the Steelyard wharf.'

Beauchêne seems almost to stagger. He puts one muddy hand on a gravestone to steady himself, the other rising to his mouth in shock.

'Merciful Jesu! How terrible for you. What manner of body?'

Bianca brushes away a bee that has taken an interest in her hair. 'A young lad – murdered. He'd been there for some time. The question I keep asking myself, Father, is: did Aksel know it was there?'

'Surely you don't think he was responsible for such a... a...'

'I pray not, Father Beauchêne,' she says earnestly. 'But we found other things there, too – things whose presence we are having some trouble explaining away. I'm beginning to question how well I knew him.'

Father Beauchêne looks perplexed. 'What manner of things, Mistress Bianca? Felonious... papist?'

'It is rather hard to explain their relevance without knowing what was in Aksel's mind,' Bianca says, knowing she must sound suspiciously evasive. 'How long had he been a member of the congregation?'

'He was praying here when I came, which was after the great massacre of Protestants in Paris. So that would have been in '72.'

'Then you would know if there had been a change in him.'

'He was much affected by the loss of his wife and child to the pestilence, if that's what you mean, but a tragedy like that is enough to change any man.'

'That was seven years ago. Have you noticed any change in the last two or three?'

'If you're asking me if he appeared to be in a disturbed humour before he died, I can only tell you that he was the Aksel we all knew. He bore his sickness bravely. He prayed. He was resigned to the knowledge that he was soon to face his maker – as we all should be. But I can tell you here, in the sight of the all-knowing God, that he did not appear to me to be a man with secrets. Does that help you, Mistress Merton?'

'In some small manner, yes. Thank you, Father, you've been most helpful. I'm sorry to have kept you from your work.'

Beauchêne smiles to let her know it has been no sacrifice. He escorts her back to the lychgate, where he takes out his knife and resumes his work trimming the holly. 'I should have set about this task a month ago,' he says. 'But I've been ministering here alone, and I haven't had a moment to myself.'

'Keeping holly in check is a battle, isn't it?' Bianca says politely.

'I had hoped for some help when the replacement for old Parson Dumont arrived. But the new fellow, young Parson Montague, is a fire-and-brimstone man. He thinks gardening a pointless pursuit while there are still sinners to be saved.' Beauchêne laughs at his own wit, cuts a small sprig of holly, and hands it to Bianca. 'Still, it's probably better not to trim it back too far – the congregation would soon complain that I was making it too easy for the witches and bad spirits to pass through.' He smiles. 'God's grace upon you, Mistress Merton. I do hope we shall meet again.'

Bianca passes through the lychgate and out into Throgmorton Street. And as she does so, she presses the holly against her breast and thinks of Aksel Leezen. It's all very well to grow a prickly barrier against bad spirits, she tells herself. But what do you do for protection if they're already inside?

✠

Nicholas has considered that he might never see Petrus Eusebius Schenk again. He is not naive. He knows that promises made in the joy of a reunion can burn brightly but cool swiftly, like embers thrown from a fire. His old friend's reticence about revealing where he was lodging has confirmed in his mind that Petrus wants only solitude, that whatever is troubling him cannot be eased with one swift jab of the lancet of companionship. First must come the practising of a slow, determined physic, one step at a time, one wound cauterized before moving on to the next. But if Petrus chooses not to present himself for curing, what hope is there?

And then, five days after Schenk's first visit to the Jackdaw, and much to Nicholas's surprise, he shows up at the Paris Garden lodgings, breezy as a summer meadow, as bright as sunlight on the surface of a woodland pool.

'Alter Freund,' he says, 'we have so much to catch up with. Time to kick the years back where they came from.'

And what a kicking the years get – worse than a gypsy cornered by a gang of apprentice boys after a football match on Finsbury Fields. After the visit to the Paris Garden, most of the meetings happen at the Jackdaw. When Nicholas returns from his weekly visits to St Thomas's hospital for the poor, Petrus Eusebius is invariably there waiting for him, ready to ask him if he remembers that time outside Zutphen when they'd almost been taken by a Spanish patrol; or inviting him to recall the day they'd emerged, refreshed and naked after a cleansing swim in a lake at Bussloo, to discover the local maids had adorned a gorse thicket with their clothes. Nicholas is only too happy to indulge Schenk, though he remembers barely half the incidents Petrus plucks from his seemingly prodigious memory.

When Bianca hears some of the stories being retold for the third time, she begins to excuse herself from these sessions. She does not object to her husband and his friend reliving their past. That's what fellows do when they have so much to catch up on. But sometimes when she passes by on whatever task the Jackdaw demands of her, or at the Paris Garden lodgings to prise Bruno away from Buffle so that he can eat or practise his writing on his hornbook, she can't help but notice an unevenness in the exchanges. Schenk is the one doing the questioning, his body leaning forward with an earnest tilt to it, the firelight making a sparse corona of his pale tufty hair. Sometimes she is inclined to think of a schoolmaster with a pupil who hasn't studied hard enough.

'You two must have been the best of companions,' she says to Nicholas one night when they lie abed. 'Yet before he turned up, you'd never once mentioned Schenk's name.'

'Hadn't I?' Nicholas replies casually, as if the thought has never occurred to him. 'I suppose I didn't want to dig up the past. It was before we met.'

'In the time when you loved Eleanor?'

'Yes, but that doesn't imply I meant to keep him a secret. To be truthful, I'd almost forgotten him. He was a soldier, I was a physician. We were friends, yes. But not exactly brothers.'

'By the tales he tells, I'm surprised you had time left over to treat your patients.'

'That's just Petrus. I think he's a lonely man trying to forge himself some comforting memories to replace the troubling ones. That's why I indulge him. When he's built himself a strong enough raft, I'll move on to the real question: why is he adrift in the first place?'

And still there is no word of Gideon Trindle, Hugh Mould or Oliver Sly.

✠

Tired of Richmond, Her Majesty removes herself and her court to Nonsuch in the heart of the gentle Surrey countryside. Nicholas is summoned. Once again it is not his physic that is required – the queen wishes to hear his thoughts and opinions on the politics of the Barbary shore, in particular Morocco and its proposed envoy to her court, Abd el-Ouahed ben Massaoud ben Muhammed Anoun. Using the simpler form – Muhammed al-Annuri – Nicholas tries to relieve the Privy Council of the onerous burden of pronouncing the ambassador's full name. They thank him for it, but nothing can prevent them from calling him what the queen calls him: plain Master Anoun. Thus, even before they arrive, is the dignity of diplomatic envoys determined by the English court.

'Mr Secretary Cecil tells us that while you were in Morocco, Master Anoun was instrumental in saving your life,' observes old Charles Howard, the Earl of Nottingham. He scratches at the corner of an eye that once glared out contemptuously upon the Spanish Armada but now weeps like a squashed grape.

'Yes, that's true,' Nicholas says, thinking he'll suggest a decoction of storax, hawkweed and gilliflower.

'I trust you didn't make any rash promises to him.'

'Promises?'

'Promises for which England or – more specifically – her Treasury might be held liable.'

'None, Your Grace,' Nicholas says, trying not to roll his eyes at the earl's generosity of spirit. 'The favour was in return for me having saved his.'

'Good,' pipes up Baron Cobham, a fellow of about Nicholas's age who is renowned at court for the modest depth of his intelligence. 'Then the Moor is morally obliged to us.'

'He'll be here in early August, we think,' says Mr Secretary Cecil, who is shorter than both Howard or Cobham, but possessed of three times their capacity. 'I'll have my secretaries write you a paper determining your duties. While he's here, it would be pleasant if nobody's life required saving.'

When the session is over, John Lumley – seneschal of Nonsuch, now that it has reverted to the queen's possession – strolls with Nicholas in the Italian garden. The classical fountains whisper their refreshing serenata over the neatly clipped privet hedges. In the cypress trees the blue tits scavenge for insects.

'I have spoken to Ned and Rose Monkton about their having a place here during the revels for the ambassador,' Nicholas tells him. 'Ned says he would be honoured. Rose, however, is needed at the Jackdaw.'

Lumley's usually wintry face brightens. 'We shall miss Rose's presence, but Ned is more than welcome. I'll need all the bodies I can get. He can travel with the women and servants from my house on Woodroffe Lane.'

'I shall let him know,' Nicholas says.

'By the way, I've made enquiries about the écorché models, but so far without result. Did you have any better luck with the banker, Gaspari?'

'None. He was out when I called. I had intended to return, but to be truthful, I've had more pressing matters to attend to.'

'Do you think Mistress Bianca would object if I confirmed my offer to purchase them?'

'Mercy, no,' Nicholas says, relieved. 'Bianca wouldn't want them back in the house.'

Lumley gives a forlorn sigh that sounds like surf on a cold Northumbrian shore. 'Women, eh. They comprehend our fascination with mechanical curiosities even less than we understand the allure of needlecraft and ribbons.'

For the sake of diplomacy, Nicholas agrees. But he decides that when he recounts his visit to Nonsuch to Bianca, he'll keep that exchange to himself.

✠

I make some noise. I am not a fellow who sleeps well.

When he stays overnight again at the Jackdaw, Petrus proves to be a man of his word. It is three in the morning when the customers in the communal lodging chamber are woken by a tortured groaning that rises towards a scream. Only a well-aimed boot ends whatever nightmare Petrus is enduring.

When the same thing happens at four, he is only saved from a beating by the intervention of Ned Monkton, who comes in like a bear waking from its hibernation. A compromise is reached. Petrus will sleep downstairs in the taproom on a straw mattress by the hearth, and the customers will receive a penny back from the fivepence they have paid for a meal and a bed.

'You see, I did not lie,' he tells Nicholas and Bianca ruefully, as he departs the next morning, ashen-faced and red of eye, for whatever beggarly shelter he has found himself. 'Now you understand why I should not accept your offer of lodgings.'

'Ain't no cause to feel shame on account of troubles you didn't ask for,' Ned tells him firmly, making sure the nearby customers at their breakfast can hear.

Ned's solicitude gives Nicholas an idea. He wonders why the notion hadn't occurred to him before. Why not enlist Ned to help his old friend from the Low Countries climb out of the dark place his mind has dragged him to? If anyone knows how to break free from dark thoughts it is Ned Monkton, who has fought his own battle with melancholy and emerged victorious. When Nicholas first encountered him, Ned had been a raging furnace of anger and pain, his daily incarceration with the dead in the crypt at St Thomas's hospital, where he was employed as mortuary porter, made bearable only by the twin balms of ale and taking violent offence at every imagined slight. But with a new purpose and Rose to guide him, Ned has put that life behind him. Surely, with a little fraternal help, Petrus could achieve the same.

Nicholas's stratagem begins almost without his own intervention, though later he will have cause to ask himself who, or what, put the idea into his head. Reason or madness? God or the Devil?

It begins with a card game.

✠

Two nights later, Petrus reappears at the Jackdaw. Nicholas suggests that Ned stands him a tankard on the house and gets to know him better. He leaves them alone for almost an hour, then slips into the bench beside Ned.

'I was hearing how you rescued this big fellow from a life amongst the dead,' Petrus says as Nicholas takes his seat.

'That was Bianca's doing,' Nicholas replies, faintly embarrassed. 'It was she who found a place for Ned here at the Jackdaw. I just steered the warden at St Thomas's in the right direction, that's all.'

'But a true resurrection, for all that,' Petrus says, looking at Ned and smiling. 'Do you see, Ned? The righteous path is clear enough when the mighty keep out of the way.'

Ned raises his tankard. 'Sound words, Master Petrus. I likes 'em.'

They're already behaving like old friends, Nicholas thinks.

'What says everyone to a game of karnöffel?' Petrus suggests, grinning as if the tortured soul of a few nights ago was someone else entirely.

Tired of the tavern's two staples, primero and hazard, he has brought along a pack of playing cards printed after the German style, with suits of bells, leaves, acorns and hearts, and picture cards of emperor, king, duke and knight. He announces that he carries the deck in his pack for his personal enjoyment, though as the game requires four participants, he seldom gets to play it. No obstacle, Nicholas tells him; in the Jackdaw, if you throw anything, you're bound to hit a card player.

The tavern is quiet tonight. Bianca agrees to make up the numbers, but only on the condition that Petrus and Nicholas don't punctuate every hand with reminiscences about soldierly japes in the Low Countries. Rose, who thinks card games are what you do when it's raining and you can't go outside to find something more interesting, watches as an observer whenever her duties allow.

By the third game it is Ned and Petrus against Nicholas and Bianca. The evening passes in good fellowship. Petrus is even persuaded to stay the night, though he insists again on a mattress by the hearth.

And that night it is Ned who, light as a wraith – which, given his size, is a feat in itself – slips almost silently downstairs to comfort the groaning Petrus as he endures whatever it is that is torturing him.

Yet not so silently that Bianca, roused from an unusually light sleep, cannot watch them unobserved from the landing: the auburn-bearded Goliath and the fallen cherub. Are they praying together? she wonders. Or plotting a path out of a shared darkness?

✠

A broiderer's son, a carpenter's apprentice and a boy-player. An unlikely trinity with little to connect them, save their similar ages and the fact that all three have vanished into thin air like mist on the Thames at sunset. They might occupy Bianca's thoughts only as might any missing child, were it not for the memories she keeps locked away behind the most solid and impenetrable doors that her mind can devise. Memories now a decade old. Memories of a killer stalking Bankside, and of her own close brush with death at Southwark's abandoned Lazar House. Her deepest fear now is that Bankside has been visited by a second scourge, and that he might strike again. Eager for reassuring news, she seeks out Bran Osborne at his lodgings by Bridge House. The constable of the watch confirms that Gideon Trindle and Hugh Mould have still not returned home, and Oliver Sly is still absent from his duties at the Globe playhouse. She decides it's time to tell Osborne about the body found at the Steelyard. The constable hears her out in thoughtful silence.

'That's a gift with a sting in the tail, and no mistake,' he says. 'Was there naught about the body that might suggest who he was or where he came from?'

'Nothing that Nicholas or I could see. We're not even entirely certain he died in Aksel's house. It is possible the body was washed into the culvert.'

'Well, there's many who die unmourned in this city, Mistress Bianca,' the constable says gently. 'That's what comes of putting so many souls into one place. But my counsel to you is this: while there's no bad news to the contrary, there's reason to hope. I've sent one of my watchmen over the bridge to tell the parishes to be on the lookout for them.'

'I worry about people too much,' Bianca confesses, though nothing Osborne has said has calmed her thoughts.

'No shame in that, Mistress,' Osborne tells her with a fatherly smile. 'No shame at all.'

✠

The return to the Dice Lane shop takes Bianca past the Globe playhouse. With no performance scheduled today it is almost deserted, the masts bereft of banners or pennants. Skirting the circular walls of rough white plaster, she enters through the main doorway. In the pit, three boy-players sit cross-legged in a patch of sunlight, mending costumes with bodkin, sharp and thread. She hopes one of them is Oliver Sly.

Will Shakespeare is on the stage, squatting by one of the gaudily painted pillars, a thick sheaf of papers in one hand, a small audience of the adult players gathered around him. She recognizes most of them from their frequent appearances in the Jackdaw's taproom.

'Good morrow, Mistress Kate,' Shakespeare says, rising to his feet. He gives her a look of pretend longing, extending a hand towards her with the fingers cupped in invitation. 'Come, Kate, we'll to bed... Better once than never.'

Bianca stops, puts her hands on her hips and looks up at him, the thrust of her chin making the dark waves of her hair fall away from her brow. '"I see a woman may be made a fool, if she had not a spirit to resist",' she recites, her tongue firmly in one cheek.

When the chorus of applause, catcalls and thumping of palms against the planks of the stage – all in Bianca's favour – subsides, Shakespeare looks down at her and grins.

'I see you know my plays pleasing well, Mistress Bianca.'

Bianca favours him with a theatrical sigh. 'That's all you actors ever do in the Jackdaw – spout your lines. That, and drink me dry of ale. Am I interrupting anything important?'

'No, lady, we're just rehearsing Henry Frith. How's the boy?'

'Do you mean Bruno?'

'Well, I wasn't speaking of Dr Nicholas – lucky devil that he is.'

'Bruno is well, Master William, thank you,' Bianca says, turning her head towards the three lads busy at their darning. 'And on the subject of boys—'

'Don't talk to me about boys, Mistress Bianca,' Shakespeare says, cutting her off. 'They're an ungrateful and incontinent rabble.'

'I take it by "incontinent" you mean unreliable.'

'That as well.'

'And young Oliver Sly?'

'Away with the fairies, the little arseworm.'

'Are you not worried for him?' Bianca says, surprised by his casual response.

'Why should I be? He's probably in Blackfriars now, playing maids for twice what we paid him.'

'If he returns, do you promise to send word to me?'

'If you wish it. But why? What is our Sly to Mistress Kate? He's no Petruchio. He's barely grown his first whisker.'

'He's missing. He may have fallen into harm, Will. I'd like to know if he returns. It will set my mind at ease.'

Seeing the concern in her eyes, Shakespeare relents. 'I'll ask my friends across the river if they've seen him. If there's word, I'll bring it in person.'

As she walks back towards the Paris Garden, Bianca cannot help but imagine the loneliness and fear of a lad lost in a big city. She can tell herself that on Bankside boys come and go all the time, and not all of them for dark reasons. But that does not prevent a cold worm of fear from crawling about inside her stomach. She thinks of the body she and Nicholas found in the Steelyard. Had his journey to an unmarked grave begun with someone noticing too late that he'd disappeared? What if he was merely a predecessor to Gideon Trindle, Hugh Mould, Oliver Sly and who knows how many other nameless victims?

From that question it is but a few short steps to that locked door, behind which she keeps chained the memories of the eviscerated bodies that began turning up around the time she met Nicholas. She remembers the razor-sharp fear, the dreadful waiting, the way the hours seemed to pass by carrying a terrible certainty with them – that tonight, or tomorrow, or the day after, another victim would inevitably be found – and knowing with a debilitating terror that you couldn't stop it happening.

16

It is a summer Sunday and July is almost spent. In the open land to the south of Bankside, the second ploughing of the fallow fields is complete. After sermon, there is dancing around the maypole in the Pike Gardens. By early afternoon the beefy pinguid scent of roasted oxen hangs in the air. Ale is drunk, rivers of it, and jugglers, mummers and fools laid on to entertain.

No public festivity would be complete without its harvest of bloodied knuckles and cheeks – not all masculine – so Nicholas spends much of the time in the company of the Southwark barber-surgeons, patching up the wounded and calming the overexcitable.

Ned has invited Petrus, who declares, 'Better even than *Mainfest* in Frankfurt' as he takes in the unfettered babel of Banksiders at their play.

Spotting a nine-pins stall, Ned suggests a game.

'I don't have the coin,' Petrus says sheepishly.

'You're a guest,' Ned tells him. 'You don't need no coin.'

Leaving the two men to their play, Rose and Cachorra steer Bruno from one amusement to the next – hobby-horsemen, fire-eaters, wrestlers... Sometimes they must contrive a sudden pretended interest in a tree or a passing bird, in order to shield the child from the blatant coupling occurring in the hedgerows. When Bruno begs to be allowed to see what's attracting a crowd jostling to get into the bear-baiting ring, she tells him it is merely a collection of fools, queuing up to wager their hard-earned coin on how loud the mastiffs can bark.

It is a little after three, judging by the last tolling of the St Saviour's bell, when Bianca decides to seek out Nicholas, thinking he might welcome some assistance. She leaves Bruno with Rose and Cachorra and goes in search of him.

Passing the nine-pins stall again, she sees that Ned and Petrus are still there. The two men are standing face-to-face in conversation, a little way off from the players casting wooden balls at the assembled skittles. Ned's length of throw must have earned them a profit, she thinks. But as she draws closer she can see that something is very wrong.

The much smaller Petrus has his back to her. Only Ned's face is visible. And to Bianca's alarm, he looks just as she remembers him when he was deep in his cups and had taken offence at someone's injudicious or careless remark. His great auburn-bearded head is tucked downwards, like a buffalo about to charge. His brow is deeply creased in anger. For a moment she thinks he's about to fell Petrus with one swipe of his fist. Only as she hurries forward to intervene does she see the reality: that whoever Ned is angry with, it is not Petrus. Indeed, he's nodding in agreement with whatever it is that Petrus is saying. And he's concentrating on it so hard that he hasn't seen Bianca approaching.

She is soon close enough to catch snatches of what Petrus is saying: '... the size of ten men, a giant... Ned, you are still nothing in their eyes... less than a worm crawling beneath their feet...'

Now, only two paces behind Petrus, Bianca calls out, 'Is all well?'

Even before Schenk can turn towards her, Ned's face rises. His angry eyes fall upon hers. Instantly the rage is gone. He is the Ned she knows. The Ned she loves.

'Aye, Mistress,' he says, with an accompanying beam of recognition. 'Better now that I can see things clearly.' He places one paw on the smaller man's shoulder. 'Thank you, Master Petrus, from the 'eart of a man what was born in ignorance. 'Ows about another game of nine-pins?'

✠

The next time Bianca encounters Ned he is alone. There's no sign of Petrus anywhere. She asks if there is something amiss between them. 'Never,' says Ned. ''E's gone to the foreigners' church, for Evensong.'

'Are our merriments too godless for him?'

It's not meant as a slight, but Ned frowns.

'Master Petrus is a God-fearin' soul, Mistress. As should we all be.'

'Of course, Ned. I meant nothing by it,' Bianca says with an apologetic smile as she walks away.

She leaves the fair shortly afterwards, to fulfil a long-standing promise to visit an elderly tanner who lives with his considerable family in a cramped tenement beside Folly Ditch in Bermondsey. Bianca is providing a regimen of syrup of dropwort in honey, to treat the weakness of the lungs that Nicholas has diagnosed. After confirming the physic is progressing well, she spends longer than she anticipated indulging the patient's several daughters and granddaughters, to whom she is a fascination. Thus she does not set off on the journey back to the Jackdaw until the light is beginning to fade. The walk is uneventful, until she steps out from the narrow alleyway almost opposite the tavern.

There's a fight going on, right outside the Jackdaw's entrance.

Odd, she thinks. Thanks to Ned's reputation – and her own, if she's honest – the Jackdaw is seldom troubled by street quarrels. She's about to issue a stern rebuke when, despite the lengthening shadows, she recognizes one of the brawlers as Petrus.

The other is a skinny lad of about fourteen in a tattered jerkin. But it's impossible to determine from the flurry of arms and fists who is the assailant and who the defender. Then the boy breaks away, one hand flailing wildly as if to ward off Petrus. The lad takes one look at Bianca and flees in the direction of London Bridge, leaving a cloth bonnet trampled in the dirt. To her embarrassment, Bianca realizes that the fracas was no quarrel, but an attempted robbery.

'Are you hurt?' she asks, glaring after the disappearing figure.

'No harm, Mistress. No harm,' Petrus assures her, dusting himself off. 'It was just a purse-diver.' He gives a wry laugh. 'Why he chose me, I cannot think. I am dressed no more richly than he. And if he was hoping for coin, he picked the wrong fellow.'

'A rude shock, to be assaulted after the calm of Evensong,' Bianca says, looking him over for signs of injury and finding none. 'You'd best come inside. I'll fetch you a glass of malmsey, to calm you.'

As she follows Petrus into the tavern, she looks back in the direction of the now-vanished thief. She knows most local cut-purses and house-divers at least by sight, but this one had been a stranger to her. She suspects he must have come across the river. A risky move. The lad had looked barely strong enough to steal washing off a windowsill, and Bankside felons don't take kindly to trespassers. Perhaps it was hunger that had driven him across the river, hoping to find easy pickings.

Strange, she thinks, to feel almost sorry for him. A thief is a thief, when all's said and done. Picturing the lad now, his weak, gangly frame flapping as he battled the resisting Petrus, her mind turns naturally to the missing boys. How much of a fight were they able to put up? she wonders. Or did they only realize what was happening to them when it was too late?

It will be some time before she has cause to think of the purse-diver again. But when she does, she will have reason to ask herself if what she witnessed was really what she thought it was.

✠

'It appears you were right,' says Mr Secretary Cecil when Nicholas is called to the mansion on the Strand to discuss how ambassador al-Annuri should be welcomed when he arrives with his entourage. 'Not a single new seditious text has appeared since your printer was killed. I think we may assume we've burned out that particular wasps' nest. By the way, I've spoken to Attorney General Coke. I'm hopeful he will order the case against your father to be dropped. I trust Yeoman Shelby has learned his lesson.'

'My father assured me there was not a more loyal subject of Her Majesty alive in England,' Nicholas says artfully.

Perhaps he should show more gratitude. There had been no imperative for Cecil to loan him a horse and write a letter ordering his father's release. He had done those things out of an apparent kindness. Yet is Cecil truly a kind man? If the printer on Gravel Lane had been taken alive instead of murdered, Mr Secretary would happily have sent him to the scaffold without a second thought. With powerful men, Nicholas thinks, generosity always has a sliding rate of exchange.

With his mind nudged by the thought of the murder, he asks, 'Are we any nearer to discovering who killed the printer? Have your informers and searchers heard anything?'

A wan smile struggles for life on Cecil's thin lips. 'When I send my intelligencers to Bankside, if they ask your compatriots there if the sun is shining, they get six different answers, and every one designed to deceive.'

'That's because they enjoy pricking the dignity of those who govern them, Sir Robert.'

The smile has a sudden brief flowering before it withers. Cecil wags a cautionary finger. 'That by itself smacks of sedition.'

'Then I take the answer to be "No".'

'And you would be right to do so. To speak plainly, I'm not much troubled. The rogue is dead, and his loathsome provocations burned wherever they are found. The fellow who killed him has done the Privy Council no small service. He deserves a remittance, not a hanging.' Cecil fusses with the inkpot on his desk. 'How am I supposed to sign documents with no ink?' he demands, as if he has a host of invisible servants floating in close attendance. He shouts at the half-open door, 'I need more ink. Tell the scrivener. And more fresh-cut nibs.'

Nicholas hears footsteps hurrying away.

'Now, where were we?' Cecil says, his interest in the printer's fate seemingly buried beneath a thousand more important things. 'Ah yes, the imminent arrival in England of the ambassador from the court of King Muly Ahmad of Morocco—'

'The king's correct style is Sultan Ahmad Abu al-Abbas al-Mansur,' says Nicholas, cutting in before he's even considered the wisdom of correcting the queen's principal Secretary of State.

'I shall refer to him as Her Majesty and her Privy Council refer to him – King Muly Ahmad,' Cecil replies tartly.

'I'm merely suggesting that may not go down well with his ambassador, Sir Robert,' Nicholas points out diplomatically. 'A Moor's name is as important to him as ours are to us.'

'Well, the ambassador will have to suffer it in silence, won't he? This is London, not Marrakech. It's Her Majesty's court he's attending, not Nebuchadnezzar's.'

'As you wish, Sir Robert.'

'Tell me, Nicholas, has your interest in the Barbary shore prospered or languished since you returned from Morocco?'

'It was seven years ago, Sir Robert. I've done my best to forget the entire enterprise.'

At once the predominant memory of his time there springs unwanted into Nicholas's mind. The gracious, oak-panelled chamber shrinks to the size of a Bankside jakes. Instead of breathing air sweetened with beeswax and pomander, his lungs are filled with air too hot to breathe. He is lying chained on top of a pile of crates, and his only hope of escape will be if his limbs melt enough to allow them to trickle out of the tight shackles, which seems entirely plausible, given the heat inside this makeshift prison. But before that happens, he believes that Muhammed al-Annuri will send someone to kill him. There are occasions, even now, when that nightmare troubles his sleep. And when he wakes, the relief of knowing how badly he had misjudged the Moor is as strong as ever.

'I hope you haven't forgotten it entirely,' Cecil says, breaking into Nicholas's thoughts. Mr Secretary leaves his desk and walks over to the Molyneux globe sitting in its frame in the corner of the chamber. He turns the lacquered sphere gently with the palm of his hand until the coast of north-west Africa and the Iberian Peninsula slide into view. 'Allow me to refresh your memory.' He positions one fingertip where he imagines Marrakech to be. Nicholas reckons he's off by a good hundred leagues. 'King Muly Ahmad, while an infidel, is fearful that Spain might one day attempt to reconquer his land. That makes him an ally.'

'As he was when you sent me there, Sir Robert.'

'Indeed. And don't think I've forgotten how much Her Majesty owes you for having helped maintain him in that position.'

'Then what has changed?' Nicholas enquires. 'I assume *something* must have changed.'

'The ambassador, or so word has it, is bringing a proposal for a joint enterprise with England against Spain.'

'A war?' Nicholas says under his breath. 'England is countenancing a war with Morocco against Spain?'

'If you hadn't noticed, Nicholas, we're already in a war with Spain.'

'But surely Her Majesty isn't considering an invasion? We couldn't possibly muster—'

Cecil interrupts him with a peal of laughter. 'Invasion? Christ's wounds, Nicholas, we can barely afford to fund our forces in the Low Countries and Ireland as it is. If we'd had a decade of good harvests, honest tax collectors and even more honest subjects, there'd still be nowhere near enough in the Exchequer to fund such a reckless venture.' Cecil returns to his desk. 'No, there will be no joint enterprise against Spain, regardless of Muly Ahmad's wishes. After a period of careful consideration, we will explain to Master Anoun that what his king proposes is out of the question. We will be regretful, contrite, but unshakeable.'

'Then why are we permitting Sultan al-Mansur's embassy to come here if we've already decided not to agree to his proposal?'

The look Nicholas gets from Mr Secretary Cecil is one of exaggerated, weary despair.

'Nicholas, let me explain something to you. Sir Thomas Gresham did not build the Royal Exchange because he had a fancy for architecture. He built it for the enhancement of commerce. For trade. For profit. Why would we prevent Master Anoun from coming into England with his proposal, when we might be able to strike a better – more profitable – accommodation with him on the matter of trade between our two realms?'

'You mean that he's going to ask for our help, and we're going to keep him hanging on while we work out how much we can sell him?'

Cecil gives an appreciative laugh. 'Your talents are wasted in physic, Nicholas. But yes, that is correct in the essentials. Her Majesty has seen fit to allow the charter she most graciously awarded to the Barbary Company to lapse. We advised her to renew it, but she chose, in her sovereign wisdom, to ignore us. That means there is no longer a formal entity to regulate the exchange of English wool for Moroccan sugar. Or, for that matter, manage the supply of Moroccan saltpetre for our gunpowder. At present, we get more squabbles between competing merchants than we do benefits. And now that we have sent the Hansa merchants packing, we must ensure our new markets are properly ordered. We need to reinstate a monopoly. And we need to ensure the right people have control of it. That will be the framework for our negotiations with Master Annuri. I expect you to employ your former relationship with the Moor to the realm's advantage.'

'Don't you mean to the advantage of the investors?'

'We are a nation that survives on our wits, Nicholas. Our ships are faster than the Spanish, and so too are our minds. Our future is in trade.'

Nicholas looks unpersuaded. 'Al-Annuri is no fool, Sir Robert. He possesses a formidable intellect. There's steel in him, too. He's austere and quite ruthless. He won't be dazzled by tricks, like a country visitor to Bankside. I would warn the Privy Council against underestimating him.'

'Come now, he's a Moor. He hails from a realm built on sand. When he sees the civilization God has gifted His children, the Privy Council is confident that Master Anoun will be too busy marvelling to notice how we take advantage of him.'

Nicholas thinks of his several audiences with the queen in her privy chamber set with Moorish cushions, and of the way London competed with itself to embrace everything Turk when al-Mansur sent an unofficial mission to England in '88. Londoners turned out in their thousands to watch the regal, exotically gowned strangers ride into the city. Within a week, if you weren't wearing harem slippers – produced in bulk by the cordwainers of Cheapside – you were irredeemably vulgar.

'I wouldn't wager on it, Sir Robert,' he suggests. 'Certainly not with your own money.'

'I have no intention of wagering my own money, thank you very much. Fortunately the Almighty was wise enough to provide the world with merchant bankers.'

The perplexed look on Nicholas's face appears to amuse Mr Secretary Cecil.

'I don't follow, Sir Robert. What have bankers to do with the visit of ambassador al-Annuri?'

An embroidered purse lies on Cecil's desk, tied at the neck with a gilded ribbon. Mr Secretary keeps it for special, private disbursements that he doesn't want to show in his accounts. He lifts the purse and jiggles it to make the coins chink. 'To exploit the benefits of trade with the Moors, Nicholas, our merchants will need backing, investment, support. They will require loans. Hence our need for merchant bankers. Of repute only, of course, and discreet, too. The Lord High Treasurer, Thomas Sackville, has already identified the perfect fellow – a member of the Gaspari banking family here in London. Master Silvan Gaspari will be attending the discussions with ambassador al-Annuri.'

On any other occasion, on hearing Cecil mention the banker, Nicholas might think, At last, I shall have the opportunity to ask Gaspari about the écorché figures. But not today. Not when his name is spoken in the same breath as the Moor's.

'I once made a mistake about Muhammed al-Annuri,' he says. 'I thought him an enemy. But I wouldn't be here now if that had been so. I am not comfortable, Sir Robert, with the prospect of gulling him.'

Cecil looks affronted. 'Gulling? We're not asking you to cheat him, Nicholas. We're expecting you to do your duty to the realm – to Her Majesty.'

'And if I refuse to be a part of this deceit?'

'We all make mistakes, Nicholas,' Mr Secretary tells him easily. 'I'm sure you lament your own with Master Anoun. Just as I would, were I to have to write to the magistrates in Ipswich telling them I'd made one of my own, in assuming the innocence of a certain yeoman farmer from Barnthorpe.'

✠

'Where's Ned?' Bianca asks Rose the following day when she visits the Jackdaw. 'The sign outside is squeaking like a piglet. The hinges need greasing.'

'Master Petrus 'as taken him across the bridge to hear a new parson preach at Austin Friars,' says Rose, holding a fardel of fresh rushes across her chest as though she were cradling an infant.

'Ned?' Bianca says in surprise. 'Ned has never been much of a hot one for the pulpit. Are you sure?'

Rose shrugs and casts another handful of rushes onto the flagstones. 'Apparently there's this new parson who's just brimming with godly zeal. According to Ned, Master Petrus says this fellow preaches not for them what already 'as their riches 'ere on earth, but for the likes of us, the little folk.'

Bianca laughs. 'If there's only one person on God's earth who cannot be described as little, it will be your Ned.'

'Aye, but if this fellow's preachin' keeps Ned's great 'ooves out of the way while I clean the taproom, 'e can sermonize to his 'eart's content. It's fine by me.'

✠

'I can make you a decoction to banish every manner of worm from the human body,' her mother had once told her, 'save for the worm of suspicion.'

There's no getting away from it, Bianca thinks; I distrust my husband's friend. I'm infected.

True, the worm had started small. It had been born at the fair. She'd felt the birth pangs the moment she'd seen Ned's face change, even though she hadn't fully heard what Petrus had said to him. And it has fed well ever since, fattened on Rose's comments about Ned suddenly choosing to attend the church at Austin Friars with him, and Petrus's refusal to tell anyone – including Nicholas – where he's lodging.

I will have to pay more attention to Petrus Eusebius Schenk, she tells herself. Because the only known antidote to a worm that size is truth.

The opportunity comes two days later, during a card game at the Jackdaw. Nicholas is as silent and tight-jawed as an alderman caught in a Bankside jumping-house. But then he's been that way ever since returning from Cecil House. Knowing Sir Robert as she does, Bianca's confident that she has a general understanding of what has happened, if not the details. Cecil has coerced him. Cecil has manoeuvred Nicholas into doing something he'd prefer not to do.

When Petrus turns up, from wherever he spends his days, she enlists him and Ned in a few games of *karnöffel*, hoping they might bring Nicholas out of himself. And now Bianca is facing Petrus across the table. Nicholas is beside her, Ned to Petrus's right.

The first thing she notices is how Petrus drinks his ale. He seems to gain no pleasure from it. After a while she becomes sure he's doing it only to please, to fit in, and that it costs him more than he is revealing. The stiffness in him makes her think he is enduring an initiation ceremony. Just like she had at thirteen, when she'd wanted so desperately to join the leading gang of girls in her district in Padua, *le Volpi*. The outward show is one of enjoyment, but the eyes tell a different story.

From there it is but a small step to noticing how mechanically he plays the card game. She is reminded of how she herself behaved when she arrived in England from Padua and attended her first Protestant church service, her presence required by law. It had taken every ounce of her composure to pretend that her heart was in the Protestant orisons that so offended her Catholic soul.

She tries to listen more analytically to Petrus's habitual recounting of stories from his and Nicholas's time together in the Low Countries. And as she does, it dawns on her that it's almost like listening to someone trying to school another with a poor memory: *Surely you remember when... Yes, of course we were there when it happened... I can't believe you've forgotten...*

Later that night as she and Nicholas lie abed, she says, 'Tell me more about your friend Petrus. I mean, *really* tell me.'

'What do you mean?' he replies, running his fingers through her hair as she lays her head against his chest, as if she's listening to see if his heart is going to lie to her.

'Your friend arrives out of the blue. He won't tell us where he lives. And now Ned seems to be his *protettore*, his champion.'

'That's because Ned knows a wounded bird when he sees one.'

Or is it the other way around? Bianca wonders. What if it is Petrus who has spotted the wounded bird?

'But who is he, Nicholas? Who is he really?'

'I can only tell you what I remember of him, and what he's told me since we met again. It's not much. In the Low Countries we were friends, not brothers.' He gently teases strands of Bianca's hair between his fingers, hanging a memory on each one. 'I know he's from a small town near Frankfurt, in Hesse. His father was *Leutpriester* of his parish – a local priest. They were a religious family, I know that. His grandfather was a passionate follower of Huldrych Zwingli, the Protestant reformer. Petrus used to boast how his grandfather got arrested for smashing up the images of the saints in Catholic churches.'

Bianca props herself up on one elbow. Her voice takes on a hard edge. 'My mother told me that Zwingli was the Antichrist personified, because he believed that worshipping images of Christ, the Holy Virgin, all the saints – even painted images of God Himself – was idolatry.'

'We can't hold the grandchild to blame for the sins of the grandfather,' Nicholas says, surprised by her vehemence.

'I'm sorry; it's just that I was raised to venerate the saints and pray at their shrines. It brought me comfort. To me, destroying holy images is sacrilege, not reform.' She lies back down beside him again, and Nicholas catches the scent of roses from the drops of oil with which she anoints her neck at bedtime. 'We've dismissed the grandfather and the father, now what about the son?'

'I think he intended to follow his father into the Church. But then Petrus decided God needed practical help in the Low Countries, quit his theological studies at Basle University, bought himself the furnishings of a soldier and presented himself to the army of Maurice of Nassau.'

'That only tells me *what* he is. It doesn't tell me *who* he is.'

'Is there a difference?'

Bianca sighs. 'Nicholas, only a man could ask that.'

Nicholas accepts the reproach manfully. 'I know what you mean.'

'Is there a wife, children? A proper home somewhere?'

'He's never mentioned them. To be truthful, Petrus was always rather resistant to allowing any of us to know him well.'

'And yet he claims you're his dearest friend in all the world. Have you thought perhaps there's something about him he doesn't want anyone to know?' Bianca suggests.

'There's the Caporetti imagination at work again,' he laughs. 'Your mother has a lot to answer for. If you want my honest opinion, Petrus is a troubled, lonely man searching for some sort of redemption. He's been through a lot that he isn't yet ready to reveal to us.'

'Like where he's living? Why is he so evasive about that?'

'Only a woman could ask that. Because he's *proud*.'

'God save us from proud men,' Bianca says to the darkness. 'Pride is my least favourite sin.'

As she waits for sleep to come, she recounts to herself all the little impressions she's formed of Petrus Eusebius Schenk since the moment he walked into the Jackdaw. And when she's done, she asks herself a question that had often troubled her whenever she'd heard Father Rossi in her local church in Padua preach against the seven deadly sins: why is it that lying was never on the list?

✠

It takes Bianca a day to contrive her plan. At first she casts herself in the leading role. She is confident she could remain unobserved. As a child she carried secret messages for Cardinal Fiorzi, messages he didn't want intercepted, messages he thought it safer to entrust to the precocious daughter of Simon Merton and Maria Caporetti. After all, who would think of challenging the familiar bright-eyed imp who always sang and skipped her way through the lanes of Padua? But she is a grown woman now, and if she were to make a mistake there would be a lot of explaining to do, not least to her husband.

If not herself, then who?

She rejects Rose, because Rose is incapable of stealth, even though Bianca knows she would agree in a heartbeat. And if Rose is eliminated, then so too must be Cachorra. How could a tall, statuesque Carib woman possibly remain unobserved by her quarry?

But only the year before – in Ireland – she and Cachorra had slipped through the lines of the Earl of Tyrone's army like sister wraiths. And as she racks her memory, Bianca cannot think of any occasion when Cachorra and Petrus have been in proximity to one another in the Jackdaw. She finds none. Nor has Petrus yet visited the lodgings at the Paris Garden.

Cachorra it must be. When Bianca puts her plan to her friend, she agrees at once. Now all that is left is to wait for a conjunction of the planets: an evening when Petrus makes one of his frequent but irregular visits to the Jackdaw, followed by a morning when Nicholas departs to fulfil his duty at St Thomas's hospital for the poor.

It comes four days later.

✠

Cachorra is ready in her position beside the public well at the crossroads, well within sight of the entrance to the Jackdaw. She has been there almost since first light. This has meant filling and then emptying her ewer from the bucket for protracted periods, much to the bewilderment of more than one Bankside woman who has stopped by for water. Now she has spotted movement at the Jackdaw's entrance.

'I'll come out into the lane with him,' Bianca had told her, 'so that you may identify him. Not that he's easy to miss. He looks like a cherub who's fallen into sin.'

But it is Master Nicholas who is emerging from the tavern now, dressed in his old white canvas doublet, a purposeful swing in his step as he sets off towards Thieves Lane and the hospital.

'Good morrow, Cachorra,' he says with a smile. 'If I need anything today, I'll send a boy to fetch it.'

This is normal, and to be expected, Cachorra tells herself. Master Nicholas always has need of medicines when he's at St

Tom's: silverweed boiled in wine for easing gripe of the belly, distillation of wild sebesten for voiding phlegm on the lungs, motherwort for driving worms from the belly... She grins and waves her greeting at him. And then he, being the fellow he is, stops to pass the time of day and gossip with her.

Inside the Jackdaw, it is a simple matter for Bianca to delay Petrus's departure for a while. She engages him in small-talk until she's confident that Nicholas is well on his way to St Tom's and unable to observe Cachorra set off on her discreet pursuit. To her horror, as she steps outside into the lane, she sees her Nicholas and Cachorra still in conversation. If Petrus follows her gaze, he'll see the two of them together. She will have to abandon the whole plan there and then.

Giving a performance that would shame anything Master Burbage could put on at the Globe, she feigns a sprained ankle, stumbling into Petrus and forcing him back into the taproom. There she buys herself a good five minutes, stretched out on a bench playing the stricken maid while Petrus hovers over her solicitously. When she detects he's keen to be on his way, she finds herself visited by a divine recovery out of a clear blue sky and hobbles valiantly with him out into the lane.

To her relief, she sees Nicholas has gone on his way.

'Are you sure you are recovered, Mistress?' Petrus asks.

'Absolutely, kind Petrus. No question about it,' she assures him. 'My woman's clumsiness has detained you too long.'

And when he releases her arm, turns and heads towards the crossroads that will take him to Long Southwark and the bridge, she stands square in the land, hands on hips, and briefly tips her head at his departing back, so that Cachorra may be quite certain of her quarry.

✠

'You had Cachorra follow Petrus?' Nicholas says in astonishment, unable to keep the harshness out of his voice. It is later that day, and they are at the Paris Garden lodgings. Bianca has returned to the parlour from settling Bruno down to sleep. She had known this was going to be a difficult conversation the moment Cachorra met her at Dice Lane after the successful completion of her mission.

'*Somebody* had to discover where he was sleeping,' she says unapologetically.

'If Petrus had wanted us to know, he would have told us.'

'I have not the slightest regret, Nicholas. I sent Cachorra after him for his own good.'

'Not to satisfy your own curiosity?'

Bianca winces. 'Well, yes, I admit that. But you've already told me you think he's a troubled man. I feel it too.'

She hesitates, knowing that she is about to tread on uncertain ground.

'When you lost your first wife and the child she was carrying, you too were so troubled that you ended up sleeping in churchyards and under hedges, drinking yourself into oblivion. Did you not value the concern your friends tried to show you then? Did you not thank them for trying to help you?'

Nicholas has but hazy memories of that time – if only because in his mind he has forced them behind a protecting screen – but even hazy memories can stab like a newly sharpened knife. 'I did everything I could to reject their help, including driving them away. I certainly didn't thank them for it.'

'But you do now.'

'Yes, of course I do.'

'Then tomorrow you will thank me for having Petrus followed.'

Nicholas is not a man to argue with the truth, at least not for long. 'Yes, alright, I suppose I will. The question is: what did Cachorra find?'

'First, she thought Petrus might be living somewhere in Broad Street Ward, up towards Moorditch. But he was heading for the Dutch church at Austin Friars.'

'There's naught unusual about that. He's from Hesse. It's natural that he would attend church there.'

'Cachorra would have followed him in, but she was worried she'd be rather conspicuous. She had to wait for him to emerge.'

'And?'

'He headed back the way he'd come. She had to play a nimble dance to avoid him.'

'Serves her right.'

If Bianca registers the admonition, she doesn't show it. 'She followed him all the way back to… guess where?'

Nicholas bites back his impatience. 'I don't know. The royal menagerie at the Tower? The Bishop of London's residence at Fulham Palace?'

Bianca ignores the sarcasm in Nicholas's voice. 'The Steelyard,' she says with laboured gravity. 'Your friend Petrus is living like a vagrant in the Steelyard.'

17

Petrus is proud, or so Nicholas says.

But is there something else lurking behind this mask I'm convinced he wears? Bianca asks herself.

She knows Nicholas is too trusting. But there are worse flaws that a husband's character could have. She admires him for it. It's proof for her that Robert Cecil's malign influence hasn't burned into his skin like spilt molten sugar.

'He's from Hesse; the Steelyard is the obvious place for Petrus to pick,' he'd pointed out to her when they'd argued the next morning over what to do. 'He's been on the road a long time. How was he to know the Privy Council had expelled the Hansa merchants?'

That had seemed entirely plausible to her. And yet...

Ever since Cachorra had discovered where Petrus was living, Bianca has been torn over what to do. Subterfuge and deceit – even as a protection against humiliation – do not sit well with her. And then there's the influence Petrus seems to be exerting on Ned. Yet he has committed no crime. All she can accuse him of is being particularly God-fearing and a little over-secretive. Besides, she cannot bear to think of a vulnerable, lonely, troubled man, far from home, living the life of a vagrant in the abandoned Steelyard. In the end, she comes down on the side she always knew she would: 'Let him lodge in Aksel Leezen's house,' she says. 'Let's at least put a proper roof over his head. He doesn't need to know what we found there.'

✠

It is an ambush, even if it is staged with good intentions. That evening Bianca and Nicholas wait until the *karnöffel* game is over and Petrus's defences are down before they make their move. In response to Bianca's offer to lodge the night at the Jackdaw, Petrus has just recounted how he walked all the way from Basle to Delft to join Prince Maurice's forces in the Netherlands, and therefore a stroll in the summer dusk to his lodgings hardly counts as a trial.

'A stroll to where, though?' Bianca says, looking directly into Petrus's eyes and thinking they look like two very small grey doors that have been soundly shuttered against a cold wind.

Petrus doesn't answer. Taking a deep breath, Bianca commits herself.

'I wouldn't want you to think we were prying into your affairs, Petrus, but Nicholas and I have been much troubled by the thought of you not having somewhere amenable to rest your head at night.'

Petrus gives her a weak smile. 'I'm fine, Mistress Bianca. I'm content with my lodgings. And Ned here deserves to sleep without having to care for a man who raves in his sleep.'

'But the Steelyard can hardly count as comfortable lodgings. Can it, Petrus?' she responds.

For an instant the shutters open, but so briefly that all Bianca can see behind them is a rapid and jumbled procession of emotions: denial followed swiftly by acceptance and, yes, fear. Then the grey doors slam shut again.

'You've been spying on me,' he says coldly.

'A friend of mine, who's seen you here in the taproom, happened to be coming from the Vintry to the bridge and noticed you entering the Steelyard. She mentioned it to me in passing, nothing more. Nicholas and I simply drew our conclusion.'

A stony silence from Petrus.

You're buying yourself time, Bianca tells herself. What for?

Beside her, Nicholas is studying his fingers, faintly embarrassed but relieved the secret is out in the open. After what seems like an age, Petrus sits back on his stool and gives a guilty smile.

'The Steelyard is Hansa to the foundations. I can fool myself that I'm almost at home in Sulzbach.'

'So my friend was correct?' Bianca presses, careful to sound anything but triumphant.

Petrus nods. 'Yes, I confess it. I am lodging in the Steelyard. Are you content now?' He looks at Nicholas. 'Suspicion is an unusual currency in which to exchange friendship.'

'We're worried about you,' Nicholas says defensively.

'The Steelyard is almost deserted, Petrus,' Bianca says slowly but with great gentleness. 'There aren't any lodging houses left there. You must be sleeping in one of the abandoned storehouses. Please, tell us the truth.'

Petrus responds with an awkward sideways jerk of the head. 'I'm not afraid of a little discomfort. Did our saviour complain when he slept forty nights in the desert?'

'Jesus only had the Devil to contend with. He wasn't troubled by London's thieves and cut-purses.'

'Bianca's right,' Nicholas says. 'We'd never forgive ourselves if something ill befell you.'

Bianca lays a hand on Petrus's wrist. 'I have a suggestion,' she says.

'I've told you before; I don't make a tolerable lodger.'

'I'm not talking about the Jackdaw or our house at the Paris Garden, Petrus. I'm thinking of the Steelyard. I have a house there. It's empty.'

The shutters in Petrus Schenk's eyes fly open so fast that Bianca half-expects to hear the bang. He stares at her in disbelief.

'You're playing with me, Mistress Bianca. Why would you do that?'

'I'm doing nothing of the kind, Petrus. I'm telling you the truth. I have a small house in the Steelyard.'

He leans forward across the table, studying her like someone trying to place a face in a faulty memory.

'I inherited it, Petrus,' Bianca says, laughing as she explains. 'It's nothing grand – just a downstairs storeroom and three chambers upstairs. It will need a little furnishing to make it comfortable. But we can buy a mattress and sheets, find you a cooking pot and plate. You'd be safe there. What do you say?'

What he says is not what she expects.

'Were you given this house as spoils, when the Hansa were expelled?' Petrus asks, almost as if he were accusing her of looting. 'Did you buy it for a fraction of its worth?'

'No, nothing like that,' Bianca protests, feeling the heat rise in her cheeks. 'It was a bequest, from a Hansa merchant named Aksel Leezen. I was a customer of his, and a good friend.'

Does Petrus think she's lying to him? Because while the rest of his face is a study in impassivity, his brow tightens involuntarily. His gaze seems to sink even deeper into its lonely fastness.

'If it's the money you're worried about, I won't accept a single farthing,' Bianca assures him, breaking into an open, girlish wishing-to-please smile. 'Say you'll accept, Petrus. Nicholas and I would feel so much better if we knew you were lodged properly, with a decent lock on the door.'

And while she waits for him to reply, Bianca decides that one ambush is enough for anyone. She will have to find another time to voice her concern about Petrus luring Ned Monkton to Austin Friars.

✠

Above Bankside the summer clouds skip downriver, borne on a mischievous breeze. In the Jackdaw's yard, his neck craned, little Bruno watches them fly past overhead while, beside him, Buffle scratches herself for fleas. Bianca and Rose are carrying out the furnishing for Petrus Schenk's new accommodation: blankets, sheets and pillows, a small selection of plate and cooking pots, and a horn lantern with a thick stub of tallow candle in it. Ned goes ahead of them, a mattress slung over his back, his great arms pinning one end over his head like an enormous monastic cowl.

'Where are those clouds going?' Bruno asks. 'They fly so quickly.'

'They're off to Rome,' says Rose, whose understanding of geography is at best hazy, 'where they will turn grey and angry and rain on the Pope's 'ead.' The words are barely out of her mouth before she casts Bianca a guilty smile. 'Sorry, what with you being a—'

'It's alright, Rose,' Bianca says hastily to prevent embarrassment. 'The Holy Father's garden could probably do with the watering.'

When the furnishings have been carefully laid in the cart, Ned subdues the mattress with an armlock. He holds it in place on top while Rose secures it to the cart with twine.

Petrus joins them in the yard. For once, he has slept soundly. Bianca puts it down to his relief at knowing he's going to have a bed to sleep on in future, instead of a dirt floor.

'You've been more than generous, Mistress,' he says, 'as good a Samaritan as a man could hope to meet. Forgive me if I sounded less than grateful.'

'I know you're of a spartan disposition, Petrus, but a little basic comfort never hurt anybody. I was planning to replace all these anyway.'

Nicholas comes out to make his farewells. 'I have patients to visit or else I'd come with you,' he says, shaking Petrus by the hand. 'Just because you now have a bed, that's no reason to forget where we are.'

'As if I could,' says Petrus.

With Rose having a tavern to manage, it falls to Ned and Bianca to help Petrus move into his new accommodation. It's not a long walk to the Steelyard – well under a mile – though the traffic on London Bridge can make the duration unpredictable. Still, with Ned pushing the cart, they have an effective battering ram. They set off past the crossroads towards Long Southwark, making small-talk as they go. After a while Bianca leaves Ned and Petrus to talk amongst themselves. She falls in a few paces behind, content to let the two men's friendship find its own path.

It happens first as they approach the Winchester House water-stairs. Bianca barely registers it. Indeed, it is only because she is following on behind with the keys – and thus has a clear view of the back of Petrus's head bobbing along beside Ned – that she notices it at all; and the fact that a trick of shadow and light has contrived to turn the sparse white tufts of his hair into a dandelion's crown, which she expects at any moment to fly away on the breeze.

On the right-hand side of the lane a child is coming towards them, a boy of perhaps twelve. He is no more remarkable than any other Bankside urchin, playing a game with himself, walking on the very edge of the open drain. One foot precisely leads the other, like a street-entertainer walking a tightrope. He seems to be challenging Fate to tip into the mire, grinning at his dextrous ability to outwit her. Seeing him, Petrus's body gives a fleeting shudder, as if he's been struck on the funny-bone. As the lad passes by, Petrus's head tracks him. For a moment Bianca puts it down to a last-minute recognition. Her mind anticipates the call of greeting: *It can't be... surely not... Is it really you?* But it doesn't come. Petrus's head snaps back in the direction of travel of Ned and his battering ram.

She thinks nothing of it. Until it happens again.

The second occasion comes as they pass Oysterhill Lane. Bianca turns her head to look down the narrow cut to where the Thames gleams and ripples like the scales of a great brown serpent sliding past the tenements along the riverbank. In the corner of her vision, she notices an apprentice boy, felt cap on head, a bolt of cloth under one arm, come out of a doorway.

Bianca is a naturally fast walker. Aware that a moment's inattention could have her colliding with the slower-moving Ned as he pushes the laden cart, her attention returns to her companions. And as it does so, she catches Petrus with his head turned towards the boy, his body seemingly braced for an expected blow. The moment is over almost before it happens. But now she recalls the first instance, and the connection lingers in her mind like an aftertaste. She has the impression she's just watched a cat consider pouncing on an unsuspecting mouse.

She knows there are Banksiders who think she possesses the second sight. In Padua, her own mother was convinced of it. In *la Volpi* the other girls would intimidate rival gangs with the threat of it: *Bianca can see what you're seeing before you see it... Bianca knows what you're thinking before you think it... Bianca is the daughter of a sorceress.* In England, she has long been aware of the danger this can put her in. Were she living anywhere but Bankside, she'd run the risk of being accused of witchcraft. Bianca herself has come to believe that it is merely an astuteness, a cognizance, an innate ability to notice those little ticks and mannerisms that constitute a personality. That, and overripe imagination. But whatever it is, by the time the third instance happens – at the corner of Stockfishmongers'

Row and Wolsies Lane – it is roaring into flame like a warning beacon lit on a dark night.

The Steelyard is less than ten minutes away. Ned is pushing his battering ram and making good-natured apologies: *Forgive, Master... My fault, Mistress... Coming through, Gentles...*

This time it is a girl of perhaps fifteen, pretty, modestly coifed in Bruges lace – the daughter of a successful merchant, or an alderman's hope for a good marriage. She walks in company with a woman who wears a silver pendant chain around her neck, jewellery that any self-respecting Bankside cut-purse would have away inside a heartbeat. The girl's expensive russet gown swings impudently over a farthingale that's far too large for her and – like her mother – she has her haughty gaze raised, to avoid having to look in the eye London's less fortunate. But from Petrus comes the same shiver. The same snap of the head. The same spasm of intensity.

By the time they reach the Steelyard, Bianca has managed to place the feeling of suspicion that has now convinced her she is witnessing a pattern. If searching for a word to describe it, she would be forced to choose *predatory*. And she's seen it elsewhere. It brings back memories from her teenage years in Padua. Memories of Lorenzo Adelardi.

Lorenzo had been a skinny boy with pustules, who'd hung around the women's bathhouse in the Borgo degli Argentieri. *La Lucertola*, they'd called him – the Lizard. At thirteen, Lorenzo was merely gauche. By sixteen, the pustules had gone and gauche had changed to over-mannered. He was handsome, though, even by Paduan standards. Bianca herself had harboured the hope that the lizard might slough off its skin and make itself acceptable, because by then she had concluded that she was prepared to make concessions in the face of undeniable beauty.

And then Lorenzo the Lizard raped and strangled poor little Gessica Corocetti behind the Piazza dei Signori.

It has occurred to Bianca that she has observed in Petrus a similar shiver, a similar snap of the head, a similar catlike flexion, ready to pounce.

It is on the corner of Church Lane that her smouldering suspicions really catch light. Someone shouts 'Cut-purse! Stop the cut-purse!' A sudden, brief blur of tumult amongst the crowd on Thames Street.

It is over almost as quickly as it starts, leaving Bianca with the merest impression of someone taking to their heels towards St Martin's. An everyday occurrence, she would tell herself on any other occasion. Just one of the risks you run in London. But not today. Because today the incident carries her back to that moment in the lane outside the Jackdaw, when she had stumbled upon Petrus and the supposed purse-diver.

A robbery – exactly like the one she's almost witnessed: that's what Petrus had claimed. But is that *really* what was happening?

She imagines the scene now: Petrus and the thief, frozen in their struggle, a tableau conjured by doubt. And suddenly human shadows begin to join her, peopling the lane. Gessica Corocetti, the Lizard's victim, is there too. So are Hugh Mould, Gideon Trindle and Oliver Sly. And they're all asking her why she hadn't opened her eyes before it was too late. Why she hadn't warned them.

The image fades. Bianca turns to catch up with Ned and his cart. And as she does so, she asks herself: what would I have observed if I'd stepped from that alleyway a minute or two earlier? Would I still have thought it was Petrus under attack? Would I have seen clearly exactly *who* was the real victim?

But that is impossible, she thinks. That's the worm of suspicion that began at the fair taking on the form of an entire serpent, for no reason other than its own vanity. Because Nicholas would never befriend a murderer. Ned would never attend sermon with a violator and a killer. And I, Bianca Merton, could not play karnöffel with a monster and not see it in his eyes.

✠

It is like having a fault in the weft and warp of a gown, she thinks – to most observers invisible, but once you know it's there, you will forever afterwards notice it. By the time they reach the Steelyard, Bianca is observing Petrus Eusebius Schenk with a discreet but determined intensity. Approaching the wharf, he stops and turns to her, his face tight with what she takes to be embarrassment. For an uncomfortable moment, she thinks he's noticed her watching him.

'Forgive me, Mistress Bianca,' he says. 'I must make a confession to you.'

Jesu, he's going to tell me why random passing lads and lasses catch his eye, she thinks. *This is going to be strange.*

Petrus clears his throat. With alarm, Bianca realizes that's what she did when she attended confession in Padua. *Forgive me, Father, for I have sinned…*

'I have been living here in some degradation,' Petrus says, wringing his hands. 'My circumstances are not what I would wish – you understand me?'

And she does understand him. A proud man cannot bear her to see the hovel he's been forced to live in. The prospect of humiliation in front of a woman – his friend's wife – is troubling him.

Or perhaps he doesn't want her to learn that he's got Gideon Trindle, Hugh Mould and Oliver Sly chained up there. Or their remains buried under his floor. After all, she thinks, they all went missing around the time Petrus Eusebius Schenk turned up at the Jackdaw.

'Ned can go with you,' she suggests. Ned is almost as large as Sackerson the bear from the baiting-ring. Petrus would never dare attack him. She waits for Petrus to deliver a reason why he doesn't want Ned to see where he's been living. That, she thinks, will be proof it's not pride behind his reticence, but guilt.

'That will be fine with me,' Petrus says, demolishing her construction in an instant. Chiding her Caporetti imagination, Bianca follows Ned and Petrus into the warren of the Steelyard.

✠

'Be careful, there's not much light until we open the shutters upstairs,' Bianca warns as Petrus follows her across the threshold of Aksel's house. 'You don't get so much of the scent of tar and pitch once you're upstairs.'

'Compared to where I am at present, it's a palace,' Petrus says.

'It has rats, I'm afraid.'

'I'll find a stray dog.'

While Ned unloads the cart, Bianca leads Petrus up the stairs to the living chambers. She opens the shutters and throws wide the windows to let the air in.

'This is the living chamber,' she says. 'The hearth will need clearing, but the chimney's sound. There's an iron frame for hanging a pot from. I don't think Aksel did much cooking after his wife died. I suspect he got his bread and meat from the counters in the Steelyard. Now they've gone, I suppose you'll have to use the traders on Thames Street.'

'I'll manage, Mistress Bianca,' Petrus assures her.

The corner of a mattress appears above the stairs, followed rapidly by Ned. Bianca opens the door to the first sleeping chamber. She checks the bed ropes, tightening the loose ones before Ned puts the mattress in place. When the contents of the handcart have been brought up, she takes two keys from her chatelaine's ring. 'These are for the street door,' she tells Petrus. 'You won't need the key for the second bedroom. It's a bit of a mess in there, so I keep it locked. If there's anything you need, you can let me know when next you come to the Jackdaw. Ned can help you fetch the rest of your belongings from... from... wherever it is you were staying. I must get back to Dice Lane.'

But Petrus appears not to have heard her. He's standing staring at the door to the second bedroom like a man looking out to sea – a man searching for the first sight of the masthead that will tell him his ship has made it home safely. That it hasn't been lost with all hands – and the precious cargo it carries.

✠

They are sitting together on the riverbank by the Falcon stairs watching the tilt-boats and wherries land their catch of passengers from the city. If the weather holds, it should be a profitable day for Bankside. And if it doesn't, well, more coin left over to spend in the taverns.

'What was it you wanted to say to me privily?' Nicholas asks, watching two boys spearing for eels in the shallows.

'It's about your friend Petrus.'

'Oh?'

'I think there's something strange about him. He worries me.'

Nicholas studies Bianca for a while, uncertain how to respond. 'I've told you before: he's troubled. I think he has a sickness of the heart.'

'It's more than that.'

She pushes the dark hair off her forehead, as if trying to let her thoughts see more clearly. 'This morning, when I went to the Steelyard with him, I noticed how he would sometimes stare at passing people.'

'He's new to London. It's a lot bigger than Sulzbach. He's bound to stare.'

'It was as if he knew them, but didn't. I can't explain. It was most odd.'

Nicholas recalls the first night Petrus had stayed at the Jackdaw, and he thinks of the following morning when they'd walked across the bridge together, saying their farewells before Petrus set off towards All Hallows Lane. He sees again in his mind the boy carrying a basket of medlars, and the way Petrus had turned his head, his body seeming to flinch.

'I can see it in your face,' Bianca says. 'You've noticed it, too, haven't you? It's not simply my imagination.'

'Only once,' Nicholas admits. 'But it could signify nothing. There could be a perfectly rational answer.'

'Such as?'

'Perhaps he's come to London in search of someone.'

'He has – *you*.'

'I mean someone else, someone he's lost.'

'I hadn't thought of that,' Bianca says. 'Does Petrus have brothers or sisters?'

'I think he has one of each.'

'Older or younger?'

'Younger. His father remarried after his first wife died.'

'Just like you.'

'That's not uncommon, is it?'

Bianca stares at the river, silently rebuking her wayward imagination. 'Well, it's an explanation I prefer to the alternative.'

'Which is?'

'That he has something to do with the disappearance of Gideon Trindle, Hugh Mould and Oliver Sly.'

Nicholas stares at her. 'Why would you even begin to think that?'

It is a question Bianca has asked herself frequently since she returned from the Steelyard. Is it her imagination running wild again? Or has a veil lifted from her eyes – a veil she put on because she didn't want to think badly of a friend of Nicholas's from the past? She takes a calming breath before setting out her case.

'Petrus arrives from nowhere, just as Gideon Trindle and Hugh Mould go missing – quickly followed by Oliver Sly,' she begins. 'Instead of choosing a lodging house – where he'd likely have to register his name and where he'd come from – he picks somewhere almost abandoned, somewhere full of hiding places. When he arrives at the Jackdaw, he won't tell us where he's staying. And then there are the nightmares he has. What if they're caused not by the terrors he witnessed in the Low Countries, but by a guilty conscience?'

'That's ridiculous. What do you think he's done with them? Buried them in the Steelyard?'

'Prove me wrong,' Bianca says bluntly.

'I don't have to. We know why Petrus chose the Steelyard. He's got very little money and it's as close to home as he can get in a foreign city. He didn't tell us where he was staying because he's a proud man. And as for suggesting he's kidnapped – even murdered – those three missing boys, well, that's laughable.'

Bianca stares at the river, not knowing whether to feel foolish or angry. 'There's something odd about Petrus Eusebius Schenk. And I don't only mean his name.'

Nicholas rises to his feet. 'This is nonsense, sweet,' he tells her with a disbelieving laugh. 'Petrus isn't a murderer. There's no proof that Trindle, Mould and Sly are even dead.'

'Then why haven't they returned?'

'There could be any number of reasons. You're imagining demons where there are none. And, frankly, I think you're treating Petrus less kindly than you might,' Nicholas goes on, turning back towards the Paris Garden lodgings.

Bianca is about to call after him, 'I let him stay in my house for free, didn't I?' But she holds her tongue.

You think you know your friend, she silently tells him as she follows. And I thought I knew Lorenzo Adelardi. But if I'd really listened to what my heart was screaming at me, I'd have warned Gessica Corocetti never to go behind the Piazza dei Signori with him.

✠

It is night, and the Steelyard is as dark as the river that runs beside it. In Aksel Leezen's house, Petrus Eusebius Schenk sits alone on the floor of the upstairs living chamber, the only light the glow from the tallow stub in the horn lantern Bianca gave him.

He has resisted temptation for several hours. He has done so partly because he knows that reunion is a joy worth waiting for, but mostly because he senses this is the moment after which retreat becomes impossible. His only break from the waiting has been to go downstairs to the storeroom and stand awhile over the trapdoor, in case he might hear the boy's ghost calling to him. But all he'd caught was the sound of the river breaking against the mouth of the culvert.

Now, he has decided, is the time to unfurl the banners, raise the trumpet to the lips, sound the call to battle. From tonight there can be no going back, only advance.

He reaches out and pulls his pack close to his knees. He unlaces it and lets the dead souls come to him.

When they are free, he rummages inside until he finds the keys that he brought with him from Zurich. He lays them beside the ones Bianca had given him earlier in the day: two pairs with solid iron shanks and bits like the stubs of tightly pruned branches. He smiles. She thinks she's so clever, that one. So *scharfsinnig*. He imagines the look on her face were she to learn where he'd got them.

He takes up the one he had used when he sought to gain access to this very house, that rainy evening when he returned to the

Steelyard for the first time in a year and a half. He lays it beside the matching one Bianca has provided. He then takes her second key, the one that opens the lock that the Lord Mayor's men had installed when they expelled the Hansa merchants. He makes a mental note of the bit before laying it down.

That leaves his second key, which matches none of the others.

Rising to his feet, the horn lantern in his left hand, the key in his right, Petrus advances on the locked door to the second bedroom. He can hear Bianca's voice in his head: *You won't need the key... It's a bit of a mess in there, so I keep it locked...*

And as Petrus slips the key into the lock, he recites out loud a verse from the Book of Revelation: *I know thy works: behold, I have set before thee an open door, and no man can shut it: for thou hast a little strength, and hast kept my word, and hast not denied my name.*

☩

Father Beauchêne pushes open the heavy door and steps inside the church to escape the sudden shower. The weak light from the lantern that he holds pools around him, a pale oasis battling against a desert of darkness. He stops and listens to the night.

The church is empty, silent save for the faint sound of the rain hitting the old hammerbeam roof high above. He peers ahead, towards the plain altar almost lost in the shadows. It looks to him more like a tomb than a place of pious celebration.

Not yet ready to let the peace of God's house come to him, he lifts the lantern as high as his reach will allow. He looks around carefully, ensuring that he hasn't missed Asher Montague lurking in the apse, or behind the pulpit, like an assassin of the Holy Spirit. Only when he's quite certain that he's alone does Beauchêne relax.

He walks slowly down the length of the nave, casting his gaze around at the ancient stones. In his mind, though they have withstood the trials of centuries, they seem bruised, almost in pain. They have been assaulted yet again. Earlier today, Montague blasted them – and the parishioners they shelter – with another of his fiery onslaughts. They will need time to heal.

Beauchêne shakes his head in sorrow. The church's continued existence is tenuous enough, he knows. The Lord Mayor and the aldermen are suspicious of foreigners worshipping here, even if they are faithful to the queen's religion. It wouldn't take much to give them an excuse to shut it down. Montague's scorching zeal – bordering on sedition – would be more than enough.

When Montague first arrived, Beauchêne had thought him an innocent. He was so young, seemingly unmarked by the tribulations that afflicted the parishioners he was meant to serve. But now he wonders if it was really God who sent the young zealot here. The Devil is clever with his tricks. It would not be beyond him to send a dark angel wearing a cloak of sanctity for disguise.

Taking a final glance around to ensure the object of his thoughts is absent, Beauchêne kneels before the altar, clasps his hands together and begins to pray.

18

A summer thunderstorm is venting its black wrath over the Strand. Hailstones the size of pomegranate seeds assault the windows of Cecil House in suicidal icy salvoes. In a chamber off the long gallery, the grand men sitting around the even grander oak table must raise their voices in a distinctly ungentlemanly manner simply to be heard.

The meeting has been convened to address the realm's trade relations with Morocco, in preparation for the arrival of the sultan's ambassador. Mr Secretary Cecil presides. With him are England's Attorney General, Sir Edward Coke, and Lord Treasurer Thomas Sackville. A dozen other privy councillors have come in expectation of finding a few scraps left on the carcass once the big beasts have filled their bellies. 'Let's pray the ambassador arrives to better weather or he'll think he's in Norway,' jokes Cecil, to the amusement of all.

The minor characters in this tableau are painted in the background, Nicholas amongst them. They sit patiently on benches set around the walls, straining their ears for the call. The signal will be subtle: the merest raising of a finger or a slight nod of the head. Then it will be up to the secretaries to provide the required figure, date or appropriate extract from whatever bill is being cited to win or defeat the argument. They will spring from their bench, moving forward at a crouch so as to appear invisible, whispering their compendious knowledge into their principal's ear, giving him the clarification, guidance or validation he requires – or rescuing him from the hole he has dug for himself. Complete attention is required. The very worst thing in the world would be to miss the call because you hadn't heard your principal above the rattling of the hail against the windows.

Nicholas is attending as Sir Robert's shield. His sole purpose is to employ his knowledge of the Moor and his ways against any criticism from privy councillors who are not of the Cecil faction. There are more of those at court than Mr Secretary cares to admit. Nicholas does not relish the prospect. The array of formal black gowns and starched ruffs gathered around the long table reminds him too much of a meeting of the Censors of the College of Physicians, called with the express purpose of disciplining a recalcitrant Dr Shelby.

Besides Nicholas, there is one other outsider present today. But even in that small fraternity they are poles apart. Where Nicholas wears a plain broadcloth doublet, the other – sitting beside him – sports a wide-shouldered short-gown and trunk-hose in expensive bottle-green velvet. Where Nicholas has a head of wiry black curls, the other boasts a mane of argent locks that fold themselves obediently on his collar like svelte greyhounds settling down beside a warm hearth. Is Silvan Gaspari an exemplar of his kind? Do all bankers smell of expensive oils?

But at least Gaspari's presence has offered Nicholas some small relief from the tedium of the conference. So far this morning he has learned that in the year to last Michaelmas, English merchants have exported to the Barbary shore linen goods worth £7,411. 3s. 6d., twenty hundredweight of tin, sixty pounds weight of opium, large quantities of red argol and more stalks of *spica romana* than they could possibly have an appetite for. In return,

England has imported, amongst other things, sixty chests of the finest Moroccan sugar expressly for the queen's use – price set by Mr Secretary's late father, Lord Burghley, at one shilling and tuppence a pound. Nicholas reflects that he has attended wakes that are more invigorating.

'And this is all trade with a poor and savage land, whose people are infidels and heathens,' announces Charles Howard, the hawk-nosed Earl of Nottingham, his voice raised sufficiently above the storm to snap Nicholas out of imminent slumber. 'Fie! That's what I say to those nay-sayers who advised against throwing out the Hansa merchants. This is undoubtedly just the start of a new world of opportunities. Why, I dare to hope that I shall live to see us one day trading with distant China.'

'The question,' says Robert Cecil, shorter by a head than any man at the table, 'is how we bring order to a situation best described as chaos. Master Gaspari, perhaps you would be kind enough to outline your concerns from a financial perspective.'

Gaspari, who has been primed for this moment, gets to his feet and walks to one end of the table, facing Cecil from a distance that Nicholas is sure must make Mr Secretary look positively diminutive. When he speaks, the meeting is treated to a confident, almost liquid voice. The Swiss accent is all but undetectable.

'Masters,' he begins with an upward tilt of the heavy head that has the silver mane swinging like the curtain on a tester-bed, 'it will be a brave man who sinks his own money into Barbary without a guarantee that any losses he might incur will be replenished from Her Majesty's mint. I myself would not do so unless there were written agreements with King Muly Ahmad that some control was imposed on rampant theft. I have clients who are pursuing a certain Master James Rives, their factor, who has absconded with imports worth six thousand pounds – goods that have been paid for, but not produced by him for loading onto any ship bound for England. Muly Ahmad has washed his hands of the matter, much to the discomfort of my clients.'

Lord Treasurer Sackville raises a bejewelled hand to interject. 'Her Majesty has already written to Muly Ahmad on this matter, enjoining him to bring this Rives to book.'

'And my clients are grateful before their maker for it,' Gaspari says unctuously. 'But that doesn't pay the interest on the loan of six thousand pounds. If there is no resolution soon, I shall have to foreclose upon those wholly innocent gentlemen who sought finance for the project.'

'You could extend the conditions of the loan,' Robert Cecil observes from the far end of the table. 'Or wait until the matter is concluded satisfactorily.'

From Gaspari's shocked expression, Cecil might have invited him on a tour of the lowest Bankside bawdy-houses, in the company of the Bishop of London. 'I am not a provider of alms for the poor, Sir Robert,' he protests with alpine frostiness. 'If I am to loan again to enterprises in Barbary, I shall need a guarantee. I can tell you, seeing good Christian men and their families brought to penury and starvation does not sit well with me. But I have other clients to whom I owe a measure of diligence.'

Cecil turns towards Nicholas. 'Dr Shelby over there knows Master Anoun well. He has even met King Muly Ahmad,' he says, for the benefit of those privy councillors who may have thought the man in the broadcloth doublet was there to serve the sugared sack when the meeting concludes. 'Doctor, do you think Master Anoun would be amenable to calling upon Muly Ahmad to expedite more formal legal arrangements?'

Nicholas stands up and takes his place beside Gaspari at the table. The banker gives him the sort of look that Nicholas suspects he might give a servant, should the man have the effrontery to enter his chamber unsummoned.

'You have to view it from their perspective,' Nicholas tells the expectant faces. 'They see us as we see them – as alien. To them, we are the infidels and deceivers. Muhammed al-Annuri and Sultan Al-Mansur will act in whatever manner they consider to be in their best interests.'

'Are you suggesting the Moor sees himself as the equal of the Christian man?' Nottingham asks, glaring down his beak at Nicholas.

'Why wouldn't he?' Nicholas asks innocently.

Nottingham looks to Cecil as if he might hold the answer. Mr Secretary Cecil gives a discreet diplomatic cough. 'I believe what Dr Shelby is trying to say is that we would be wise to put ourselves in their shoes. Is that correct?'

'It is, sir. Without attempting to treat with ambassador al-Annuri in an honest and open way, you will make little progress. Otherwise he will have no incentive to assist us. Especially if we intend to reject his master's approach in the matter of—'

Cecil raises a cautionary hand to cut him off. 'Stop there, please, Dr Shelby. I believe you are about to raise a matter to which some in this chamber are not privy.'

'Forgive me, Mr Secretary,' Nicholas says. 'I assumed we were speaking openly.'

'There is open and then there is gaping, Nicholas.'

'But Dr Shelby does speak soundly,' Gaspari says, turning his leonine head in Nicholas's approximate direction. 'I have some experience of dealing with the Moors myself.'

'You lend to them?' says Lord Treasurer Sackville. 'I thought they abhorred usury.'

'Mercy, no! I sell to them.'

'And the nature of the goods?' Sackville asks.

'Paper. And printing presses,' Gaspari replies. 'Or to be more precise, I facilitate the sending of quality paper and I finance the construction of printing presses.'

Why, in the presence of some of the most powerful men in England, Nicholas asks himself, has Silvan Gaspari chosen to lie? What profit does he expect to earn by deceit? 'May I ask something, purely for clarification?' he says to Robert Cecil, though the question is really intended for the silver-haired, velvet-clad man at his side.

Cecil's reply seems to take a while to reach him from the far end of the table. 'If you think it might assist us, Dr Shelby.'

'I was wondering what profit there might be in financing printing presses in the lands of the Moor?'

'Is that of relevance to this discussion?' asks Nottingham.

'It might be, given that I spoke earlier of plain dealing.'

Cecil waves a hand at him. 'Carry on, Dr Shelby. Ask your question.'

When Nicholas speaks, he does so to Cecil, rather than to Gaspari. He thinks it less of a confrontation. Confrontations, he suspects, are not welcome amongst such august company.

'Forgive me if I am mistaken, but I was under the impression that printing is prohibited amongst the Moors. They believe that a mechanical device would make it too easy to falsify their holy texts. The practice is therefore outlawed. Perhaps Master Gaspari could clarify.'

As if on cue, the rattle of hail against the windows dies away, leaving an uncomfortable quiet in which Nicholas is painfully aware of his raised voice.

Gaspari turns to him, his heavy face colouring. 'Are you questioning my integrity before these noble gentlemen?' he says, his accent hardening.

'Not at all. As I say: for clarification.'

Gaspari addresses the table with all the hurt pride of a cuckold. 'Noble sirs, Dr Shelby is quite correct in what he says. The printing presses that my family finance are in places like Constantinople, Aleppo and Marrakech. They are used by the Christian and Hebrew communities there to print all manner of texts. These communities do not fall within the proscription Dr Shelby speaks of. The science of printing is not a cheap endeavour. Presses, type and paper cost money. I am proud that the Gaspari have a long tradition of supporting the printing and dissemination of learned works throughout Europe and, indeed, the lands of the Turk.'

For a moment there is silence while the black cloud of Gaspari's indignation rolls down the table towards Robert Cecil like the storm just past. But this time there is no accompanying hail. Mr Secretary disarms the banker with an indulgent smile. 'I'm sure Dr Shelby meant no insult by his question – which you have answered in full and to everyone's satisfaction. I think we may rest this matter. Let us move on to the subject of interest.' A hard look straight into Gaspari's prosperous face. 'Given that there may well be several gentlemen here, or indeed at court, who may wish to avail themselves of commercial activities with the Moor, what figure do you think appropriate, Master Gaspari – given the nature of the risk?'

'Ten in the hundred, Mr Secretary,' says Gaspari.

'That is the limit imposed by law, is it not?' Sackville chips in.

Gaspari's expression suggests he's being asked to give up the last florin in his purse. 'Trading with the Barbary shore is a risky business,' he says. 'As I have previously stated, I am not a dispenser of alms.'

'Ten would be tolerable, especially on the sugar,' says Nottingham.

But Nicholas is party to none of this. His mind is elsewhere. He is still braced against the squall even though the storm has moved on. The ringing in his ears is not the departing thunder.

It is what Silvan Gaspari said barely moments ago, in his defence to Nicholas's own injudicious question: *The science of printing is not a cheap endeavour. Presses, type and paper cost money.*

Why had it not occurred to him before? When he was standing in that tenement on Gravel Lane, observing the tortured corpse of the printer with what he had believed then to be rational dispassion, why was he imagining every question but the one he should have been asking?

How did an impoverished printer, living hand-to-mouth on Bankside, find the money to possess such an expensive and complicated engine as a printing press?

✣

Never burn your bridges, or so Yeoman Shelby has told his sons on more than one occasion. Nicholas has cause now to wish he'd listened. When the meeting ends, he attempts to speak to Silvan Gaspari about the écorché figures. But the banker has taken deep offence. 'I have no time to speak to the likes of you, sirrah,' he says loftily even before Nicholas opens his mouth. 'I have business at the Royal Exchange – with men of quality.'

Worse still, Nicholas is forced to wait two hours before he sees Mr Secretary Cecil again. He begs a plate of manchet bread and cheese from the kitchen to sustain himself, then returns to the long gallery and waits to be called.

'If you've come to apologize for insulting Master Gaspari, you've wasted your time,' Cecil tells him when Nicholas is ushered into Mr Secretary's study. 'The fellow is no less a rogue than all his kind. But we have need of him, so tongues must be bitten, I'm afraid, Nicholas. Tongues *must* be bitten.'

'I hadn't intended to apologize, Sir Robert. It was merely that something he said made me wonder if you had been looking in the wrong place for your seditious printer.'

'Are you telling me the fellow on Bankside was innocent?'

'No, I still think he was the source. But as Gaspari says, a printing press and its paraphernalia are expensive items. Someone must have been supporting him.'

Cecil considers the proposition. 'We believe there to be some sixty printing presses in England. We have visited every single one we could find. We discovered nothing to make us believe any of them were the source of seditious material.'

'Did your searchers visit Bankside? Did they speak to Symcot?'

'No. He wasn't known to us. Not every printer is officially approved.'

'I believe Symcot and his press arrived on Bankside around December '98,' Nicholas says. 'Someone must have financed it, because the printer himself didn't appear to have a penny to his name.'

'What are you proposing, Nicholas?'

'Let me make enquiries. I'll see if I can find out who it was. They may be the true source of your seditious texts.'

A look of amused distrust flickers across Cecil's pale face. 'And why would you bother? We've found no more of those tracts. The call to insurrection is silenced; the danger is past. Besides, I thought you'd rejected the notion of serving as my intelligencer? Did you stay to tell me you've changed your mind?'

Not this side of the Second Coming, Nicholas thinks. But until I find who was responsible for those tracts, your hold over my father remains as claw-like as it ever was.

But he has already spoken incautiously once today. And so he simply smiles and says, 'In my professional opinion, Sir Robert, it is always best to finish a course of medicine to the last drop. Giving up too early is never a wise idea.'

✠

Asher Montague has ordered that the congregation will no longer sit when he delivers his sermons. Sitting – or, worse, kneeling – before a priest in holy vestments is little better than pagan idolatry. Stand up! Let God see you as he made you: that is now the sentiment at every service he holds at the Dutch church in Austin Friars. Consequently Ned Monkton has become, by a head, the most identifiable member of the congregation.

Never in all his life has Ned heard such preaching. How can this young priest see so clearly what is in his heart? How can Parson Montague look into his soul?

Ned has always attended sermon not because he is particularly pious but because that's what everyone does. It's the law, and money is not so easily come by that he would waste it on a fine for non-attendance. But until now he has seen churchgoing only in terms of how it reaffirms his own place in God's order on earth.

In Ned's mind, he is at the bottom of an immutable hierarchy: first the queen, then her lords and bishops, next the priests, the gentlemen, and at the bottom the ordinary folk. Even amongst them there is a rank, and Ned Monkton would not place himself very high on it, even if he has come up in the world from his former estate. Were it not for Bianca Merton and Nicholas Shelby, he would probably still have for his daily company those at the extreme bottom of this imaginary pyramid: the dead. He might still be trapped in the crypt at St Thomas's where, as mortuary porter, he spent his days amongst the human detritus of the city, using the same single winding sheet, the same single coffin, to send those even more unfortunate than himself to their unmarked graves. When he had wrapped them and placed them in the single coffin, he would bid them farewell. Then he would wait until the sheet and the coffin were returned to him for the use of the next poor soul who had fallen through the cracks in heaven's floorboards. And while he was waiting, he would speak soothingly to the silent, give names to the nameless, a last measure of friendship to those who would find no more of it in this world.

At first Parson Montague's uncompromising scouring of the congregation had unsettled Ned. He hadn't needed Montague to tell him he was damned. He took that for granted. He knows he has done bad things in his life, even if they were for the right reasons. On his right hand he carries a branded M, to show that he has taken a man's life, for which he came closer to hanging than he cares to remember. He is a sinner, plain and simple, and one day he will have to answer for those sins. But until he heard Parson Montague's extraordinary preaching, he has never truly believed there was an alternative to damnation. Or that martyrdom could be so alluring. He stands before Asher Montague in an almost trance-like state, listening to the hurricane of promised resurrection. Montague's body is arched, arms thrust wide, in an ecstasy that Ned can only imagine. He is the future. He is justice. He is the burning bush, and it is not his voice, but God's, booming around the church like summer thunder.

'And lo, though the flames licked the skin of John Hooper like the tongues of the serpent in Eden's Garden,' Asher Montague roars in a voice too profound for one so young, 'even until his limbs burned through and fell into the ash, the martyr raised himself above the torments of the ungodly! And the Almighty smiled upon him. The Almighty sent him balm, so that although he burned, he would feel no pain. Who amongst you will not embrace that fire if it brings you everlasting life in heaven?'

The sermon is over. The congregation is wrung out like wet linen slammed against a rock. They leave the church at Austin Friars and disperse to their homes, some in silent contemplation, others roused and overwrought like the victors of a violent street brawl. Asher Montague stands in the porch and watches them go, eyes moist with fervour, an ecstatic bloom on his face.

'I know what's in your heart, Ned Monkton,' Petrus says as they walk away. 'I felt it too. Don't be afraid. Be joyful. A man could travel to the ends of the world and not hear such preaching.' He tugs at the sleeve of Ned's jerkin to pull him back. 'Do you not find it a revelation?'

'Aye, he 'as a true gift.'

'My heart was lifted when he quoted from the Book of Isaiah, "Even the captivity of the mighty shall be taken away, and the prey of the tyrant shall be delivered." I thought to myself, Ned: that's *us*. We are in captivity to the mighty. We are the prey of the tyrant. And we *shall* be delivered.'

Ned scratches his head in wonder. 'I didn't know such words was in the Holy Book. I can't read scripture, see.'

Petrus raises his eyes to heaven, and in them is reflected not sunlight, but bliss. '"And I will deliver thee out of the hand of the wicked, and I will redeem thee out of the hand of the tyrant." Have you ever heard such inspiring words, Ned?'

Ned confesses that indeed he has not.

'"He that oppresseth the poor to increase himself, and giveth unto the rich, shall surely come to poverty",' Petrus whispers in rapture.

'It would be about bloody time,' Ned says. 'God can't intend 'onest folks to live the way some of us 'ave to.'

'It's not God, Ned,' says Petrus. 'It's those false idols, those graven images that set themselves between the humble man and his maker.'

'I 'adn't thought of it like that,' Ned muses. 'But now you lay it out so clearly...'

Petrus gives Ned's jerkin another tug. 'Come with me. I think it's time I introduced you to Parson Montague.'

19

Not for the first time Nicholas thinks how easily the printing press on Gravel Lane could be mistaken for an engine of torture. The carriage looks just as much like a rack as the last time he'd seen it. Beneath the platen – now raised to permit the extraction of the victim's head – the dried blood has added a dark patina to the oak. The H-frame with its vertical wooden screw the diameter of a young tree wouldn't look out of place on Tower Hill, as a new instrument of slow execution for the entertainment of the crowd.

'What are you looking for, Dr Shelby?' Constable Osborne asks. 'I thought you'd seen all that you required to see when last we were here.'

'I'm not looking for anything tangible,' Nicholas replies. 'I want to understand what it must have taken to transport this machine across the river and set it up on Bankside. It was certainly beyond the resources of the man who operated it. Think of it: metals for the type, fuel for the furnace to cast it, paper, ink, maintaining the working of the frame. That's no small enterprise. Yet the poor fellow who ended up under that platen appeared to be as impoverished as a roadside beggar.'

Osborne's canny eyes widen. 'Perhaps he wasn't a very good printer. All he did, apparently, was print pages from the gospels to sell on street corners.'

'That's my point entirely. Is there any news of a perpetrator?'

Osborne shakes his head. 'There's a baker he owed money to... A neighbour who accused him of blocking the street sewer... But they all have alibis. The Surrey coroner put it down to a quarrel with someone across the river. Someone unknown.'

Nicholas walks slowly around the press, gauging the weight of the thing. The two main beams of the H-frame are as tall as he is, solid baulks of squared-off timber. Lifting them would require more strength than one man alone could bring to bear. 'Who paid for the labour? Who arranged for the transport?' he asks, though his question is directed more to the press than to Osborne. 'Who provided the metalworkers to make the bolts, hinges and straps that hold all this together? Who did all that, and then gave you just enough to live on while you ran off pages of scripture that you sold for farthings? Was it the man who turned the handle while your head was pinned beneath the platen? Or was it someone else – someone who wanted to learn his identity?'

'Have you seen enough, Dr Shelby?' Osborne asks.

'You'd need a wherryman who was used to carrying sizeable loads across the river,' Nicholas says. 'You wouldn't hire just anybody. You wouldn't want to see your investment floating down towards Deptford like so much flotsam, would you?' He turns to the constable. 'Bianca says that someone told her Symcot came here two winters ago.'

'Aye, that's what his neighbours say.'

'That would be about the time Master Shakespeare and his players took down their old place in Shoreditch, before they brought the timbers across the river to build the Globe,' Nicholas says, for his own benefit as much as Osborne's, as if he were tentatively laying out planks across a patch of swampy ground, wanting to be sure they were secure before trusting his feet to them.

'Are you suggesting Master Shakespeare might have something to do with this?' Osborne says doubtfully.

'No, not at all,' replies Nicholas. 'But if you're going to transport the entire frame of a playhouse across the river, you're going to pick the best wherrymen you can find to do the job. Someone who would also know how to take care of something as expensive as a printing press.'

✠

Nicholas makes his way down a narrow passage and over a small wooden bridge thrown across a ditch that flows into the river between Bankside's bear-baiting ring and the Clink house of correction. He stops at a terrace of modest timber-framed buildings whose upper floors lean out towards the houses opposite as if with lascivious intent. Indeed, the whole area is considered racy. This is where many of Southwark's players choose to live, for its convenience to the Swan, the Globe and the Rose, and the proximity of many of Bankside's better taverns and inns, including Mistress Merton's Jackdaw. At its liveliest, it is a babel of recitation, rehearsal, argument and insult. Even the hardest-nosed local doxies are known to drop their prices for a spirited but pecunious roaring boy from the theatres. But today it is quiet.

'Can't spare you long, Dr Nicholas,' says Will Shakespeare as Nicholas steps across the threshold. 'I've to meet Master Henslowe in a quarter of an hour. He needs to learn that a playwright isn't like a weaver – you don't thrash a loom for an hour and then announce, "There you are, three yards of tragedy, comedy, history or pastoral to pull the groundlings in, as ordered." What can I do for you?'

'It wasn't a weaver I wanted to speak to you about, it was a printer,' Nicholas says, looking around at the chaos of paper, pounce-pots, books and half-burned candles.

'Don't talk to me about printers. Thieves and pirates, the lot of them. I went to that fellow on Gravel Lane last year, to see if I could get some sort of control over the printing of my plays. Saucy rogue told me he'd have nothing to do with the lasciviousness of the playhouse. *Lasciviousness* – I ask you! Cheeky fardel. So I said, "What are you doing on Bankside then?" And he said… well, never mind what he said, he's dead now.'

'It was him I wanted to speak to you about,' Nicholas says.

'Have they caught the fellow who killed him?'

'Not yet.'

'My money's on Ben Jonson. He probably said much the same sort of thing to Ben. Sticking someone's head under a platen – that's just the sort of thing Ben would do, if he'd had a few.'

'I'm trying to determine who brought that press across the river.'

Shakespeare studies Nicholas for a brief while, as though trying to read his thoughts.

'Ah,' he says with a stage wink, 'for a certain little arseworm of a fellow with crooked shoulders who lives in a big house near Covent Garden? If I lie, spit in my face and call me a horse.'

Nicholas sighs. 'You're not the first person on Bankside to suggest it, Master Will. It's common knowledge that I serve him as his son's physician. But that's all.'

Shakespeare laughs and claps Nicholas on the shoulder. 'Don't worry, sweet Nick. No one around here thinks you're an informer.'

Nicholas chooses not to answer. He has long ago resigned himself to accepting that secrets cannot be kept for ever. On Bankside a week would be stretching your luck to breaking point. 'This is mostly a personal matter,' he says. 'My father was accused of possessing one of the seditious tracts that were issuing from that press.'

'That's confirmed, too, is it – that it was Symcot who was printing them?'

'Not exactly. But it seems likely.'

'And your father – is he alright? They haven't dungeoned him, have they?'

'They did, but he's free now. If I'm going to prove his innocence, I need to find out who was the real force behind that press, because I don't believe Symcot was. I thought I'd start with whoever brought it across the river.'

'How do you think I can help, Nick?'

'I've established that it came across in December '98. That's about the time you struck down your playhouse at Shoreditch, before you brought it across the river, isn't it?'

'Yes. It was snowing hard for days. We froze our whirligigs off taking that bloody theatre to pieces at Shoreditch. We had to store the timbers on the north side, while we prepared the ground and laid the foundations for the Globe. It was too wet to start at once.'

'When you brought the timbers across, who did you use?'

Shakespeare trawls his memory for a moment. 'Dick Burbage arranged most of it. But if I recall things aright, the boatmen we hired were Peter Powtrell, Jack Henham, Will Thorne and... that fellow with the missing ear... What's his name? I've forgotten.'

Nicholas recalls one of the Jackdaw's customers, a burly man in his fifties whose ear had been trimmed for petty larceny. 'Daniel Swale,' he suggests helpfully.

'That's the one – Dan Swale,' says Shakespeare. 'For the really heavy timbers we used Rob Tucker's barge.'

'Where did you store the timbers, before you brought them across? I presume you needed somewhere reputable and secure. They must have been worth a lot of money.'

'Without question. That's why we wanted to keep them for the building of the Globe,' Shakespeare replies.

'So who did you use? Should I ask Master Burbage?'

'Mercy, no; I can tell you that. We used a master carpenter, fellow named Peter Street.'

The name means nothing to Nicholas.

'He oversaw the Globe when we raised it up,' Shakespeare says, seeing the blank look on his visitor's face. 'His storehouse is on the north bank of the river, by the Bridewell water-stairs.'

✠

Before Nicholas goes to see Peter Street, first he walks across London Bridge to St Paul's Cross. This is where Londoners gather in the open air to hear the great theologians preach. More than a few punches have been thrown here when competing dogmas excite the audience beyond endurance. In the time of Her Majesty's late father, a sermon preached here led to the Evil May Day riots against the city's foreign population. But today there are few people about. The pulpit stands empty, a summer pavilion with a leaded half-onion dome for a roof.

Nicholas makes his way around the perimeter of the church and past the dean's house to the guildhall of the Worshipful Company of Stationers, in the area of the city where, by tradition, the booksellers, scriveners, binders and printers have their stations. Just as he did when he first visited the printer Symcot on Gravel Lane, he offers the liveried clerk the fiction that he's proposing to write a book on physic. What he's really after is evidence of where printer Symcot's press was before it crossed the river to Southwark, and who might have been funding it.

'Before this proposed book of yours is printed, it will have to be approved by the Privy Council,' the clerk says, his suspicions rising as he takes in Nicholas's plain doublet and tousled black hair, his broad shoulders and his limbs well fashioned from a childhood on the land. 'Are you sure you're a physician?'

Whether it's the queen or a common clerk, it's always the same, thinks Nicholas. *You're too young... too unrefined... too impecunious... Your beard isn't luxurious enough... You've no grey hairs...*

'Quite sure, thank you. If I could simply see the roll of permitted presses here in London, I'd be eternally grateful.'

'And if there was such a roll, I'd be happy to show it to you,' the clerk says. 'But no such thing exists. We license books approved by the Church authorities and the Privy Council, not the printers of them.'

'That's a pity,' Nicholas says, trying to keep the disappointment out of his voice. 'I was hoping there might be a list. I'm trying to locate the owner of a press that was moved across the river two winters ago.'

The clerk shrugs. 'I can't help you. The only lists we keep are of membership fees and fines paid for transgressing the Company's statutes. I'm sorry, but all I can suggest is that you visit some booksellers. Choose a book that you consider pleasing in style, and you'll find the name of the printer shown on the title page. Then you can contact him yourself.'

'I don't suppose you would care to scrutinise your list of transgressors, to see if a man named Symcot is listed there,' says Nicholas. 'He's the printer who crossed the river to Bankside. I wouldn't want to commission anyone disreputable.'

'It will cost,' says the clerk.

And indeed, it costs sixpence. And takes a good half hour. But the result is worth its weight in gold.

'Here he is,' says the Clerk. 'Symcot, fined one shilling for publishing unauthorized biblical texts of an inflammatory nature. But he didn't pay the fine himself.'

Of course he didn't, thinks Nicholas. A shilling would have kept Symcot in bread for a month.

'Then who did pay it?'

The clerk peers at the roll of parchment, then lifts his gaze to meet Nicholas's. 'A Master Hooper,' he says. 'Address not given.'

Leaving the Stationers' Company, Nicholas again passes the empty open-air pulpit at the Cross. He pictures in his mind the anonymous author of the seditious tract railing at his congregation from beneath its wooden dome. It is Asher Montague that he sees. But the fiery peroration bursting from his mouth is not from the sermon Nicholas heard him preach at Barnthorpe. It is from the sheet of paper Cecil had shown him at Richmond: *Let Hooper, the glorious Martyr, be thy touchstone and thy comfort, even when the task seems beyond the strength of thine arm. Be the first to raise thy hand...*

But raise it in what cause? And to what end?

✠

The London premises of master carpenter Peter Street lie on the north bank of the Thames, where the noisome Fleet ditch spills the ward's detritus – human waste, the corpses of cats and dogs and occasionally people – into the river. But to Nicholas's joy, entering the interior of the warehouse is like stepping into a freshly coppiced orchard, the sappy scent of wood shavings and sawdust hanging in the air like the heady fragrance of a Southwark bagnio.

Street is a short, well-set fellow in his late forties, his shoulders and his arms out of scale with his legs, which Nicholas puts down to a lifetime of hoisting heavy baulks of timber. He has a pedantry to his actions and is precise in his movements, as though his body is checking itself against an invisible rule, try-square or plumbline. He wears a leather apron, and his bare forearms carry indecipherable marks, presumably made by the large splinter of charcoal that he carries lodged in the cleft above his right ear.

'If you want a job done, I'm afraid we're fully committed, Master,' Street says when an apprentice fetches him from behind a vast pile of roughly hewn logs. 'I'm up to *here* at present, working on Master Henslowe's new playhouse on Finsbury Fields. I can't take on another job until at least September – it's a shortage of labourers that's the problem. All the carpenters who really know an adze from an augur are down at the queen's dockyards building galleons. An' these days it's nigh on impossible to find an apprentice without a squint or two left thumbs.'

'I'm just after some information, that's all,' Nicholas says, introducing himself. 'Master Will Shakespeare told me you might be able to help me. It's about storage and transportation.'

'*Oohh*,' Street drawls, makes a theatrically pained face and rocking one hand back and forth like a seesaw. 'Your storage is going to be a problem. First, there's the floor space – as you can see, I've very little available. Then there's the transportation. If it comes across the bridge, I have to warn you the freightage toll has gone through the roof.'

'It's nothing like that. I only wanted to know if you had ever been asked to store a printing press in your workshop. It would have been around the December before last. Did anyone named Hooper pay you to store such an item?'

'A printing press, you say?'

'I do.'

'Hooper?'

'Yes.'

'After the martyr?'

'That's what he called himself – John Hooper.'

Street scratches the back of his neck. A paper-thin curl of planed wood falls out of his hair and onto one shoulder. He brushes it off and shakes his head. 'N-o,' he says slowly. 'Can't help you, friend.'

'With the press or with Hooper?'

'Both, as it happens. There's a Horton on St Andrew's Hill, but he's a souse-head – wouldn't know a printing press from a spokeshave. I'm sorry I can't help. Was it important?'

'Just an enquiry. I'm sorry to have taken up your time.' Nicholas is about to leave when a thought strikes him. 'Are there any other workshops or storehouses around here, Master Street?'

'Not this side of the Bridewell, but beyond Salisbury Court there's a small one. It's down by the river, between Water Lane and the Whitefriars stairs.'

'Do you know who owns it?'

'No one called Hooper, that's for sure. As far as I know, it's empty. It's on the riverbank, but I can't recall seeing any vessels moor there, not for a long while anyway.'

✠

The tide is coming in fast. Rather than risk walking along the shore, Nicholas walks north along the Fleet ditch and then cuts through the open courtyard of the Bridewell, once a royal palace but now serving as a house of correction, a hospital and a poorhouse. A low archway brings him out into Water Lane. He turns south again to the riverbank.

Just as Master Street had told him, he finds the storehouse close by the river, below the old Carmelite friary now turned into private dwellings. On the far side, beyond the Whitefriars water-stairs, he can see the treetops in the gardens where the law students of the Inner Temple take ease from their studies. Or bring their sweethearts for a little distraction when the thrills of the *De Laudibus Legum Angliae* and the *Liber Assissarium* prove too racy a diet.

On first inspection, the building looks well on the way to dereliction. There are holes in the tiled roof and the windows have been boarded up. A mossy green patina nourished by damp and river mist is slowly but insatiably consuming the brickwork. Nicholas pushes at one of the planks nailed to the inside of a window with no glass in it. Barely held in place by rusted brads, it falls inwards, landing with a moist thud. When he peers in, it takes a while for Nicholas's eyes to pierce the gloom. Eventually the weak light spilling through the holes in the roof and the gaps in the river-facing doorway allow him to see an empty dirt floor. He hears the agitated thrashings of feathers high up in the rafters as nesting birds object to his intrusion. But even though he searches the interior as best he can, he can see nothing that might suggest anything has been stored here for years.

Walking around to the side of the building, he comes to a pair of wide doors, a rusted chain looped across the central join and secured by an equally rusty lock. He looks up at the lintel, hoping to see a sign that might announce who owns the place. But the only marks on the timbers are the discoloured grey pennants left by the gulls.

Perhaps someone across the garden at the Inner Temple might know who owns the place. But he is running short of time; he will have to leave any further enquiry for another day. Disappointed to have come so far only to be thwarted, Nicholas turns back towards the bridge of the Fleet ditch.

And as he does so, he feels something small and hard beneath the sole of his shoe. At first he thinks he's stepped on a pebble, or an acorn or nut from the surrounding trees. But it's the wrong time of year for acorns to fall. And when he steps off, the object remains partially embedded in the leather. Raising his foot, he tugs it free.

He knows at once what it is. Sitting in the palm of his hand, protected from the elements by a layer of dried ink, is a small shank of metal about the size of the nail on his little finger. He moistens the thumb of his other hand and rubs one end, revealing – once the dirt has come away – the raised letter K at one end. He is looking at a single piece of iron type.

20

'**W**hat do you mean, Ned has changed? Has he shrunk? Surely he cannot have grown any larger.'

It is market day at St Saviour's, and Bianca Merton and Rose Monkton are browsing the stalls. Carts full of summer vegetables and fruit brought in from the Surrey fields vie for their attention.

'It's not funny, Mistress Bianca,' Rose says, rejecting a punnet of overripe gooseberries. 'I'm worried about 'im. Last night 'e said we were all damned unless we stood up to Pharaoh the way the Israelites did.' She bursts into a series of distressed honks that have the geese in a nearby pen responding in alarm. 'My Ned wouldn't know Pharaoh from... from... Oh, I don't know – Old King Lud!'

Bianca lays down her wicker basket and takes the other woman in her arms. 'Rose, Rose, whatever is the matter?'

When Rose has recovered enough to speak, she says, 'Ever since Master Petrus started taking 'im to 'ear that parson at the Dutch church preach, Ned's been like it. It's as though 'e's taken all the troubles of the poor on 'is shoulders, an' even Ned's shoulders ain't broad enough for that. He gets angry at every urchin an' vagrant 'e sees, an' God knows there's enough of them on Bankside. 'E blames the bishops an' the lords, and if he thought no one was listenin', I'd wager 'e'd blame the queen 'erself. I'm afeared 'is old anger is coming back to trouble 'im. An' 'e's not even Dutch!'

'I'm confident it won't last, Rose,' Bianca assures her. 'Ned's never going to make a Puritan, is he? It's not in his nature.'

Rose gives a watery snort. 'If it were a doxy what 'ad turned 'is head, why, I'd go up there and give 'er a proper slappin'. But you're not allowed to slap parsons or else you get excommendicated.'

'Excommunicated, Rose.'

'That too.'

Bianca takes a handkerchief from the sleeve of her bodice and dabs at Rose's face. 'Have you spoken to Ned about this?'

''E tells me I should come an' listen, make up my own mind.'

'Why don't you?'

'I got the feelin' Master Petrus don't want me to. They're like two boys who've found a shiny 'alf-angel in the mud by the Mutton Lane stairs an' don't want to share it with anyone. Least of all a woman.'

'You're not just a woman, Rose, you're his wife.'

'And as such I must defer to 'im, mustn't I?'

Bianca tells her breezily, 'We never did that sort of thing in Padua. My mother was a Caporetti. It was all she could do to bring herself to defer to the Pope.'

Rose manages a strangled laugh. 'But this is England. A wife is meant to 'onour 'er 'usband with obedience. That's why the queen has never married, ain't it? 'Cause she wouldn't never defer to no one.'

'That's what they say, Rose. That's what they say.' Bianca thinks of her own growing disquiet where Petrus Eusebius Schenk is concerned, and of the fate that so nearly befell Nicholas's father. 'I'll ask Nicholas to speak to Ned,' she says. 'We'll see if he can break whatever spell this new preacher at Austin Friars seems to be weaving.'

Rose seizes her friend's hands. 'Oh, would you please? I know 'e'd listen to Master Nicholas.'

'In the meantime, try to stop worrying yourself. The bishops and the Privy Council are always careful not to let firebrands preach beyond what is permitted. I'm sure this new preacher wouldn't risk overstepping the mark.'

Bianca makes a final tour of Rose's face with her handkerchief and returns the damp linen to the sleeve of her bodice. As she leads Rose to the next stall, she thinks perhaps it might be worth a visit to Austin Friars – if only to see what all the fuss is about.

✠

Sunset, and in the western sky heaven appears to be burning, the clouds glowing crimson and orange. Across the Paris Garden the bats are hunting, their darting black shapes bringing yelps of outrage from the mastiffs in the baiting-ring kennels. From the Falcon water-stairs comes a burst of drunken ribaldry as a late wherry takes the last of the revellers back across the river.

'I think I'm making a little headway in discovering who is behind Symcot's printing press. If I'm successful, I can break Robert Cecil's hold over my father,' Nicholas says as he and Bianca lie together, the window open to let in the cool evening air.

'Is that why you were so sharp a few nights ago, when you came home from Cecil House? I had a feeling the Crab had got his claws into you again.'

'If I can find out who was responsible for those tracts, I promise I'll be done with Mr Secretary Cecil. He can find another physician for his son. I want no more of him. I want *us* to have no more of him. He's been nothing but a malign influence on our lives.'

'Speaking of malign influences, Nicholas, I think you should have a word with Ned.'

'Ned? Why?'

'Because he listens to you.'

Nicholas brushes a strand of hair from her face, the better to see what is in her eyes. The dying light throws a ruddy wheal across her cheek. 'What's wrong?' he asks.

'Rose is worried about him,' Bianca says, propping herself up on one elbow, the wide neck of her nightshift slipping down over one shoulder. 'I know that people are inclined to step over to the other side of the lane when they see Ned coming, but you and I both know that underneath that fearsome exterior is a gentle soul. And an impressionable one.'

'That's true,' Nicholas replies, caressing the pale patch at the crest of her shoulder where the twilight catches it.

'Remember when you first came across him?' Bianca says, as a tiny winged silhouette darts across the patch of sky framed by the window and pulls her memory after it. 'He was convinced that I could turn myself into a bat, or poison him with my voice alone. He was sure that I was a witch.'

'Don't tell me that's not a fact?' Nicholas says with a gentle laugh. 'It'll come as a terrible shock to half the people in Southwark.'

'This isn't a joking matter, Nicholas. What would happen if Ned found himself in the same position as your father?'

Nicholas frowns. 'Why should he? What's he done?'

'It's not what he's done, it's what's been done to him,' Bianca says. 'It sounds to me as if this Parson Montague at the Dutch church has been turning Ned's head. He's been going there rather a lot, with your friend Petrus. Or hadn't you noticed? Do you want to risk the same thing happening to Ned as happened to your father?'

Nicholas sighs. 'Very well, I'll speak to Ned.'

Bianca kisses him chastely on the forehead. 'Now tell me what the Crab did to upset you.'

'He wants me to gull Muhammed al-Annuri when he comes,' Nicholas says. 'I'm to keep him happy while the Privy Council and a banker named Gaspari make some potentially very profitable deals with Morocco. But underneath, they have no intention of giving him what he wants, which is to enlist our help against the Spanish. I'm supposed to be the sugar they add to the wine, so that he doesn't notice they're serving it to him sour.'

'You've never really told me what happened when the Crab sent you to the Barbary shore.'

'It was years ago. Best to leave the past sleeping.'

Bianca knows better than to press him. She has long held the suspicion that finding out the truth about what befell Nicholas in Morocco would be far worse than anything her imagination can conjure.

'But you owe this al-Annuri a debt?' is all she thinks it wise to ask.

'Yes. And I'm not going to gull him as if he were a green-pate fresh from the country come to Bankside on May Day.'

'You'll do what you think is right,' she says, before leaning over to give him a second kiss, this time not on the forehead and certainly not chaste.

And I shall do the same, she thinks in the moment before her lips meet his. Starting with Parson Asher Montague.

✠

Two men stand by the lychgate at the Dutch church in Austin Friars watching the parishioners pass through. Sextons, Bianca assumes; though why gravediggers should be checking the congregation she can't imagine. They look as though they'd be handy in a quarrel at the Jackdaw.

'Good morrow, Mistress, and welcome to God's house for the righteous in a foreign land,' the larger of the two says to Bianca, in an accent that she would place somewhere north of Milan.

'Are you from this parish?' asks the second, his English as native as the soil beneath his feet.

Bianca has not expected a challenge. Her intention had been to remain unnoticed, even by Father Beauchêne. To that end, she has dressed herself in an old gown that she never wears in the Jackdaw's taproom, and a hood with a veil to cast shade over her features. She knows that Ned will not be in the congregation – Rose has managed to contrive enough chores at the Jackdaw to keep him safely in Southwark today – but Petrus might be here. If he were to spot her, she would have a hard time convincing him she wasn't spying, mostly because that's exactly what she is doing.

Making a quick check to see that Father Beauchêne is nowhere to be seen, she adopts a thick Veneto accent, to misdirect the man who has just this moment stopped her.

'I from Cheap-aside. I 'ear very good about Padre Montague. I come to see 'im.'

The guise seems to work, because she is asked no more questions and is hurriedly waved through the lychgate to avoid holding up the queue. As she crosses the trodden grass to the porch, Bianca tells herself that a lie told for a good purpose isn't quite the sin it might be – even if it is committed in a holy place. After all, there's more than one church in Padua that she's had to enter with her eyes lowered in guilt.

Taking her place at the back of the church, she checks the heads of the worshippers for Petrus's pale halo of hair. She cannot see him anywhere. She turns her attention to the church itself.

She has the same reaction whenever she enters a Protestant church – as though she's discovered that someone has stolen her purse. She's been robbed. Plain whitewashed walls... severity... no roodscreen worth the carpenters' efforts... no heady smell of incense. Where is the shrine to the Holy Mother? Where are the vividly coloured statues of the saints? Where is the grandeur of God's glory? What have you done with all the beauty? she wants to cry out.

Bianca has long since reconciled herself to praying amongst the heretics. She's sure God understands. He's all-knowing, after all. He will have calculated that the recusancy fines for not attending church would ruin her inside six months. He couldn't possibly blame her for the priests dressing so plainly, or because they believe bread is only bread and wine is only wine, and not the living flesh and blood of His son. It's not her fault that the congregation has no imagination. What would her old friend Cardinal Fiorzi in Padua make of it? He would probably wag a stern finger at her and warn her she was playing a game of hazard with her immortal soul. But God can see she still has a faithful heart, and in Bianca's mind that's all that matters.

Today at least, judging by the voices she can hear making conversation around her, there's a good smattering of English in attendance. Have they too been attracted by Asher Montague's growing reputation? Or should it be his notoriety? Clearly Ned Monkton isn't the only one susceptible to the new parson's oratory. She tries to imagine what this Old Testament firebrand might look like. She imagines an angry, grey-haired rock of thunderous piety.

And then an angel in a plain black surplice walks in. An angel with a face too young and too innocent to have even an ember of zealotry burning in it. An angel with a frame that looks too slight to bear the heat of God's fire.

The congregation falls silent, cowed even before Montague has placed one boyish foot on the steps to the pulpit. He lifts his arms. The congregation rises as one, Bianca just a beat behind the rest.

'You are not slaves,' he announces in a voice that has the sweetness and clarity of a finely tuned bell. 'You were not brought into this world to fall upon your knees and worship graven idols!'

Bianca thinks: this is going to be interesting.

✠

When she steps out of the little church at Austin Friars, Bianca feels as though she has been carried, helpless, on a great flood – a piece of driftwood tossed by the tempest, swallowed by the deep and then spat out again. And she doesn't much care for it.

Nor does she care for the way so many amongst the congregation had been complicit in Parson Montague's dangerous ecstasy. He has preached obedience and rage in equal measure: uncompromising obedience to God; rage for the bishops, the Privy Council, the Lord Mayor, aldermen and sheriffs great and small, and for everyone else who seeks to come between a soul and its creator. These functionaries of the Devil, he told them, were responsible for every injury received by the common man or woman since the first stone was laid in the city of Sodom. Now she understands why those two men were on duty at the lychgate. They'd been scrutinizing the gathering congregation for unfamiliar faces, outsiders, informers who would report what they'd heard to the Bishop of London. She smiles with pleasure at her minor triumph. It hadn't occurred to them that the only real spy they should be on the lookout for was a woman in a plain kirtle, a veil obscuring her features and an overdone Italian accent on her tongue.

As she makes for the lychgate again, Bianca sees Father Beauchêne at work pruning the ivy on the churchyard wall. When she calls to him and he turns, he is at first unable to recognize her.

'Why, Mistress Merton!' he says when she has removed her hood. 'What are you doing here?' He glances at the church. 'Surely you're not one of Montague's followers.'

Bianca takes the strand of ivy that Beauchêne is battling with, pulling it taut for him. The blade of his knife slices diagonally through the stem, leaving a sappy wound. 'A friend of mine has been coming here rather a lot when Parson Montague is preaching. I wanted to see what all the fuss was about.'

'Fuss? That's an understatement.'

'I take it you don't approve of Parson Montague.'

Beauchêne attacks another strand of ivy. He doesn't look at her. 'I had hoped the replacement parson would take away some of my more onerous duties. I didn't expect him to leave me with little to do but the gardening.'

'He's taken over?'

'More or less.'

'Who were those two fellows keeping watch at the lychgate when I arrived?' Bianca asks. 'Are they sextons?'

'No, they're acolytes of Montague's. They run errands for him, protect him if anyone has the temerity to object to his sermons – not that anyone does any more. I don't know where they come from, or where they go when the sermon is over. Montague won't tell me. In fact he appears to think I don't exist.'

'You mean they're his bodyguard?'

Beauchêne gives a surprised laugh, as if the idea has never occurred to him. 'I suppose you could say that. One's local, I believe. As for the other one, all Montague would tell me is that he's from Zurich.'

Somewhere north of Milan. I was right, Bianca thinks.

'Do you perchance know of a man named Petrus Schenk who prays here?' she asks.

Beauchêne breaks off from his work, lowering the knife until it rests against his right knee. 'Last time you were here, you were asking about Aksel Leezen. Today it's someone else. I'm beginning to think your visits aren't entirely concerned with religious devotion, Mistress Merton.'

'They're connected, in a manner of speaking.'

'How so?'

'This Petrus Schenk is lodging at Aksel's house – well, *my* house now.'

Beauchêne watches her, trying to read her face. 'Yes,' he says, 'I know Master Petrus.'

'Do you know him well?'

'No better than any of the other transients in the congregation. I seem to recall that he started attending church around the time Parson Montague took up his position.'

'Have you formed any opinion of Master Schenk, Father?'

'Should I have done?'

What can she tell him? That Petrus Eusebius Schenk troubles her? Father Beauchêne probably spends his days amongst troubled people. It's his calling in life to ease them of their troubles. But what power does he have to ease hers?

'I'm concerned for a friend of mine,' she tells him. 'Master Petrus brought him here to see Parson Montague preach, and now he can't seem to stay away.'

'I'll grant you, Parson Montague has an appeal to some of the more impressionable amongst the congregation,' Beauchêne says.

'Have you ever heard him cross the line between preaching and sedition?'

Beauchêne doesn't answer. He returns to his pruning.

'My friend is a gentle, simple soul,' Bianca tells the back of his head. 'He has had a hard life. On the surface he seems as strong as an oak, but at heart he's an innocent. I don't want him being led astray by wild sermonizing.'

At that moment Asher Montague emerges from the church porch, glances in their direction and disappears around the side of the church in the direction of the adjoining prior's house. Beauchêne turns to watch him go, giving Bianca only his profile. But she can see the priest's jaw stiffen with distaste.

'If he troubles you as much as I suspect, why don't you report him to the Bishop of London?' she asks.

'And give the Privy Council the excuse to shut down this place of worship, the way they shut down the Steelyard?' Beauchêne says. 'We are foreigners in this city, Mistress Merton. We live here on licence. Besides, you know what can happen to those who step beyond the limits set by the queen's religion. I would never deliver a man of God to such a fate – not even one as incendiary as Parson Montague.'

'Thank you,' Bianca says. 'I think you've told me what I need to know.'

Beauchêne turns to face her again. The shadow cast by the ivy-covered wall makes black brushstrokes of the furrows on his brow.

'If your friend is as impressionable as you say, Mistress, my advice to him would be to choose another church,' Beauchêne says under his breath, as though, even out of sight, Montague has the acute hearing of a wild animal in the forest. 'That man says he's spreading God's word. But if you care for my opinion, words from the wrong mouth may carry poison just as easily as they may carry the promise of salvation.'

✠

It is warm, and Bianca's hood is a trial she can do without. Having thrown it back during her troubling conversation with Beauchêne, she elects to let it lie about her shoulders as she walks through the lychgate and sets off back towards Bankside.

In her mind, she rehearses what she is going to say to Nicholas. Having witnessed Montague's fiery preaching, her concerns for Ned Monkton have now increased tenfold. The very last thing she wants is for Ned to suffer the same fate as Yeoman Shelby.

As she crosses Throgmorton Street, intending to turn down Finch Lane towards Gracechurch Street and so to the bridge, she stops dead in her tracks. On the opposite side of the street, walking in her direction, is the very man from whose attention Bianca has prepared so carefully to hide herself: Petrus Eusebius Schenk.

She freezes. How will she explain her presence here? Her hands scrabble for the hood and veil draped around her shoulders, but her fingers seem to have forgotten the shape of her own body. Should she call out a friendly greeting? Will he see the lie in her eyes? *Mercy! Master Petrus, what a coincidence – how are you settling into the Steelyard? I've just dropped off some curative distillations from my shop on Dice Lane at St Anthony's hospice, right there – on the corner...*

Her mouth dries as the words glue themselves to her tongue. He's going to notice her. He can't fail to.

A waggon piled high with bales of wool is coming the other way. It might provide enough cover for her to make the shelter of Finch Lane unobserved.

But even in her relief, her mind tells her that the waggon is slowing. The spokes of the wheels are barely moving. The horses are turning into statues before her eyes. Is it stopping? Or is fear playing tricks with time? Either way, Bianca is convinced it will never reach her in time.

And then her vision is full of canvas bales, and the sound of iron wheel-rims turning on the cobbles shocks her out of her panic-induced torpor. She sprints for the shadows at the entrance to the narrow alleyway, flattening herself against the wall of the first house she reaches. Gathering her breath, Bianca looks back over her shoulder.

Quite why, she will later be unable to say. It would have been so much wiser simply to put her head down and keep going. But then she would never have seen what happens next.

Perhaps it is because the troubling sermon has set her senses on edge. Perhaps Father Beauchêne has heightened her concerns. Or perhaps it really is the second sight in play – because she will later tell herself that she was sure something was going to happen, even as the wool cart passed out of her immediate view.

For a moment she thinks Petrus has seen her after all, because he is turning. He even beckons to her. And then she realizes that the subject of his interest isn't her at all, but a lad of around fifteen in a cream cloth jerkin, fair-haired and rosy. Petrus completes his turn. He faces the lad. They exchange a few words together. Bianca gets the impression that Petrus is asking where the boy is going, because the lad points in the general direction of Austin Friars. Then, as he resumes his journey, Petrus falls into step beside him. Bianca watches them disappear around the corner towards Capel Court.

What have I just observed? she asks herself. An innocent meeting or something else entirely? Because her mind has taken her back to that evening, not so very long ago, when she'd interrupted Petrus struggling with an unknown lad in the lane outside the Jackdaw. And now she's wondering if her assumption then had been correct. Had Petrus really been the target? What if, in fact, he'd been the attacker, and the skinny boy she'd seen fleeing in the direction of London Bridge the victim?

Have I witnessed another abduction?

The voice in her head doesn't want to believe it. But it can't compete with the Caporetti instinct racing in her heart. Petrus must be behind the disappearance of Hugh Mould, Gideon Trindle and Oliver Sly. And now there's a fourth name, as yet unknown, to add to the list.

21

On the far side of the courtyard, the door to the Jackdaw's brew-house lies ajar. Nicholas pushes it open and enters. At once he inhales the bucolic smell of hops, barley and the herbs that Bianca adds to the ale. Whenever he comes here, he imagines he has walked into Oberon's fairy bower.

And there is Ned Monkton, Oberon himself, perched on a throne of casks, making notes on a slate with some chalk. Even the characters he makes are like fairy symbols – Ned hasn't the writing and must use his own invented notation.

'Good morrow, Ned,' Nicholas says. 'Have you time for a word?'

Ned lays the slate and chalk on the top of a cask and slides down onto his feet. 'Aye, Master Nicholas. Always time for a word with you.'

'I've heard Parson Montague preach,' Nicholas begins uncomfortably, as though from a prepared script. 'I attended one of his sermons at Barnthorpe.'

Ned might be lacking in reading and writing, but he's no fool. 'An' you've come to give me a warnin', Master Nicholas?'

'Does it have to be a warning, Ned?'

'That depends on what you 'as to say next.'

Nicholas smiles at his own feet, feeling outsmarted already. 'As I say, I've watched and listened to Asher Montague – in Barnthorpe – and I have to say, he walks a very fine line.'

'Maybe he does raise the rafters a bit,' Ned admits. 'But shouldn't a good song be sung loud?'

'I thought Parson Montague disapproved of singing. Doesn't he think it's the Devil cackling?'

A conflicted frown passes over Ned's fiery features. It's not too late, Nicholas thinks. We haven't lost him yet. 'The point is, Ned,' he continues, 'Montague's preaching might be compelling, but it's also dangerous. My father ended up under the threat of losing a hand.'

'But that ain't Parson Mont'gue's fault, is it?'

'We're not suggesting that you're easily gulled, Ned. No one's saying that. But it's easy to get swept up by a high tide if you don't read the river right.'

''Oos this *we*, might I ask?'

'All of us, Ned. All of us who care about you. Me, Bianca, Rose...'

Ned scratches his great auburn beard. 'Well, I thanks you all for your concern, Master Nicholas. But Parson Montague 'as made me see things I 'adn't seen afore.'

'What things, Ned?' Nicholas asks, fearful of what lifting this particular stone is going to uncover.

''Ow those what call themselves our betters ain't our betters at all. God didn't set them over us, they put themselves there. An' they ain't got no right to it. In God's eyes, I'm as good a man as they.'

'No question of it, Ned,' Nicholas assures him. 'But have you heard the story of the Sirens?'

Whenever Ned looks puzzled, Nicholas is always reminded of a bear trying to work out how to get at the honey. He's wearing that expression now.

'They're characters in a myth from ancient Greece, Ned,' Nicholas explains. 'The Sirens were women with the most beautiful voices. They sang to passing sailors from the shore. The sailors were so bewitched by the loveliness of their song that they rowed closer – right onto the hidden rocks. Sometimes alluring songs are sung for a dark reason. Have you thought of that?'

But Ned is not persuaded.

'An' what if the fellow what owns this boat is forcin' these sailors to do the rowing? What if 'e's enslaved 'em? Wouldn't it be right for 'em to take their chances with the rocks? I reckon it'd be better to risk drownin' with a beauteous song in my ears than spendin' the rest of my days rowin' some rich bugger about.'

Nicholas cannot but agree with him, though he confines his response to a wry smile. He knows what Robert Cecil and the Privy Council would tell Ned Monkton, were he standing before them at this moment. He can almost hear them delivering their sentence: You have defied God's order. You have challenged the immutable structuring of man and woman according to His plan: monarchs, princes, bishops, lords, gentlemen… and at the very bottom, ordinary fellows like you. To seek to change it is not just a denial of authority, it is a denial of the Almighty's will. And such denial must be punished. Severely.

Knowing he sounds less like a friend and more like a schoolmaster, Nicholas says, 'Be cautious, Ned. There are some things we cannot change. And if someone tells you otherwise, they might not be doing so with your best interests in mind – however sweet the song.'

But as he leaves Ned Monkton to his work, Nicholas cannot help but think himself a coward, and wonder what happened to the young man who set off all those years ago to the Low Countries to help in the fight against imperious Spain, the seal on his medical degree barely set hard and the rage against cruelty and injustice burning bright in his heart. Where did you go? he asks himself. And what did you forget along the way?

In the days since her narrowly avoided encounter with Petrus at Austin Friars, Bianca has waged a losing battle with her suspicions. For Nicholas's sake she has tried to give him the benefit of the doubt. And for Ned's, too, because the growing bond between him and Petrus cannot be denied. But she has failed.

The result gives her no comfort. Suspicion is a sin. If the queen's bishops had not ruled the confessional to be nothing but a doorway to papist ritual – and thus prohibited – she would already have lightened her conscience with the help of a priest. But no matter how many times she tries to impose reason on her thoughts and admit her lack of actual physical evidence, Bianca has concluded that Petrus Eusebius Schenk is a monster.

There are just too many doubts in her mind to ignore.

First, there are those strange responses she'd noticed when Petrus passed apparently random strangers in the street. Cachorra and Nicholas have seen them, too. Hence they cannot be figments of her imagination.

Second, there's her conviction – based on his behaviour – that Petrus is hiding something.

Third, and most damning of all: no sooner does Schenk appear on Bankside than three lads go missing in quick succession. Bianca is almost sure now that she has witnessed Petrus attempt two other abductions: of the so-called purse-diver outside the Jackdaw, and of the unknown lad near Austin Friars.

Which brings her unavoidably back to her first damning observation – and tells her that what she and Cachorra had perceived in Petrus Eusebius Schenk was not some harmless quirk of a man's behaviour, but the conscious appraising of his next victim.

✠

'I'm not one for dissembling, Ned. May I speak plainly?'

Bianca has managed to contrive a moment alone with Ned Monkton at the Jackdaw. Rose is overseeing a repair to the bread-oven before the evening rush. She knows she doesn't have much time.

'I'd not wish it otherwise, Mistress,' Ned says, looking up from the leather tankard he's cleaning.

'Does Petrus ever make confession to you?'

'I don't know what you mean.'

'Does he ever tell you the sort of things he would only tell a priest, for instance. Or God?'

Ned looks confused.

'I mean, has he ever expressed any... any...' – Bianca struggles to find the words – 'any *desire* for young men?'

'Desire?' echoes Ned, the wall of his brow furrowing. ''Course he ain't. Sodomy's a crime punishable by death – 'less you're rich, of course. Then it's just readin' verse to each other.'

Wishing the earth would swallow her up, Bianca changes tack. 'When we were at the fair, at the nine-pins, I thought Petrus had said something that had made you angry with him. But I was wrong. It wasn't anger, it was agreement. What was he telling you?'

Ned might look like one of Bankside's bears, but he's too wise to be baited for long. 'Is this to be like that sermon Master Nicholas read me a while back in the brew-house, about Parson Mont'gue?'

Bianca sighs at being read so easily. 'Was it Parson Montague's preaching that Petrus was speaking about? Is it his sermonizing you were agreeing with? Was it his talk of injustice that was making you angry?'

'Petrus and Parson Mont'gue talk of things I ain't thought about afore,' Ned tells her, almost proudly. 'Things I should 'ave thought about.'

'Oh, Ned. I've heard this Montague preach. He might look like an angel, his words might cause a passion to burn in your heart, but he's *dangerous*.'

'What d'you mean by "dangerous"?'

'Men have gone to the scaffold for letting others lure them into misguided anger. You know that, Ned. For Rose's sake, if not mine, don't be one of them.'

For a moment Ned seems to her like a man on a riverbank watching two friends drowning, knowing he can only save one of them. He looks from her to his tankard, then back again. With pain in his eyes and a catch in his throat, he gives her a surprisingly formal look and says, 'I thank you for your concern, Mistress. An' Master Nicholas, too. You've done so much for me. I owe you both my life. But I owe God even more.'

⳨

Bianca plans the unmasking of Petrus Eusebius Schenk with all the caution of a seasoned general faced with a well-defended bastion. This will be no frontal assault with trumpets blaring and banners flying. She must use stealth and cunning. Curbing her impatience, she will wait until the next occasion when Petrus comes to take Ned Monkton to the Dutch church. A careful conversation with Ned confirms that will be four days hence. To her good fortune, it coincides with one of Nicholas's sessions at St Thomas's hospital.

In the meantime, she calculates how long it will take the two men to walk to Austin Friars, attend Asher Montague's sermon and for Petrus to return to the Steelyard. She assumes the lightest traffic on London Bridge and no lingering after the sermon. Experience tells her that she is being laughably cautious, but the last thing she wants is for Petrus to surprise her while she's in Aksel's house.

To minimize the risk of being seen, she decides to launch her sally not from the Jackdaw itself, but from the Dice Lane shop. The night before, she will entrust Rose with the task of letting Bianca know that Ned and Petrus have left the Jackdaw. That will give her time to take up position at the end of Dice Lane and mark her quarry from a safe distance as they make their way to the bridge. There will no repeat of the incident on Throgmorton Street. If the worst were to happen and either man were to spot her, she will say she is on her way to see a merchant at Petty Wales by the Tower because she's running low on some ingredient or other. Once she is sure Petrus is leading Ned north towards Austin Friars, she will take Stockfishmongers' Row west towards the Steelyard.

What does she expect to find in Aksel Leezen's house? Her imagination paints an ever more lurid procession of tableaux. Petrus has filled it with child slaves... Petrus is running a harem of young catamites... Petrus has buried the bodies of the three missing lads beneath the storeroom floor... The culvert is filled with the floating bodies of his victims, bobbing like apples in a tub on All Hallows' Eve...

'What's wrong, sweet?' Nicholas asks when her silent night-time fretting wakes him.

She prays he won't notice the dampness her sweat has left on the bed sheet. 'It's nothing, Husband,' she tells him. And hates herself for lying to him.

✠

The day before the planned assault, Nicholas and Bianca take their Jackdaw family to the Globe playhouse. The Lord Chamberlain's Men are performing *The Tragedy of Julius Caesar*. Petrus comes, too. Bianca would prefer to watch a comedy, but little Bruno, Ned and Rose are up for a gory assassination, and

Will Shakespeare has reserved them good seats. Bruno, though he's only five and too young to fully understand what's going on, is by no means the only child in the audience. He cheers loudly when the tyrant falls, taking his cue from Ned and Petrus, whose approval, to Bianca's mind, is a little too enthusiastic. Glancing at her husband's friend, she notices that his face is flushed with excitement, as if he's imagining himself among the assassins, revelling in the frenzied stabbing. He seems utterly engrossed. I'm right, she thinks. I know I'm right.

Cachorra, who is still getting used to the excitement of the English playhouse, is astounded during the storm scene when thunder rolls around the theatre and lightning flashes, even though she has only to look up to see an almost clear sky.

'It was a cannonball in an oblong wooden box set on a small seesaw, hidden away above the stage,' Nicholas tells her afterwards. 'And the lightning is made by firecrackers sliding down a cable.'

'How ingenious the English are,' Cachorra exclaims appreciatively, 'to make bad weather even when the sun is shining.'

Petrus, however, has another perspective, one that sends a cold chill through Bianca's blood as she overhears it.

'The young lads who played Calpurnia and Portia,' he observes to no one in particular, 'were so artfully done that I could have sworn they were truly women.' He turns his gaze on the audience standing in the pit. And as Bianca watches, his face darkens and he begins to whisper a passage that she assumes is from the Bible. 'Neither shalt a man put on a woman's raiment, for all that do so are an abomination unto the Lord thy God.'

She thinks she's heard it before. But it is not until later that night, lying in bed beside a sleeping Nicholas, that she remembers where. It had been in Padua. After Mass one Sunday – she would have been around thirteen – when Father Rossi had railed against the young men who dressed as women to sell themselves to strangers behind the Palazzo Bo. It was a passage from the Book of Deuteronomy.

✠

Bianca finds the first part of her plan easier than she had expected. To begin with, all goes well. Rose arrives at the Dice Lane shop shortly after the St Saviour's bell chimes the eighth hour, with news that Ned and Petrus have left for Austin Friars.

'Why did you want to know?' she asks. 'You were most insistent last night. "The very moment they leave" – that's what you said.'

'I needed to hear they were on their way, Rose. I want to search Aksel's house while Petrus is away. I didn't want to risk following him from the Jackdaw in case he saw me.'

'I *knew* it would be something like that,' Rose says with a conspiratorial grimace. 'I've never trusted that Petrus. There's being God-fearin' and there's using piety as a mask. An' I know which is which.'

'Well, let's see what I discover at Aksel's house,' Bianca says, heading for the door and waving the keys she's brought from the Paris Garden lodgings.

'How long will you be gone?' Cachorra asks from behind the shop's mixing table.

'I'll be back before they return from Austin Friars,' Bianca says. She pauses before stepping into the lane and looks back at her two friends. 'If all goes well, we'll soon have Master Schenk trussed up like a Michaelmas goose. Then we can start work on breaking his hold over poor Ned.'

✠

She spots the two men almost exactly where she'd expected to, near the ruins of the Bishop of Rochester's lodgings, close to the Winchester water-stairs. All she needs to do now is stay well back, using the city traffic for cover, and follow the summit of Mount Monkton striding purposefully in the distance. It won't be difficult. Ned is a good head higher than anyone else walking the city streets at this hour.

She manages to remain unseen all the way to the junction of Fish Street Hill and Thames Street. Flattening herself into the shadows of the Fishmongers' guildhall, she watches Ned and Petrus continue their journey northwards, until even Ned is lost to sight. Then, no longer in need of caution, she hurries west into Stockfishmongers' Row. In well under half an hour after leaving Dice Lane, Bianca halts outside the house Aksel bequeathed her.

The Steelyard is deserted as far as she can tell. Summer seems to have joined her in this secretive enterprise. It has hidden itself, too. The sky is corpse-grey and a brisk wind off the river sends dust-devils swirling in angry eddies down the narrow cobbled lanes of the former Hansa compound. Even the few vagrants living here seem to have vanished. A solitary mangy cat hunts in the drain-ditches, watched by the ossified skeletons of the wooden cranes along the wharf. Out on the river the bargemen brace themselves against their oars. The wherries and tilt-boats plying cross-current are having a hard time of it, their passengers draped over the gunwales like wilting flowers as they add their spew to the general filth of the river.

Taking the keys from her chatelaine belt, Bianca inserts one into the original lock and turns it. Then she uses the second on the lock that the Lord Mayor's men installed while they waited to see if Aksel, even in death, owed them any taxes he had forgotten to pay. She steps into the darkened ground-floor storeroom.

✠

‘Could it ever possibly come ’bout?’ Ned Monkton asks. ‘A fellow like me standin’ afore God with the same chance of salvation as the Bish’p of London? Or Sir Robert Cecil? Or the queen ’erself?’ He lowers his eyes towards the downy head of Petrus Schenk with the wonder-filled eyes of a child. The two men are striding up Gracechurch Street towards Austin Friars, Ned every now and then making a little shuffle to shorten his stride so that Petrus can keep up.

‘We believe it so, Ned. In God’s eyes, we’re just the same: all sinners.’

‘I’ve tried not to sin, Petrus – fuck knows I ’ave.’ Ned puts his hand to his mouth. ‘Sorry. Cursin’s a sin too, ain’t it?’

Petrus looks up and gives him an angel’s smile. ‘God sees how plain men like you and I are driven to sin by those who think themselves our betters. These men talk about God’s order, about how we are placed in rank according to His wishes, but they lie. They put themselves up as false gods to confuse us, to trick us into subservience. You’ve understood what Parson Montague has explained to us in the privy sermons that, in his generosity, he’s allowed us, haven’t you?’

‘Aye. But I ain’t understood *all* of it.’

‘But you will, Ned. You will, one day. And on that day, you and I shall stand side-by-side in the battle of the good man against the tyrant. Are you up for that, Ned?’

And Ned, imagining in his mind the bloodstained body of Julius Caesar falling beneath the daggers of the just, swears silently in his head that he is ready. More than ready.

✠

The same smell of pitch, hemp, old timber and abandonment. The same sepulchral stink of river that wells between the flagstones and up from the hatch to the culvert. Bianca stands in the semi-darkness and wonders how she could ever have thought Aksel's gift was anything but a test of her nerve, a monstrous burden she could do without. I'll get rid of it, she tells herself. I'll sell it to anyone who'll have it. I'll even give it away – as soon as I know the truth. A scuttling in the gloom tells her the rats are still in residence. A dreadful image forces its way into her mind: the culvert seething with them as they feast on the corpses of Gideon Trindle, Hugh Mould and Oliver Sly.

She forces herself to approach the trapdoor, unlocks the bolt and raises the hatch a few inches, certain she is going to hear the crunch of rodent teeth gnawing on human bone.

All she hears is the lapping of water at the bottom of the ladder.

Perhaps he dropped them off the wharf at high tide. Surely, then, at least one would have washed up on the riverbank.

But how would I know? Who would tell me? Bodies turn up along the Thames almost every day – drunkards falling in, mariners slipping off barques, victims of quarrels, robberies or neglect... No one thinks of passing the news to Bianca Merton. It is only when a corpse turns up in the river mud of your own parish that word spreads.

Perhaps he's got them locked in the bedchamber, upstairs. But then she remembers Petrus doesn't have a key for the bedroom with the effigy of the child in it. Besides, if she stands very still, holds her breath and tries to calm the thumping of her heart, she can hear no movement above the ceiling beams.

Perhaps he's killed them and spends his time here living beside their decomposing corpses. She shudders. To find out if she's right, she will have to climb the stairs.

Bianca is halfway up when her rational self tells her she's a fool. If there were bodies here, the stench of human decay would be as heavy as the mist that sometimes hides one bank of the Thames from the other.

A pale wash of light floats down like an apparition from the top of the stairs. The upper-floor windows are unshuttered. Surely an abductor – a murderer – wouldn't go about his business with the windows letting in the light.

A sudden creak beneath her feet brings the fear jumping into Bianca's throat like the sudden sour taste of rising bile.

Get a grip of yourself – it's just a loose board.

Reaching the living chamber, Bianca sees its current occupier has added not a touch of his own presence. The space still has the bare, ascetic simplicity of a monk's cell. The few domestic utensils she gave Petrus lie by the hearth. Looking into the sleeping chamber, she sees the bed is neatly made.

Neatness, caution. Laudable in some, proof of deceit in others. You can't abduct three lads and keep them – or their bodies – hidden without paying attention to detail.

The compunction to check the locked second bedroom comes over her like a fierce venom flowing into her body from a serpent's fangs. It is impossible to fight. It can have only one end: the entire paralysis of her will to resist. Even as she approaches the door, she knows there is no reason to think Petrus has ever entered it. He has no key.

So why can I not stop myself?

The key turns in the lock almost by its own agency, as though the room wants her to enter. She pushes cautiously at the door, though she knows there can be no one inside – except perhaps the ghost of the young lad whose body Nicholas discovered in the culvert.

Bianca steps inside.

The room is as cold as an ice-house. The wind off the river has somehow found a way through the plaster-and-lath walls, biting its way into Aksel's house, spilling up through the floorboards as though the river was in flood. She shivers.

The effigy of the little girl still lies by the bolster of the bed, just where Bianca had left it. The flat, painted eyes seem to regard her with disappointment. She half-expects the unfinished part – the left cheek, ear and brow up to the hairline – to colour itself in as she watches, making a complete living face.

Welcome back. I thought you'd forgotten me.

And then Bianca feels the scream rise out of her lungs.

The little girl is not alone.

Ranged on the floor around her are six other children, three on either side, like infant mourners around a deathbed. Two girls, four boys, their flat, dull features executed in the same style as that of the girl on the bed. Bianca feels their painted eyes boring into her.

Where have you been? they seem to be saying to her. *We've been waiting.*

PART 3

✠

Exits and Entrances

22

Bianca feels no triumph as she stands before Nicholas in the parlour of the Paris Garden lodgings, breathless from her journey back from the Steelyard. Her face is flushed, her hair awry; she is certain that every person she passed on the way here must have believed she was either distraught or insane. The wherryman who picked her up at the foot of Dowgate Street and brought her across to the Mutton Lane water-stairs asked if she was fleeing a violent lover and whether she needed protecting.

'It's alright,' Nicholas says soothingly. 'Calm yourself. Take a while and then tell me all that again. I caught about one word in six.'

'I need a glass of malmsey,' she says with an outrush of breath.

Nicholas takes her by the shoulders and gently pushes her down into a chair. He fetches a clay bottle and two glasses from the Flanders sideboard and pours two good measures. Bianca keeps gulping until the sweetness of the wine steadies her tremors. Then she holds out the glass for a refill.

'I tried to warn you,' she says. 'I *knew* there was something troubling about your friend. But you wouldn't listen to me.'

Nicholas gives her a consolatory look. 'I'll ignore that you went behind my back to spy on Petrus. But start from the beginning again.'

Bianca drains the second glass almost as quickly as the first. She tries to compose herself, with only limited success. She tells him again of her growing doubts about Petrus, his story, his behaviour, his mystery. She recounts her visit to the Steelyard. But when she comes to the point where she had entered that second chamber, her voice almost breaks.

'It's obscene! Petrus has made himself an entire crypt of painted effigies, all like the one Ned and I found. All children, arrayed together like a tableau of the dead – in a *locked* chamber. I didn't give him a key, Nicholas. And I certainly didn't say to him, "Feel free, pick the lock, set out your monstrous satanic pageant in the spare sleeping chamber of Aksel's house." It's a damning discovery, whichever way you look at it. Especially if you consider that we also found a body there!'

'Slow yourself, sweet,' Nicholas says, trying to calm her. 'Petrus can't have had anything to do with that. The body had been there a while, and Petrus hasn't been in England before.'

But his soothing only makes Bianca more determined. 'That's what *he* told you. How do we know he's not lying? How do we know he's not responsible for the disappearance of those three lads?'

'Now you're just being irrational. You didn't find any trace of them at the Steelyard, did you? Go on, admit it.'

'No. But that doesn't mean—'

'If you didn't give Petrus a key to that chamber, then how did he get in?'

'Perhaps he picked the lock.'

'And *un*picked it afterwards? You said it was locked.'

'He must have got hold of a key. *Somehow.* Why are you defending him?'

'Because Petrus is my friend.'

'A friend who breaks into a locked room and turns it into a sepulchre?'

Nicholas shakes his head in disbelief. 'I'm sure Petrus will have an explanation.'

Bianca feels the chain keeping her emotions anchored begin to fail. 'An explanation! What sort of explanation? That he's a practitioner of the dark arts? A necromancer?'

'That's not the Petrus I know.'

'Nicholas, you don't *know* him at all. And I don't know how he came by those awful effigies, but he must be responsible for the first one, too. Which means Petrus must have visited Aksel's house in the past, even though he claims never to have been in England before.'

She pauses to force an order on the competing terrors swirling in her thoughts. 'Perhaps it was Petrus who put those awful écorché figures there. He's probably responsible for killing that lad you found in the culvert. And as for Oliver Sly, Hugh Mould and Gideon Trindle—' Bianca's hands fly to her eyes, to shut out the horrible image that has sprung into her mind. 'Face it, Nicholas! Your friend murders people, then makes effigies of the dead like trophies.' Removing her hands from her face, she gives Nicholas a look that is colder than any she has ever given him. 'Who is he going to stare at next, Nicholas? Our Bruno?'

Nicholas waits until he thinks it safe to speak.

'You probably won't understand this, but Petrus and I have faced hardship and danger together. We have experienced the worst of human folly and cruelty. We have a friendship forged in battle and adversity. I once saw him weep over a dog the Spanish had slaughtered alongside the Dutch Protestant family whose pet it was. He was as grieved by that as he was at the human suffering. He goes to church. He wants a better world than the one in which we live. Petrus *isn't* a murderer. I'm sure of it.'

'I'm going to see Constable Osborne,' Bianca says harshly. 'You've befriended a monster.'

'Once a parish law officer is involved there will be no going back for any of us,' he cautions. 'If we hand over Petrus to the queen's law without being certain, we could be delivering an innocent man to the hangman's noose.'

'Christ's holy blood, Nicholas! What more do I have to do before you see the truth?'

Unable to withstand her vehemence, Nicholas concedes ground. 'Very well. But we must challenge him ourselves. And we must allow Petrus to defend himself. That's how a friend would behave to another.'

'That's how a *fool* would behave,' Bianca snaps.

Nicholas does not rise to her bait. He says calmly, 'If appearing a fool saves a friend from the noose, then I'm happy to be called foolish. But if he admits it – if you're proved right – then we'll hand Petrus over to Constable Osborne.'

Bianca looks directly into Nicholas's eyes, even though she's afraid that her own have become too much of a mirror glass for her emotions. 'God help you if another lad goes missing before then,' she whispers. 'And from now on, I'm not letting him anywhere near Bruno.'

✠

The final unmasking of Petrus Eusebius Schenk takes place two afternoons later. Petrus and Ned return from one of their private sermons with Parson Montague at Austin Friars. The taproom at the Jackdaw is almost empty. Bianca has primed Rose to draw Ned away by raising a fictitious query about the tavern's accounts. But she wants him in sight, just in case. When he's moved off, she and Nicholas slide into the booth where Petrus is sitting in quiet contemplation over a cheap pamphlet of passages from the scriptures.

'We need to speak to you,' Nicholas says, facing his friend from the opposite bench.

'How may I serve you?' Petrus asks innocently.

Bianca has brought a cup of small-beer with her. She slides it across the table. 'I know you don't really care for this, Petrus, and that you only sup to fit in around here. But you might need this after you hear what we have to say.'

Schenk's gaze flits from her to Nicholas, as if seeking an ally, then back to Bianca. 'What is this about? What's the matter?'

Bianca takes a steadying breath and launches her assault, carefully at first, as if to test the mettle of his defences.

'Petrus, I went to the Steelyard yesterday, while you were with Ned at the Dutch church—'

His fallen-angel eyes hold hers for a moment.

'You were *spying* on me?'

'It's my house, Petrus. I can go there when I choose.'

'And you chose a time when I was elsewhere. How thoughtful of you not to trouble me.'

There's nothing for it now, Bianca thinks, other than to storm the breach. 'I suspect you know what I found there – in a chamber that I know for a fact was locked.'

'I wish I did,' says Petrus, taking a slow pull at his ale to show how untroubled he is. 'But you'll have to tell me. I'm a simple Hessian. I've never understood the appeal of riddles.'

'If anyone is perplexed by a riddle, Petrus, it is us,' Bianca says. 'Can you explain the presence of painted images of children, hidden away in a chamber to which you don't have a key?'

'If I don't have a key to this chamber, how can I?'

Nicholas looks on as if he were a bystander in a street quarrel, unsure where his aid should be directed.

'Please don't try to tell me you don't know what I'm talking about,' says Bianca. 'We're not green-pates, Petrus.'

'You didn't lock the door, Mistress Bianca. How else could I have entered?'

'So, you admit it?'

For a moment, Schenk says nothing. Again his eyes shift from Bianca to Nicholas. But this time Nicholas does not return his gaze. 'I think you should answer Bianca's questions honestly, Petrus,' he says. 'I'm deeply troubled by what she has told me – what she found in that chamber.'

Petrus gives him a brittle smile. 'My old friend from the field of battle distrusts me because his wife has a suspicious nature?'

Bianca cuts in angrily. 'Master Petrus, you do me a dishonour. When you came here, I welcomed you. I took pity on your plight. I gave you free lodging. And in return you've played loose with my charity, deceived my husband and sought to poison the mind of a dear friend with seditious mischief. Admit that those images are yours?'

Petrus takes a slow draught of beer. Bianca cannot tell if he has confession or denial in mind. Or whether he's planning to hurl the cup at her and make a run for it.

'There are three young lads missing,' she says coldly.

'And you think I have something to do with that?' Petrus says, his eyes widening.

'I must tell you that I've watched your head turn when sometimes you see a youth pass by in the street. Nicholas has seen it, too. So has Cachorra. I even saw you engage in conversation with one, near Austin Friars. You led him away towards Capel Court. Where were you taking him – to join Gideon, Hugh and Oliver? Are they even alive? Petrus, *what* have you done?'

Again Petrus remains silent. Like a supplicant at an altar, he lays down his cup and steeples his fingers in front of his face, as if he's about to start praying. His expression has taken on the look of a suffering cherub.

'Yes,' he says, 'the effigies – they're mine.'

To Bianca, her own intake of breath sounds like a rushing wind. She stares at Petrus, challenging him to continue.

'I carry them with me in my pack wherever I go,' he says softly to the printed pamphlet in front of him. 'They are my family. There are my ghosts.'

'Ghosts?' Nicholas enquires, his eyes locked on his friend.

'You know what Holland was like, Nicholas – the bestiality that is the truth behind the supposed glory of war. You were there.'

'Yes, I was,' Nicholas replies. The forlorn hopelessness in his friend's eyes catches him like a blade thrust between the ribs.

'Well, after you left, as I told you, it got worse. Much worse.'

'You have to explain, Petrus,' Nicholas says, 'for everyone's sake.'

'You were able to leave, Nicholas,' Petrus continues. 'You could turn your back upon the Low Countries and leave the ghosts behind. I could not. They began to follow me wherever I went. They would never let me rest. In the end I had to give them shape and form, accept them, invite them to travel with me wherever I went – become my family. I contrived to make images of those who were foremost in my mind, the ones I'd seen before decay turned their faces into something I couldn't bear to see. It was easy enough. I have a little skill with saw, knife and a paintbrush. They're of little weight, barely heavier than the souls they represent. It is no burden for me to carry them.'

'Do you mean these images are memories? Memento mori?' asks Bianca.

'They are my atonement. I carry them with me so that I can be certain I will never forget.'

'But you have nothing to blame yourself for, Petrus,' Nicholas says. 'You were an honourable soldier. Your cause was just.'

Petrus gives a cruel laugh. 'Is that what you believe? Our princes and our generals were no better than the papists. I know the Spanish were monsters, but we dealt out our own share of the monstrous. We burned Catholic churches. We crucified the priests. We drove Catholics from their houses, hanged them from trees like unpicked fruit left to rot in the sun. And we killed their children, too. How many infants on the ends of pitchforks does a man need to see before the ghosts of those he's slain begin to keep him company even when he's awake?'

'Is *that* what you're seeing in the street – when your head turns?' Bianca asks, every certainty her imagination has contrived over the past weeks turned into a cold stone of guilt in her heart.

'*Every* day,' Petrus says, now close to tears. 'I can tell you this, Mistress Bianca, I don't need darkness to see apparitions.'

'But the first image of the child – the one that was in the room before you came. Explain that to me, if you've never been in England until now.'

With a hurt smile he says, 'I knew of Aksel Leezen before I came here. We're both from Hesse. My father sent hemp to him, for resale in England. When I heard he had lost his wife and daughter to the pestilence, I made him one of my ghosts and sent it to him as consolation.'

'Did you know we found a body,' Nicholas adds, 'inside the culvert under the wharf?'

'A body, you say?' replies Petrus, looking like the mould from which innocence was cast.

'You know nothing about that?' Bianca enquires.

'How could I? I've never been in Leezen's house before.'

'And how did you get into the chamber?'

'The door was unlocked.'

Bianca frowns. 'I'm sure I locked it,' she says, surprised by the pique in her voice. She looks at Nicholas for support. 'I *know* I did – after that dreadful fellow Dankyn and the watch removed the body.'

'We were troubled by what had happened, sweet,' Nicholas says evenly. 'It would have been an easy mistake to make. It's of no consequence.'

'There are still three young lads missing, Petrus,' Bianca says defensively. 'What about the lad I saw you with by Capel Court? And that supposed robbery in the lane outside – who was really being attacked?'

Petrus's mouth gapes in hurt astonishment. 'The lad you saw serves at the Dutch church. I happened to encounter him on the way there. Did you see him protest? Did he struggle?'

'No, I didn't, but...' Bianca senses the heat spreading across her cheeks.

Petrus points to the door. 'And what you saw out there was me getting assaulted in this godless city of yours.'

Nicholas speaks, his voice sounding like a judge dismissing a badly argued case. 'I was sure you'd have an answer to these charges, Petrus. I'm so sorry we doubted you – that Bianca doubted you. I know myself what grief can do to a man.'

In Bianca's mind the doubt turns to anger. *Stai mentendo! Ingannatore! Bugiardo!* She is convinced the man sitting before her is as trustworthy as Lucifer's arse-wiper. If a dressmaker had offered her a kirtle with that many holes in it, she'd have thrown it back. She is about to say so when a shadow falls over the table and a familiar voice stops her in her tracks, a voice she knows well. A voice familiar to her from the taproom and the Bankside playhouses.

'Mistress Kate, I hope I am not intruding in something privy.'

Looking up, she sees Master Will Shakespeare standing in the entrance to the booth. She composes herself, smoothing the top of her gown as though she's been caught in an indiscretion behind the bushes.

'Master Will, I'm afraid now is a very poor time. If it's ale or victuals you're in search of, I'm sure Rose will take care of you.'

'I've come because of Oliver Sly,' he says. 'You insisted you wanted to know if there was news—'

Jesu, they've found his body, Bianca thinks. Perhaps they've found all three. I was right all along.

'You'll be glad to hear he's safe,' Will Shakespeare says. 'Him and the two lads with him. I did hear their names, but they're not known to me. Trundle and Mildew, something like that.'

'Gideon Trindle and Hugh Mould,' Nicholas says, though Bianca is sure there must be something wrong with her ears, because her imagination is refusing point-blank to accept what it's hearing.

'That's it. They're the ones.'

'Where were they?' Bianca hears Nicholas ask.

Shakespeare jabs a finger over his shoulder in the general direction of the north bank of the river.

'Blackfriars. Those rogues at the playhouse there have been taking young lads off the street to appear on-stage and serve the patrons their ale and oysters. They cited the Privy Council's letters patent permitting the master of the Chapel Royal to enlist boys for the queen's revels. Thought they'd get away with it, too, the scoundrels. Dick Burbage had to get a warrant from the magistrate enforcing Sly's release, or else he'd still be there – and the others. It's an outrage, that's what it is.'

'Abduction most assuredly is,' Nicholas agrees.

'No,' says Will Shakespeare. 'I meant poor Sly having to perform with that bunch of talentless wastrels at Blackfriars. Now, how about a jug of knock-down and a coney pie to celebrate their safe return?'

✠

Nicholas has said barely a word to her since what Bianca has decided to call 'the catastrophe'. Petrus himself has responded with hurt detachment and a contrived politeness that she finds almost insulting. She has never felt so humiliated.

Lying in bed, with Nicholas's back towards her, his breathing slow and measured as if he were trying to subdue his anger, she recounts in her mind the foundations on which she had built her premise. Even now they seem to her unassailable. Yet Schenk has demolished every single one.

'I'm truly sorry,' she says to the darkness.

For a moment Nicholas does not answer.

Are you asleep? Or are you punishing me?

At length he murmurs, 'You've said so to Petrus. For our friendship's sake, let's hope he believes it.'

Whose friendship do you mean? Yours or ours?

'I don't know what else to say.'

'Then best say nothing.'

If that's what will make you happy...

Unable to sleep, Bianca lets her mind return to the Jackdaw's taproom. She imagines herself and Schenk facing each other across the table-board. Nicholas and Will Shakespeare are elsewhere, somewhere undefined, distant. Steadying her breathing, she throws her accusations at him once more – not like a hurried handful of dirt snatched from the ground, but each one a carefully chosen and well-aimed stone.

Not one of them punctures his smooth exterior. They bounce off Petrus Eusebius Schenk as if he himself were made of granite. They don't even break the sanctimonious smile he wears.

Yet even in defeat, Bianca tells herself she is still her mother's daughter, and generations of her line have gone to their maker convinced they would trust the fabled Caporetti second sight over anything a man might tell them, however plausible it sounds.

23

Ned Monkton towers over Asher Montague. Yet there is no mistaking who is the teacher and who the pupil. Ned is on his knees before the altar at the Dutch church at Austin Friars, his great head bowed, his auburn beard spread across his chest like a pelt. It is the day after the confrontation in the Jackdaw. The sunlight slants through the windows and onto Ned as though it shines only for him and the priest and, as far as God is concerned, the rest of the world can spend its days in darkness. Montague has his hand on Ned's right shoulder. They have just this moment said their amens after Montague has recited the Lord's Prayer. Ned feels closer to the divine than at any time in his life.

'A soldier for the Lord must be a practical man,' Montague tells him after an appropriate silence. 'He must be observant, always on the watch for sin. The Devil is clever at hiding his dung. But a righteous nose will always sniff it out. Can you sniff, Ned Monkton?'

Ned has never considered sniffing the Devil's dung in the service of God. But he's a Banksider, and there are stenches there enough for a man with nostrils a foot wide. 'I reckon so, Parson,' he says proudly.

'Then let us see how observant you truly are. Let us put your memory to the test. The Lord needs His warriors to have a good memory.'

'Long as you don't ask me to write nothin' down,' Ned says humbly. 'I 'aven't the skill at it.'

'No writing needed, Ned,' Montague replies. 'Your strength will lie in the reliability of your mind.' He lifts his hand to tap his own boyish forehead, indicating where this arsenal for the Lord's coming battle may be found. 'Now, let us begin. You spent some time at Nonsuch Palace, I understand from Master Schenk.'

'I did, Parson – me an' Rose, when the pestilence came in '93. Dr Shelby arranged for us to shelter there.'

'Good. Then Nonsuch will be our test,' Montague says. Then, almost as an afterthought, 'You can test the answers you give against the true facts, when you return there for the revels for the Moor ambassador – see how much you've got right.'

''Ow do you know about that?' Ned asks, surprised.

'God knows everything, Ned. Let us begin with the layout of the palace. How many floors are there in the outer gatehouse and how are they reached?'

✠

When Ned steps out of the church, Petrus is waiting for him, leaning against a headstone.

'How did you do, Ned?'

He grins. 'Right well, accordin' to Parson Montague.' Then his face clouds over. 'But I's not sure I should be tellin' things what Master Nicholas 'as said to me. I don't know as 'e'd want me to.'

'You need not fear, Ned,' Petrus assures him. 'There are no secrets a man can keep from the Almighty. And Parson Montague is doing His work, just as you are.'

'Master Nicholas isn't 'appy that I'm coming 'ere,' Ned says, his eyes betraying the struggle going on inside him. 'Nor is my Rose. I don't like keepin' things from people.'

Petrus moves away from the headstone. He puts his hand over Ned's, like a parent soothing a child. It covers barely half. '"A seduced heart hath deceived him, that he cannot deliver his soul, nor say, Is there not a lie in my right hand?"'

'From the Bible?' Ned says. He doesn't know why. Almost everything Petrus and Parson Montague say is from the Holy Book.

'From the Book of Isaiah.'

Ned repeats the quotation in his head, hoping its meaning might become a little clearer. But like so many of the passages that Petrus and Asher Montague have read to him since he started coming to Austin Friars, the refreshing water in the brook is a little too muddied for him to see the bottom clearly.

✠

'I've never felt so awful in my life,' Bianca tells Cachorra in the shop at Dice Lane. 'When Will Shakespeare delivered the coup de grâce, I didn't know where to look. Petrus was all for quitting the house in the Steelyard, because I'd dared to doubt him. I had to grovel, insist that he stay. Otherwise, Nicholas would have thought I had a vendetta against him.'

'And have you? After all, those lads are all safe and returned.'

'I just want Nicholas to accept the truth: Schenk is lying to us. The problem is, I don't know about what.'

'Then how can you be sure?'

'That dreadful image of the little girl – the first one, the one he claimed he sent to my friend Aksel as a commiseration – it doesn't have the right hair colour. Aksel's daughter's hair was blonde, not dark. And the effigy wasn't even finished. Who in their right mind would send an uncompleted memento mori? What's more, I think Petrus has been to the house before, even though he says he hasn't. I know I locked the second bedchamber. He must have already had a key. And who would give him that, save for Aksel himself? Because I certainly didn't.'

Cachorra is crushing a sprig of wood-sage for a distillation that Bianca is making to ease the discomfort of Widow Blundell's ulcerous left shin. She lays the herb and the pestle aside. 'But what do you do about it?' she asks. 'If you ask these things to Master Petrus's face, your husband will...' Searching for the correct English word and failing, she makes an explosive gesture with her hands. 'He will... *explotará!*'

'Nicholas will indeed *explotará*,' Bianca replies. 'So I must be cautious.'

And caution, she thinks, will require enlisting someone who knows how to keep a confidence. Someone like a lawyer, for instance. A lawyer who dealt with Aksel Leezen's Will. A certain lawyer from the Consistory Court.

✠

The Austin Friars lychgate is unguarded, no sign of the two men who had stopped her the last time she was here. Bianca finds Father Beauchêne alone in the vestry. The air is sultry. It carries the dry, mineral scent of a mason's workshop, as if the old stones are slowly leaching out the dusty breath of centuries.

'Yes, of course I recall Master Woolrich. He and I had many conversations on the matter of Aksel Leezen's Will. Why do you wish to speak to him? Don't tell me there's another problem with the bequest. I thought that was all settled.'

'No, there's no problem,' Bianca assures him. 'I'm interested in the history of the house – who lived there before Aksel came. Now that the Hansa merchants have all gone, there's no one to ask.'

'Then ask the parish,' suggests Beauchêne helpfully. 'The house will have been assessed for tax. Look at the Subsidy Rolls. They should tell you who was living there.'

'I've had experience of asking parish officers for help before. It's hard enough on Bankside; Dowgate will be ten times as hard. I can hear them now: *It is not a woman's place to scrutinize parish records. Away with you! Back to your embroidery.* No, I need a lawyer.'

Beauchêne's face creases into an understanding smile. 'The Consistory Court abides with the High Court of the Admiralty and the Court of Arches by St Paul's. There's a large stone building to the west, where the lawyers work and lodge. It's called the Doctors' Commons. You can't miss it. You might find Master Woolrich there.'

'Thank you, Father Beauchêne, that's most helpful.'

'Of course he could be at Canterbury.'

'Canterbury – in Kent?'

Beauchêne wrings his hands apologetically. 'The London Consistory Court falls under the jurisdiction of Archbishop Whitgift,' he explains. 'That is where most of the court's business is transacted. You'll have to take your chances, I'm afraid.'

✠

Bianca arrives at the Doctors' Commons as St Paul's bell rings the second hour of the afternoon. Just as Father Beauchêne told her, the building is easy to find, its imposing stone frontage standing out amongst the huddle of timbered houses on the Ludgate Hill side of the church. Ignoring the glances of the lawyers taking their ease around the entrance in the sunshine, she marches in.

'Master Woolrich, you say?' intones an elderly clerk, the bone frames of his reading spectacles pinched against each nostril. 'I shall have to see if he's in his chamber. Is he expecting?'

'Not unless he's been keeping a very great secret from you.'

The clerk adjusts his lenses. He stares at her blankly with weary, moist eyes. 'I beg your pardon?'

'It was a joke. If he was *expecting*...' She gives up. 'Never mind. Would you tell him that Mistress Bianca Merton wishes to see him, about a house left to her in a Will.'

She waits until her right foot decides on its own account to start tapping the floor, conscious of a slow gathering of lawyers come to peer at the woman with the crown of dark hair and the amber eyes, who is standing in their Commons with all the studied dignity of the Attorney General himself.

'You're out of luck,' says the clerk when he returns. 'Master Woolrich is at Canterbury. Perhaps you would care to leave a letter for him. Can you write, or would you like me to take down the words on your behalf? There would be a scrivener's fee, of course.'

Biting her tongue, Bianca writes a brief note to Master Woolrich and – determined not to let the disappointment show on her face – strides imperiously past the gawping lawyers towards St Andrew's Hill and then onwards along Thames Street towards the bridge and home.

24

It is the height of summer, but in the Paris Garden lodgings there is a lingering frost. Nicholas is almost glad when Robert Cecil calls him to the Strand to discuss the arrival of Muhammed al-Annuri. It is over a decade since the first, unofficial visit to London by envoys of the Moroccan sultan. Memories require refreshing. Half the Privy Council is there.

'What manner of ceremony will the ambassador expect when the ship carrying him anchors in Dover harbour?' asks the Lord Chief Justice, Sir John Popham. 'Would a Moor consider a cannonade fired in his honour to be a welcome or an act of aggression?'

'Will his entourage expect horses or camels to convey them to London?' enquires Baron Hunsdon.

'Where are we going to get camels from?' counters Sir Thomas Egerton, Master of the Rolls, testily.

'There's a couple in the royal menagerie,' Mr Secretary Cecil advises. 'But they are monstrously unpleasant beasts. I'd advise any man who thinks of riding one to make his Will first.'

'Provide carriages,' suggests Charles Howard, the Earl of Nottingham, a practical man. Then he immediately casts doubt on his own suggestion. 'Do Moors even know of carriages? Might they think them prisons on wheels?'

Nicholas assures the committee that horses will do fine, if they are handsome, well caparisoned and of a fiery temperament. 'Put them on common palfreys,' he says, 'and they'll believe we think them effeminate.'

'Will they bring their own altars?' asks the cleric from Fulham Palace. 'Because the Bishop of London cannot possibly be expected to approve heathen worship carried out in public view. There will be riots.'

'If we tell them which way Mecca lies, they will be content to make their orisons modestly and without show,' Nicholas says, trying to be helpful.

'Does it matter?' Cecil asks.

'If you were to ask me to point to Jerusalem, Sir Robert, and I pointed instead towards Ipswich, would you consider me a friend or a deceiver?'

A sudden rush to study Mr Secretary's Molyneux globe ensues. Charles Howard – in his capacity as Lord High Admiral of England – provides the approximate compass bearings.

'Do Moors eat meat like we do?' the representative of the Lord Mayor of London wants to know.

Nicholas reassures him that they do, but it's likely they will bring their own cooks with them. If not, he knows a young man by the name of Farzad Gul, presently in the kitchens of Lord Lumley's Nonsuch Palace, who could assist.

And it is to Nonsuch that the deliberations take Mr Secretary Cecil next, with Nicholas in tow. When the court accompanies Her Majesty there for the diplomatic talks and the revels that will follow, where will everyone sleep? The courtiers will be accustomed to finding themselves wedged into the accommodation like too many shoes stuffed into a boot-chest, but where to put the Moors when they come? 'Do Moors even sleep indoors?' asks the Dean of Westminster. 'Do they not prefer to take their slumber on the sand, gazing up at their starry Arabian firmament?'

When the discussion turns to entertainment, Charles Howard points to the stucco images of biblical and mythical creatures set into the white walls of the inner courtyard. 'They'll think they're at home,' he opines. 'Perhaps we could transport the beasts in the royal menagerie here and treat Master Anoun to a lion hunt in the deer park.'

No one is quite sure whether he's joking.

Mr Secretary Cecil decrees that the talks – and the revels to follow – will take place in the banqueting house, a fine building set some four hundred paces from the palace on the crest of a small hill with pleasing views of the surrounding Surrey countryside.

'What shall we give them?' asks Sackville, the Lord Treasurer.

'Why not a performance of Master Shakespeare's *Titus Andronicus*?' suggests Charles Howard, who likes his plays gory.

Nicholas respectfully points out that a tale that includes a Moor as a villain – whose fate is to be buried up to the head in sand and left to starve – might be considered by the ambassador somewhat less than diplomatic. Having seen it only a few days before at the Globe, Nicholas suggests *Julius Caesar* instead, on the presumption that as both realms have known Roman rule, there will be a common appreciation of history.

'I'll order the Master of the Revels to commission the Lord Chamberlain's Men,' Mr Secretary Cecil says, favouring Nicholas with the merest hint of a wry smile.

Farzad Gul is summoned from the Nonsuch kitchens and consulted on dishes for the welcoming feast. Nicholas cannot help but smile to see how the young Persian lad, who washed up on Bankside some seven years ago after being rescued from Arab slave-traders by English sailors, has turned into a strikingly handsome young man with a solar smile and an assured but gentle manner about him. They instantly fall into happy reminiscences of Farzad's time in the Jackdaw's kitchen until Robert Cecil intervenes with, 'Yes, yes, this is all very endearing, but will the Moor eat sturgeon? Do they even know of fish in the desert?'

It is during this visit that Nicholas speaks again to Lord Lumley. Nicholas is descending the steps that lead from the banqueting hall to the Grove of Diana with its statues, spring and leafy grotto when Lumley takes him by the arm. 'I owe you an apology,' he says.

'Why so, my lord?'

'As you might expect, I've been a little busy preparing for the arrival of Her Majesty and the Moor ambassador. I haven't had time to make enquiries about your écorché figures.'

'I'd almost forgotten about them,' Nicholas replies diplomatically.

'If Mistress Bianca is still happy for me to have them, I'll pay you before you leave. Would four pounds be acceptable?'

'That's most generous of you, my lord. I'm sure she'd be only too happy to be rid of them. But what if you discover the true owner?'

Lumley smiles. 'There's no document to indicate such a person, is there?'

'No, we found nothing.'

'Then don't worry; I won't ask for the return of my money.'

Nicholas leaves Nonsuch at dawn the next morning. Cecil offers him a place in his coach. The journey takes five hours, his spine jarring at every slam of the wheels against the baked ruts of the London road. Dozing is impossible. Crossing the Thames by the Lambeth horse-ferry, Nicholas gets out and stretches his aching limbs. He thinks that when they reach Cecil House he will walk back to Bankside rather than sit for one minute longer than necessary on a hard seat. He might even take the opportunity to stop at the Inner Temple on the way and ask about the deserted storehouse he saw after his visit to master carpenter Peter Street.

Preparing himself to get back into Cecil's coach, he watches a pair of swans drift majestically past the lumbering raft, their pristine plumage gleaming in the morning sunshine. The sight gives him an idea: he'll spend some of the money John Lumley has given him for the écorché figures on new gowns and petticoats for Bianca, to thaw the frost that has sprung up between them. Her unfounded accusations against Petrus have hurt him, yet in his heart he knows her to be the least vindictive person he's ever met. He can guess how hard it has been for her to apologize, and in truth he feels more than a little guilty for his own withdrawal from her. Perhaps it's time to put things right. Even so, he suspects four pounds will be nowhere near enough to soften the temper of her Italian pride, or her mistrust of his friend from Frankfurt.

✠

Crossing the Fleet ditch, Nicholas enters the gardens of the Inner Temple. Out on the river, a gilded barge is heading towards Whitehall, the wherries and tilt-boats playing chance with it like terriers snapping at a badger. Though the rivermen are proud of their guild and their loyalty to the Crown, if the queen is not aboard they cannot resist having their sport by trying to throw the royal oarsmen off their stroke.

It is warm, even in the shade of the trees. Nicholas can hear the thrumming of bees and the whisper of the wind in the grass. Approaching the dirt area around the storehouse, he looks out for more discarded pieces of metal type, but sees none. Nor can he see any sign that someone has been here since his last visit. The space where the window board fell in when he pushed it still has the black, vacant appearance of a missing tooth.

He is thinking about making his way up to the building of the Inner Temple and beginning his enquiries when he feels a sharp jab against his back. His head snaps forward, his left temple striking the window frame, so that the voice and the pain arrive at the same moment.

'Oi, what the fuck are you about, you saucy fellow?'

As he turns, Nicholas brings his hands up, balling them into fists, ready to defend himself.

He is looking at a short, bushy-bearded man in a broadcloth tunic stretched to tearing-point over an ample stomach. In his right hand is a cudgel, responsible, Nicholas presumes, for the pain in his back and the bruise on his temple.

'You could have asked without resorting to *that*,' he says angrily. 'I was only looking.'

'Speak up, I'm a little hard of hearing,' the man says belligerently.

'I said I *was only looking*.'

'By what authority?'

'Do I need authority? This is hardly Richmond Palace, is it?'

'It's privy land,' the man announces grandly. 'And I'm charged by the master of the Inner Temple for keeping out them what has no business being on it.'

'Are you afraid I'm going to steal the Flemish hangings and the silver plate?' Nicholas says sourly.

'Very funny. But you've no business being here. So, like I said, you can fuck off.'

'That's no way to attract business, is it?' Nicholas says, an idea springing into his head. 'I'm sure the master of the Inner Temple wouldn't be averse to renting out this place, if the price was right. I haven't met a lawyer yet who'd turn up his nose at the prospect of an income for no outlay.'

The man looks doubtful, but not because he hasn't heard Nicholas properly.

'You want to rent this hovel?'

'Yes. I need to store some timbers, and Master Street's place over there is full. Of course I would also need a fellow to keep watch on the place. I wouldn't want the student lawyers breaking in and thieving from me. No need to tell the master of the Inner Temple. How does one gold half-angel a month sound?'

The man studies Nicholas carefully, and then transfers his cudgel to his left hand, holding it behind him as though to hide the evidence. 'I hope I didn't cause you any hurt,' he says. 'It's just that we've been troubled by vagrants sleeping in the orchard. Not that you look like—'

'Have you been keeping watch on this place long?' Nicholas asks, hoping the answer is 'at least two years'. He smiles to show that it takes more than a prod with a cudgel or the accusation of being a vagrant to cause him insult.

'More than ten years, sir – since I was paid off by the Lord High Admiral, after we trounced the Don's great armada. Master Murfin, sir, Obadiah Murfin – former gunner's mate aboard the *Stag*.'

That explains the deafness, thinks Nicholas. 'And still a man who knows his business, I can tell,' he says admiringly.

'I like to think so, sir,' beams Murfin.

'So you were here two Decembers past – in '98?'

Obadiah Murfin gives him a pained look. 'Only in a manner of speaking, sir. To be honest with you, that December I was unable to perform my duties as I would have wished.'

'You were absent?'

'I was abed – from Advent to Twelfth Night, recovering from a flux of the fundament.'

'Pity,' Nicholas muses.

'You're telling me. Thought I was turning inside out. Feared I'd never see the new year. But God smiled, and here I still am.'

'Indeed you are. You don't happen to know if anything was stored here during that time, do you?'

'Stored?'

'A printing press, for instance.'

Murfin's face contorts with the effort of remembering. He shakes his head. 'Can't say as I do. Not that anyone would bother to tell *me*. I just guard the place.'

'Would the master of the Inner Temple know?'

'Probably not. The Temple don't actually own this corner, sir. I'm paid to keep watch on it because it's an easy way for a miscreant to get into the Temple gardens. It's hard enough keeping the young lawyer gentlemen from treating the place like a bawdy-house without every other slippery trick sneaking in and trying to filch the apples and the coneys.'

'I don't suppose you happen to know *who* owns it?'

'Oh yes, sir. The owner's been here once or twice over the years, to look the place over and talk to the Temple about selling it. Haven't seen him for a while, though. I hear he went off to the Low Countries with the late Earl of Leicester, to fight the Dons. No idea what became of him. Probably still there, for all I know – or slain. He was a gentleman, I remember that. What was he called now? Sir Thomas somebody. Wriggly? Rayleigh?'

Even though the sun has now slipped behind a cloud, Nicholas feels his cheeks hot with exultation. 'Wragby?' he prompts, hardly daring to believe it. 'Was the name Thomas Wragby?'

'*That's* it,' Obadiah Murfin says with evident satisfaction that his memory hasn't gone the way of his hearing. 'I knew I'd remember it in the end. A gentleman from Suffolk, I believe. Wragby. Sir Thomas Wragby.'

25

Nicholas waits on the Whitefriars stairs for a wherry to take him across to Bankside. Though the late-afternoon sun is shining, for him the city seems enveloped in fog, the boats on the river, the buildings at his back, the far bank all are only half-seen, obscured by the swirling, competing thoughts in his head.

If Wragby is the man behind the seditious pamphlets, Nicholas reasons, then Yeoman Shelby might not have been the victim of circumstance. What if Wragby – or someone connected to him – had been so monumentally foolish as to leave one of the texts lying around in the church at Barnthorpe? Had Wragby panicked when Asher Montague told him the tract had been handed in? Had he used Yeoman Shelby as a scapegoat, to divert attention away from the true source of the sedition? Nicholas can easily imagine the consternation Wragby must have suffered when he learned that the very man he had hoped would bear the penalty for his own carelessness was in fact the father of the queen's physician. Nicholas almost smiles. How could Wragby have known what an exaggeration that was, and that Yeoman Shelby's son was the very last person at court with the power to send the Privy Council's interrogators his way?

And what of Parson Montague? Was his role in the affair as innocent as the priest had maintained? Were Wragby and the printer, Symcot, merely the instruments, and Montague the inspiration? If anyone was going to be behind the seditious texts, it would be the angelic firebrand Asher Montague.

Like a beacon shining through the fog in his mind, Nicholas suddenly recalls what Montague had told him at Barnthorpe. *My father was a follower of John Hooper, Dr Shelby... When Hooper burned, he fled across the Narrow Sea... I watched the hope fade in his eyes as a Catholic Queen of England tried to burn the one true faith out of these isles... I know well enough the terrible price God sometimes asks us to pay for entry into His glory...*

Is it Asher Montague who has taken Hooper's name as a disguise... or is it Thomas Wragby? Nicholas asks himself as he grows impatient at the wait for a wherry. Is he one man or two? Again, the words from the pamphlet ring in his ears, just as they were intended to ring in the hearts of impressionable readers: *Be our masters ever so mighty... Cast them down into the fires of Hell where they belong... Let Hooper, the glorious Martyr, be thy touchstone and thy comfort, even when the task seems beyond the strength of thine arm... Be the first to raise thy hand...*

What if John Hooper is not a single person but a conspiracy? What if the tracts are not simply a clarion call, but a plan?

As Nicholas's frustration at the wait becomes too much to tolerate, he decides to walk back to Bankside. His bones still ache from the ride in Robert Cecil's carriage and the effort will do him good. It will also, it occurs to him, take him past the Steelyard.

✠

The door to the lower storehouse is locked and Nicholas is forced to wait until Schenk answers his calls. 'Vagrants,' explains Petrus when at last Nicholas is admitted. 'I have few enough possessions. I don't want to lose them to thieves.'

He leads Nicholas up to the living chamber. Nicholas sees the little wooden effigies of children arranged around the walls, as though this is a nursery frozen in an instant by some bewitching spell. He understands now why Bianca found her discovery so unsettling.

'Don't be alarmed,' Petrus says, seeing the look on Nicholas's face. 'As I told you when you challenged me, my ghosts keep me company. If they were not with me, I might forget their faces, and then I would think myself the guiltiest man on earth.'

'I'm sorry Bianca leapt to the wrong conclusion. There must be a way we can put this darkness in your mind to flight, Petrus. Some men find prayer helpful. Or the comfort of a wife.'

'I've tried everything, Nick: whores, drink, anger. Just like Ned Monkton. I hear you rescued him from a life lived amongst the dead.'

'And look at Ned now – married, content. Free.'

'Ned's not free, Nick. None of us are. God determines from the day we are born how our lives will be lived. He knows from the start who is damned and who is saved. Prayer is not enough to save me. And a wife could not bear a man like me.'

'But it can't help to surround yourself with'– Nicholas indicates the little painted effigies – 'with these.'

Petrus gives him a smile that seems, to Nicholas, almost contented. 'They are my family now. They will always be with me. I know it might be hard for Mistress Bianca to comprehend, but they give me comfort. It is the insubstantial that I find harrowing. Making a dream solid, giving it shape and form, that helps me. I can look on them when I choose, instead of having them ambush me.'

'If I can help in some way—'

'You're the one who looks as though he needs help,' Petrus says, breaking in. 'You look as though you've come second in a wrestling match.'

'I've been sitting in Robert Cecil's coach for hours,' Nicholas tells him ruefully. 'And before that, I was at Nonsuch almost until dawn answering foolish questions. Mr Secretary and the Privy Council seem to think I'm the oracle to consult on the Moroccan ambassador. What does he eat? What does he drink? What does he sleep on? For the entertainment, they wanted to offer him Will Shakespeare's *Titus Andronicus*. I can just picture Muhammed al-Annuri's response to the portrayal of a Moor as a villain and a murderer. We'd be at war with Morocco as well as Spain!'

Petrus laughs, his dark mood seemingly forgotten. 'Surely they're not going to take the ambassador to a Bankside playhouse.'

'Mercy, no, he'd be robbed blind before he sat down. The revel is to happen at the Nonsuch banqueting hall. And I'm going to look like one of the gardeners, unless Mr Secretary has me properly attired. He'll probably want me looking like a real gallant, ruff and all. And I hate ruffs. They make me look ridiculous.'

'I don't know how you can stomach being around such frippery and show.'

'I grit my teeth and invent uncomfortable ailments for them.'

'I approve of that, Nicholas,' Petrus says conspiratorially. 'I imagine it will a grand occasion. Apart from the ambassador, who will be there?'

'Oh, the queen of course; then the Lord Keeper of the Great Seal, the Chancellor of the Exchequer, the Lord Treasurer, the Lord High Admiral... Mr Secretary Cecil, that goes without saying... the Bishop of London, probably the Archbishop of Canterbury... the Attorney General, the Lord Chief Justice... all the courtiers... If that's not enough to convince al-Annuri to give up diplomacy and retire to his favourite *riad*, I can't imagine what would.'

Petrus stares towards the window, a far-away look on his face. 'A man could live a thousand years and never see such sights or know what it is like to walk in the gardens of a palace like that,' he muses.

Nicholas glances at the grim effigies set around the room, the proof – even if not actually living – of a man in agony.

'Why don't I take you there?' he says, as the notion strikes him. 'When the queen is not in residence, it's a tranquil place. The gardens are glorious. It's a good place for lifting a man's spirits. I should know; when I first went there, I too was living in darkness.'

Petrus turns away from the window. 'Would you do that? For me?'

'Of course I would. It would have to be after the ambassador's visit.'

'I was thinking of leaving London – returning to Hesse. I don't think there's much for me here. Could we go before?'

Petrus turns away from the window. 'Would you do that? For me?'

'Of course. I'll have to make another visit before the ambassador arrives anyway.'

To Nicholas's surprise, Petrus embraces him. 'You're a good friend, Nicholas. You always were.'

When Petrus releases him, Nicholas gives an embarrassed smile. 'I'll ask only one favour in return. A simple one.'

'"Ask, and it shall be given you; seek, and ye shall find; knock, and it shall be opened unto you." From the Book of Matthew,' says Petrus with a soft smile.

'Stop taking Ned Monkton to Austin Friars to hear Asher Montague preach.'

For what seems an age, Petrus doesn't reply. Then, with a look of infinite sadness on his face, he says, 'What good would that do, Nicholas? When a man is ready to open his ears to receive God's voice, nothing on earth – not even your queen and all her fine ministers – can block out that wondrous noise.'

✠

Will he call, or is visiting an apothecary shop on Bankside beneath the dignity of a lawyer from the Consistory Court?

Bianca tries to picture Master Nathaniel Woolrich galloping back from Canterbury, reading her note and, without pausing even to brush the dust off his boots, spurring his flagging horse across London Bridge, down Long Southwark, right at the Tabard inn and so into Dice Lane. But the image is no sooner in her head than it is replaced by another: of Woolrich almost buried under a mountain of legal tomes, laboriously – and with the energy of an exceptionally aged snail – going about whatever it is that lawyers are paid to go about.

Time is running out. It cannot be long now before the Moor ambassador's ship sails into the Narrow Sea, and Nicholas will be summoned to Nonsuch for the official conference and the revels that will follow. And Bianca wants her proof before that happens.

Closing the shop, she and Cachorra return to the Paris Garden lodgings. They are upstairs settling Bruno to his sleep when Nicholas returns home.

'How was John Lumley?' Bianca asks when she greets him in the hall. 'Did you see Farzad?'

'I did. Farzad is preparing the feast for ambassador al-Annuri when he visits. By the way, Lord Lumley gave me four pounds for the écorché figures. You'll need something appropriate to wear at the revels. We can go shopping on Cheapside, if you'd like. I thought a new gown might thaw this frost that has grown between us.'

She takes his hand and kisses it. 'There is no frost, Nicholas. Just concern.'

'Concern for what?' he says, going to the sideboard and pouring two glasses of sack.

'A moment ago I was listening to Cachorra tell Bruno tales

about her Carib island. He's decided he wants to be a sailor and carry her back home, bless him. He has your sensibility.'

'What do you mean – my sensibility? I don't understand.'

Bianca takes a sip of her wine. 'How many has it been now? First there was Elise Cullen, then Samuel Wylde, then Hella Maas... and now your friend Petrus Schenk.'

'Would you rather I had no compassion in my heart at all?'

She takes his hand. 'Of course not. It's what I love about you most. But you must admit, it's taken us to some dark places.'

'I wouldn't be a physician if I didn't want to heal the sick.'

'But it's not just the sick, Nicholas. It's also the lost. And you can't try to save *everyone*, simply because you couldn't save Eleanor and the child she was carrying.'

The wine is beginning to wash some of the dust from his mouth. Yet he finds it harder to speak than he expected. 'Is that what I'm doing?'

Bianca lays aside her glass and folds her arms around him. 'Be careful, Nicholas. There's nothing wrong with compassion, provided it doesn't leave you blind to danger. Now, upstairs with you and say goodnight to your son, so that he may dream undisturbed.'

Her gaze follows him up the stairs. She is more relieved than she can admit that the rift between them seems to have closed, yet she is frightened out of her wits by the secret she has managed to keep hidden in her heart. She could call it stubbornness. She could call it the Caporetti second sight. But whatever the cause, the truth cannot be denied: her suspicion of Nicholas's friend is burning as fiercely as it ever did.

✠

Early next morning Nicholas attends the Clink prison. He has been called to treat a warder who has been assaulted by an inmate for stealing the victuals the prisoner's wife was providing for the easement of his confinement. He cleans the man's wounds with a wash of Saracens' consound and splints and wraps his broken fingers. In payment, the warder – a notorious bully – offers Nicholas a bottle of sack and a chicken joint. He accepts and promptly returns them to their rightful owner.

Feeling pleased with himself, he then takes a wherry to the public water-stairs by Ivy Bridge Lane on the north bank of the river below the Strand. He walks to Cecil House and seeks an audience with Mr Secretary.

'Please be brief, Nicholas,' Robert Cecil says as Nicholas rises from his chair in the long gallery. 'I'm due at a Privy Council meeting in five minutes.'

'I require your approval, Sir Robert, to tell a certain Puritan priest to vacate the realm and return whence he came.'

'Are we speaking of this new fellow at Austin Friars?' Cecil asks perceptively. 'I hear he's very clever at walking a tightrope.'

'Yes. His sermonizing is turning the heads of two friends of mine. They're both good men. But I'm a physician, I've seen how mountebanks and charlatans can twist good men's reason and make them buy cures that are really nothing of the sort.'

Cecil's eyes hold his as Mr Secretary digests Nicholas's request. 'He hasn't preached against Her Majesty's religion, has he? I'd have heard about it if he has.'

'No, Sir Robert. Not from what I've heard.'

'Has he called Her Majesty the Devil's whore?'

'No, of course not.'

'Or demanded the Pope reign in her place?'

'No.'

Cecil passes the papers he's been reading on his march down the gallery to an attendant secretary and gives Nicholas a regretful smile. 'Then it's a matter for the Bishop of London. I can't go around turfing parsons out of their pulpits on hearsay.'

'I think I'm getting close to proving who was behind those seditious tracts, Sir Robert,' Nicholas says, feeling the opportunity slipping from his grasp.

'Montague?'

'Perhaps. I'm not sure.'

Cecil's thin lips part in a puff of exasperation. 'I shall need more than that, Nicholas. If you think there is a significant threat to the realm, then say so. Master Topcliffe and his interrogators are more than competent when it comes to extracting confessions.'

Mr Secretary's mention of the Privy Council's most efficient torturer reminds Nicholas how dangerous making an unproven accusation can be. What if he's wrong? Denouncing innocent men, condemning them to suffer white-hot irons and the rack is a crime in itself – one that a man dedicated to healing would find it hard to bear.

'As I say, I need more time.'

'Then you'd best hurry. My agent in Morocco writes that the Moor embassy is preparing to sail. Given the dispatch was prepared three weeks ago, that means he's already at sea.'

And with that, he leaves Nicholas gazing helplessly at his scuttling back as he disappears around the corner at the end of the gallery, his black velvet gown swirling like wind-blown laundry on a washing line.

✠

It is dawn, and upriver beyond the bridge the sky glows a golden orange, though the sun is not yet over the horizon. Nicholas has hired two horses from the Tabard inn. He and Petrus ride south down Long Southwark and into the Surrey countryside towards Nonsuch Palace.

'It's like being back in the Low Countries together,' says

Petrus, 'only without the Spanish to shoot their bows and their firing pieces at us.'

'And no ghosts to trouble you, I hope.'

'Not yet,' Petrus replies with a self-conscious laugh.

It is a more direct journey than from Cecil House and, without the jolting torture of the Cecil coach, a deal more comfortable. Within three hours they are riding through the deer park. Ahead of them the white towers of the Nonsuch outer gatehouse rise above the wide bowling green where a team of servants is busy trimming the grass, so that when the ambassador and the court arrive, they will be sure their bowling balls run fast.

Nicholas tells Petrus to wait in the middle archway, beneath King Henry's great golden sundial that fills most of the wall above. He goes in search of John Lumley, finding him in the queen's apartments, overseeing the preparations for her arrival.

'Let your friend bide awhile in the Italian gardens, or down in the Grove of Diana the huntress,' Lumley tells him when Nicholas has explained why he's come. 'God knows, I've dwelt there enough times to reflect on my own sorrows and come away a far more contented man.'

'I'm sure he'll be grateful, my lord,' says Nicholas.

'The gratitude should be the realm's,' Lumley replies. 'We'd have far fewer poor fellows sleeping under hedges and begging outside churches if we took better regard for what men must endure in war. Is he a useful fellow?'

'Without question.'

'Well, if work would distract him from melancholy, I need every man and woman I can find. Nonsuch might seem almost empty now, but when the queen and the court are here we must find board, bed and service for hundreds. If I had to maintain a permanent staff to cope with that, I'd be bankrupt inside a week.'

For the rest of that day and until the following afternoon, Nicholas and Petrus remain at Nonsuch. They walk together between the fountains, the classical statues and the cypress trees in the Italian gardens; they lie and reminisce in the long grass of the Wilderness that isn't a wilderness at all, but a clever artifice; they engage in loud but good-natured competition at the archery butts. Nicholas allows his friend some time on his own and goes in search of Elise Cullen, one of Lady Lumley's chambermaids. He first encountered Elise ten years ago. Then she had been a mute – too terrified to utter a sound in case the two monsters who had murdered her brother came back for her. Now she is a pretty, assured young woman of twenty-three. She throws her arms around him, much to the amusement of the other chambermaids at work in the royal chambers.

'Dr Shelby, how happy it makes me to see you,' she says. Then, to the other women, 'This is Dr Shelby. He gave me back my voice, and justice for my little Ralph. He is the best man on God's earth.'

The servants have heard it all before. But they enjoy her pleasure, and the sight of Nicholas blushing.

'He's handsome,' pipes up one of the newer women, 'for a physician.'

'Fie, Sarah Holcombe,' Elise says. 'Mistress Bianca is a beautiful sorceress. She might turn you into a slippery eel.'

'Can she cast a spell to keep the goose feathers inside these bloody mattresses?' enquires Sarah.

Before they depart, Petrus asks if there is a chapel where he might pray. 'I would ask the Lord that He allow the peace I have found here to follow me back to London.'

'Of course. There's Lord Lumley's private chapel,' Nicholas tells him. 'It's where Bianca and I were wed. I'll ask him if you might spend a while there.'

'Then it is a lucky place, as well as a holy one.'

The chapel is on the ground floor, with windows overlooking the privy garden. Just as Nicholas remembers, the wainscoting smells of beeswax and incense, the latter the only clue that this is where Lord Lumley and his wife Elizabeth privately practise their Catholic faith. He leaves Petrus alone and waits outside, reliving that blissful and overwhelming day when Bianca became his wife.

When they begin the ride back to London, Petrus seems a changed man.

'See, I knew this would do you well,' Nicholas says. 'Sometimes the best physic is simply beauty and a change of scenery.'

'And I even have employment for a while, thanks to you,' Petrus grins. 'Nicholas Shelby, old friend and brother-in-arms, you cannot know what a service you have done me.'

✠

The day after he returns from Nonsuch, Nicholas and Bianca spend the morning on Cheapside, searching out a gown for her to wear at the Nonsuch revels. In the afternoon Bianca goes to the shop on Dice Lane while Nicholas attends a patient, one of the few on Bankside who pay him in coin. The man is a member of the Mercers' Guild named Crepin. He has a belly the size of an overstuffed cushion and the habit of grandiloquence. Nicholas has been visiting him for over a month. He's sure Crepin's condition – gallstones – is imaginary. Nicholas can detect no jaundice in the man's flesh, or pain, for that matter; only a film of greasy sweat that sticks to his probing fingers like wet varnish on a bad painting. He is sure Crepin only calls him in the hope of hearing some titbit of court gossip that he can recite to his friends at the Mercers' Hall. Crepin's only other topic of conversation is a repetitive lecture on the benefits of throwing the Hansa merchants out of the Steelyard. England, he assures his physician at every opportunity, will soon be as mighty as Spain, now that we are rid of the foreigners and their deceitful tricks.

Nicholas endures it for almost an hour. Then he says, 'Well, Master Crepin, I think the time has come to face facts. If we are going to relieve you of your discomfort, I fear we will have to resort to the traditional method.'

'What do you propose?'

'Simple. We have you lie on a trestle with your legs supported and make an incision between the testicles and the anus. Then we purge the corrupted matter within. If the stones are substantial, we can drill them or break them up with a small chisel. The great Moor physician, al-Zahrawi, has left us a fine description of the process. I myself have studied at Padua, and I can tell you the norcini are very skilled at it.'

'The who?' asks Crepin, looking truly jaundiced for the first time since Nicholas has been attending him.

'The norcini – travelling butchers. Those fellows can wield a knife faster than any man of medicine I've come across. I could have a barber-surgeon do it for you if you'd like, but they won't have had the benefit of watching the Italians. Whereas I could probably have the whole thing finished inside five minutes.'

'Five minutes? Will it hurt?'

'Intolerably, I imagine. Of course I can't be sure – I've never tried taking a sharp blade to my own perineum.'

Crepin turns a funereal grey. 'I think I'll get a second opinion.'

Feeling confident that he will likely hear no more from Master Crepin, Nicholas walks back towards the Paris Garden. On the way he stops at Constable Osborne's house and spends a while outlining the plan that he's contrived on the ride back from Nonsuch. Osborne agrees, with only one provision. 'No rough stuff,' he says. 'The Bankside constable has no real authority in Broad Street Ward.'

Nicholas assures him that rough stuff is the very last thing on his mind. Then he continues his journey home. When he reaches the porch of the Paris Garden house, he sees a man in Cecil livery waiting for him.

'Dr Shelby, I have a message from Mr Secretary Cecil,' the man says, rising at Nicholas's approach.

'I trust his son William is not unwell?'

'No, sir,' the man says. 'The Moor ambassador's caravel has been sighted off Start Point. The party to welcome him is to ride for Dover the day after tomorrow. I am to command you to be at Cecil House, ready in all respects, no later than eight in the morning.'

✠

Bianca is asleep, breathing softly. In the pale light from the open window, Nicholas can see the sheen on her body left by their love-making. Her last question before her eyes closed was, 'How long will you be away?'

'Perhaps a week,' he had said. 'Long enough to bring al-Annuri to London. Then I'll accompany him to Nonsuch for the official talks. John Lumley says his steward at the Woodroffe Lane house will send word when you should follow on. You'll be travelling with Will Shakespeare and his players, along with the rest of Lord Lumley's servants. If they offer the coach, say no.'

He watches her now, remembering the All Souls' Day morning – almost ten years ago – when he had woken from insensibility after his attempt to end his own life. He still recalls the exact words she spoke: *I imagine you must be hungry. Can you manage a little breakfast? There's larded pullet. We have some baked sprats left over, too. I'll have my maid Rose lay out a trencher downstairs.*

He smiles. A new gown is nowhere near payment of the debt he owes her. But he can, at least, make another instalment. He can ease her concerns for Ned Monkton.

If Sir Robert Cecil isn't prepared to banish Asher Montague and his dangerous sermonizing, then he, Nicholas, must take matters into his own hands. And he has one day left in which to do it.

No rough stuff, Bran Osborne had said.

But why would members of the Bankside watch need to employ rough stuff against a man-child preacher? Nicholas asks himself with a satisfied smile. Especially if they're posing as emissaries from the Privy Council.

26

The five men enter the lychgate of the foreigners' church at Austin Friars just as the bell rings noon – Nicholas, Constable Bran Osborne and three of his sturdiest fellows. The watchmen are wearing their leather tunics, their official cudgels hanging from their belts. They have cost Nicholas sixpence per man, though Osborne has refused to take his share. Rules have been set; Nicholas is to do the talking. There will be no threats of violence. Parson Asher Montague must be treated as the sanctity of his station requires.

'I simply want him to think that the Privy Council have taken notice of him,' Nicholas has explained on the walk from Bankside. 'I will remind him that they can be very unforgiving when it comes to seditious preaching. I will suggest it would be better if he chose somewhere else to preach. But that's all.'

Because the writ of the Bankside watch does not run in Broad Street Ward, Constable Osborne has laid out his own conditions. If anyone with Church or parish authority challenges them, he will do the talking. Nicholas is to say nothing other than that he is in the service of Mr Secretary Cecil, which is close enough to being the truth. He is not even to give his name. Nicholas is more than happy to agree, knowing that Bianca has already been here to speak to Father Beauchêne.

Beauchêne himself is tidying around the gravestones when Nicholas leads the party into the churchyard. 'God give you good morrow, gentlemen,' he says, getting to his feet and meeting them on the path to the porch. His watery blue eyes take in the watchmen's cudgels and their owners' air of muscular determination. A flicker of alarm plays across his boxy jaw. 'You're a little early for evensong,' he observes cautiously, 'but the Almighty will be pleased by your enthusiasm.'

'We're here on Privy Council business,' Nicholas says, deepening his Suffolk burr to sound ponderously official. 'Tell us, where may we find Parson Montague?'

Beauchêne's artless face flinches as if Nicholas has thrown a punch. What little colour there is in his complexion washes out like unfastened dye.

'We are all good Christians here,' he says. 'We are loyal subjects of Her Majesty. We have nothing to hide.'

'And *you* have nothing to fear, Father,' Nicholas says. 'It's Asher Montague we're after.' He feels a rogue for frightening an innocent man, but Beauchêne's reaction confirms his belief that it should be easy to convince Asher Montague to leave.

Beauchêne begins to wring his hands. 'I *knew* that man would bring trouble here. I swear, in the sight of the Almighty, that neither I nor most of the congregation here abide the fieriness of his preaching. I've been meaning to speak to the Bishop of London about it, I swear it.'

'The Privy Council is aware of that, Father Beauchêne,' Nicholas says reassuringly. 'If you would just tell us where we may find Parson Montague...'

Beauchêne gestures towards the porch. 'He's in there, at prayer. It's almost all he does. I swear I've never seen him eat or sleep. Is he to be arrested? I suppose I should send word to Fulham Palace. But if you're here, I suppose they already know. I hope the Lord Bishop doesn't think—'

Leaving Beauchêne staring anxiously after them, Nicholas

leads the small party to the porch entrance. Stepping into the cool interior of the church, he finds it has been boarded in two, a makeshift wooden wall rising on his right as far as the hammerbeam roof. To his left are a dozen or so rows of pews set in two banks, separated by a central aisle. At the far end, Asher Montague is kneeling before the altar, deep in an ecstasy of contemplation. A shaft of sunlight slants through the chancery window, softening his already cherubic features and giving him a martyr's halo. Nicholas can't help but think of Archbishop Becket. No rough stuff, he reminds himself.

He has his speech prepared. He will tell Montague that the Privy Council has decided his preaching has crossed the line, that if he doesn't douse the flames of his zealotry he will face a charge of sedition. If Montague stands his ground – as he did when Nicholas went to see him in the little church at Barnthorpe – he will tell the priest that the Privy Council suspects him of being behind the tracts that issued from printer Symcot's press, and that he could be considered by association an accessory to Symcot's murder. If even that fails, he will invoke the name of Richard Topcliffe, the Privy Council's master of the cruel arts.

We'll see just how deep your embrace of martyrdom goes, he says to himself.

'Parson Montague, a word, if you please.'

For a moment Montague doesn't move. Then, slowly, he drops his arms to his side and rises from the flagstone, turning to see who has had the temerity to interrupt his orisons.

'I know you,' he says in his soft West Country cadence. 'You're the fellow who came to see me at Barnthorpe.'

'Yes, I am.'

'I remember – the queen's physician. Your father was the one who was arrested.'

'I am here at the behest of her Privy Council,' Nicholas continues in the most officious manner he can muster. 'I am here to inform you that Her Majesty's Privy Council—'

Whatever reaction Nicholas has been expecting, what Asher Montague does next is completely unexpected. There is no warning sign in the priest's eyes. No sudden tensing of the limbs in preparation for flight. One instant Montague is facing him with a look of mild curiosity on his face, the next he is away like a spooked coney in a desperate attempt to get to the porch and the open door.

Nicholas has only a moment to think, *So much for your talk of facing martyrdom with the courage of John Hooper*, before the watchmen behave as watchmen always do when the subject of their interest suddenly makes a break for it. One of them lunges after Montague, his hands closing on thin air as the priest dodges sideways and springs up onto the nearest pew, vaulting over into the next row. A second watchman sprints back towards the porch to block Montague's escape route from the church.

'We mean you no hurt,' Nicholas calls out, as Osborne and the third watchman each take a row of pews, with the aim of flushing Montague out into the nearest aisle. They chase after him like sidesmen following a parishioner who's just snatched away the collection plate.

But Montague either doesn't believe Nicholas's assurance or panic has got the better of him. There follows a graceless dance as he tries desperately to evade his pursuers, the quiet of the church assaulted by the shriek of wooden pews rasping on the flagstones and by the blasphemous curses of the Bankside watchmen. Montague seems to possess an energy fired by desperation. Nothing Nicholas can say will calm him.

'What, in the name of Jesu, is this unholy disturbance?' calls

Father Beauchêne from the porch, attracted by the noise. 'What is this rioting in God's house?' But the watchman guarding against Montague's escape slams the porch door in his face.

With one last frenzied burst of energy, Montague jumps down into the side-aisle, dodges the outstretched arms of the much larger Bran Osborne – who is trying to tackle him as if this were a Midsummer Day football match – and races towards a low archway set into the church wall.

The archway gives entrance to a small vestibule. The archway gives onto a small vestibule with a door that Nicholas realizes must open onto the churchyard. Beside it, cut into the chamber's righthand wall, a narrow flight of stone steps leads up to the bell-tower. As Nicholas closes on him, Montague tugs desperately on the door's iron ring.

But the door stays shut. Locked.

Cornered, Montague turns to face Nicholas, his open, boyish face contorted by what Nicholas can only think is a mix of revulsion and terror.

'Stand still, Father,' Nicholas urges. 'I simply want to speak with you. You need fear no violence from me.'

But he might as well be speaking the language of distant Ethiope. Montague reaches into the folds of his black gown and draws out a knife, jabbing it towards Nicholas like a man trying to puncture a bladder. He clearly has no skill with it. But a lucky thrust doesn't need skill.

'Mercy! What manner of priest carries a blade?'

Nicholas hears Bran Osborne's voice at his shoulder. Then he's rudely shoved aside as the constable steps forward and, with a practised swing of his official cudgel, sends the knife clattering around the stairwell. Montague screams in pain, clutching at his wrist. With nowhere else to go, he turns towards the steps and begins to climb.

'Don't follow him, Bran,' Nicholas says, knowing that Osborne is too big a man to easily navigate the narrow, winding space. 'Let me.'

He plunges after the fleeing Montague, the stuffy gloom of the winding stairway echoing to the two men's frantic footsteps.

In the past, Nicholas has visited more than one patient in this part of London. He knows about Austin Friars. The church is not what it might appear when seen from the outside. Overall, it is a substantial building with a high steeple. But foreigners are confined to one end, the rest turned over to common storage long ago, in the reign of the queen's father. And the two sections are divided by the partition wall Nicholas had seen on his entry. He is not concerned that Asher Montague might escape onto the roof. Unless his zealotry has been rewarded with angel's wings, where could he go? Nicholas's fear is that Montague might know a way over the partition and into the other part of the church. And if he's this desperate to escape, then there's something more to Asher Montague than overblown piety.

The priest is only a few steps away from him now. As the stairway curves, Nicholas catches fleeting glimpses of the hem of the priest's black gown, itself a defiant challenge to the white required by the queen's religion. He lunges out to snare a fleeing ankle, only to have his hand swept aside by the flailing heel of Montague's boot. He stumbles. The edge of a step rushes out of the semi-darkness towards him. By instinct alone, he prevents his teeth getting smashed in, a sharp stab of pain flaring the length of his right forearm.

And then the steps give onto a narrow landing directly below the steeple. Nicholas sees Montague's gown seem to shrivel in the gloom, as if the priest was disappearing before his eyes. It takes him a moment to understand that Montague has crouched to pass through an even smaller arch than the one that led to the vestibule. Nicholas knows now that he was right: Montague has no intention of letting himself be trapped on the roof. The little arch, he guesses, would have given the monks access to the high stone gallery that runs around the inside of the church close to the roof.

Squeezing through, Nicholas sees that he is now on the other side of the makeshift wall, standing on a wooden floor that has been strung across the void just below the bottom of the gallery and over the storage space beneath. The boards feel dangerously insecure, little more substantial than loose planks laid on cross-beams. At its highest point there is barely six feet of headroom between the planks and the ridge of the friary's hammerbeam roof. Shafts of weak light slant down from the tops of the cut-off windows, the glass uncleaned – Nicholas can imagine – since the queen's late father threw out the Augustinian friars. He can make out the dark clumps of birds' nests in the spaces between the hammer-posts and arch braces. Droppings splash the rafters, as though a drunken labourer has staggered past with a brush and pail of whitewash.

Montague is in the centre of the space, below the crown of the rafters so that he does not have to stoop. He is making for the far end of the building. Ahead of him, Nicholas can make out what looks like the top of a wooden ladder. If Montague can get down to the lower level and out of the friary, he can disappear amongst the tenements and gardens along the ancient city wall around Bishopsgate.

Nicholas has abandoned his earlier intention of simply scaring Asher Montague into leaving Austin Friars. Now he is sure that the priest is something a deal more danger-ous than an overly pious zealot. He has known it from the moment Montague drew that knife. If Bran Osborne hadn't struck the blade out of his hand, would the priest have used it? Is Montague not just a firebrand, but a killer? And is he still armed? Ducking under an arch brace to get to better head-room, Nicholas resumes his pursuit.

Clouds of dust rise up as the planks judder to the impact of pounding feet. Nicholas has the impression he is chasing Montague into a dark and misty marsh – a marsh that could swallow them both in an instant.

And then, above the sound of his own breathing and the roaring of his blood, Nicholas hears the awful squeal of rending planks. A grunt, as though someone has been punched in the gut. His knees buckle. For an instant he thinks he's falling. He throws out his arms to steady himself.

But it is not Nicholas who is falling. Ahead of him, he sees two lengths of a fractured plank spinning through the gloom like trapped birds beating their wings in panic. Asher Montague is sliding into the void they leave, dropping like a man in the instant of his hanging. As he disappears, the hem of his black surplice snags on the jagged edge of the hole. Nicholas hears the thud as the priest's falling body is checked, then pulled, inverted, sus-pended head-down above the void. He reaches the spot in three strides. Even before the last one is complete, Nicholas's body is sinking to the floor, his hands reaching out to pull Montague to safety.

But he is an instant too late. The fabric of the priest's gown rips even as Nicholas's fingers touch it. He thinks he sees the body disappear into the darkness as if Montague were plunging into deep water. Drowning. But in the gloom, it could just be his imagination. What is indisputable – what will be his abiding memory of his doomed attempt to simply warn Asher Montague away – is the sound of the priest's head striking the flagstones thirty feet below.

27

Father Beauchêne has a key to the blocked-off part of Austin Friars, given to him by the parish for access in the event of fire or vandalism. It is Constable Osborne who locates the body, lying where it had fallen, in the space between two rows of stacked crates.

'If he'd gone left or right a little,' the constable says, 'he'd have landed on the top of that lot – barely a ten-foot drop.' He looks down at the body, a pool of blood spreading about Montague's head, which itself is bent at a fatal angle against one shoulder of his black surplice. 'Looks to me as though he didn't have God's ear quite the way he thought.'

'Jesu!' Nicholas whispers. 'I only wanted to warn him off. I just wanted to put an end to his pernicious influence over my friends. I didn't mean him to die.'

Osborne shakes his head in wonder. 'I've apprehended more than a few rogues in my life,' he says. 'But I've never yet had a priest pull a knife. Still, there's got to be a first time for everything. What made him do it?'

'This is going to take some explaining, Bran. I'm sorry I got you involved.'

'I think what happened here is quite clear, Dr Shelby,' Osborne says in a matter-of-fact tone. 'This poor fellow was clearly the victim of an unfortunate accident, when he unwisely chose to walk across a floor too rickety to bear his weight.' He leans closer to Nicholas so that Father Beauchêne cannot hear. 'But I would respectfully suggest that you discreetly take yourself hence and pretend you were never here.'

'And how are you going to explain the presence of the Bankside watch in Broad Street Wards?' Nicholas says doubtfully.

Bran Osborne gives him a look of angelic innocence. 'I'd heard he was a fine and compelling preacher. We came to hear him give sermon. We're all good Christian men on Bankside, Dr Shelby. There are no recusants among my watch. Wouldn't abide it.'

Nicholas looks up to the gaping rent in the makeshift planked ceiling. 'There will be footprints in the dust up there – evidence that I chased him.'

'Oh, those are mine,' says one of the Bankside watchmen. 'I went up there to inspect the hole the poor fellow fell through, didn't I?'

Nicholas turns to Father Beauchêne. 'This rather depends upon your wishes, Father. You're the one who's going to have to tell the parish and the Bishop of London.'

Beauchêne looks up at the damaged ceiling, then down at the body. 'This is a church for foreigners. It exists only for as long as the city permits. Parson Montague's wild sermonizing could have led to the Privy Council closing us down. I think it is wise in this instance to invoke Psalm one hundred and nineteen.'

Nicholas stares at him blankly.

'"Thy word is a lantern unto my feet, and a light unto my path",' intones Beauchêne. 'Clearly, on this occasion, the Almighty chose not to light His lantern. He would have done that for a reason. That is good enough for me.'

Nicholas lowers his head for a moment as if in prayer, though in truth he is trying not to smile. Then he says, 'I don't suppose you could show me where Parson Montague lodged, could you?'

✠

The cloisters at Austin Friars have long since been torn down and turned into tenements for the residents of Broad Street Ward. But the prior's house remains, attached to the side of the church. Asher Montague's simple stone chamber is on the ground floor. Father Beauchêne has a key for this, too.

Nicholas has pictured the interior on his walk with Beauchêne around the side of the friary: austere, humble, a monk's cell, even though monks are no longer welcome in England. And as he enters it now, it is exactly as he pictured. The bed is a straw mattress laid on the stone floor, a single woollen blanket and a canvas bolster the only signs of surrender to the sin of luxury.

Remembering how the printer, Symcot, had made a hiding place for the seditious tracts, Nicholas refuses to be hurried by either Father Beauchêne or Bran Osborne's suggestion that he leave as swiftly as possible. At first inspection there is nothing to see, other than a small chest that contains Montague's spare shirt and breeches and a meagre collection of utensils and personal effects. Nicholas takes them out and taps the sides and bottom of the chest to check it has no false compartments that might contain seditious tracts or any evidence to connect Montague with their production. He finds nothing. Pulling the mattress away from the wall, he inspects it for tears through which such items might have been pushed. Again, he finds nothing.

Next he checks the flagstones and masonry, looking for loose edges or missing mortar. It takes time to do it properly, but even with Montague's body cooling in the church, he will not be hurried.

When he has searched the chamber to his satisfaction, and found nothing out of the ordinary, Nicholas asks Beauchêne, 'Was Parson Montague the only person to lodge here?'

'Yes. I have my lodgings in the old refectory.'

'Did he have visitors? Anyone you hadn't seen before?'

'He had two fellows who appeared to be assistants. I suppose you could call them bodyguards. But I don't know where they lodged. Somewhere in the tenements, I should imagine.'

'A priest with bodyguards? Did you not think that was odd?'

Beauchêne looks uncomfortable. 'He used them to keep watch for your people.'

'My people?' Nicholas queries.

'Privy Council watchers, come to see if he was overstepping the mark. I told him I wanted nothing to do with any of it, Master...' Beauchêne pauses. 'You haven't told me your name. I shall need to know with whom I am dealing when I make my report to Fulham Palace.'

'All you need know is that I am in the service of Mr Secretary Cecil,' Nicholas says, trying to sound suitably mysterious. 'These two men, do they attend Montague closely? Why were they not with him when we arrived?'

'There were here about an hour before you came. I saw them speaking to Montague in the churchyard. I presume they're off on some commission for him.'

'So they could return at any moment?'

'I imagine so.'

Nicholas glances at Osborne, who discreetly shakes his head to remind him that the Bankside watch have no authority in this ward.

'What about the other chambers in this building? Are they open?'

'No, they are all kept locked.'

'Did Montague have a key?' Nicholas asks, fearful that the answer will be yes, and that he will have to search them all.

'Only I have the keys.'

'Do you ever leave them unattended?'

'Not habitually. Can you tell me what Parson Montague is

suspected of doing, other than preaching overly hot sermons? What are you looking for?'

'You must have heard about the seditious tracts that were being found in the city a few weeks ago,' Nicholas says, hoping this will make him sound even more plausible.

'Oh, you think he had something to do with those?'

'It's a possibility. Are there any communal chambers here that Montague would have had access to?'

Beauchêne shakes his head. 'Only the jakes.'

✠

One floor up, in a recess set into the outside wall of what was once the prior's chamber, a narrow, vertiginous stone shaft runs down into a cesspit. As deep as the eye can see, the sides are stained with the emanations of seven centuries of Augustinian monks. A narrow wooden bench spanning the void is the only concession to comfort. The package, wrapped in sailcloth, has been well hidden below the rim, in a cavity behind a brick that protrudes just enough for a man's fingers to grip.

'I think we'd best be gone,' says Bran Osborne when Nicholas emerges from the prior's house. He turns to Beauchêne. 'You don't have a bottle of communion wine to hand, perchance, Father?'

Beauchêne looks appalled. 'Bending the truth for you fellows is one thing, but drinking in celebration of a man's death—'

Osborne lays a friendly hand on the priest's shoulder. 'I've had my fellows do a little housekeeping up there. Now it simply looks as though Montague was in his cups. Empty the bottle. Leave it somewhere convenient for the coroner's men to find. When we've gone, wait until it's time to ring the next hour, then discover the body. That will give us time to reach the bridge.'

✠

You are not to blame… you intended him no harm… If he'd had the sense not to bolt like a startled deer, Asher Montague would still be alive. It was his choice, and his alone, to risk an escape route than any man in full possession of the faculty to reason would have rejected immediately as fatally unsafe…

Nicholas hasn't needed Bran Osborne to remind him of these arguments, though the constable has done so unemotionally more than once on the journey to London Bridge. But he cannot dismiss the gnawing sense of guilt that has accompanied him like an invisible sixth member of the hurrying party.

Montague's death gives him no comfort. From the very start he had baulked at denouncing the priest to Robert Cecil, knowing the methods the Privy Council would employ to interrogate and then punish the very whisper of sedition. Now, as a direct result of his intervention, Asher Montague is dead.

Why did he react in such an unexpected way? Nicholas wonders. *I told him he had nothing to fear from me, that I desired only to speak to him.*

But even more concerning is Montague's reaction when cornered in the stairwell. What manner of priest carries a knife concealed in his surplice, and draws it when he thinks himself threatened?

Nicholas tests the weight of the sailcloth parcel he is carrying. It certainly feels as though it contains nothing but papers. He hasn't opened it yet; it would be just his luck if a gust of wind scattered the seditious texts all over Fish Street Hill. But he can be sure now that Montague and Sir Thomas Wragby were complicit in them. He remembers his first confrontation with Montague, at the church at Barnthorpe, when he had gone to see for himself what manner of man had so entranced his father. Montague had been calmly dismissive then. He can recall the man's words exactly: *I know well enough the terrible price*

*God sometimes asks us to pay for entry into His glory... I can assure you
I am not at all afraid to pay it.*

A man so certain of his courage would not have fled. He would
have had the fortitude to stay and bluff his way to freedom. After
all, thinks Nicholas, until you ran, the proof I thought I had was
little more than circumstantial.

What has changed between that day and now? What is it that
made Asher Montague decide he would risk anything rather than
stand his ground?

✠

'He drew a knife on you?' A look of horror makes a mask of
Bianca's face. 'You could have been killed!'

She throws her arms around Nicholas and holds him tightly, horrified by the image of him lying on the flagstones at Austin Friars, a
spreading tide of blood carrying away his precious life. After only
a moment or two, he is forced to ease her away simply to breathe.

'Constable Osborne was with me, sweet. I was never in any
real danger.'

'You might have left me a widow!' she says, displaying her fear
in anger. She glances up the stairs of the Paris Garden house to
where Bruno is sleeping. 'And our son without a father. What
were you even doing at the Dutch church?'

Nicholas gives her a penitent smile. 'I might not have a
Caporetti's intuition, but I'm not blind. I know you distrust
Petrus, even though he proved his innocence to you that night
at the Jackdaw. So I thought I might at least be able to quell the
fears you and Rose have for Ned. And I thought the easiest way
was to warn off Montague, remove his influence.' He rolls his
eyes towards heaven. 'I didn't plan for him to *die*.'

'Remove his influence? Well, you've certainly achieved that.'
Bianca places her hands on either side of his face and shakes her

head in perplexed relief. Then a thought hits her. 'Nicholas, what manner of priest carries a knife?'

'That's what I was going to tell you. I was right about that illegal printing press. I'm certain Asher Montague and Sir Thomas Wragby – the magistrate who committed my father to the Ipswich assizes – were involved.'

'Involved? How?'

'Wragby paid for the press, and I suspect Montague wrote the seditious tracts. That's why he ran.'

'But how did your father get mixed up in it?'

'It's my guess one of them was foolish enough to drop a copy in Barnthorpe church. My father handed it in to Montague. In order to divert attention, Wragby laid a charge of sedition against him. I can imagine their alarm when Father told them his son was the queen's physician.'

'But why would they go to all that trouble? Why not just burn the tract your father handed in?'

'Because he'd shown it to others. It was only a matter of time before word got out and the Privy Council searchers turned up at Barnthorpe. Montague had only been there a few weeks, but he already had a reputation for fiery preaching. The searchers would have wondered if he might not be responsible for the tracts. Far better for him and Wragby to appear as the courageous defenders of the queen's faith.'

Bianca considers this for a moment. Then she says, 'That doesn't explain why the printer was murdered. Perhaps you're wrong about his press being Wragby's. After all, you didn't find any tracts there.'

'No. That continues to puzzle me.'

'Is that what's in there – more sedition?' Bianca asks, indicating the parcel he's brought with him from Austin Friars, lying unopened on the table.

'I imagine so. I'll give it to Sir Robert tomorrow, before I leave for Dover. He can boil the contents in saffron sauce and eat them for supper, for all I care.'

'But you haven't opened it. How do you know it contains the tracts? It could be something else.'

In the evening light from the latticed window the waxed sailcloth gleams a dull golden colour. Nicholas cannot help but think it looks like bullion lifted from a sunken ship. 'It feels about the weight of a ream of paper. I just assumed.'

'What's that phrase your father has, about finishing a job?'

'Always sow to the end of the furrow.'

Bianca gives him a wry look. 'Then you'd best cast a few more seeds, hadn't you?'

The package is secured with twine. Picking carefully at the knot, Nicholas unwraps it and pulls the covering aside.

The contents are not quite what he is expecting. They are documents, but not identical copies of the wild clarion call that Robert Cecil had shown him at Cecil House. These look more like letters. But they are not written in any language he can understand. He can see no fiery words calling for the death of all who worship false gods, for the removal by force of bishops and princes. These are nothing but blocks of what appear to be random letters and symbols, each one unemotional and utterly incomprehensible.

'They're written in a code,' Nicholas says with a disappointed shake of his head. 'No matter. Mr Secretary employs plenty of clever fellows skilled in the breaking of ciphers. Sooner or later, they'll work out what these contain.' He sighs. It has been a momentous day. 'In the meantime, I need to sleep. Dover is a goodly ride away, and I'm told it's impolite to be late for the welcoming of foreign dignitaries.'

✠

The courtyard at Cecil House is seldom empty. On most days there will be secretaries, messengers, petitioners, informers and spies hurrying back and forth, coming or going, mounting or dismounting, eager or fearful, depending on the success or otherwise of their own mission for Her Majesty's principal Secretary of State. On this August morning, with the soft light of a clear dawn striking the stained-glass Cecil crests set high in the mullioned windows, it is especially busy: the official welcoming party for the first ambassador from the Barbary shore to the court of Her Sovereign Majesty, Elizabeth, is preparing to depart. Horses snort loudly. Hooves rattle impatiently on the gravel. Grooms chatter as they tighten leather girths against polished buckles. Sleeping late is all but unknown at Mr Secretary's London headquarters.

A habitual early riser himself, Sir Robert has come out to inspect the company.

'Dear Jesu,' he laments as he takes in Nicholas's plain canvas doublet and unadorned riding cloak, 'he'll think you're the apprentice farrier. We'll have to get you something for Nonsuch. You can't appear at the revels looking like a tradesman.'

'Asher Montague is dead,' Nicholas says, sidestepping the rear of a horse that is objecting to the clumsy way its rider is climbing into the saddle.

'Who?'

'The firebrand priest at the Dutch church. I went to speak to him yesterday. He bolted like a house-diver caught trying to work the lock. I'm sure he was involved in the printing of the seditious tracts.'

'God's wounds, don't tell me you killed him?'

'It was an accident. He fell, trying to escape.'

Cecil gives him an arch look. 'Escaping from you? In your capacity as a physician? What were you doing, attempting to present your bill?'

Nicholas ignores the jibe. He hands the sailcloth package to Cecil. 'I found this hidden not far from his chamber.'

'What is it? More calls for the overthrow of God's ordained order?'

'At first that's what I thought. But no, it's a collection of what I think might be correspondence – in code. I thought you'd want to have it deciphered.'

Cecil takes the package. 'Do I need to send someone to have a word with the Broad Street coroner?'

'It's taken care of. It was a genuine accident. If necessary, I can provide witnesses who will confirm it.'

'I'm relieved to hear it. Still, one less firebrand Puritan in this city is cause for celebration.'

Cecil gives Nicholas one last despairing appraisal. 'When you return, before the diplomatic conference begins, you might care to come up with a way of looking more like a proper representative of our sovereign lady Elizabeth, and less like the fellow who sells oysters at Charing Cross.'

28

The pretty square-rigged caravel sails into Dover harbour on a brisk August breeze. She comes in company with two English pinnaces, sent out to ensure she is not mistaken for a Spaniard and fired upon by mistake. From the castle comes the roar of a cannon, fired in salute to welcome her in. The entire town has turned out to watch. Even the women stacking sheaves of grain in the surrounding fields come to the clifftops to gawp.

England has sent her Knight Marshal, Sir Thomas Gerard, to welcome the Moroccan ambassador. For the occasion he has attired himself in a bright-blue velvet doublet, Venetian hose, and sports a wide-brimmed felt hat crowned with a plume of peacock feathers. Gerard is England's second choice. His superior in heraldic rank – the Earl Marshal – is the disgraced Earl of Essex, and Elizabeth wouldn't favour *him* to take delivery of the contents of her close-stool of a morning.

Nicholas knows Gerard as well as any present. The two met when Robert Cecil sent Nicholas to be his spy at Essex's headquarters in Ireland, during last year's disastrous campaign. Sir Thomas has made it plain all the way from London that he does not much care to have Nicholas in the official receiving party. As they stand together on the quayside, a delegation of gentlemen of the court at their backs, Nicholas can see by the stiffness in his jaw that Ireland still rankles.

With the caravel's crimson sails furled and the cables made secure to the quay, the first ambassador from the court of Sultan Ahmad al-Mansur, King of Morocco, to the court of Elizabeth, by the grace of God Queen of England, France and Ireland, steps ashore, followed by a retinue of about a dozen attendants.

Like his companions, Abd el-Ouahed ben Massaoud ben Muhammed Anoun is plainly dressed in a flowing white *djellaba*, exactly as Nicholas has always remembered him. A similarly plain turban covers his head. The long nose has the same imperious set to it that Nicholas had once mistaken for a sign of cruelty, and the deep, dark eyes still dazzle when he smiles.

But it is to his accoutrements that the welcoming party must look if his status and wealth are to be properly judged. The jewels stitched to the tasselled strap across his chest – from which hangs an equally embellished black leather scabbard containing a wickedly curved sword – sparkle brighter than the August sun shining on the water of Dover harbour.

'Physician, it is good to see you again,' he says directly to Nicholas in Italian, one of two languages he uses when speaking to Christians, the other being Spanish. 'Has your queen sent you to greet me? Has she made you a prince already?' He looks Nicholas up and down, then does the same to Gerard. 'If they have, I shall have to tell my master that the English are cheap when it comes to dressing their top men.'

'I'm still just a physician, Excellency,' Nicholas replies, grinning. 'My only consolation is that, in England, doctors are allowed to think themselves princes.'

'Your Italian has improved,' al-Annuri says with an admiring nod.

'I have my wife, Bianca, to thank for that.'

'I shall look forward to meeting her. Is she your favourite wife? How many others do you have?'

Nicholas laughs. 'There's only one Bianca.'

'What's he saying?' asks Gerard, trying to look as though he doesn't care.

'He says he's honoured to set foot at last on English soil,' Nicholas says, bending a knee to the ambassador in formal greeting.

Gerard does the same. As he bends, the peacock feathers swish across his lowered face like a curtain caught in the draught from an open door.

'Tell Master Anoun that I welcome him to our shores in the name of our gracious sovereign lady, Elizabeth. We will convey him directly to London, where he and his gentlemen will be lodged in appropriate comfort.'

'Who's the pigeon in the foolish hat?' the ambassador asks Nicholas.

'Sir Thomas Gerard, England's Knight Marshal.'

'He is England's champion?' al-Annuri asks, looking concerned. 'He fights her battles – alone?'

'It's a courtesy title,' Nicholas explains.

'Allah be praised for that,' al-Annuri replies, looking relieved. 'Otherwise, we've no hope of forging an alliance against the Spanish. Is he a eunuch?'

'What's he saying?' Gerard asks again, adjusting his hat.

'His Excellency says he's looking forward to seeing London.'

As Gerard and the ambassador set off along the quayside to where a mounted escort waits, along with grooms preparing the horses for the ambassadorial party, Nicholas falls in between – and just behind – the envoy and the Knight Marshal, ready to translate when called upon. Al-Annuri's arrival has brought mixed emotions. It is good to see again the man who saved his life on the Barbary shore. The debt has been paid, like for like. But to Nicholas the exchange now seems uneven. How could it not, given that he knows the Privy Council has no intention of offering the ambassador England's assistance in the fight against their mutual enemy?

✠

'His Excellency wishes to pay his compliments to my wife,' Nicholas explains to Gerard when the party rides up Kent Street towards the southern end of London Bridge.

The Knight Marshal's hands tighten on the reins so much that his horse tosses its head angrily in response. 'You're suggesting that I expose the ambassador to a Southwark bawdy-house?'

'It's a tavern,' objects Nicholas. A respectable tavern, too, he insists – or as respectable as any on Bankside. And so a rider is sent ahead and a detour made. By the time they arrive, Bianca has put on her best kirtle and her cornelian bodice and, after a brief skirmish, has subdued her hair to a state marginally appropriate for the hosting of passing dignitaries. A reception line is organized: Bianca, Rose, Cachorra, Ned, Timothy and the potboys and serving maids. The lane outside is packed with Banksiders, all eager to catch a glimpse of the strangely dressed tawny gentlemen from a land that not one of them, save Bianca, could find on a map.

Al-Annuri is the very model of dignified courtesy. Ned, usually unshakeable, is as nervous as if the queen herself had dropped by for a jug of knock-down and a hand or two of *primero*.

'Don't they have taverns in the desert?' asks George Solver, one of the Jackdaw's regulars and husband to Jenny, owner of the loosest tongue on Bankside. 'Now that's an enterprise I wouldn't mind investing in. We could make a fortune if we introduced the heathens to ale.'

From the Jackdaw it is across the bridge and into the city of London, where the Lord Mayor and his aldermen wait to formally welcome the ambassador to the city. A crowd has gathered on Fish

Street Hill to see the strangely attired Moors arrive. They follow the party as it rides up Lombard Street to the Royal Exchange. For the most part they are good-natured, like excitable children at a country fair. But Nicholas still catches the occasional shouted insult: *Be gone, you godless heathens... Away with you! This is a Christian realm...* If al-Annuri catches the timbre of the words, he does not deign to turn his stately head.

At the Exchange, Nicholas translates the official speeches as best he can. The ambassador's quiet but imposing demeanour is in stark contrast to the noisy flummery of the welcoming committee.

And afterwards, when His Excellency and his entourage are safely lodged in a fine house nearby, made available by one Alderman Ratcliff – who has his aldermanic eye on the same prize as everyone else who's signed up to engage the Gaspari banking family to advise on the wonderful opportunities to be hoped for on the Barbary shore – Nicholas is summoned to Cecil House to report.

'And Master Anoun's present disposition?' Cecil enquires. 'Do we face an uphill struggle?'

'That depends on what you offer him. He is not a man accustomed to being taken for a country green-pate. He is learned, astute and won't take kindly to any deceit.'

'Well, that's for the Privy Council to decide,' Cecil says dismissively. 'You are simply there to reassure him of our good intent, and to relay to us his moods.' He pours two measures of sack from a silver jug and hands one glass to Nicholas. 'While you're here, I thought you might care to know that those enciphered documents you recovered from Austin Friars are giving my fellows quite the headache. Most of them are devilishly clever. We've only broken a few, and even those not entirely. Tell me more about our friend, Asher Montague.'

Nicholas takes a sip of the sweet wine. It tastes almost too expensive to drink. When he swallows it down, he feels like a man who's deliberately thrown a full purse into a midden.

'I believe Montague and Sir Thomas Wragby are – were – behind those seditious tracts,' he says. 'They didn't print them, but they were the inspiration. One of them, I believe, was careless enough to leave a copy lying around Barnthorpe church. When my father handed it in, Wragby and Montague were worried it might attract the attention of the authorities. They trumped up a charge of sedition against my father to make any investigation look elsewhere. When he told the Ipswich assize magistrates about me, they fortunately decided to refer the case to you.'

'What prompted Montague to make his unwise decision to bolt?' Cecil asks. 'What was he afraid of?'

'I was trying to warn him off. Two friends of mine who attended his sermons were in danger of falling for his zealotry,' Nicholas explains. Then, lowering his eyes in an admission of guilt, he adds, 'I made him think I was there on behalf of the Privy Council.'

Cecil's 'Ah, I see,' is laden with sudden understanding. 'Then I think it's time I invited Sir Thomas Wragby in for a privy conversation. The last thing we need in these uncertain times is a resurgence of radical Puritanism.'

'Wragby was a soldier of fortune for the Protestant cause in the Low Countries,' Nicholas points out. 'He won't fold easily.'

'I can't put him to the hard press, Nicholas. Not yet. Besides, all this is supposition. You have no actual proof. If I start applying hot irons to magistrates, the Lord Chief Justice will have something to say to Her Majesty about it. And you might have noticed that we're all rather consumed at present by Master Anoun's visit. It will have to wait until the official conclave is over and the ambassador has had his audience with the queen.'

Cecil reaches out for Nicholas's glass, a sign that the audience is over. Then he stops, as if he's just remembered something. Withdrawing his hand, he asks, 'This rogue Montague, was he a foreigner?'

'Not unless foreigners have West Country accents,' Nicholas says, hurriedly downing his sack in case the hand returns.

'Then why was he communicating with a brother in Zurich named Albrecht?'

Nicholas's eyes widen. 'I thought you said you were having difficulty breaking the cipher?'

'Ciphers, Nicholas – the papers are encoded in more than one. If I were of an optimistic temperament, I would probably describe our progress as slow.'

Remembering his confrontation with Montague in the church at Barnthorpe, Nicholas says, 'Montague told me his father was an admirer of John Hooper, the martyr. When Hooper was burned, his father fled to the Low Countries – then to Switzerland. That's the only connection with Zurich that I can think of.'

'Zurich is a hotbed of extremism,' Cecil says. 'I suppose we should be grateful it's Protestant extremism and not papist.'

'The phrases in the seditious tracts might be a way into the code,' Nicholas suggests. '"Let Hooper, the glorious Martyr, be thy touchstone and thy comfort, even when the task seems beyond the strength of thine arm."'

'That's how we've made the little headway we have,' Cecil tells him with a weary smile. 'We've also considered the possibility that the Book of Deuteronomy might provide a breach; the tract ended with a reference to chapter thirteen. We've tried that too, without success. The key may be elsewhere in Deuteronomy, but it's thirty-four chapters long. I have the utmost faith in my fellows, but it will take a while and they have an irritating need for food and sleep.'

'That use of the word *task* – that's interesting,' Nicholas says, reflectively studying the bottom of his wine glass. 'Does the author mean task as in the general struggle to be godly? Or does he have something more specific in mind? And that verse you showed me at Richmond – the one about the worship of false gods and being the first to put idolators to death—'

Cecil's uneven shoulders give a little twitch, like a raven drying itself after a rainstorm. '"The enticers to idolatry must be slain, seem they never so holy,"' he quotes. '"If thy brother... or thine own son, or thy daughter, or the wife, that lieth in thy bosom... entice thee secretly, saying, Let us go and serve other gods... thine hand shall be first upon him to put him to death..."

Nicholas says ominously, 'Perhaps those tracts weren't simply a clarion call from a deluded firebrand embracing extreme Puritanism, but a reference to something more specific.'

'Such as?'

'An assassination. If anyone would qualify as an idolator or a worshipper of false gods, it would be Muhammed al-Annuri.'

For a moment Nicholas thinks Mr Secretary is about to burst out laughing.

'I think that is rather unlikely, Nicholas,' Cecil says with a shake of his little head. 'It would take considerable resources to arrange such an attempt. Besides, how could a few deranged Puritan extremists in Zurich have knowledge of the ambassador's itinerary? The prize wouldn't be worth the effort of winning. Anyway, while he's within the royal verge, Master Anoun is probably safer at Nonsuch than he is in Morocco.'

✠

'He's very striking,' Bianca says casually from the bed. Through the open window a handful of stars gleam in a sky still holding out against the coming night. 'Eyes like a hawk's, but they do twinkle so.'

'Should I use some of John Lumley's four pounds to invest in a *djellaba*?' Nicholas asks, unlacing his doublet and tugging his shirt over his head. He starts to wash himself with scented water from the bowl Bianca always places in their chamber before bed.

She turns her attention from the dusk to her husband. She likes watching him prepare himself for sleep, or for lovemaking. The strength that a boyhood spent working the land has put into his limbs has not yet faded, despite his years in the city. There's nothing wrong with admiring something you find beautiful, she tells herself – though to save him from the sin of vanity she says, 'Don't be foolish. With your English complexion, you'd look like a ghost in a winding sheet.'

'Never mind a winding sheet, I am instructed to purchase a new doublet, by order of Mr Secretary Cecil. He said I looked like the fellow selling oysters at Charing Cross. We can pick up your new gown from the dressmaker at the same time.'

Bianca claps her hands. 'Mercy! So that's what it takes to get you to buy a new doublet – a diplomatic emissary from a foreign power. Let us pray you don't need new boots any time soon.'

He laughs at her teasing. 'Remember, you're to be at Lord Lumley's house on Woodroffe Lane no later than eight in the morning, the day after tomorrow. The ladies are travelling to Nonsuch by coach and waggon, along with most of his London servants. You should be pleased. Her Majesty doesn't usually favour wives being at court. I think the exception is because she wants to impress the Moors with the flower of English womanhood.'

'Oh, good, an entire day spent bouncing about like a pea in a farm cart.'

Nicholas rolls his eyes at her stubbornness. 'Think of the company you'll be in when you finally get there. People will be dropping into the Jackdaw for weeks wanting to hear you tell of it. Poor Jenny Solver will have to give up gossiping.'

'Who will be present?'

'Apart from ambassador al-Annuri? Just about everyone in the realm we're required to make the knee to: Mr Secretary Cecil... the Attorney General... the Lord Chief Justice... the Lord Admiral... the Privy Council... more bishops than you can shake a crozier at... Oh, and the queen.' Nicholas lays aside the washing bowl and cloth and climbs into bed beside her. 'But most important of all – and outshining even the most luminous of them – will be one Mistress Bianca Merton of Bankside.'

'The woman with paste for pearls and glass for jewels,' Bianca says. 'You know how courtiers do so like to look down their noses.'

'Take your inspiration from Muhammed al-Annuri – style and dignity through simplicity.' Nicholas kisses her on the forehead. 'By the way, Petrus will be travelling with you. John Lumley has promised to take him on as a temporary servant, to help during the time the court is there. He needs all the hands he can get.'

'Oh, wonderful,' Bianca murmurs. 'A day in a cart, and your strange friend for company.' She leans against his chest, feeling a sudden shock from the coldness of the droplets of water that he hasn't entirely dabbed from his skin. 'To be honest, what will make me truly happy is seeing Farzad, and John and Elizabeth Lumley again. And I can't wait to see what your fine Moor ambassador makes of an English revel.'

'And I can't wait to see you in your new gown. You'll be the brightest jewel there, by a mile.'

Bianca kisses him. 'There are *some* lies I'm prepared to forgive, Husband.'

But inside, she is thinking: *the day after tomorrow* – which means time has almost run out. If Master Woolrich of the Consistory Court does return from Canterbury tomorrow, she will have to wait until the revels at Nonsuch are over, if she is to have any hope of proving her suspicions about Petrus Eusebius Schenk are correct.

✠

'Is beautiful – *exquisito*,' Cachorra says in wonder. 'You will look very much *elegante*, more so even than the queen, for sure. Has Master Nicholas seen you wear it?'

It is noon the following day, and Bianca has only now unwrapped the orange mockado gown with green-and-white puff sleeves that she and Nicholas bought on Cheapside, laying it out on the table for Cachorra to see.

'Only the dressmaker,' she says. 'I wanted Nicholas to have to wait until the night of the revels to see me in it. I want it to be a surprise.'

Cachorra laughs. 'It is always good to keep your best hound just a little hungry. Let me see how it looks on you.'

Bianca is about to start untying the points of her bodice when there comes a brisk knocking at the street door. Cachorra, who by mutual consent has become part companion, part maid – with all the attendant ease and none of the subservience – volunteers to lift the latch. She returns with a puffing Nathaniel Woolrich.

'I understand from the Inner Temple that you've been asking after me,' the lawyer says, bending a knee with all the formality of a clerk appearing before Chief Justice Popham. 'I fear I was called away to Canterbury. How may I assist?'

'Good morrow, Master Woolrich,' Bianca says, breathing a sigh of relief that the plan she was beginning to think was drawing its last breath has suddenly had a miraculous recovery. 'What a fortuitous appearance.'

'You wish perhaps to launch a suit against someone?' Woolrich enquires, taking off his cap. 'If so, I can assure you that we Consistory Court lawyers are as ferocious as a bear at a baiting.' He bares his teeth in an attempt at an ursine snarl. With his plump shiny cheeks, he reminds Bianca more of an irritated squirrel.

'I need your help, Master Woolrich – and your discretion,' she begins.

'For you, Mistress, I would happily swim the Hellespont.'

'A walk across London Bridge to Dowgate Ward will be enough,' Bianca says, dashing the young lawyer's hopes in an instant.

'For what purpose?'

'I need to discover if there were ever any persons other than Aksel Leezen and his family living at his house in the Steelyard. The Hansa merchants have all gone, and presumably taken their records with them. I thought you might be able to assist.'

'Speak to the parish, Mistress. No need for a lawyer.'

Bianca gives him a disappointed smile. 'If only it were that simple, Master Woolrich. Sadly, in my experience, parish officials tend to look askance on a woman asking to see the records. Men do seem to like to guard their little secrets.'

Woolrich makes a slow, lawyerly nod as if he were conceding defeat on a point of jurisprudence. 'I would suggest, then, that we try the Subsidy Rolls – at the city Guildhall and at the Court of Exchequer in Westminster. Are you in any hurry for this information?'

'As a matter of fact, yes. And I was hoping for something a little less official. I'd like to be as discreet as possible.'

'The wards themselves will have the original tallies from which the official records are made. I could begin there.'

'That sounds ideal. May I accompany you? Time is a little tight.'

Woolrich smiles hungrily. 'And what, Mistress, might I expect in return? A lawyer's gown does not purchase itself.'

Bianca adopts a look of theatrical innocence. 'What are you suggesting?'

'Something more tempting than mere coin, perhaps,' Woolrich says, looking at the gown lying on the table.

Bianca senses Cachorra stiffen. Towering over the young lawyer, she looks like a serpent readying to strike.

'Master Woolrich, have a care,' Bianca says sternly. 'I am a married woman.'

'I meant no dishonour, Mistress,' Woolrich says hastily. 'But this is Bankside. I'm sure you understand my drift.'

Bianca notes the beads of sweat breaking out on his brow and the hungry look in his eyes. She puts a confiding hand on his wrist. He almost jumps out of his boots. She wonders if the day will ever dawn when dealing with the Master Woolriches of this world becomes less easy.

'They do say,' she begins, with an enticing smile, 'that Messalina, the wife of the Roman emperor Claudius, entered a competition with her ladies to determine which of them could satisfy the carnal lusts of the most gladiators in a single day. Messalina emerged the victrix – *twenty-four*.'

Young Woolrich seems to be finding it hard to swallow.

Bianca gives a conspiratorial glance in the general direction of Bankside's more salubrious stews. Her voice drops to a whisper.

'Within a hundred paces from this very spot, I could introduce you to a certain house that would consider *that* to be little better than unskilled labour. The quicker we depart, the sooner you can be back.'

Inside an hour, Bianca is standing in the vestry of All Hallows in Dowgate Ward, running her finger down an unrolled strip of parchment covered in the careful script of an anonymous clerk she will never meet, but whom she will thank with all her heart for being a diligent and meticulous man.

29

The white walls of Nonsuch Palace shimmer in the August sunshine. Seen from a distance through the haze, the carved gods and heroes of antiquity carved in relief on the stucco panels seem almost to have come alive, as though waking from their slumbers in the glare of a fine Aegean morning. In the surrounding fields the scythe blades swing through the high stalks of wheat left standing after the harvest, cutting them down for fodder. From the woods and coppices of the park the deer watch cautiously, as wary of a man with a scythe as they are of one with a bow.

Ambassador al-Annuri is mightily taken with Nonsuch. Walking together in the Italian garden with its statues and fountains that shoot, through clever mechanisms, cooling spray into the sultry air whenever someone passes, Nicholas gives a translation of John Lumley's commentary. Several courtiers have come to watch, gawping from the shelter of the hedges, bushes and fake Roman pillars.

'My lord is saying that the palace itself was built after the French style, rather than the Italian, by Her Majesty's late father, King Henry. It was gift for his third wife, Mistress Seymour—'

'His third?' queries the ambassador with an almost imperceptible lift of a coal-black eyebrow.

'Indeed, Excellency. He had six.'

Al-Annuri purses his lips. 'And yet I understood that it was the Christian fashion only to take *one* wife.'

It is John Lumley who rescues Nicholas from further explanation. 'Perhaps the ambassador would care to see the library. We have some fine translations into the Greek and Latin of works by the great physician of antiquity, Avicenna.'

When Nicholas translates Avicenna's name into the Moorish original, Ibn Sina, al-Annuri shows the first real animation anyone has witnessed since he arrived at Dover. But his enjoyment must wait, he explains. It is almost time for his party to observe the *Dhuhr*, the midday prayers. While the Moors retire to their accommodation, Nicholas accompanies Lumley to his library to choose what to show the ambassador when his attention has returned to the temporal.

To his discomfort, Nicholas finds William Baronsdale and Silvan Gaspari already there. The two men break off their conversation as Nicholas and Lumley enter. The banker gives him a look of utter contempt. He clearly hasn't forgotten their quarrel at the Privy Council meeting.

'Forgive us, my lord,' Baronsdale says. 'It is such a rarity to find so extensive a collection; we could not constrain ourselves.'

'It would be a worthless collection of mere paper if it were not meant to be consulted and enjoyed,' Lumley says pleasantly. 'Don't let us disturb you.' Then, turning to Nicholas, he says, 'Perhaps the ambassador would find it of interest to see the écorché figures.'

Overhearing, Baronsdale raises one eyebrow. 'You have écorché figures, my lord? May I see them?'

Lumley goes to a heavy oak cabinet and takes out a parcel wrapped not in the old cloth covering that Nicholas remembers, but in fine Flanders linen. Laying it on the top of the cabinet, Lumley unwraps it and lays out the contents for inspection. In the sunlight lancing through the windows, the painted plaster limbs gleam like freshly cut meat on a butcher's block.

'They're very fine,' observes Baronsdale. 'May I?'

'By all means,' says Lumley. 'You'll note the rendering of the tendons is particularly clever.'

Baronsdale picks up the figures one by one, inspecting them as if he were a cook choosing the best cuts for a feast. 'I don't suppose they're for sale,' he says. 'I've been after some of these for two years or more.' He turns to Silvan Gaspari and says, pointedly, 'Haven't I, Master Gaspari?'

The banker raises his hands defensively. 'Such items are extremely rare, Master Baronsdale. I've explained to you before, I'm still searching. Sometimes it can take months just to discover the fellow that one is dealing with is nothing but a manufacturer of cheap statuary. Things haven't been made any easier by the merchant I used as an intermediary having the bad grace to die on me.'

A discreet cough from John Lumley stops the spat in its tracks.

'My apologies, sir,' says Baronsdale. 'My passion for the collection of such fine items as these made me forget where I was.'

Gaspari says nothing, but still manages to look as though he's suffered a mortal insult.

To Nicholas, however, the banker's injured sensibilities are the last thing on his mind.

'This merchant you speak of – was he named Leezen, by any chance?' he asks Gaspari. 'Aksel Leezen?'

Gaspari stares at him with the astonishment of someone watching a Bankside sleight-of-hand trick. 'Yes, that's the man. A Hansa trader. How do you—'

'My wife found those figures in Leezen's house, in the Steelyard,' Nicholas says.

'Then they could very well be mine,' Baronsdale announces.

'The house had been locked for some time,' Nicholas points out. 'There was a dispute over the Will. Perhaps that's why they were never transferred to Master Gaspari.'

'Did they come with any bill of account or sale?' Gaspari asks.

'No. We found nothing,' Nicholas says. 'I understand from my wife that all Leezen's account books were originally held by the Consistory Court. But they were sequestered by the Lord Mayor's men. You'd have a hard task finding out.'

'Master Baronsdale, did you by any chance pay Master Gaspari in advance?' John Lumley asks pleasantly.

'No. I did not.'

'Well, there you have it, Master Baronsdale. I have already paid for them. They are mine, by right of purchase.'

Used to the customary reverence shown to him by the Fellows of the College of Physicians, Baronsdale finds it a little hard having to defer to John Lumley. 'But my lord,' he says with forced courtesy, 'it was I who ordered them.'

'They weren't made to your specific order,' Silvan Gaspari points out spitefully.

'And I do rather like them,' says Lumley, enjoying his moment. 'They really will suit my collection of curiosities very nicely.'

Baronsdale turns on Nicholas, his anger barely constrained. 'You had no right to sell these items to Lord Lumley. They are mine. Give them to me.'

'I don't own them,' Nicholas says, his voice devoid of apology. 'I sold them to his lordship. I can show you the receipt if you'd care to visit Bankside.' He notices Lumley's grey spade-cut beard twitch slightly as the custodian of Nonsuch tries not to smile.

'Master Gaspari,' Lumley says diplomatically, 'would you care to see an edition I have of Johann van Calcar drawings, printed by Oporinus? The book is dedicated to the Gaspari family.' He goes to a shelf and returns with the book he and Nicholas had consulted when Nicholas first brought the écorché figures to Nonsuch. He opens it to show Gaspari the title page.

Gaspari reaches into an expensive belt pouch and withdraws a small silk bag. Taking out a set of reading spectacles, the banker perches them on his fine aquiline nose.

And Nicholas would probably smile, if only to himself, at the dent that having less than perfect eyesight must put in Silvan Gaspari's vanity – were it not for the fact that he is too busy staring at the design on the silk bag. It's the same emblem he'd seen on the tunic of Gaspari's servant, at the banker's house on Milk Lane: an exaggerated letter G, embellished with fronds, folderols and curlicues – the lower part of which is identical to the etching on the blade Nicholas pulled from the body at the Steelyard.

✳

Having directed Nathaniel Woolrich to his reward at the sign of the White Goose, Bianca hurries on towards the Paris Garden. In her mind she recites the names she read from the Subsidy Rolls at All Hallows in Dowgate Ward barely forty minutes ago. There can be no equivocation now, she tells herself. The proof is undeniable, clearly shown in the official record for tax assessment for every inhabitant of the Steelyard, collected in the year before the Privy Council ejected the Hansa merchants.

The first line had been precisely what she had expected, though, in the manner of English official record-keeping, somewhat loose in style and accuracy:

13. Akal Lees. Hausa merc. £6. 12s. L: 14s.

The first number – thirteen – the parish clerk had informed Woolrich, as Bianca stood at his shoulder, was the property's position in the tax assessor's progress around the Steelyard. The next entry was the official's clumsy attempt to record the owner's name: *Akal Lees* – Aksel Leezen. Bianca can easily forgive the error; ever since she arrived from Padua she has understood that foreign tongues do not lie easily in English mouths.

Then had come Aksel's occupation: *Hausa merc*. 'Hausa', a similarly corrupted version of 'Hansa'; 'merc', an abbreviation of the Latin *mercator*, for merchant.

Next in line was the assessment of Aksel's business for tax purposes: six pounds and twelve shillings for the year. And finally the subsidy raised on it: fourteen shillings – around one-tenth.

After the assessment there had been a list of those residing in the property besides Aksel. There had been no mention of a wife or daughter; both, Bianca knows, had been lost to the pestilence some years before.

Then had come the lightning clap, the thunder that had rung in her ears until she had feared the ceiling would fall in.

On the day the Subsidy assessor came, Aksel Leezen had not been living alone at the property in the Steelyard. And whereas the other entries in the Rolls had recorded names with the appellation *serv*. – indicating servants – the next two lines had shown his lodgers to be anything but.

> Peter Shank – stranger
> Asha Mountjoy – revd.

Stranger – as in foreigner; *revd* – as in reverend father. As in wild sermonizer with a guilty secret, now dead. And both men so confident in their security not to have bothered giving the assessor false names, even if his lazy recording had almost done the job for them.

Our Lord's holy mother, Bianca mutters to herself as she approaches the lychgate at the Dutch church at Austin Friars. Did you know who they were, Aksel? Did you know you were opening your door to a liar and a firebrand Puritan?

But what truly sends the icy meltwater surging in her stomach is the image of a young lad's decayed corpse lying unwrapped on the floor of Aksel's house. A corpse that could well have gone into that culvert around the time Petrus Schenk and Asher Montague were living there.

30

I t is later that afternoon before Nicholas manages to speak to Silvan Gaspari alone. He finds the banker in the company of a treasury clerk. The two men are sitting at a bench in the south walk, working in the shade of a plane tree whose canopy is trimmed to a near-perfect circle. At first Gaspari is disinclined to speak, claiming he is busy drawing up an estimate of the net profit likely on the Moroccan enterprise for Lord Treasurer Sackville. Nicholas persists.

'I know there has not been harmony between us of late,' he says, 'but I confess I need your help. The matter is of some significance. It involves a death.'

The colour drains out of Gaspari's face, almost as if the banker has been expecting – *fearing* – this moment. He excuses himself to the clerk and walks a few paces away for privacy. Nicholas follows, perplexed. When Gaspari stops, his body tenses as if he is expecting a blow that he has no chance of avoiding.

'What is this about?' he says brusquely, yet with a trace of unease in his voice.

'The design on your spectacle bag, and on the livery your servants wear—'

'What of it?'

'Is it employed anywhere else – such as on plate, or knives perhaps?'

'Why do you ask, Dr Shelby?'

'Because I've seen the design elsewhere – on the blade of a dagger.'

As Gaspari holds his gaze, Nicholas sees the smoothness, the confidence, the superiority drain out of him.

'I discovered a blade with an identical design at the scene of a murder, at the Steelyard in London,' Nicholas continues. 'The tip was embedded in the victim's vertebrae. There was a sheath attached to a belt, but it was empty. I concluded he was stabbed from behind, probably while the killer was embracing him. Have you any notion how a knife bearing the Gaspari emblem might have ended up in such circumstances? Was he one of your servants perhaps?'

For a moment Nicholas thinks Gaspari has suffered an attack of apoplexy. He staggers, almost falling against the foliage of the bower. Regaining his balance, he buries his face in his hands. Nicholas can hear a muffled moaning escaping through the banker's trembling fingers.

'Master Gaspari,' the clerk calls from his bench, 'is everything alright? Are you unwell?'

Gaspari removes his hands from his face and waves the clerk to silence. He stares at Nicholas. There are tears in his eyes.

'No, Dr Shelby. He wasn't a servant. He was my son.'

✚

In a more secluded part of the south walk, away from prying eyes, Nicholas learns the truth about the body recovered from the culvert at Aksel Leezen's house. Silvan Gaspari sits on the stone rim of a fountain, the sun making the tears in his eyes glint like ice-crystals.

'Are you truly certain about the blade, Dr Shelby?' he asks.

'Quite certain, I'm afraid. How old was your son when he went missing?'

345

'Louis was almost sixteen. He was due to travel to Basle the very next week, to enrol at the university there.'

'When was this?'

'Louis went missing just over a year ago, Dr Shelby,' he says, barely in control of his emotions. 'It was a Monday, the day after Trinity Sunday. I sent him to the Steelyard to carry a message to a Hansa merchant there. He never returned. I had all the men of my household search for him. We called the local watch. But we found nothing – not a trace. How is it that you were able to do so?'

'It was chance,' says Nicholas. 'My wife inherited the property. I found the body in a culvert that connects the house to the edge of the wharf.'

Gaspari puts his hands to his face again. 'The dagger wasn't really for defence. It was a present, for his fifteenth birthday. I should have sent someone with him. I chastise myself for that failure every day – every single day.'

'Was it to Leezen that you sent him?'

Gaspari drops his hands and looks at Nicholas. 'If you're thinking Leezen might have been the man who murdered my son, Dr Shelby, you're wrong. Leezen was an old man, and quite ill. He wouldn't have had the strength to prick a rosebud, let alone a fit fifteen-year-old youth. Where is Louis's body now, Dr Shelby? I should like to see him when I am done here.'

'In the graveyard at All Hallows in Dowgate Ward,' Nicholas says. 'I understand he was given a proper Christian burial.'

Gaspari lets out a long, slow sigh, as if exorcising all the demons he has been wrestling with since his son went missing. 'Thank you for telling me, Dr Shelby. I pray that you never know what it is like to lose a beloved son.'

Nicholas does not respond immediately. He could tell Gaspari about Eleanor, his first wife, and the child she was carrying. But he fears it would only sound as though he were trying to trump the banker's grief. In the end he says, simply, 'I can imagine it, Master Gaspari. And I would not wish it on my worst enemy.'

✠

As evening sets in, Bianca entrusts to Ned the parcel containing her new gown and bids him a temporary farewell. He is to collect Petrus Schenk from the Steelyard before going on to John Lumley's London house on Woodroffe Lane in the north-east of the city, above Tower Hill. The two men are to remain there overnight, assisting the preparations for tomorrow's move to Nonsuch. Bianca has promised to be there by first light.

Lying to Ned does not come easily to her. She consoles herself with the fact that it is a white lie, and a small one at that. She has told him she needs a night's sound sleep if she is to endure the long, uncomfortable ride in a carriage. But sleep is the last thing on Bianca's mind. Giving Ned an hour's head-start, she is soon weaving through the crowd on London Bridge.

Nicholas is sure to listen to me now, she tells herself. Petrus has lied to us. I have the proof, clear as daylight. It's there for all to see, in the Dowgate Ward Subsidy Roll. He and Asher Montague were lodging together at Aksel's house in the Steelyard. If Nicholas is right in his theory that Sir Thomas Wragby and Asher Montague were responsible for the seditious tracts that got Yeoman Shelby imprisoned – and very nearly cost him his right hand, or worse – then Petrus Schenk is very likely also involved.

And what of the young lad whose body she and Nicholas discovered there? Both Schenk and Montague could well have been there around the time the boy was killed. Were they complicit in his death? Did they in fact murder him? If so, for what reason?

That question brings her to the murder of the printer, Symcot. Could Schenk and Montague be connected to that, too?

Bianca struggles to fathom out what could have motivated them to kill the man whose skill they needed to print the sedition in the first place. And then the Caporetti second sight lifts the shade from her mind's eye. The light blazes. The realization strikes her like a physical blow. The tracts were Symcot's idea all along. He was murdered not because of what he was printing, but for what he *knew*. He was killed because Wragby, Schenk and Montague feared that his dabbling in sedition would bring down the attention of the authorities upon him, and through Symcot upon *them*.

Bianca smiles with satisfaction. Nicholas is going to be astounded when she tells him. Her only regret is that she was with him in Ireland when Schenk and Montague were back in London preying upon her old friend while he was dying. If Robert Cecil hadn't forced Nicholas to go there on his commission, she might have been able to intervene. Another reason, she thinks, to despise the Crab and all his works.

She knows tomorrow's journey to Nonsuch is going to test her resolve to the limit. It will take every ounce of her composure to endure the ride in Schenk's presence. She takes strength from the knowledge that she'll be travelling with the remaining women from Lumley's London household. With luck, and a little caution, she should be able to avoid Schenk entirely.

In the bag she carries slung across one shoulder is a bundle of dried rushes from the Paris Garden house, a tinderbox freshly stocked with tinder and flint and a stub of tallow candle. Because when she reaches her destination, Bianca is going to drag the mattress she loaned Schenk out onto the empty wharf, place upon it those loathsome wooden effigies and set fire to the lot. Tonight she intends to exorcise every trace of Petrus Eusebius Schenk and the malign shadow he and Montague have cast across the memory of her old friend, Aksel Leezen.

When she reaches the Steelyard, she notices the wharf is not empty. A small barge is moored there, the tip of its single mast describing a lazy orbit as it moves with the current. It does not trouble her. One or two of the abandoned storehouses have been expropriated by the Lord Mayor and the Corporation of the city. Without giving the barge more than a cursory glance, Bianca heads for Aksel's house.

Dropping the bag from her shoulder, she takes out the ring of keys. It takes a moment to turn the twin mechanisms, but Bianca soon has the door unlocked. Taking a deep breath to calm the fluttering in her stomach, she steps inside.

The first thing she notices is that she can hear water sloshing at the foot of the steps to the culvert. The hatch is open. How can that be? She locked it the day Nicholas discovered the body there.

Beside the trapdoor stand two wooden casks. Much smaller than ale barrels, they look to her like the sort of containers the Jackdaw might receive from the Vintry, containing a few gallons of malmsey or sack.

And then a voice from the gloom beside the door almost propels Bianca's feet straight out of her shoes.

'Well, look what we have here! I could swear it's the maid from Austin Friars.'

Spinning around, she sees two figures step forward towards her. She recognizes them at once. They are the two men who were checking the parishioners at the lychgate the day she went to hear Asher Montague preach.

31

The shock forces its way into Bianca with the efficiency of a butcher's knife. The stabbing fear seems to loosen muscle from bone, tear away sinew, prise flesh from the meat beneath. Her whole body feels as if it's being expertly filleted. Bianca drops her bag. But with the instinctive ferocity of a former member of la Volpi, she turns to fight.

Despite the gloom, her first strike hits the taller of the two men almost where she had intended, in the groin. But only almost. Her foot lands on the inside of his right thigh, but just an inch or so too low. It is enough to send him reeling, but not to incapacitate. And while she is cursing her luck, his companion lands a blow to her cheek that drops her to her knees and sends lightning bolts chasing their tails around the inside of the darkened storeroom.

When Bianca regains her senses, she is sitting propped against the storeroom wall. The man whose groin she had tried to destroy is squatting before her, his dagger pointing towards her throat. The tip of the blade wavers alarmingly, though whether through the holder's pain or anger, she isn't inclined to ask. She suspects it's both.

'What are you doing here?' the taller of the two asks. 'This property belongs to the mistress of the Jackdaw, on Bankside. Who are you?'

Bianca is about to protest that she is that very person – and demand to know what these men are doing in her property – when she remembers how she had attempted to disguise herself to them at the Austin Friars lychgate. She falls into the exaggerated Italian accent she adopted then, hoping that she might be able to talk her way out of the danger she has stumbled into.

'I only come 'ere to find Signora Merton, for the *medicina*. She live 'ere, no? She very fine *farmacista*. If she no 'ere – I go.'

Her words seem only to add to the two men's confusion. The one with the knife stands up and turns his back on her, so that she can't overhear the whispered conversation with his companion. But by the way his shoulders move, she can tell they don't know what to do with her. She considers making a bid to reach the door. But as if the knifeman has eyes in the back of his head, he holds out the blade to warn her against trying to escape.

Bianca glances at the two kegs by the trapdoor. Are these men smugglers?

After a minute or so they appear to reach a conclusion. The knifeman nods, then turns back to her, resuming his guard over her. The taller one upends the cloth bag that Bianca dropped when they startled her. He retrieves her keys and goes upstairs to the living chamber. She hears the floorboards creaking and guesses he's checking that the bar across the shutters is locked. A moment later he comes down and closes the trapdoor, locking the bolt in place. Then he hoists one of the wooden casks over his left shoulder, takes it to the street entrance, opens the door with his free hand and places the cask down outside on the cobbles. He comes back for the second cask.

'Who knows that you've come here?' asks the knifeman.

'Only my 'usband, Umberto,' Bianca says, plucking a story out of thin air. 'An' my two cousins, and my brother. I 'ave to go to them now. They get angry if I no there to cook. Big men, they get *lunatico* when they no eat. They soon come 'ere to ask why Lucretia is lazy, good-for-nothing *cagna*.'

'God's luck to them,' says the knifeman, his eyes showing more than a little doubt, 'because they'll have to break that door down, won't they?' He nods to where his companion is waiting in the alley. Rubbing the place on his thigh where Bianca's foot had landed, he says harshly, 'But if you're lying to us, we'll know soon enough. And then I'll come back and take my pleasure how I fancy.' He turns his back to her and joins his companion.

Bianca does not move. She sits against the wall nursing her bruised cheek, tasting the ferrous seasoning of blood in her saliva while she watches the sliver of dusk-light disappear as the door closes. She hears her own keys rasping as they turn in the two locks, and voices fading in alleyway. And then she is alone in the darkness, the only sound the slapping of water in the culvert, as though she were trapped in a sinking ship.

✠

On Woodroffe Lane, to the north of Tower Hill, the lanterns are burning at Lord Lumley's town house. The servants are busy loading up, in preparation for a departure at first light. Already the street to Crutched Friars and Aldgate is half-blocked by open-topped waggons.

Tonight, the London staff are assisted by additional hands borrowed from other households across the city. Tomorrow, they will journey together to Nonsuch to make up the numbers needed to serve an expanded and demanding court, the Privy Council and the ambassador's entourage.

His lordship's steward is overseeing the operation. He has placed the extra help under the supervision of the senior members of the household, in case one or two of them have larceny rather than service in mind. The two exceptions to this are Ned Monkton and the fellow with the strange name that Ned brought with him a couple of hours ago. The steward knows Ned well, having served with him at Nonsuch in the year the pestilence came to London. He trusts the giant with the auburn beard implicitly.

When Petrus Schenk comes to him with the news that two fellows from the company of players hired to perform at Nonsuch tomorrow night have turned up bearing items accidentally left behind, the steward is minded to accept the approach at face value. But he is also a cautious man.

'Who will vouch for them?' he enquires.

'I will,' says Petrus. 'I know them. I've seen them working at the Globe on Bankside.'

The steward looks for Ned Monkton, for confirmation. But Ned is inside the house.

'How big are these casks? We don't have much room left.'

'Not large. About the size of a man's torso. A rundlet or so,' Petrus explains, gesturing to show the dimensions. 'They're stuffed with costumes. These fellows want to travel with them, lest they go adrift.'

'Well, I suppose the Lord Chamberlain's Men cannot perform before Her Majesty in their undershirts,' the steward says. He points to the last waggon in the convoy. 'There should be room enough in that one. Tell them they can stand guard tonight, in recompense for their masters' forgetfulness and my amenability.'

✠

'We weren't to know who she was,' protests the knifeman as his friend hoists the two casks into the waggon. They and Petrus are at the tail end of the line of carts, sufficiently far away from the Nonsuch servants not to be overheard. 'We thought she was an Italian from the Broad Street Ward.'

'Are you sure she can't escape?' Petrus demands to know.

'Every lock was made fast,' says the taller fellow, jumping down from the waggon.

'What about the trap to the culvert?'

'That, too,' says the knifeman. 'Unless she can burrow through flagstones, she's confined. If it'll content you, we'll go back and put an end to her.'

Petrus considers this for a moment. It would be sensible to do as the man suggests, but he can't risk anything going amiss tonight. If someone were to offload the casks because they questioned their presence in the waggon, or there was no room left for his companions when they returned, all could be lost. Besides, he knows the inside of the Steelyard house well enough to be confident that if the locks are set, there is no way Bianca can escape and raise the alarm.

'No,' he says. 'Stay here and guard those. That's the most important thing. I doubt anyone will come looking for her. Shelby is already at Nonsuch. She'll have been acting on her own. She's that type. I wonder what else she keeps from her husband.'

'And when we get back, what then?' asks the knifeman.

'When *you* get back,' Petrus says calmly, 'you can have what sport you like with her. I shall be getting *my* reward in a far, far higher place.'

✠

It is night in the Steelyard. Bianca knows this because within moments of her captors leaving, her eyes had become accustomed to the gloom. She had then been able to pick out the thin slivers of grey around the doorway. Now they have faded away entirely. There is nothing left but darkness. Her only consolation is that having taken her keys, her captors have left behind her bag containing the stub of tallow candle and its attendant tinderbox.

But Bianca has not been idle. First she has spent a considerable time at the main door to the storeroom, calling for help. But slowly the hope of an answer has faded, leaving her with nothing to show for the effort but a sore throat.

Then – not wanting to waste the candle stub, in case her incarceration lasts longer than she expects – she has gone upstairs to make a careful touch-tour of the upper floor, with the intention of finding some means of escape. As she expected, the bar across the upstairs shutters was down and securely latched. She braced one foot against the wall beneath the window and tried to wrench the bar from its housings on each side. This time she gained nothing but sore hands.

Without hope or expectation, she returned to the storeroom to test the bolt on the hatch to the culvert. That was the most futile effort of all, because she had seen it being locked. So now she is sitting beside the hatch, dejected and more than a little afraid, listening to the grumble of the river a few feet away and knowing that even if she were able to force the bolt, escape by that route would be impossible.

There's nothing for it now, she thinks, but to wait for Cachorra.

Before setting out, she had left Bruno with her friend at the Paris Garden lodgings. She had taken the precaution of saying where she was going. Eventually Cachorra is bound to come looking for her. Bianca prays she'll have the sense to fetch the set of spare keys that Rose keeps at the Jackdaw. And that she'll arrive before Schenk's friends return.

She knows the waiting will be all the more unbearable in darkness. By touch alone, she takes the stub of tallow from her bag. It feels even smaller than she thought, which vindicates her decision to leave lighting it for as long as possible. Then she retrieves the tinderbox and lays it close beside her.

Placing the candle stub between her teeth, with the wick outwards, Bianca draws her feet towards her, making an apex of her knees. She pulls back her gown and under-shift so that her legs are bare, reaches down to locate the tinderbox and places it between her knees, holding it in place with a gentle pressure from her thighs. She waits a moment, setting her body's position in her mind, taking a measure of the tension in her muscles.

Taking the tinderbox very carefully between the fingers of her right hand, she parts her knees and lowers the box to the floor, pressing it down on the flagstones. Again she waits while she frames the curve of her spine and the extension of her arm in her mind. Then, confident that she has made for herself a spot in the darkness that she can reliably reach, never having to search more than an inch or two, she lets go of the tinderbox.

When she next reaches down between her legs, she finds the small metal box at the first attempt. Cautiously turning it upside-down, she spills tinder and flint onto the flagstones. She makes a pile of the tinder, again by touch, then takes a flint between her fingers and starts to strike it against the hard stone. Tiny flashes dance in the darkness like shooting stars reflected in a deep, dark pool.

It takes some time, but suddenly a tiny flame shows her the nest of tinder on the floor between her knees. She cheers in triumph as it catches.

Bianca is about to take the tallow stub from between her teeth and apply the wick to the burning tinder when the most extraordinary thing happens.

A sudden gust of air from beneath the edge of the culvert trapdoor scatters the burning tinder. Before she can cry out in frustration, a brilliant white light turns the darkness into day, showing her the inside of the storeroom in eye-searing brilliance. It shoots in a line perhaps another yard or so back to the hatch, filling the air with yellow sulphurous smoke. Bianca scrambles away to stop herself choking, shading her eyes with her hands.

Almost as quickly as it bloomed, the light dies. All that is left is a trail of glowing specks on the flagstones to show where the casks were dragged.

But there is no mistaking the rancid stink of gunpowder in the air.

32

In the modest timber-framed house on the northern edge of the Paris Garden, close to the river and the Falcon water-stairs, Cachorra has reached the limit of her equanimity. As the hours have passed, her concern has grown until now it can no longer be constrained. Bianca should have returned hours ago. Her gown lies packaged and tied next to a small travelling chest containing a clean under-shift, her beautifying pastes and oils, and the ivory comb Nicholas bought her at Epiphany because a wooden one wasn't a match for the thickness of her hair. Now Cachorra is convinced something ill has befallen her friend.

She knows the route Bianca intended to take to the Steelyard, because Bianca told her before she left. Now she is sure there is nothing for it but to set off in her friend's footsteps. It is late, but the sky is almost cloudless; the moonlight will help her find her way. But first she must wake little Bruno and lead him through the lanes of Bankside to the Jackdaw, leaving him with Rose.

It is only a ten-minute walk. Roused unceremoniously from his sleep, Bruno does not complain. He is too excited by the pros-pect of spending the rest of the night curled up beside Buffle, the Jackdaw's dog.

'I wish Ned were 'ere,' Rose says. ''E'd come with you.'

Cachorra assures her there's not a cut-purse in London who would dare insult a six-foot-tall Carib woman going about her lawful business. Even so, as she sets off towards the southern end of London Bridge, she hopes she might run into Constable Osborne's Bankside watch. It would be good to conscript one of his fellows to accompany her, because the concern gnawing with icy teeth at her vitals is growing with every step. She can't remember feeling this unsettled since the day the Conquistadores sailed into the peaceful Hispaniola anchorage where her village lay. She had been eight years old then, and something inside her had known at once that her world was about to change for the worse. She has the same feeling now.

Cachorra reaches the southern gatehouse of the bridge without encountering the watch, or anyone else for that matter. She hurries along the thoroughfare that runs across the bridge, the buildings on either side making a tunnel that seems to bear down upon her oppressively.

On New Fish Street she encounters a group of drunken gallants leaving the Sun tavern. She endures their dull wit with indifference; they're too deep in their cups to trouble her. On Stockfishmongers' Row she passes a whore with her cully, tupping vigorously beneath the overhang of a house. Fifty if a day, and painted as thickly as the upperworks of a Spanish galleon, the woman watches her pass, wondering if competition has arrived.

On the corner of Church Lane, barely minutes away from the Steelyard, Cachorra runs into the Dowgate Ward night-watch. Not just one, but four of them. And accompanying them is the largest mastiff she has ever seen.

'Has a woman with dark hair passed this way today?' she asks pleasantly, trying to bury her Spanish accent as deep as she can. 'A handsome woman. She come this way, I think, a few hours ago.'

The leader of the watch is a short fellow with a belly that swells his leather tunic like a fair wind swells a sail.

'We don't need no foreign whores on our streets, corrupting good fellows with their filthy perversions,' he says aggressively. 'Specially not Blackamoors. Decent Christian doxies find it hard enough to make a livin', without the likes of your sort taking the bread out of their mouths.'

Cachorra resists the urge to point out the contradictions in his argument. Instead she says calmly, 'I am not a whore. I am looking for my mistress, Bianca Merton. I think she come this way before.'

'She's Spanish, ain't she?' says another of the watchmen to his leader. 'She's a fuckin' Don.'

'Probably a spy, come here to take the measure of the city's bastions,' suggests another. 'Why else would a Don be skulking around the streets after dark?'

Cachorra considers running, but one glance at the slavering mastiff convinces her otherwise.

'Please, let me go about my business,' she pleads. 'I fear for my mistress. I must find her.'

But her words fall on deaf ears and flinty hearts. Despite her increasingly loud protestations, within ten minutes Cachorra is sitting in the dark in a noisome cellar, the slamming of the iron grille ringing in her ears, and an ocean of despair threatening to overwhelm her.

✠

Over the Surrey fields, sunrise paints the sky a gentle rose-pink. Thin bands of cloud lie like scattered grey pebbles cast into blood-stained water. In the Nonsuch chapel, the Bishop of London, Richard Bancroft, has hurried from the queen's side to lead the Privy Council in prayer. In their separate accommodation in the wing that King Henry had hoped would house his queen, Jane Seymour – had she not died before the roof was on – ambassador al-Annuri and his entourage have stolen a march on the piety of their hosts by observing their own Fajr before sunrise. Now the talks must begin, and Nicholas is in a quandary.

Does he go along with the scheme to manoeuvre the Moors into agreeing to the trading enterprise being touted by the Privy Council and Silvan Gaspari? Or does he tell al-Annuri the truth? Does he warn the Moors that there is not the slightest chance they will get what they've come for: a joint campaign to invade Spain? If the former, he will be deceiving the man who saved his life. If the latter, he will betray his country and his queen. Despite the luxurious surroundings, Nicholas feels wretched.

After breakfast, the parties process through the gate in the privy garden, across the carefully manufactured fiction of the Wilderness, past the Grove of Diana the huntress, and up the little hill to the banqueting hall. After formal expressions of eternal friendship between Her Majesty Queen Elizabeth, Defender of the Faith, Queen of England, Ireland and France, and His Highness Ahmad Abu al-Abbas al-Mansur the Golden, Conqueror of the Songhai, Commander of the Faithful, the talks commence.

The ambassador praises England for her efforts in the fight against their common enemy, Catholic Spain.

Mr Secretary assures the ambassador that England will stand by Morocco if the papists ever think about returning her to the dominion of the Portuguese.

Nicholas translates.

Before al-Annuri can launch upon his master's wish for the two realms to embark on an enterprise against the Spanish, Robert Cecil is talking trade. How better it would be for everyone, he explains, if the sultan were to offer monopolies to a select group of English merchants whose financial strength is assured, thanks to the august house of the Brothers Gaspari, bankers to anyone with enough money to pay the interest, and friend to all those in possession of a blind eye.

'I have come here expecting to meet lions, but all I see before me are street hawkers,' al-Annuri whispers to Nicholas, as Lord Treasurer Sackville embarks on a long list of English produce that the Moors might care to purchase in return for the monopolies.

Nicholas studies his hands. The one event he can look forward to with any pleasure is the imminent arrival of Bianca with the convoy from Woodroffe Lane.

✠

Bianca knows it is morning. Slivers of daylight are again pushing their way through the gaps in the street door and around the shutters in the living chamber. The sound from the culvert had changed, too, telling her that the tide is turning.

The meagre light has allowed her to pick out the scorch marks from the trail of black powder that Schenk's fellows must have spilled when they carried those two casks up from the culvert. She wishes she had never lit the tallow candle. Because now she cannot un-know what is in those casks, and she can all too easily guess where they're bound. She can hear Nicholas's voice clearly in her head, answering her question about who was going to attend the performance at Nonsuch after the diplomatic talks: *Apart from ambassador al-Annuri? Just about everyone in the realm we're required to make the knee to: Mr Secretary Cecil... the Attorney General... the Lord Chief Justice... the Lord Admiral... the Privy Council... more bishops than you can shake a crozier at... Oh, and the queen...*

And she can remember all too well a line from the seditious tract that Nicholas had recited to her before he left for Barnthorpe to save his father: *Away with the vile servile dunghill of those ministers of damnation... Destroy that viperous generation, those scorpions, those puppets of the Antichrist, the murderers of the soul... Let God's hand strike those who worship false gods...*

It is the first time that hearing Nicholas's voice – whether in his company, in her mind or in her dreams – has caused her to very nearly vomit.

33

Cachorra, too, has found sleep almost impossible. But it is concern for Bianca, as much as the hard floor of the little chamber, that disturbs her so. She has tried sitting, but the cold stone floor quickly made her bones ache. She has tried curling up on the floor, stretching out, curling again, turning herself onto one side and then the other. No position affords her the slightest comfort.

Is this a prison she is in? If so, where are the other inmates? She does not know if it is still night. It could be morning, or after-noon, or the next evening since she was taken. At one moment it feels as though she's been incarcerated for little more than an hour, the next as if she's been here a month. But the very worst feeling of all is utter helplessness. She should be out searching for Bianca. Instead she's trapped – caged in much the same way that the Ciguayo raiders caged her when she was eight years old, before they sold her to the Conquistadores. Cachorra is a woman not much given to weeping. But at this moment she could weep tears of rage as much as of self-pity.

And then, somewhere nearby, a door opens. A wash of light fills the narrow space beyond the iron grille and an elderly, benign-looking fellow in a rust-coloured jerkin waddles into view. Behind him is the man from the Dowgate watch who accused her of being a spy and a whore.

'So, what have we here?' the older man says, peering at Cachorra through the bars. 'Mercy, an exotic animal indeed. Are you sure you haven't arrested one of the creatures from the royal menagerie, Constable Terrill?'

Cachorra's eyes narrow. Would you speak in such amiable tones if you knew I was named after the Spanish for a leopard cub? says the voice in her head. I scratch. I *bite*. She glares at him. 'Where am I? Let me out. I must find my friend, Mistress Bianca Merton. Why have you imprisoned me?'

'Anon, anon; all in good time,' says the man in a soothing tone. 'I am Master Warbersley, Common Councillor for the Dowgate Ward, and you are in the crypt of All Hallows-on-the-Cellar, which is where we detain miscreants before sending them onwards to the Compter or Wood Street Counter.'

'But I am not a criminal,' Cachorra protests.

'Constable Terrill believes you are a Spanish spy and a doxy.'

Cachorra's face hardens. 'I am no spy, nor a whore. I am in the service of Mistress Merton, at the sign of the Jackdaw on Bankside. Also, I learn with her to be *boticario*, for making apothecary.'

Warbersley smiles. 'Constable Terrill does have a mind sometimes taken by wild fancy.'

'Then you let me go?'

'If your mistress lives on Bankside, what were you doing late at night on this side of the river?'

Cachorra nods in the constable's direction. 'I tell your rude little *enano* there, I was searching for my mistress. She goes to the house she owns in the Steelyard. But she does not come back. So I must look for her. I might already find her yet, if that *eunuco* had not put me in here!'

Warbersley considers this in silence for a moment. 'Have you anyone who will confirm what you have told me?'

Cachorra seizes the iron bars of the grille and tries to shake them. 'Yes! My friend, Rose Monkton. She is also to be found at the sign of the Jackdaw. But hurry! I think my mistress is in danger.'

'I shall return when I have established the veracity of what you have told me,' Warbersley says in an official tone. 'If you are speaking the truth, I might be persuaded not to forward your case to a magistrate.'

'I have no *case* to answer,' Cachorra snarls. 'Let me go, so I may find my mistress.'

But Councillor Warbersley has concluded the interview to his evident satisfaction and is already halfway to the door.

✠

A pause has been called for the ambassador and his entourage to perform the Dhuhr, their midday prayers. Not wishing to appear the less pious, Bishop Bancroft summons the Privy Council to the Nonsuch chapel, delivers a sermon on speaking truth and being honest in dealing with others – which Nicholas finds a little rich, in the circumstances – and leads everyone in prayer.

On the way back to the banqueting hall Nicholas sees the Lord Chamberlain's Men have arrived and are setting up their paraphernalia on the gentle slope, ready to move inside when the talks are over. The players are walking around or sitting on the grass, reading their parts aloud, some to themselves, others to their fellow actors. Will Shakespeare is in animated conversation with his foremost actor, Dick Burbage. Nicholas's heart lifts. If the players have arrived, the convoy from Woodroffe Lane can't be more than an hour or two behind. He waves, receiving a friendly response from both men as he re-enters the hall.

But again his mood is soon soured. Taking his place beside Muhammed al-Annuri, he marvels at how the ambassador can keep such a serene countenance. Surely he must understand by now that he's being played.

Over the following two hours al-Annuri tries on numerous occasions to pin down the Privy Council on the matter of his sultan's hopes for a joint enterprise against Spain. On every occasion one or more of Her Majesty's councillors has an answer that allows them to return to the matter of trade. The queen's dockyards cannot produce enough ships. The rebellion in Ireland has priority over the muster of soldiers. The queen's ordnance is depleted. Steel for breastplates and morion helmets is hard to come by. Nicholas half-expects al-Annuri to ask why England doesn't just send a letter of surrender to Madrid and be done with the whole sorry business.

When the hands of King Henry's great golden horologe on the face of the inner gatehouse show three in the afternoon, word comes that the queen will receive His Excellency for a private audience. Nicholas is not required because Elizabeth is fluent in Italian. Mr Secretary Cecil, however, instructs him to gauge the ambassador's mood when the meeting is over.

Nicholas fills the time by wandering back to the banqueting hall. The Lord Chamberlain's Men have moved inside and are setting up for their performance of Master Will's *The Tragedy of Julius Caesar*. The carpenters have built a platform some ten feet deep and a foot high and have contrived some painted pillars to represent the Capitol. A curtain painted with an imagined impression of Rome has been hung behind the stage, serving both as a backcloth and as a wall for a tiring room, in which the players may change costume or rest when not required to appear before the audience.

'When the storm happens, won't the firecrackers you use to effect lightning set fire to the curtain?' Nicholas asks Will Shakespeare.

'No firecrackers tonight, Dr Nick. The Master of the Revels has decreed it. He doesn't want Her Majesty choking on the smoke, or the ambassador to think he's being assassinated. Fucking placeholder. What does Sir Edmund-fucking-Tylney know about performance?'

Nicholas lends a hand with the preparations until one of John Lumley's grooms arrives to tell him the ambassador's audience with the queen is over. He catches up with Muhammed al-Annuri in the privy garden below the windows of the royal apartments. The Moor is walking with two of his most senior advisors. Nicholas can tell at once that he's angry.

'Why does your queen treat me like a child?' al-Annuri asks as he passes. 'I expected more plain speaking from one of such reputation. Yet all I hear is *perhaps...* and *maybe...* and *if it might be contrived...*'

Nicholas takes a deep breath. How should he answer? How much longer can he keep the truth from the man who saved his life? How cheaply can Robert Cecil buy his conscience? He is saved only because the Moor has already moved on.

✠

Less than an hour later, the procession of carts and waggons arrives from London. Nicholas hurries to the outer gatehouse to welcome Bianca to Nonsuch. He sees Ned Monkton helping to unload the possessions of the ladies of Lord Lumley's London household. At the rear of the convoy he spots Petrus. But looking around, he can see no sign of Bianca.

'Where is she?' he asks Ned.

'I thought she was with you,' Ned replies, assisting a brace of maids down from their waggon. 'I've brought 'er gown, though.'

'What do you mean? She was supposed to be with this baggage train.'

'I were told this mornin' that she'd decided to ride down with the last of the players.'

'Who told you that, Ned?'

'Lord Lumley's steward.'

Nicholas searches out the fellow.

'I got word from one of the grooms,' the steward says. 'I didn't ask who told him.'

'Is the man here?' Nicholas asks.

'No, he was assigned to stay. The Woodroffe Lane house still has to function while we're away.'

As the horses drawing the now-empty carts and waggons are led away to the Nonsuch stables and the passengers disburse to their temporary accommodation, Nicholas is left standing alone by the gatehouse, looking impotently out across the bowling green, the great park and away towards the London road, with a mounting sense of dread swelling within him.

34

'Yes, of course this is Mistress Cachorra,' Rose Monkton says, peering through the bars of the grille.

'Are you sure?' asks Councillor Warbersley.

Rose jams her fists against her hips and turns to him, her black ringlets bouncing around her plump cheeks. 'Am I sure? Marry! How many six-foot-tall tawny Amazons do you think there are in London?'

'And you can vouch for her probity?'

'Without reserve. She's a friend of Mistress Merton, who owns the tavern that your saucy fellows came visiting, thinking they'd get free ale in return for my coming here.'

'She told us she was a friend of the queen's physician. How can that be true? She's a Blackamoor.'

'You're a councillor, Master Warbersley. You'll have seen the queen progress through the city on more than one occasion. You know she has Blackamoors amongst her servants. Why then should her physician not count one amongst his friends?'

Warbersley emits a long, grudging sigh. 'Very well, I see no reason to detain this person longer. Constable Terrill, fetch the keys!'

Inside five minutes, having learned from Councillor Warbersley that the Dowgate watch have arrested no one fitting Bianca's description in the past twenty-four hours, or learned of any who might have fallen prey to cut-purses or accidents, Cachorra and

Rose are hurrying along Thames Street towards Church Lane and the Steelyard. On the assumption that Cachorra would have received no food during her detention, Rose has brought some bread and cheese with her, which Cachorra eats as she strides.

'Do you think some mischief has befallen her?' Rose asks as she struggles to keep up.

'I don't know. I pray not.'

'Did she tell you why she was going to the house in the Steelyard?'

'Only that she had learned something about Master Nicholas's friend, and that she wanted to search the house once more before she told him. Then she was going to come back and sleep awhile before setting off for milord Lumley's house.'

'If she's not at the house, what are we going to do?' Rose asks.

'We shall have to retrace our steps and start the knocking on the doors. Maybe someone can tell us what has happened to her.'

As they march on, almost breaking into a run, neither woman will look at the other. Each knows that an exchange of glances will only confirm their worst fear: that in one of the side-lanes they have passed, Bianca is lying either hurt and insensible – or dead.

When they reach the house in the Steelyard, Cachorra marches straight towards the double doors and pushes hard against the upper lock-plate. The door does not move. Only now does she dare glance at Rose – and sees in her friend's eyes a mirror for her own dread.

'If she never even reached 'ere—' Rose begins, her voice trembling.

Her words are cut off by the sound of Cachorra's fist striking the door so hard that despite the thickness of the timbers it shudders in its frame.

'Bianca! Are you there?' Cachorra bellows in a voice that sends the gulls rising from the wharf in squawking agitation.

And to her immense and everlasting joy comes a reply, delivered first in Italian because that's the language Bianca habitually calls upon when emotion gets the better of reason, and second in English.

'*Finalmente! Dove sei stato?*' About time! Where have you been?

'Is all well?' Rose calls out. 'We've been worried to distraction. Let us in.'

'I can't,' Bianca shouts back. 'The bastards have locked me in and taken the keys.'

'What bastards?' Cachorra asks, rubbing the sore edge of her hand.

'I'll tell you in a moment. Have you brought the spare keys?'

'No,' says Rose. 'I didn't think to. I never imagined you'd be locked—'

'*Le piaghe di Cristo!*' comes the cry from behind the door. 'Go back to the Jackdaw and fetch them. Take a wherry – it's faster than walking. Tell the oarsman to charge it to the tavern. Most of them know us well enough. And Cachorra—'

'Yes, *hermana?*'

'Go with her. While Mistress Moonbeam is fetching the keys, go straight to the Tabard and tell the ostler I want to hire the two fastest horses he has. Tell him I'll pay extra if he can find a pair with wings.'

✠

Oliver Sly, the Lord Chamberlain's Men's newest and youngest player, is sitting in the makeshift tiring room inside the Nonsuch banqueting hall, knees bent, the handwritten pages of his part propped on his thighs. He is wearing the one broadcloth jerkin he owns. In a while he will don a white cloth gown and paint his face with ceruse to achieve a fetchingly feminine look, highlighting his cheeks and lips with vermilion paste, and thus transform himself into the lady Calpurnia, wife to Julius Caesar, Emperor of Rome. Nearby, the company's seamstress, a rotund soul named Abigale Glossop, who has a reputation as a formidable tavern brawler, is checking the lengths of cloth the company will employ for Roman togas.

Through the open door that leads out onto the gently sloping grass of the hill, Oliver can see the musicians checking their instruments and the other players rehearsing their lines. It is the first time he has performed before the queen and the court. The butterflies in his stomach feel as large and as vigorous as inebriated starlings. He knows he can't afford to make mistakes tonight. Another round of teasing, like the one he's had to endure after his kidnapping by the company at Blackfriars, is more than he could bear.

'"When beggars die there are no comets seen; the heavens themselves blaze forth the death of princes",' he says in his best Roman-matron voice.

He expects Abigale – who knows most parts backwards and often acts as cue to the players when they rehearse – to respond as Caesar, proclaiming, "Cowards die many times before their deaths; the valiant never taste of death but once."

Instead a man's voice answers. 'We're instructed to stow these here, by order of Lord Lumley's steward.'

Looking up, Oliver Sly sees two men, one tall, the other short, standing in the doorway. Each has a small cask on his shoulders.

'Sand,' says the shorter man. 'In case you silly buggers set fire to the hangings.'

Sly shrugs. 'Put 'em where you like. I'm Caesar's wife, not the fucking fire-watch.'

35

It is early evening, and the setting sun paints the sky to the west a luminous coral. In the Nonsuch banqueting hall the servants are removing the silver platters and gathering up the worst of the soiled rushes from the floor. The Nonsuch cooks, headed by Farzad Gul, have produced fifteen courses of wonder. The salted pike cooked in verjuice has been decreed a triumph, the roasted venison from the deer park deemed the tastiest in years, and the woodcock served in a sauce of mustard and sugar generally considered beyond praise. The Persian dishes produced by Farzad to please the ambassador and his party have found particular favour. Nicholas has eaten little. His mind is too occupied with concern for Bianca. Where is she? Why has she not come? What ill has befallen her?

Before the feast he had asked Mr Secretary Cecil if he might return to London, in case she had suffered an accident, or some other misfortune that had prevented her from reaching Woodroffe Lane in time. Cecil's answer had been a blunt '*no*' – followed by a brief lecture about fulfilling one's duty to the queen.

'Is Master Anoun showing himself amenable to our proposals?' Cecil had then asked.

In reply, Nicholas had also wanted to answer, 'No – and nor should he, given how you're trying to gull him.' But there are some opinions Principal Secretaries do not care to hear. So Nicholas had answered in the same evasive way that the Privy Council had dealt with al-Annuri's own questions throughout the day.

The queen has not attended the feast. Elizabeth has taken her meal in the privacy of the royal apartments. Only when she is ready will she lead her ladies-in-waiting from the spacious chambers that her father had built for Jane Seymour, along the southern panelled gallery, down the staircase in the south-west tower, out through the privy garden, across the orchard that lies below the pretend Wilderness and up the hill to the banqueting hall, her only male attendants being Mr Secretary Cecil, George Carey the Lord Chamberlain and an escort of the yeoman of the guard. Entering the banqueting hall – the table boards and benches now cleared away – she will take her place in the centre of the front rank before the stage, flanked by her senior ministers and ambassador al-Annuri. Her ladies will settle themselves at her feet like bejewelled spaniels, sitting decorously on cushions, expected to remain as immobile as the stucco figures of ancient heroes that adorn the outer walls of the palace.

The next row back will accommodate the rest of the Privy Council, along with Richard Bancroft, the Bishop of London (accompanied by two chaplains – his own and the queen's), and the ambassador's entourage. Behind them will come the second-rank courtiers. Peering over their shoulders will be the last of the quality: the wives and the other women of the various households, permitted – unusually, because our sovereign lady doesn't care much for competition – to attend purely in order to show the Moors the beauty and finery of English Christian womanhood.

Regarded as barely more than a royal servant, Nicholas would normally have his place in the very last row of all. But tonight he is to sit beside ambassador al-Annuri, acting as translator, and is expected to report any unguarded opinions to Sir Robert Cecil. He is conscious that if he looks back over his shoulder, there will be one face he does not see. Where is she? What has befallen Bianca?

While the boards and benches are being cleared away, Nicholas follows the last of the diners out onto the grassy slope. The night is warm and languorous, scented with pine and myrtle. Two rows of small iron braziers set on posts flank the broad stone steps leading down the gentle incline, making a corridor of light. From the darkening sky, swallows dart down to snatch unwary insects entranced by the flames.

To walk off the torpor of the feast, Nicholas decides to take a stroll. There will be plenty of warning of the queen's approach. It is almost five hundred paces from the door of the south-west tower of Nonsuch Palace to the banqueting hall, and at nearly sixty-seven it is advancing years, not royal dignity, that incline Her Majesty towards sedateness.

As he walks, Nicholas sees al-Annuri speaking with a brace of privy councillors and the Bishop of London. He catches fragments of Italian and Spanish as they attempt to make themselves understood to the Moor, even a line or two of Latin from Bancroft. From the English side, prevarication in three languages, he thinks.

By the path that leads down to the Grove of Diana the huntress, set amongst the trees on the western edge of the Wilderness, two yeomen of the guard are sharing a joke together. Nicholas never fails to be surprised by how lax security is at Nonsuch when the queen is here. Perhaps because she considers it more a home than a palace, there are seldom more than around thirty yeomen of the guard in attendance. He has seen no sign of their captain, Walter Raleigh. Sir Walter, he assumes, is still in the west, where – as all London knows – he has sulked for months because he thinks Elizabeth has slighted him by not appointing him vice-chamberlain of her household.

From the trees comes the mournful call of an owl preparing for the coming night's hunting. Thinking of the play he is about to see again, Nicholas recalls his Latin master at school telling the pupils that the owl, in ancient times, was a bird of ill omen, and that its cry heralds an imminent death. Suddenly the warm evening air doesn't seem quite so comforting.

✠

The ostler at the Tabard has proved himself a sound judge of a horse. The two chestnut mares are bold and fast. Bianca and Cachorra canter their mounts through the lengthening shadows of Long Southwark towards the open Surrey countryside.

After Rose had left them to return to the Jackdaw – she cannot even sit on a horse at rest without experiencing a toppling of the senses – there had been a brief delay while a pair of men's saddles was fetched; the ostler had assumed his customers would be riding as he thought women should: side-saddle. Bianca had held her impatience at bay by drinking a long draught of spring water from the Tabard's well and gobbling down – in a very unladylike manner – some brawn and bread; she has had nothing to eat or drink for twenty-four hours. Now, thinking herself at least back in the match, the discomfort of her incarceration is forgotten. Only the fear remains.

Should she go first to Cecil House? She had swiftly rejected the idea. There was no time to waste on convincing a phalanx of disbelieving Cecil secretaries that she wasn't suffering from a woman's frenzy of the mind. Nor has Bianca allowed herself the luxury of considering exactly what Petrus Eusebius Schenk plans to do, or for what twisted reason. All she knows is that he is a zealot, very probably a killer, and in possession of two casks of black powder, and that he is likely already at Nonsuch.

She urges her horse into a gallop. She feels the summer air flowing around her face. The sound of pounding hooves and the wild breathing of her mount fill her ears. She feels as though she could be flying. Beside her, Cachorra vanishes, then reappears as her own horse strives to keep pace. This, Bianca thinks, must be how the hawk feels as it plunges towards its unsuspecting prey. She imagines her talons slamming into Petrus Schenk, lifting him up and away before he can achieve whatever evil lies in his corrupted mind.

Nonsuch is some fifteen miles away. In her heart, Bianca knows her mare cannot possibly keep up this pace until they reach it. She will require rest if she is not to drop, exhausted, far beyond her destination, leaving Bianca to walk the rest of the journey. Looking ahead into the sunset, Bianca picks a lone tree beside the track some distance ahead at the top of a small rise. That, she decides, will be the spot where, reluctantly, she will bring the mare back into a walk.

But not yet. For a few more heady moments Bianca intends to stay on the wing.

✠

The white walls of Nonsuch have turned a fiery amber in the setting sun. Perched on its gentle hill, the red-brick banqueting hall stands apart from the palace like a russet moon cast adrift, throwing its long shadow towards the queen's procession as it crosses the orchard. In addition to the avenue of lit braziers, a myriad of candles set in portable sconces on the window casements gleam against the glass. The whole building is aglow. Flanking the main entrance, musicians in fine livery play gentle airs that echo sweetly in the hazy twilight. A troop of yeomen of the guard in crimson tunics embroidered with the Tudor rose come smartly to order.

Down the slope and onto the flat ground, two opposing lines of courtiers, interspersed with more yeoman halberdiers, flank the stone steps to welcome their sovereign lady to the performance.

Nicholas stands in the right-hand line, next to ambassador al-Annuri. The Moor has made no comment to him about the day's disappointments. Nicholas suspects he would rather be on his way back to Dover to take ship for home.

Looking across the steps, he sees Silvan Gaspari, his silver mane of hair turned a lurid pink in the light from a nearby brazier. He looks dispirited. Nicholas draws some small comfort in the fact that, if England has not given al-Annuri what he came here for, al-Annuri has similarly withheld his favour over the monopolies.

As Elizabeth reaches the foot of the steps, the musicians strike up a martial blast on their trumpets and pifferi. Mr Secretary Cecil offers her his hand. Sir Robert is the shorter of the two by a good couple of inches. His queen's piled auburn wig, topped by a lace caul studded with jewels and pearls, serves only to highlight the contrast. Together they rise – the monarch and her crab. That's what Bianca would probably whisper in his ear at this moment, Nicholas thinks, were she here. Which serves only to double the sense of worry that has been gnawing at him with its icy teeth ever since Ned Monkton arrived with the convoy from Woodroffe Lane.

✠

In the Nonsuch kitchens, set beside the eastern edge of the middle gatehouse, Farzad Gul is directing the servants drafted in from Lord Lumley's London town house as they assist the regular household in washing the salvers, plates and dishes from the feast. The cooks and their assistants have laboured for hours in heat stoked by three great open hearths and a bank of brick ovens. Most of the male staff are stripped to the waist. Once again, Ned Monkton has done the work of four men.

'You shall be the first to take his ease, Master Ned,' Farzad tells him with a grin. 'You have shamed my fellows long enough. You've

379

time to reach the banqueting hall before the players begin. I'm sure Lord Lumley will not object if you slip in at the back to watch.'

Ned wipes his great brow with the back of his arm. 'That's kind, Master Farzad. But I've seen the play afore, not that long since – with Master Nicholas an' Mistress Bianca.'

'Then take your leisure somewhere else, Ned. Somewhere cool. You've earned it.'

Ned thanks him and ties the points on his jerkin in preparation for going outside into the dusk. He looks around for Petrus but cannot see him.

Reaching the inner courtyard, Ned stands awhile gazing at the pale ashlar walls panelled with scenes of ancient heroes, real and mythical: Augustus... Hercules... Alexander... Neptune... Whenever he comes to Nonsuch he is always subdued by a sense of awe. It is as if these figures are a tableau revealing to him the order that God has imposed upon the world: first the mighty – amongst whom he counts the queen – then the nobles, of whom John Lumley is one, and then – scurrying to and fro in the background – the ordinary people, the grooms, the servants, the maids. And at the very bottom, the likes of Ned Monkton himself, son of a poor poulterer from Bankside, a man whose voice and account rank as nothing.

But Petrus has made him think again. Petrus has lit a flame in him. Why should a man such as himself not count in God's eyes as highly as any other?

He remembers the time he had pointed out to Petrus – after one of Parson Montague's fiery sermons in which the priest had railed against the nobility – that Lord Lumley had only ever shown him grace and friendship. He had explained that if John Lumley hadn't taken him and Rose in during the pestilence of '93, then both might now be remembered on Bankside only by their headstones.

'But you will live a thousand lives, Ned, and never find yourself living in a palace,' Petrus had replied. 'They will see you hanged at Tyburn before they give you that chance.'

Looking up, Ned sees the first star of the evening glinting in the purple sky. It seems to be mocking him, telling him that no matter what he does, whatever he endures, whatever he might dream, he can no more change his estate than sprout wings and fly to that glimmering jewel.

⚜

In the makeshift tiring room, the Lord Chamberlain's Men are ready. On the other side of the curtain, Dick Burbage is oozing his way through a dedication of tonight's performance to Elizabeth, his queen. Listening to his muffled voice, Will Shakespeare thinks his best actor might be about to twist himself into a knot of deference. Slick as an eel is our Richard.

Shakespeare has only a small part to play tonight, that of Flavius the tribune. After the first short scene he will be off-stage. On difficult performances like this, playing before the monarch and on a makeshift stage to boot, he prefers it that way. It is only twelve feet from the curtain to the edge of the platform and the first line of the audience, and not much more in the other direction to the open door leading out onto the grassy slope. Actors, he knows, are by nature an ill-disciplined and rowdy bunch. He will have his work cut out to prevent the audience hearing any raised voices from backstage, and it's almost inevitable that someone will fall over the thunder-making box and very probably roll under the curtain and into the full and unforgiving glare of the queen.

Burbage brings his peroration to a close. The musicians play a stirring fanfare. Will Shakespeare gives the signal. The players flow around both sides of the curtain and onto the stage. As

Shakespeare makes to follow, accompanied by the actor playing his fellow tribune, Murellus, he notices the two small casks standing against the inside face of the curtain.

'What are those doing there? They're not ours, are they?'

'Sand, I'm told,' whispers the other player. 'Orders, apparently, from Lord Lumley – in case someone sets fire to the curtain and the queen's wig takes alight.'

Will Shakespeare lets out a dismissive grunt. 'My mistake,' he replies. 'I mistook them for Phil Henshawe and one of his fellows from the Rose, trying to act. I suppose they'd better stay.'

✠

The Grove of Diana the huntress is set in a secluded, tree-lined cleft barely one hundred and fifty paces from the banqueting hall. The whisper of water tumbling from a natural spring fills the artificial grotto, making it the perfect place for contemplation. Or making one's peace with the world before leaving it.

In a short while, after he has composed himself and begged God to absolve him of his sins, Petrus Eusebius Schenk intends to take the taper he has stolen from the Nonsuch kitchen, walk as casually as he can manage to the steps to the banqueting hall and light it from one of the braziers. He will then enter the tiring room where, from earlier observation, he knows the general bustle will make it unlikely he is challenged. Hidden in the general backstage confusion, he will lay the two casks on their sides, the tops facing the tiring-room curtain. Removing the small wooden bungs from the twin holes drilled in the sides of the casks, he will allow a little of the black powder to spill out. Then, after a brief final prayer, he will apply the burning taper.

To his own specification, the casks have been lined with a thin layer of beaten tin. Even if they don't fully explode, the expulsion of igniting powder through the lids will drive the layer of packed musket balls inside out towards the audience with enough force to kill anyone nearby. Schenk himself does not expect to survive.

At first, when Asher Montague had come to him in Zurich to tell him about the Brotherhood of the First Hand, Petrus had been sceptical. He already knew that he was damned. The things he had done, or been party to, in the Low Countries had made that inevitable. But Asher had convinced him that the wounds his mind had suffered there were honourable scars, earned in the service of God. Asher had shown him a way out.

There were only two types of sinner, the Brotherhood had explained to him later. The first was the sinner who was damned even as he was born, carrying with him into the world the mark of that original sin, disobedience to God's law. The second was the sinner who, if he was prepared to repent and give up his own life as a sacrifice, could move the Almighty to mercy, and himself to redemption. Thus Petrus is sure that what he is about to do is not self-destruction, but martyrdom. And he won't even have to endure almost an hour of unbearable torment like his inspiration, John Hooper. It will be over in a moment. What better path could he take to redemption than to destroy those false deities who put themselves between a poor sinner and his maker?

Before he had committed himself to the work, he had asked Asher if it was not also a sin to take the lives of the innocent in the process. Montague had explained that God would look upon their unwitting sacrifice with favour. Their own martyrdom would count when He considered their immortal future, too.

'God will look upon their martyrdom with great favour,' Asher had told him. 'You will be doing them a service beyond price.'

What a tragedy, then, that Asher panicked when Nicholas Shelby had gone to him at Austin Friars. The priest had so much more still to do, Petrus thinks. A tear begins to well in the corner of one eye. Does a soul gets to sleep in heaven? It will be good to sleep uninterrupted, he thinks. To rest without nightmares. He cannot remember when he last did so.

He is not at all afraid. Indeed, he is eager. He knows that when he touches that taper to the powder, not only will all his sins be expunged, but he will stop seeing ghosts wherever he looks.

One more prayer and I will be ready, he tells himself with unshakeable certainty.

Ready to be the first to raise my hand.

✶

The setting sun turns the sheen of sweat on the mare's neck crimson. Bianca will not glance down because it looks too much like blood spilling from a wound. Her gaze is directed ahead, watching for anything that might cause the horse to shy or fall. She can feel the dust clinging to her face. Grit forces its way between her lips and into her nostrils, sometimes into her eyes. When that happens, she is forced to shut her eyelids for a moment or two and trust implicitly the mare's instinct for survival. When she reaches Nonsuch, the gatekeeper will think himself confronted by a wild-eyed, dirt-streaked harpy. But she dares not stop to wash her face in a stream or pond, not now, because she expects Nonsuch to come into view at any moment. And the closer she gets, the more she fears that, when it does, she will see a column of smoke rising above the pale walls, spreading out into the darkening sky, an enemy banner taunting her for being too late to the battle.

Cachorra is a few lengths behind, her horse carrying the heavier load. Bianca glances back over her shoulder. 'Not far now, only a couple of miles,' she shouts. But her voice is drowned by the wind and the pounding of her mount's hooves.

The ground begins to rise. Meadows of wild flowers fly by on either side. A stand of oaks lies on the ridge ahead. With the sun now almost below the horizon, they look as if they're cooling after a great fire has swept over them.

Reluctantly Bianca brings the mare back to a trot. When she reaches the oaks she intends to let the horse rest for a few precious minutes. Then she will ask her to dig deep into her spirit for the final gallop down into Nonsuch.

Reining in beneath the canopy of trees, Bianca eases herself into the saddle. She is tired, dirty and afraid. She looks down from the ridge. Across the parkland, the palace looks peaceful and serene in the twilight. The high walls are darkening even as she watches, the roofs beyond losing their outline against the purple sky. A sudden flash of light makes her heart jump into her throat. I'm too late, she thinks. Petrus has achieved whatever diabolical plan he has set himself. She braces herself for the sound of the explosion. But it does not come. The flash is only the last of the sun's rays striking the domed top of one of Nonsuch's gilded towers. Without waiting for Cachorra to reach her, Bianca sets her heels to the chestnut's flanks and almost sails off the crest.

✠

Elizabeth is sitting with regal stillness in her canopied chair. For all the interest she has shown in the performance, she could be a stuffed effigy, thinks Nicholas. Muhammed al-Annuri seems equally indifferent, his aquiline face as mobile as dried mortar. Only when Oliver Sly first appeared as Calpurnia had the ambassador shown a flicker of curiosity, turning his head to ask Nicholas if having a boy play Caesar's wife was meant to reflect what he had heard about English noblemen – that they preferred the company of their catamites to that of their wives. Nicholas had been forced to explain that it was against the law for a woman to be an actor.

But now al-Annuri is leaning forward, his dark eyes fixed on the players. It is the start of scene two of the second act, and the thunder box is working its spell. From behind the curtain comes a long, deep rolling rumble to signify the storm.

'"Nor heaven nor earth have been at peace tonight,"' begins Dick Burbage, playing the part of Caesar.

Nicholas does his best to translate as the scene plays. But as Oliver Sly's Calpurnia recounts the terrible omens the night-watch has witnessed in Rome's streets, he finds his Italian barely up to the task.

'A lion has whelped in the streets... graves have yawned and yielded up their dead... dying men did groan...'

And when Calpurnia ends her speech, 'Oh Caesar, these things are beyond all use, and I do fear them,' Nicholas finds himself – in what a moment before had been the almost unbearably stuffy banqueting hall – suddenly ice-cold.

It is as if the warnings are meant not for Caesar, but for him. And as if they are coming not from a sixteen-year-old lad wearing ceruse and a blush made of egg-white, cochineal and alum, but from the missing Bianca.

✠

'Christ's wounds – WHOA!' the Nonsuch gatekeeper shouts as Bianca drives the mare under the arch and into the outer court-yard. She pulls the horse to a halt so violently that the poor beast almost sits on its haunches. Gravel flies like musket balls. As Bianca jumps down from the saddle, Cachorra comes through the arch behind her.

'Why the frenzy, Mistress?' the guard asks, seizing the reins. 'Have you come to tell us the Dons have landed?'

Bianca bristles at the mockery in his voice. 'I must see Lord Lumley at once. Where is he?'

As the guard's eyes linger on her dishevelled state, Bianca can see that he doubts John Lumley would entertain her presence in his fine palace for a minute. 'Anon, Mistress, anon,' he cautions. 'All in good time. First, tell me your name and condition.'

And then, to her immense relief, Bianca sees a giant figure striding towards her from the inner gatehouse. She can't make out his face in the gloom, but she knows it can only be Ned Monkton.

'Ned, thank Jesu it's you,' she shouts. 'Tell this clod-pate who I am.'

As Ned breaks into a run, he calls out, 'You can leave Mistress Merton' an' 'er friend with me. I can vouch for 'em. She an' 'er 'usband is known to 'is lordship.'

The gatekeeper shrugs and heads back to his post.

As Ned reaches her, his eyes widen. Even in the dim light from the lanterns around the courtyard he can make out her sweat-dampened hair and the dust and dirt that streak her clothes.

'Mistress Bianca! Where 'ave you been? Me an' Master Nicholas 'ave been worried to our bones.'

'I must speak to Nicholas. Where is he?'

Struck by the urgency in her voice, Ned says, 'Up at the ban-quetin' 'all, with the queen an' the Moors, an' all the others. They's watchin' Master Will's play – Julius Seesaw.'

'And Petrus?'

'I ain't seen 'im for a while, to be honest.'

Bianca bends forward slightly, placing her hands behind her head and taking in a deep draught of evening air, as though pre-paring herself for some physical trial that she knows will take all her stamina. When she straightens again, Ned sees a look of fierce determination on her face.

'We must stop him,' she says. 'We must stop him now, before it's too late.'

She waves at Cachorra to follow her and strides towards the inner gatehouse. She knows Nonsuch well; it was in John Lumley's private chapel that she married Nicholas. She knows the route to the banqueting hall: past the great fountain at the centre of the inner courtyard, with its rearing marble horse... through the door at the base of the south-west tower... across the privy garden and the orchard... past the track to the Grove of Diana... Just a few minutes' brisk walk.

But tonight a few minutes might be more than she has. Bianca breaks into a run.

'Mercy, Mistress, what's amiss? Why the 'urry?' Ned asks, loping along beside her.

'You came from Woodroffe Lane with him, didn't you?'

'Aye, this morning.'

'Did Petrus have two fellows with him – one short, one tall? They would have brought something with them: a pair of wooden casks.'

She can see the surprise on Ned's face. It's the look he gives her when he suspects her second sight is in play. He's wondering how she can know of something she wasn't there to witness. But this time she isn't amused by his reaction. She's terrified by it.

'They weren't with 'im as such,' Ned says, frowning. 'But I did see 'im talkin' with two such fellows. An', aye, they was carryin' a couple of casks. I saw them bein' unloaded right there.' He gestures towards a spot close to the inner face of the gatehouse.

'I don't suppose Petrus told you who those men were?'

'No, but Lord Lumley's steward said they was from Master William's acting company. They 'ad summat what'd been forgotten, so they was bringin' it along afterwards.'

'Do you know where they took those casks, Ned?'

'I 'eard them asking the way to the banqueting hall – to where the players were settin' up. Why, what of it?'

Now comes the invisible barrier Bianca has suspected she would have to overcome ever since leaving the house in the Steelyard – forcing Ned Monkton to choose between one future and another. She takes an extra gulp of air to steady herself.

'Ned, Petrus isn't the friend you think he is.'

'I've 'ad the same from Master Nicholas—'

Bianca cuts him off. 'You must face it, Ned, he's lied to us all.'

Expecting resistance, she is surprised when Ned says evenly, 'I know you don't care much for 'im, Mistress. But 'e's been good to me. 'E's made me think things I've never thought of afore.'

'He's used you, Ned. Just like he's used me and Nicholas – all of us. And you're going to have to choose between him and us, because I fear he's about to commit an act that defies all Christian pity. And he's going to do it in God's name. I think it's time you heard the truth about Petrus Eusebius-bloody-Schenk.'

✠

He is resolved. He is at peace. He is ready.

On the slow walk from the Grove of Diana, Petrus has passed a yeoman guard patrolling the grounds, several servants hurrying about their duties, and a groom and his love emerging self-consciously from behind a neatly trimmed hawthorn hedge. Not one of them has had the face of a corpse.

Reaching the stone steps that rise towards the rear entrance of the banqueting hall, he pauses beside the first brazier. Taking the taper from where he has hidden it in the left sleeve of his jerkin, he thrusts the tip into the flames. He waits a moment until it ignites, then withdraws it, blowing on the end. He starts to climb, accompanied by this single dancing firefly that seems to lead him onwards by the hand.

At the top of the steps he can see a rectangle of dim light where the door stands open. A group of players are milling around outside in the darkness. They pay him no attention as he reaches the top of the steps, their thoughts firmly on their next cue. Beyond them, he can see that the little tiring room is crammed with players.

Petrus has calculated that the act itself will take only seconds, and so he decides to wait until there is more room to cross the ten or so feet to the casks of black powder. Because the players backstage are quiet, he hears a young lad's voice reaching out into the nightair as the boy playing Portia calls out in a feminine exhortation, 'O Brutus, the heavens speed thee in thine enterprise…' The words are like a valediction to him.

It occurs to Petrus that this is the last time he will ever look up and see a night awash with stars. He lets his gaze travel slowly across the sky, calmer and more contented than he can ever remember being.

�֍

Ned has been silent since Bianca completed a brief recounting of what she has discovered about Petrus. He had said nothing when she'd told him about Schenk and Asher Montague having lodged at Aksel Leezen's house around the time the boy whose body Nicholas had discovered in the culvert died. Not a word had passed his lips when she'd told him about Nicholas's investigation into the source of the seditious tracts and the murder of Symcot the printer.

'It all adds up, Ned,' she says breathlessly, dropping back into a walk as they approach the steps to the banqueting hall. 'You must face it. I was right all along. It's just that I didn't know what it was that I was right *about*.'

She wishes she could see his face better, but it's too dark now to see much other than his ursine silhouette, the great beard thrusting forward as he runs. She can sense him fighting a battle of loyalties in his mind, because under that alarming exterior she knows a kind and trusting heart lies.

'Our Nicholas is in there,' she says, almost pleading. Then, more brutally, 'If we don't find those casks before Schenk carries out his plan, he'll be amongst the dead, too.'

For a moment all she can hear is her own breathing. Then Ned says gruffly, 'I'm by your side, ain't I? I was never elsewhere.'

Bianca expects there to be a yeoman guard at the entrance to the tiring room. There's usually at least one at every entrance anywhere the queen is present. But she sees no reassuring scarlet tunic. She guesses that they're guarding the main entrance, because they know the Lord Chamberlain's Men by sight, and understand the half-controlled mayhem that goes on behind the scenes at every performance put on for their sovereign's entertainment. Her heart sinks even further into the icy slush that it's wallowed in since she realized Petrus Schenk's intentions.

At the top of the steps sits a young lad. In his hand is a cloth. He is using it to wipe away the pale ceruse from his face. He looks up as Bianca hurries towards him.

'You're one of the actors, aren't you?' she asks.

'I'm playing Calpurnia,' Oliver Sly says proudly, looking up at her. 'Got to wipe all this shit off, 'cause I'm meant to be back on soon as second plebeian.' He grins, which makes his streaked face even more alarming. 'What'd you want? Have you come to bury Caesar or to praise 'im?'

'I need to know if there are two wooden casks in there,' Bianca says, using her hands to indicate the size. 'About this big.'

'That's right. Sand. Orders of Lord Lumley. Oi! Where you going?'

Striding past Sly, Bianca orders Cachorra to go the main entrance to the banqueting hall and seek out Nicholas. 'Tell him the performance must be abandoned and the hall cleared at once. Hurry!'

The tiring room is a place of silent shadows. What little light there is comes from the candles in the banqueting hall spilling around the side of the curtain. The small space is crowded. On either side of an impromptu corridor just wide enough for a man to pass freely from the curtain to the door, the actors whisper the lines they will soon be called upon to deliver, stagehands wait to turn senators into citizens, plebeians, servants and soldiers by the speedy replacement of togas with jerkins, caps, breastplates and fake swords. Will Shakespeare stands close to the curtain, a small lantern in one hand, a prompt-book in the other, ready to call out if someone forgets their lines. No one is speaking. All are concentrating on what is going on beyond the curtain.

On the stage, Dick Burbage's Caesar is entering the last moments of his life.

'"The skies are painted with unnumbered sparks, they are all fire and everyone doth shine..."'

In the time it has taken to reach the banqueting hall, Bianca's sight has become accustomed to the dark. She looks around, searching for the casks. But her view is obstructed by the silhouettes of people's legs.

And then a star seems to dance in the gloom of the tiring room. Detaching itself from a cluster of stagehands, a glowing red pinprick of light starts to move across the right-hand edge of Bianca's field of view. As her head turns to follow, she sees that the star seems to be attached to something much larger – the shadow of a man. A man moving towards the curtain.

'There!' Bianca cries out. 'Ned, he's there!'

Heads snap in her direction. Out on-stage, Caesar is dying. The assassins grunt and curse as they strike him down. The queen's ladies-in-waiting gasp and squeal in terror. '"Liberty! Freedom! Tyranny is dead!"' cries the actor playing Cinna, one of the conspirators.

In the tiring room Ned Monkton barges through the actors and stagehands, knocking them aside like skittles. He slams into Petrus, knocking him off his feet, sending him sliding almost under the curtain and onto the stage. Seizing one thrashing leg, Ned hauls him back into the tiring room.

Thinking one of their own is being assaulted by a madman, two of the stagehands jump on Ned Monkton, trying to pull him away. Petrus squirms free of his grasp. Bianca is now so close to him that she can see the wild determination in his face. With his pale halo of hair, he looks to her like a demented fury risen from the grave.

And he's still holding the burning taper.

As Petrus turns in preparation for a final, desperate lunge for the nearest cask, Bianca seizes hold of his arm and sinks her teeth into his wrist. He screams. The taper falls. Bianca closes her eyes in anticipation of the blinding light that will be the last things she ever sees.

But this time there is no sudden flare of powder as there was in the Steelyard, just a wild confusion of bodies in the semi-darkness. As Bianca opens her eyes again, Petrus tears himself free from her bite. Grasping his wrist with his uninjured hand, he plunges out into the night, kicking aside Oliver Sly and leaving Bianca with a heart that's pounding fit to burst through her chest, and the iron tang of blood in her mouth.

36

Henry's great clock has just struck midnight. Sir Robert Cecil has made Lord Lumley's privy chamber his headquarters. Nicholas and Bianca are there with John Lumley and Walter Raleigh's temporary replacement as commander of the yeomen of the guard, a taciturn officer named Gatrell, whose permanently angry face is tipped by a beard with a waxed point that looks sharp enough to stab through flesh.

Nicholas can't stop himself glancing at the wheel-lock pistol that Gatrell carries at his belt. He knows there is a ban on carrying a firing piece anywhere near the queen's presence, a prohibition in force since Prince William of Orange was assassinated in Delft six years ago. Gatrell would not dare sport a firing piece here unless Mr Secretary had suspended the order. It seems Cecil is taking no chances.

From the way Sir Robert Cecil's little head turns sharply whenever someone enters with news of the search for Schenk and his accomplices, it would be easy to think he was engaged in a conspiracy of his own. Listening to Cecil's conversation with John Lumley, Nicholas has learned this has some truth in it. The queen's principal Secretary of State has so far managed to keep word of the near-catastrophe from his sovereign, the rest of the Privy Council and the ambassador. Save for a few raised voices from behind the curtain separating the banqueting hall from the tiring room, none of the audience had noticed anything amiss. By the time a yeoman guard had discreetly called Nicholas from his place beside al-Annuri to confirm that the tall Carib woman waiting outside wasn't some deranged fantasist, Ned Monkton had carried the two casks of black powder away to a safe distance. Now Cecil has no intention of causing a panic amongst the royal household and the privy councillors until the would-be assassins are caught.

'Christ's holy blood, Nicholas,' he says, turning from Lumley and fixing Nicholas with a melancholy glare. 'How could you have allowed that viper to get so close to England's beating heart?'

Nicholas stares at his feet. He has no answer.

Cecil shakes his head in disbelief. 'What manner of monstrous fanatic would even think of committing the sin of self-destruction as a means of murdering the government of this realm and its sovereign lady? Only the Devil himself could devise such a strategy.' He turns his baleful eyes on Bianca. 'As for you, Mistress, I confess I know not whether to have you confined to the Tower for being party to all this, or to petition Her Majesty to give you every reward you can think of for saving her from destruction. If you had been even a moment delayed—' He stops, unable or unwilling to consider the implication.

'It was Ned Monkton who stopped Schenk, Sir Robert,' Bianca says. 'And my husband is guilty of nothing but the loyalty that comes with friendship. Perhaps you should ask all those informers and searchers you employ why none of them were able to learn of Schenk's intentions. You'd have found him out quickly enough if he'd been a Catholic.'

For a moment Nicholas thinks Cecil is about to spontaneously ignite.

The door opens and one of Gatrell's men enters. 'No news, I fear, Mr Secretary,' he says directly to Robert Cecil. 'We're extending the search beyond the deer park, but the sky is clouding over. The moonlight is becoming unreliable.'

Gatrell turns to Mr Secretary Cecil. 'Sir Robert, it would be speedier if you ordered more of the yeomen of the guard to assist. The household servants are an ill-ordered lot.'

John Lumley shoots him a scornful look but says nothing.

'No,' snaps Cecil. 'My orders remain: a yeoman guard at every door. And never fewer than five directly outside Her Majesty's bedchamber – even if they have to take a piss up against the Flemish hangings in order to remain at their post. There could be a third madman out there. I can't run the risk.'

'All the doors are locked, Sir Robert,' John Lumley says in his Northumbrian lilt. 'Her Majesty is quite safe now.'

'That is your opinion, my lord,' Cecil says, unconvinced. 'But I would remind you that the assassins came here on a convoy from *your* London house. When the queen awakes, I intend to advise her to return to Richmond or Greenwich. I'll suggest the Tower to her if I must, if we haven't caught the bastards by then.'

'One or two in Her Majesty's household have noticed the activity,' Lumley points out. 'What shall I tell them if they ask me what's in play?'

'Tell them a couple of rogues amongst the temporary servants have made off with some of the Nonsuch silver,' Cecil suggests brusquely.

'And how shall I account for the increased presence of the guard?'

But Cecil is in no mood for discussion. 'If they'd rather risk having their chattels stolen, they're welcome to stand guard themselves.'

Nicholas gives a discreet cough. 'If it pleases, Sir Robert, I would like to assist in the search. After all, I brought Schenk here.'

Cecil levels one index finger at him from across the chamber, as if he were taking aim with Gatrell's wheel-lock pistol.

'Yes, Nicholas. You did. And finding him might go a *very* small way towards any possible redemption. Away with you!'

Nicholas and Bianca take the staircase down from Lumley's privy chamber towards the lower floor where a broad gallery, panelled on one side, windows giving onto the western edge of the privy garden on the other, runs almost the entire side of Nonsuch. They head towards an external door at the far end that is blocked by a yeoman guard, his halberd held across his body, the blade reflecting the light from a candle set on one of the window casements. Outside in the darkness, lanterns and torches move through the night, seemingly by their own agency.

'The Crab was being unfair, Nicholas,' Bianca says. 'You couldn't have known what Petrus was planning.'

'But *you* managed to work it out,' he replies despondently.

'Only when by chance I set light to the black powder they'd spilt at Aksel's house. Until then, I thought Petrus might be guilty of something else entirely.'

'I should have listened to you.'

It gives Bianca no pleasure to hear him admit it. 'Abandoning a friend is never easy – certainly not one whose friendship was forged on the battlefield.'

'I thought perhaps there was hope for him. When Petrus came here to Nonsuch the first time, it seemed to me that he had found a little peace. How wrong I was.'

Even as the word 'peace' leaves Nicholas's lips, the realization rocks him on his heels like a well-aimed fist. He stops, still some way from the yeoman guard and outside the range of his hearing.

'That's it!'

'What is?'

'*Peace*. I think I know where Petrus is.'

John Lumley's privy chapel lies in the opposite wing of Nonsuch. It is close by the Queen's Stairs, named not for Elizabeth, but for Jane Seymour. There are two entrances, one on the first floor, leading to a small upper gallery where members of the household and visitors may sit, and a second on the ground floor, giving direct access to the pews and the altar. As they approach the lower entrance, Bianca says, 'I still don't understand how you can be so certain. How could Schenk have got inside? The doors are all guarded.'

'There was plenty of time between Petrus fleeing the tiring room and Cecil ordering guards posted. The assumption was that he'd head for the Wilderness or the park.'

A few paces from the chapel door, Nicholas drops his voice to a whisper. 'Wait outside. Petrus might think you've come to bite him again.'

'This isn't a joke, Nicholas. He's a killer. A madman.'

'He won't harm me. What would be the point?'

Bianca shakes her head in exasperation. 'Christ's nails, even now you're defending him. He was prepared to let you die in an explosion!'

'I'm not defending him. But I do need to talk to him, for the sake of my own conscience.'

'If you're right, and Petrus is in there, you realize I will have to tell Robert Cecil?'

'I know. All I ask is that you walk back to John Lumley's study. Don't run.'

'Surely you're not thinking of helping him to escape,' Bianca says, horrified.

'I don't think he wants to escape. But I need answers from him. Once Cecil has him, I won't get to ask the questions.'

Shaking her head again, this time in disbelief, Bianca stares up at the moulded plaster ceiling. 'Merciful Jesu, this is where we were wed. Now there's a devil standing in the place where we made our vows before God.'

'*Please*. Just give me a few moments.' Reaching the door, Nicholas calls out, 'Petrus, it's me. It's Nicholas. I'm unarmed. I'm coming in.'

Lifting the latch, he steps into the darkness, closing the door behind him but leaving it ajar. For a moment he can see nothing. Then the glass in the chapel window gleams as a burning torch passes by outside. Nicholas catches the shape of a man kneeling before the altar. The light touches a halo of white hair and then moves on.

'I thought this is where you might be,' Nicholas says gently.

For a while Petrus does not answer. Then, having finished whatever prayer he thinks could possibly bring forgiveness for what he has attempted to do, he rises. Now Nicholas can make out his full silhouette. He appears to have his wounded wrist held across his chest.

'It is not where I had expected to be,' Petrus says with a cruel laugh. 'I should be standing before my maker now, not waiting for His enemies to descend upon me.'

'What happened to you, Petrus, to set you on this monstrous course?'

'Monstrous? Is that what you call it?'

'For want of a more damning word, yes.'

'What can be more monstrous than those whom that wife of yours has saved from their just punishment, Nicholas?'

'You mean all those people you were prepared to slaughter?'

'They are the ones who set themselves between the people and their god. I was about to do His work. I was going to sweep them away. I was going to help clear the path to righteousness, bring down the wall, let in the light. How can that possibly be monstrous?'

'Bianca has told me everything she's learned about you, Petrus – how you and Asher Montague were working together, the blade and the hilt of the same weapon. But who set you on this course?'

Petrus considers this for a moment, as though he's not sure Nicholas can be trusted with the knowledge. At length he says, 'They are people who understand that the only way the sons and daughters of Adam can save themselves from damnation is to sweep away the false gods who put themselves between the faithful and the glory of their Lord.'

'You mean to tell me there are others out there who helped you plan this?'

'They did more than help me. They sent me. They are called the Brotherhood of the First Hand.'

'Deuteronomy, chapter thirteen,' Nicholas says, tilting his head back in realization.

'"The enticers to idolatry must be slain, seem they never so holy",' quotes Petrus. '"Thine hand shall be first upon him to put him to death."'

'And you think you are that hand, Petrus? Is that what all this is about?'

'I was a soldier once, Nick. I didn't understand it at the time, but I was serving in the army of the deceivers. Then, in the midst of my torment, the Brotherhood found me. I became a true soldier of God, and a true soldier knows how to obey orders.'

'And where is this Brotherhood to be found, save amongst those whose wits are distempered and whose mercy has been corrupted? Tell me that, Petrus.'

'Amongst the stronger of the exiled Puritans in Zurich, Geneva, Frankfurt... all the places where those of the true faith gathered when England turned her back upon them and cast them out.'

The certainty in his friend's voice is unshakeable. Nicholas knows he has no hope of breaching a defence as strong as this.

'But you carried images of the dead in your pack,' he says. 'You saw them in the faces of those you passed in the street. And yet you were prepared to kill again. I don't understand.'

'Those faces I saw were the faces of the innocent, Nick. They were the guiltless. Their images were my penance for serving a false god. A child is not a false god. Surely a man of medicine can see the difference.'

Nicholas puts his hands against his cheeks in disbelief. 'I was sitting next to ambassador al-Annuri. I would likely have died, too – and Bianca, if she hadn't suspected you.'

'And then you would have both faced your Lord as martyrs, Nick. Martyrdom is a glorious thing. We have the saints to prove it so: Paul the Apostle... St Peter... St Stephen... It's a shame your queen's faith does not revere them as highly as does the Pope's. You would have had cause to thank me.'

'And when the queen and her bishops and the Privy Council were dead, what did you expect would happen then?' Nicholas asks, having to brace himself against the other's fanaticism as if it were a howling wind.

'A new world, made in the true image that God intended. A world without bishops and princes to distort His word, and to keep a man from his creator.'

'But there would simply have been a new monarch enthroned: Arbella Stuart, or the Scottish James, or some other person with a claim. And there would be new bishops, new councillors...'

'Oh no, Nick. The Brotherhood is well prepared,' Petrus says, the pride clear in his voice. 'Sir Thomas Wragby has recruited six hundred fine, God-fearing men from amongst the Protestant armies in the Low Countries, Switzerland and the Palatine – all true Puritans. With the Brotherhood to lead them, they will march on London and put to death any who seek to stand between a man and his God. England will be the first pure realm on earth.'

Nicholas would consider laughing at the ambition, if he didn't already know how stretched England's power really was. The Privy Council finds it hard enough to muster enough men to fight effectively in Ireland and the Low Countries as it is. A lightning strike on London to take the Tower, followed by a call to arms to every Puritan in the realm, could easily create a force large enough to achieve the Brotherhood's aims.

'And who pays for this?' he asks. 'Sedition of that scale requires a treasury.'

'The Gaspari family have made their resources available to us.'

Nicholas is stunned. 'Are you saying Silvan Gaspari is a member of this Brotherhood?'

Petrus lets out a harsh laugh. 'Only by association. He thinks the Gaspari are making loans to princely houses in Zurich and Frankfurt, supporting the publishing of books, the collection of art. Bankers don't bother to ask what the money is really for. Their only concern is the interest they charge: ten on the hundred. They're going to get a shock when we refuse to repay the loans – even more of one when we tell them that usury is against God's law and that, in His new realm, it is punishable by hanging.'

'And what was Silvan Gaspari's son to you? Another martyr?'

Even in the darkness, with only weak moonlight outside to outline his face, Nicholas can sense Petrus's features contorting in shock.

'Louis? You found Louis's body? How?'

'I'm guessing you and Montague dropped it into the culvert at Aksel Leezen's house, after he was murdered. You thought it would be carried away on the river. It wasn't. That's where we found him.'

Again silence, while Petrus marshals his thoughts. Then, 'We didn't wish to kill him, Nicholas. You have to believe me.'

'What happened? Did he find out what you were planning?'

'Louis was a pious boy. Asher tried to recruit him to the Brotherhood. At first he was willing. But eventually he threatened to tell his father what we were about. We couldn't let him do that.'

'And the printer, Symcot – did you kill him, too?'

'He was recruited to be the Brotherhood's voice in England. His task was to print our call to arms, and the orders that would follow. But he was only supposed to do so once we had cut off the Hydra's head of this godless tyranny. Symcot took it into his head to act on his own. He started printing tracts we hadn't authorized. We had to stop him before he brought the Privy Council to his door. They would have put him to the rack. He would have talked.'

'And before he died, you tortured him to find out if anyone else knew what he was doing?'

'He gave us weak thanks indeed for all the effort Sir Thomas had put into maintaining his press for the day we would need it,' Petrus says contemptuously.

'And what of my father?' Nicholas asks. 'Why did he have to suffer incarceration and the threat of mutilation or death? Was it because Montague was careless enough to leave one of those tracts lying about in his church? Was it to misdirect the authorities?'

'Mercy, no! That wasn't carelessness, Nick. That was to lure you to Suffolk.'

'Me?'

'You were our way into the Hydra's lair, my old friend. When we heard that you were getting close to the queen—'

'How did you know that?'

'There are like-minded friends here in England who keep us informed. The send us news of which way the wind is blowing. When we heard of a new physician having access to the queen – a younger physician with a humble background, the son of a yeoman farmer – it didn't take much to identify who that fellow might be. But Asher and Sir Thomas did not know of you the way that I knew of you. They needed to see the mettle of the man who would give us access to the altar of the false gods. I told them that if your father was in danger, you wouldn't hesitate to come. And come you did.'

Nicholas stares at Petrus in silence as he digests the enormity of what he's learned. Then he asks, 'Why are you here, now? Why didn't you flee into the darkness after the banqueting hall? Why didn't you try to escape? You must know I'll have to tell them where you are.'

'Because I am damned, Nicholas. Like most of us, I was damned at birth. I was damned again after the Low Countries. When a man sees the faces of the dead when he looks at the living, he knows it well enough. Only through martyrdom can I have any hope of salvation. The Brotherhood taught me that.'

'You know what they'll do to you, Petrus. It won't be a speedy death.'

Petrus's voice has taken on the calm certainty that Nicholas had once heard in Asher Montague's. 'You have no cause to fear on my behalf,' he says. 'I have the glorious John Hooper as my guide and inspiration. I would have preferred to have been victorious, but the end for me will be the same as it most assuredly was for him – bliss and everlasting joy in the presence of the Almighty.'

And then, almost as though some supernatural command has caused a beam of holy radiance to pierce the darkness, a streak of reflected torchlight falls over the face of Petrus Eusebius Schenk.

It reveals to Nicholas a calmness and a certainty that he has only ever seen on the faces of the painted plaster saints that adorn Catholic churches. Looking up and back, he finds its source in the little gallery of the chapel – a burning torch carried by a yeoman guard. Beside him stands Captain Gatrell, his wheel-lock pistol aimed downwards into the body of the chamber. And beside Gatrell is the small, crooked form of Sir Robert Cecil.

'Step aside, Nicholas,' Cecil calls. 'Give Captain Gatrell a clear shot.'

Now Nicholas understands. There is to be no trial. No drawn-out, torturous end on Tower Hill to remind the queen's subjects of the bloody price of treason. No public martyrdom for the man who would follow in John Hooper's shadow. Better for all that Petrus never leaves Nonsuch.

'I said step aside, Nicholas,' Cecil calls again.

Now the chapel is full of light, as though the sun has risen early. More torches dance just beyond the windows. Looking over Petrus's shoulder, Nicholas catches glimpses of crimson tunics and bearded faces in the night outside, and steel blades so pol-ished that the flames dance in them like stars reflected in clear black water.

'Do as Mr Secretary commands, Nicholas,' Petrus says with a tenderness that catches Nicholas off-guard.

But Nicholas finds he cannot move. His limbs have staged a rebellion of their own. He seems frozen to the spot.

Petrus reaches out and begins to gently push him aside. 'It's best this way, old friend,' he says.

And then three things happen almost simultaneously.

A roar of thunder fills the night, so loud that Nicholas – if his senses were able to function that quickly – might wonder if perhaps Petrus had managed to smuggle a third cask of black powder into Nonsuch and detonate it here in John Lumley's chapel. He feels himself propelled forward by a blow so violent that for an instant he and Petrus are joined like lovers, or mortal enemies engaged in a fight to the death, breast-to-breast, face-to-face. And then the burning torches and the people beyond the chapel window fade from his sight, leaving behind them nothing but a darkness as black as sin.

37

Robert Cecil and John Lumley walk together in the privy garden below the windows of the queen's apartments. It is late afternoon. The drizzle that came with the dawn has lingered all day, leaving the walls of Nonsuch glistening like wet ivory.

'I've had to tell Her Majesty at least something,' Mr Secretary Cecil says ruefully. 'Too many people heard the shot.'

'But did you tell her *everything*, Sir Robert?'

'Mercy, no. We'd all be confined in the Tower by nightfall.'

'Then what *did* you tell her?'

'That a rogue intruder took advantage of the revels last night to pass himself off as a servant and gain entry. A fellow of deranged wits. Fortunately, Dr Shelby happened to be passing and attempted to apprehend the rogue, giving Captain Gatrell enough time to dispatch him with his firing piece. Unfortunately, Dr Shelby was also struck by the same ball.'

'And she believes you?'

'There have been numerous such disturbances during her reign, my lord. Such an event is, sadly, not rare.'

'And the broader conspiracy?'

'She doesn't need to know about that. After all, it was no more than a wild fantasy dreamed up by disgruntled Puritans with nothing better to do than sit in Zurich, Frankfurt or wherever else they gather and whip themselves into a dangerous religious fervour. It could never have succeeded.'

'But the first part very nearly did, Sir Robert.'

'Which is why I have ordered a company that was destined for Ireland to march instead to Suffolk. They will remain there until we're sure that Wragby's mercenaries aren't planning to follow their vanguard. In my experience, such fellows are brave enough in the plotting, but tend to drift away at the first hint of failure.'

'And what of Wragby?'

'I've issued a command to the Lord Lieutenant of the county to have him arrested.'

'And the Moors? What do they understand of this?'

'I have assured Master Anoun that our robust and determined precautions ensured that Her Majesty – and his own person – was never at risk.'

The two men reach a fork in the gravel path.

'Tell me, Sir Robert, did Captain Gatrell give fire upon your command, knowing that Nicholas was directly in his aim?' Lumley asks.

Cecil considers his reply. 'Wheel-lock pistols can be notoriously unpredictable, my lord,' he says. 'And it *was* dark.'

'And what of Mistress Bianca?' Lumley asks.

'Naturally, she is somewhat distraught at the harm that has befallen her husband,' Cecil says. He brushes beads of drizzle from the left shoulder of his black gown. 'But she is a woman of rare enterprise, and I suspect she will already be telling William Baronsdale his business.'

✠

'The ball struck you at a tangent just above your right ear, Shelby, on a downward path,' William Baronsdale says as he lifts the plaister that Bianca has prepared from herbs taken from the medicinal plot in the privy garden. 'It chipped away a tiny amount of bone before plunging into the assassin's breast. Even a whisker further to the left and it would have entered your skull.'

Nicholas is lying in bed in what he takes to be the only chamber in Nonsuch – outside the queen's apartments – that is not occupied by more people than it was ever meant to accommodate. He suspects the unaccustomed luxury is because Robert Cecil doesn't want him accessible to too many visitors with loose tongues.

'Can you open your mouth to drink?' Bianca asks, offering him a cup of white willow, meadow rue and vervain boiled in wine. 'This should ease your discomfort.'

Nicholas tries. A searing bolt of pain shoots down the right side of his face, but he manages to drink without spilling too much over John Lumley's fine Dutch linen bed sheet.

'What of Petrus?' he manages.

Bianca shakes her head.

Baronsdale gestures her away from the bedside so that he can inspect his handiwork. 'I'm not common a seamstress,' he mutters. 'This really is the purview of a barber-surgeon, not a former president of the College of Physicians.'

'Then I'm bound to discover you've stitched my earlobe to my neck,' Nicholas counters.

Baronsdale announces himself satisfied and replaces the plaister. 'Well, at least this scandal will terminate your present favour with Her Majesty,' he says sourly. 'Such recklessness in her proximity cannot be permitted to endure. I shall see to it – personally.'

Happily bearing the discomfort, Nicholas says, 'I seem to recall, when the ambassador first came here, hearing you say in Lord Lumley's presence that you employed Silvan Gaspari to source those écorché figures for you, Master Baronsdale.'

'What if I did?'

'It means you were dealing willingly with a man who was financing treason and sedition. I must remember to mention that to Her Majesty when next she summons me.'

Baronsdale lets out a sound that falls somewhere between a grunt and a retch. He turns on his heels and, without speaking a word, departs, carrying the remains of his affronted dignity with him.

'How is Ned?' Nicholas asks.

'I suspect he feels betrayed.'

'As we all do. But is he the new Ned or the old Ned?'

Bianca gives him just the hint of a relieved smile. 'When he was called upon to choose, Husband, he didn't hesitate. We may assume, therefore, that Ned is the Ned he always was.'

✠

It is early evening when Robert Cecil comes to the chamber, his second visit since Nicholas recovered his senses yesterday. His mood appears to have softened somewhat. Nicholas puts it down to regaining a measure of control over the situation.

'As usual, I received my overnight dispatches from London this morning,' Mr Secretary says. 'My clever fellows have managed to decipher more of the documents you found at Austin Friars. They seem to validate much of what Schenk told you before Captain Gatrell gave fire. It seems the conspiracy was deep and well advanced. By the way, we've also taken Schenk's two accomplices. They were caught near Ewell, pretending to be farm labourers.'

'Are you sure it's them? It wouldn't be the first time that hot iron has been applied in error to innocent men.'

'The hot iron will come later, Nicholas. But you needn't fret. They couldn't name a single farm or manor in the whole of Surrey.

In the end, Ned Monkton identified them as the two who joined the convoy from Woodroffe Lane.'

'And Wragby?'

'He should be arraigned before nightfall.'

'Have you arrested Gaspari?'

Cecil looks evasive. 'I've spoken to him, but the Privy Council sees no necessity for an arrest. Gaspari swears he was ignorant of the plot.'

'Do you believe him?'

'I see no reason not to. Besides, there's no point in unnecessarily making enemies of one of Europe's most influential family of bankers, is there? One never knows when one might need them.'

Nicholas shuts his eyes for a moment. Expediency, he thinks, can sometimes be as corrosive as vitriol.

'Then it's over?'

Cecil gives him a wan smile. 'Thanks to God's providence, and with a little help from your wife and Ned Monkton.'

'I should have listened to her,' Nicholas says ruefully.

'In my experience, there's a danger that accompanies a close bond between men,' Cecil tells him in a rare display of introspection. 'Sometimes it blinds one to the obvious faults of the other – and to one's own. I held the Earl of Essex in warm regard, once.'

He leaves before Nicholas can ask Cecil if he gave Gatrell the order to fire knowing that Nicholas was still in the line of shot.

✣

Ned Monkton comes to see him and brings Farzad Gul. Everyone dances around the real reason why Nicholas is abed with his head bandaged. Elise Cullen drops by and bursts into tears on Bianca's shoulder at the thought that Nicholas might have died. John and Elizabeth Lumley spend a while trying to convince him that he has no blame for anything that happened. Their efforts lift his spirits a little.

As dusk falls, Muhammed al-Annuri slips quietly into the chamber like a wraith. 'I believe the balance of our debts is now unbalanced – in your favour. Cecil tells me nothing. What happened?'

'There was an attempt to behead the power of the realm,' Nicholas explains. 'It was a crazed and wild conspiracy, the design of a deeply troubled man manipulated by others. Fortunately, thanks to the determination of my wife, it failed.'

Al-Annuri digests this information in silence. He appears disinclined to know more. He seems to have lost all inquisitiveness into the machinations of the infidel. Before he leaves, he says, 'There is to be one last meeting tomorrow. I anticipate further prevarication.'

Nicholas draws a deep breath. 'They're playing you, Your Excellency,' he says. 'The Privy Council means only to exploit your hopes for its own commercial ends. The queen's ministers see Morocco as nothing but a marketplace where they might sell their wares at a better price, and profit from the monopolies they want from your king in exchange. They're no more likely to agree to a joint enterprise against Spain than they are to invite the Pope to preach at St Paul's.'

Al-Annuri fixes Nicholas with his customary dark, unreadable gaze. This is what it must feel like, Nicholas thinks, to be pinned down by a falcon that can't make up its mind if it's hungry enough to bother with you.

Then the ambassador gives a slow, appreciative nod. 'At last,' he says. 'I have found an honest man in this island.'

Nicholas can only give an embarrassed shrug. He knows he has betrayed his country and his queen. And he doesn't much care.

✠

It is early September. In the countryside around London the harvest is in. The yield is better than it has been in past years, worse than it could be. Looking out from Robert Cecil's study to the cropped fields of Covent Garden, Nicholas – now fully healed – thinks of his father. Cecil has just told him that in light of Sir Thomas Wragby's treason, all charges against Yeoman Shelby have been dropped, by order of the Attorney General.

'Wragby and his two co-conspirators are for the scaffold,' Cecil says, breaking into his thoughts. 'The death-warrants were signed last night. My agents in Zurich and Frankfurt are even now seeking out the leadership of this so-called Brotherhood of the First Hand. We may expect a temporary increase in the number of unexplained slayings in the darker alleyways of those cities.' He hands Nicholas a sheet of thick vellum with a heavy seal attached. 'Speaking of Wragby, you might care to read this.'

Nicholas's eyes fall to the handwritten lines:

> To our well-beloved and faithful servant, Nicholas Shelby of Barnthorpe in the County of Suffolk, greetings.
>
> Be it known that it is our desire and pleasure to gift unto the said Nicholas Shelby the estate of Hasketon Manor in that county, along with all its moveables, lands and revenues, and to confirm him in the estate of Gentleman, the better that he might receive and enjoy the station befitting a physician to the person of our High and Sovereign Majesty.
>
> Elizabeth R

Nicholas reads the letter twice more before asking, 'Is this real? Are you certain it's not the product of one of your clever forgers?'

Cecil looks affronted. 'Wragby won't be in a fit state to enjoy his possessions when he's been hanged, castrated, disembowelled and quartered, will he? Not unless your skills at surgery are a deal more impressive than even I give them credit for. Of course you'll need to buy yourself some decent clothes.' He gathers the papers on his desk in preparation for the next pressing duty he must perform as Elizabeth's principal Secretary of State. 'By the way, Ned Monkton is to receive a pension of twenty pounds a year. That should be enough to keep him in a degree of comfort. Of course it's conditional upon him not telling anyone what it's in reward for.'

'I'm sure he'll agree – for thirty.'

'Twenty-five. That's the most I can prise out of Lord Treasurer Sackville.'

'And Bianca? After all, it was really all down to her perseverance and courage.'

Cecil lets out a snort of laughter. 'If we start rewarding women for services to the safety and peace of the realm, before you know it, they'll be demanding seats on the Privy Council. Then where will it end? Look on the bright side. As the wife of a royal physician, now she'll have a use for that fine gown you bought her. At least one of you will be appropriately dressed.'

From Cecil House, Nicholas walks east along the Strand, through Temple Bar and into the city. The summer heat has long since faded, driven off by an early autumnal wind. He heads south down St Andrew's Hill until he reaches Thames Street. Entering the Steelyard, he finds Bianca and Father Beauchêne waiting for him on the wharf. They are standing beside a small, unlit bonfire scavenged from the surrounding empty buildings.

The wind is stronger this close to the river. It snaps at Bianca's gown and Beauchêne's surplice, ruffles the cloaks of the passengers in the tilt-boats and wherries out on the water, fills the sails of the barges.

Stacked on top of the knee-high pyre, their faces gazing upwards with blank serenity, lie the small wooden painted images of several children.

'Sir Robert confirmed it to me this afternoon,' Nicholas says, looking at Bianca. 'His investigation' – a poor word, he thinks, to describe the methods Mr Secretary's people employ – 'has shown Aksel Leezen was innocent in all regards.'

Bianca gives a nod of relief. 'I was just telling Father Beauchêne how Aksel was preyed upon for his kindness by two men who had nothing but evil in their hearts, even as they professed their piety.'

'It is a truth I do not like to admit to myself,' Beauchêne says in agreement. 'But some amongst us convince themselves that it is God speaking to them, when in truth it is the Devil.'

'Have you decided?' Nicholas asks Bianca.

'Yes. I'm going to entrust the house to All Hallows for a rent of one penny a year,' she says, 'on the condition they use it as an almshouse for soldiers home from the Low Countries and Ireland, and sailors discharged from the queen's navy – men who have no immediate aid or ease and need shelter. I know it's only a small house, but at least it will keep a few from immediate vagrancy and penury.'

Nicholas nods in appreciation. 'Aksel would approve, I'm sure.'

'And your visit to the Crab?'

'Ned will be pleased. Otherwise, nothing of importance. I'll tell all later.'

Bianca hands him her replenished tinderbox. Nicholas kneels and sets to work. It requires patience and no small effort, because the wind keeps scattering the sparks. But eventually one small flame becomes two and then three. Trails of white smoke begin to weave inside the pyre, snatched away by the breeze whenever they poke their heads out.

As the fire begins to burn, Father Beauchêne recites a blessing, his voice battling against the sound of the river and the crying of the wind. "'And God shall wipe away all tears from their eyes, and there shall be no more death, neither sorrow, neither crying, neither shall there be any more pain...'"

Now the flames are strong, gaining a life of their own. They reach the bottom of the little pile of images. The wooden limbs begin to smoke, the paint starts to blister. And then, almost as if they are eager to be free of their imprisonment, they ignite as one, flaring like a beacon, blazing brightly until they blacken and disintegrate, leaving behind a mound of ash that slowly turns to grey, before the strengthening wind bears it away towards London Bridge.

Historical Note

Just five years after this story ends, a group of embittered Catholics attempted to detonate thirty-six barrels of gunpowder beneath the Palace of Westminster. If successful, the plot would have decapitated the power of the state at a single stroke. For readers who might think the security at Nonsuch during al-Annuri's visit unfeasibly lax, Robert Catesby and his fellow conspirators were able to assemble their considerable store of explosives undetected until almost the last moment.

The idea for the painted effigies that feature in the story came from two images of Elizabethan children to be seen at Castle Drogo in Devon. Known as dummy boards, these curiosities, originating around the time of this story, fell out of fashion in the Victorian era. While wholly innocent, they exude a rather unsettling aspect.

The characters of Oliver Sly, Hugh Mould and Gideon Trindle are fictional representations of Nathan Field, Salmon Pavy and Thomas Clifton, who were among several teenagers who were essentially kidnapped to perform, or work, in London's playhouses during the time in which this story is set.

The Brotherhood of the First Hand is a fiction, although there were indeed extremist sects amongst the Puritan movement. In the middle of the seventeenth century the Fifth Monarchy Men used violence in support of their desire to establish a purely theocratic English government following the English Civil War.

Puritans continued to suffer suppression because of the existential threat to authority contained within their beliefs: that minister and bishops – even the monarch – were artificial barriers set between the pious and God. Many chose to leave England for the New World, where they could practise their faith freely.

Muhammed al-Annuri was ultimately unsuccessful in promoting his sultan's plan to persuade Elizabeth to join the Sultan of Morocco in a joint enterprise against the Spanish. After the talks at Nonsuch, he was invited to the Accession Day jousts at Whitehall. While several European ambassadors sat close to Elizabeth, al-Annuri and his entourage – being infidels – watched from a specially built canopy amongst the populace. He left England in early 1601, six months after he arrived. It is believed by some that he was the inspiration for William Shakespeare's Othello. His enigmatic portrait hangs today in the Shakespeare Institute in Stratford-upon-Avon.

Acknowledgements

This is the sixth adventure of Nicholas, Bianca, Rose and Ned, and it would be remiss of me not to express my deepest gratitude to Team Jackdaw for helping me tell it: the two Sarahs – de Souza and Hodgson – and everyone else at Corvus who has worked on the series. I must also express my appreciation to my literary agent, Jane Judd, for her wise counsel and tireless endeavours on my behalf. Likewise, I am indebted to copy editor Mandy Greenfield, who has saved me from more howlers of my own making than I can possibly count; I'm convinced that in a previous life she was a Premier League goalkeeper.

For this iteration of the Jackdaw Mysteries, thanks are due to Dr Ruth Frendo, archivist at the Worshipful Company of Stationers and Newspaper Makers, for unravelling the mysteries and complexities of Elizabethan printing; and to Michael Winship, whose work on the history of Puritanism, *Hot Protestants*, was of immense assistance.

Finally, I am again – as always – grateful beyond measure to Jane, my wife, for her belief in my writing and her unstinting encouragement.

Look out for the brand new novel
from S. W. Perry . . .

BERLIN DUET

From silent era Hollywood and the nightclubs of pre-war Vienna to the ruins of Soviet Berlin, discover the story of two people whose devotion for each other is tested by forces beyond their control. . .

In 1938, English spy Harry Taverner and Jewish photographer Anna Cantrell spend the night dancing at Berlin's most elegant hotel. Anna is married to another man, the shadow of the Nazis is rising over Europe, and neither expects they will ever meet again.

Years later, the pair reunite in the ruins of Berlin, where Anna is searching for her missing children. With the blockade tightening and the Soviets set on conquest, Harry walks a treacherous line between love and duty. And when a stunning revelation exposes a dark secret, it threatens to destroy everything Anna and Harry hold dear.

Berlin Duet is a sweeping, ambitious historical epic of love and war from the Kindle-bestselling author of *The Angel's Mark*. Perfect for fans of Sebastian Faulks and Alice Winn.

Available from Corvus in 2024